I0763576

Companions in Prophecy

Companions in Prophecy

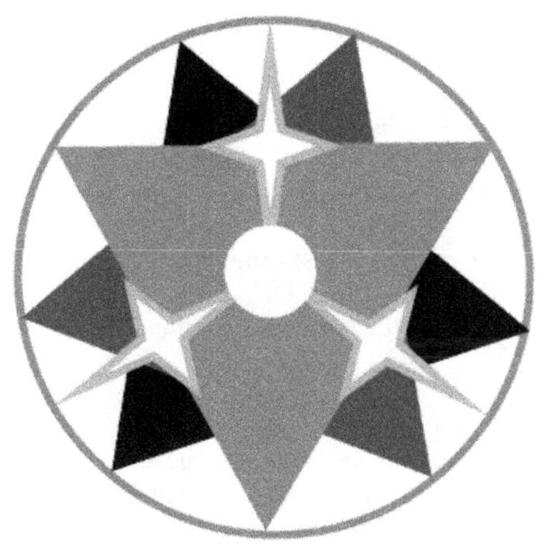

Book 2 of

Heirs to the Taxiarch

Terry Lee Martin

Primary BISAC:
FIC009020 Fiction / Fantasy / Epic

Additional BISAC:
FIC009090 Fiction / Fantasy / Romantic
FIC009120 Fiction / Fantasy / Dragons & Mythical Creatures
FIC071000 Fiction / Friendship

ISBN: 978-1-7320138-5-8 (Hardcover)
ISBN: 978-1-7320138-6-5 (Paperback)
ISBN: 978-1-7320138-7-2 (E-book)

First Edition

Library of Congress Control Number 2021916486

Companions in Prophecy is Book Two of the Epic Fantasy Series:
Heirs to the Taxiarch

Cover art, Symbol of the Meicalian Orders, and map by Terry Lee Martin

Contact the author:
tmartin@silvergobletpress.com

1251 Briarcliff Ct.
Gallatin, Tennessee, 37066
USA

www.silvergobletpress.com

For Drew

Companions in Prophecy

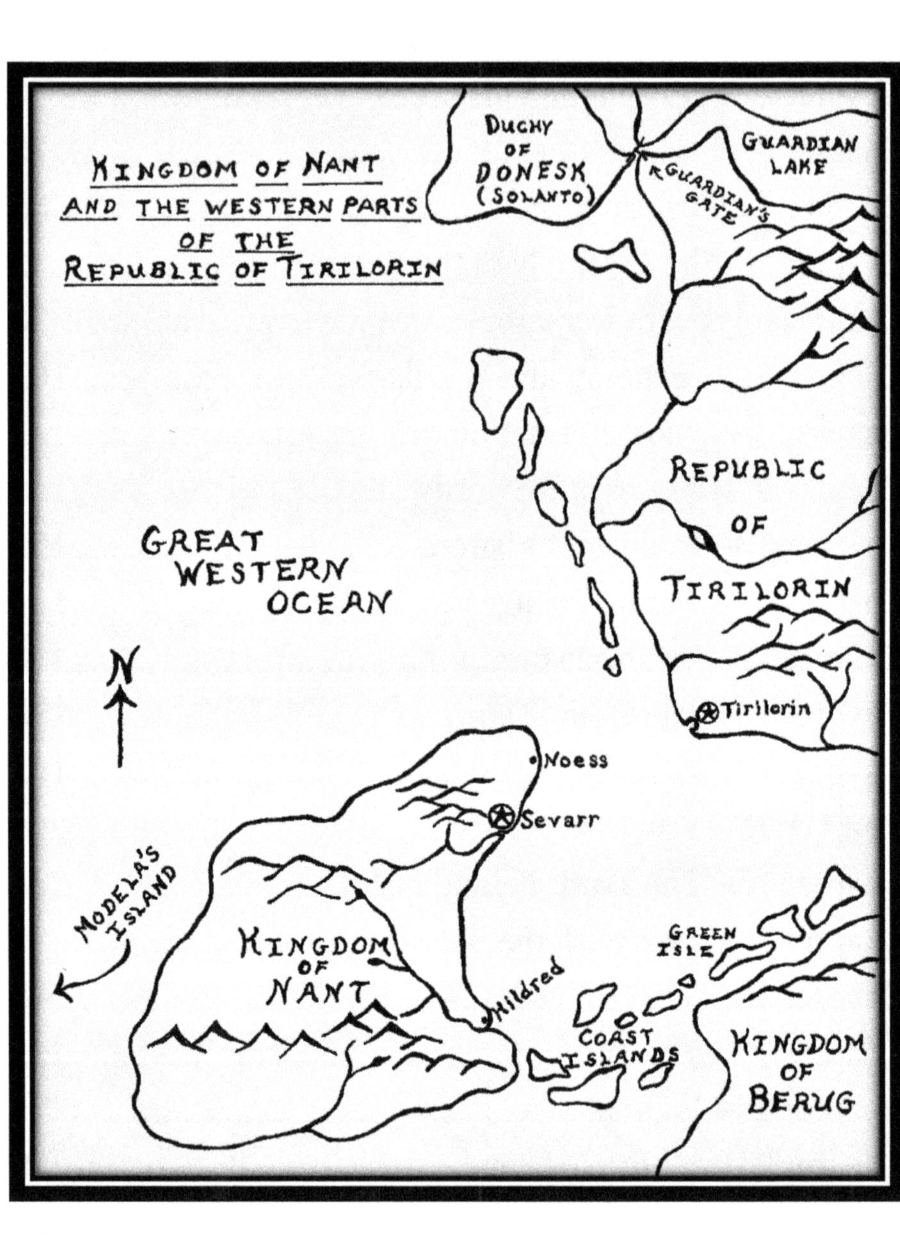
KINGDOM OF NANT
AND THE WESTERN PARTS
OF THE
REPUBLIC OF TIRILORIN
DUCHY
OF
DONESK
(SOLANTO)
GUARDIAN
LAKE
GUARDIAN'S
GATE
REPUBLIC
OF
TIRILORIN
Tirilorin
GREAT
WESTERN
OCEAN
N
Noess
Sevarr
MODELA'S
ISLAND
KINGDOM
OF
NANT
Hildred
GREEN
ISLE
COAST
ISLANDS
KINGDOM
OF
BERUG

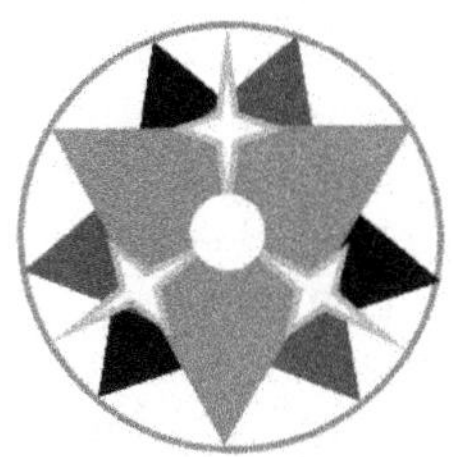

Chapter 1—Fateful Bliss

A midnight breeze drifted silently across the lake. Bright stars and a young Solvermoon cast soft shadows on the wall. Through an open balcony, owls called, and crickets played fiddles.

The cadence of this chamber music did much to soothe Nikal. He had grown more accustomed to other melodies. The sea performed a ballad dramatic and melancholy. The battles he fought in the east conducted a dissonance of glory and duty on the one hand, pain and loss on the other.

He breathed in her lavender scent, her face resting on his shoulder. Dira had drifted off following their bliss earlier in the night.

Oh, how he had missed her. He would Bond her tomorrow morning if he were allowed. He would have done so long ago.

Without permission, and in spite of the peaceful nighttime tunes, Nikal's mind wandered upon the reasons that prevented this one happiness. Crown Prince Lekktor must choose his life-mate first, a ridiculous decree passed down by their jealous grandfather when their great uncle, as the result of an Aura, Bonded the very woman their grandfather had wanted for himself. It should not have been an issue, yet it turned into a tortuous struggle, and since that time the legalities of Aura Bondings had been set aside among the royals and nobility of Nant. Among the great families, Matrimonials were only summoned now to perform the actual Rites, and the Gifted were forbidden to interfere with the powerful men who chose and contracted their Bondmates for reasons usually not related to love.

Other Disciplines too had slackened amongst the highest classes over the last fifty years or so. Women had few rights in this kingdom dominated by men. Nikal was ashamed to recall a loathsome side of himself as a teen: heartless sexual indulgence and drunken orgies, alongside his brother, with young women the servants would bring to their bedchambers. The unfortunate circumstances of these poor girls eventually broke through to Nikal's conscience, and he came to despise his actions, chastening himself in order to someday be made worthy of something higher and better. His view of women was transformed.

He credited the old Sage for his turn-around. Sage Antonin was a good man and understood his struggles. Antonin said he had had a Vision from the Guardian concerning Nikal—that through him there was hope for a brighter future for the Kingdom of Nant. He provided a repentant Nikal with Absolution and more than anyone taught him about the Principles and true manliness. Together they outlined an appropriate Discipline to which Nikal could adhere and live up to.

It was many years, however, before Nikal had the occasion to encounter that higher love he longed for in the person of the daughter of Duke Rothee. Nikal had come to the port of Noess after fighting in the east for two months. He'd returned to persuade the nobles to send more ships and men, for the Easterners needed better expertise in those early days against the Alkhan. The duke invited him to rest a few days at his estate. So, for the first time, Nikal met Dira, with her dark hair of long ringlets and perfect oval face, and when he heard her musical voice of welcome, he was smitten to the core.

And quite obviously, so was she. They grew to know one another over a peace-filled week. Near the end of his visit, he rode out on a pleasure jaunt through her father's estate. Indeed, he had quite deliberately followed her out secretly, and in a romantic fantasy come true, she led him to this same quiet hunting lodge on tiny Lake Winnettt.

That was now ten months ago.

Two more times the prince returned from the eastern war, and he would come to Noess first. It was convenient, for the city was on the common route from Tirilorin to the Nantian capital, Sevarr. He would sit offshore and wait for his trusted General Aron to make arrangements, and when all was dark and quiet, Nikal would row secretly to shore, mount the horse Aron had provided, and make his way to Lake Winnettt. There she would be, at her father's hunting lodge, waiting for him.

Just like tonight. The wars and other responsibilities occupied the greater portion of Nikal's life, but those few times together were pure joy in an otherwise hard year. She made him feel human, helped him heal, body and soul, and allowed him to experience true love and peace and contentment.

His desire to legally Bond her would have to wait. Lekktor must choose first. And the moment he did so, Nikal would declare for Dira.

As his confidante, Aron in his funny manner would warn him every time of the possible *consequences*, but being a prince had some advantage in the law. The rules in Nant were strange, and though Nikal did not care for them, he would take advantage of them if he had to. In the unlikely event he should become ruler of Nant, he would change them back to the way they were when Meicalian Principles and a common Discipline held full sway. In other countries the rules were looser, for women had as much choice in the matter of mating and Bonding as men. Not in Nant. In Nant, among the upper echelon, men held all power. Nikal was considered the great warrior and general of his age, but he could only hold his authority by playing the games of the powerful noblemen of Nant. In the meantime, Nikal would treat Dira as well as he could.

Someday, he thought, all would be well for them. He could wait, and she was committed. *Damn, Lekktor,* he said to himself. *Hurry, you fool of a brother.*

Perhaps in her sleep his lover detected his silent expletive. She stirred and opened her eyes. "Slumber evades you, dearest?" She asked sleepily, reaching up with her fingers to caress his short black beard.

He drew her close. Her smoothe skin against his own nakedness felt glorious. Though it was warm with windows open, a low flame in the fireplace cast a flickering glow upon her tender face. "Yes. Wishing."

She observed him through sleepy dark eyes. "I know what you wish for. The same as I."

"Yes." He looked at her steadily. Was there anyone more beautiful in all the world? More understanding? More loving? He kissed her and circled his fingers around and over her breasts, charming her out of her sleepiness. "But this moment is a good one, love. You never told me whether it was difficult to get away here tonight."

For a minute she lay back allowing him to perform his magic, now with his tongue and the tickling hair of his face. Her nipples hardened, and she sensed an eager relaxation in her groin. Sleepiness was exchanged for anticipation. "Father has gone to Sevarr. Mother likes you. She always has."

Nikal paused in his administrations and leaned up on his arm. "Your mother knows about us?" That would be news.

Dira giggled as she pushed him back down. She began kissing him lightly in his own key places, encouraging a body she knew needed what she could give. "She caught sight of you last time. She will keep our secret. In fact, she knows we are here, tonight. She says you are different than most men. She maintains that those who truly love one another should...love one another."

He reached behind her and traced his fingers down her spine and to the curves of her hips. He was happy, knowing what their bodies were about to repeat from earlier. "It is that way still among most. The Matrimonials move freely among the common folk, outside of Sevarr anyway, and I hope that never changes. I am often sorry for being born a royal. And for you as a high lady. It would be much easier if I were a shopkeeper, say, and you a farmer's daughter."

"Ah, yes," she said. "A Matrimonial could have Bonded us long ago. On the other hand, you would not be my prince, and you would not be the great hero and general of Nant. You could set it all aside and I would still love you, but it all makes you into the man you are. I would not want you to be any less than that. I tell you, dear, Meical the Guardian walks with you."

Nikal was enchanted by her words, for they spoke to his heart. He kissed her fervently.

"You are still willing to go into seclusion...should it become, eh, necessary?" He placed a palm on her belly.

"How sweet of you to ask, considering all." She said, teasingly. And to reassure him, she leaned over, caressed his groin, and applied her tongue and lips upon his stiffening virility. She knew he needed this, ached for it, and she needed him just as much.

Nikal leaned back with his hands behind his head so to allow her gift. "I often fear."

"I do not. I am quite content should I bear a child. We risk this every time you come here, of course. Should I go into seclusion, it will only be until your brother finally chooses his life-mate. And while in seclusion, I would be raising our child. I would not be lonely. Mother will be pleased, and Father will take the news in stride. He is not a fool. He has often wished that our family would connect to yours. He practically gave you his permission when he invited you here that first time. He tends to shade his eyes. In all ways I am freer than other women of my station. Have no fear, my dear. Cast it aside." She returned to pleasuring him, listening happily to his soft groans.

After a time, he reached up, beckoning. She cast the blanket off the bed and leaned up astride him, kissing him again and running her cool hands over the muscles of his chest and down the hair of his abdomen.

He sighed in perfect satisfaction as she lowered her warm body onto his. Her seductive curves captured all his senses. "Oh, my love!" he softly exclaimed.

"You like this?" she asked teasingly, as she raised and then lowered herself in slow rhythm.

"Ah...ah! D...d...don't speak! Y...y...you n...n...know the answer!" He stuttered as his body dampened the unnecessaries of speech in favor of that pleasure designed in the Molding of the sexes at the dawn of history.

"You're beginning to sound like Aron!" She said, giggling. But then her own voice faltered as he reached with a large thumb to apply extra pressure to her most sensitive spot. "Oh...oh!"

"Shh...sh...shh. Th...th...at's what you g...get for th...that quip!" He was as happy as he had ever been, and he wished it could go on forever.

Morning came, and with it came General Aron, alone on horseback.

"Y..yyour Highness!" he called out. Aron drew out his words in a somewhat inconsistent stammer. As a boy he was teased for it, but all in all it had no effect on his leadership skills. Those who knew him well, such as the prince, barely noticed it anymore.

Nikal and Dira had already participated together in a quick swim at dawn, and he now stood alone, bare-chested on the verandah. He was listening to the sounds of an unconcerned morning, looking out over the lake with its light mists rising, and drinking the hot herb tea Dira had made for him.

"Why, Aron! Eh, the lady inside is not presentable. Not to you, anyway. Keep your distance."

The man chuckled. "I'm sure."

"And why are you here? I sent a message. Her father is away. I intend to stay three nights more."

"Y..yyour hawk, er, your hawk is not lost, sir, and I...I...I got the message. And of all people y...you should know that I have no desire to interfere with...ah...yourrr pleasures. Ah, you deserve them." He looked around. A loon called across the lake. "Grr...rand place. Lovely."

"Yes, and quite private. That is until you rode up. Now why did you not take the message seriously?" It was at that moment that Letti, the Common Grayhawk the prince and Aron used to send messages to one another, called out shrilly and landed on the balustrade. Nikal looked at it. "Hunting, were you?"

The bird looked at its trainer with no visible emotion in its sharp eyes.

"I...I say I did take the mmm...message seriously, Your Highness!" Aron replied in slightly aggrieved tone. His speech difficulty was more noticeable when he was nervous. Yet in the heat of battle, it oddly disappeared, never a detriment. In this case, however, he did feel a bit anxious in this unannounced interruption. "But odd nn...news has been heard in Noess, and I deemed it ah...imperative you hear it from me. A...ah...Berugian messenger has flown to the capital with the nnn...news to expect a delegation. And considering the distance and timing for the mm...messages, I should say they will arrive in three more days."

Nikal set his cup on the balustrade, stepped down the stairs and approached the rider.

"Etoppsi are coming to Nant? The Meicalian Feast is months away! Whatever for?"

"The ah...news isn't plain, Yy...your Highness, but it would mm...imply something regarding the war."

"Westrealm has made a move? The Alkhaness?"

Dira emerged through the door in a long dressing gown. With chivalric instincts Aron dismounted and bowed. "Mmm...my lady! It is ah...pp...pleasurable to see you again. Do you know this scalawag? If not, I shall gladly throw down a challl...lenge to him."

Dira laughed as she stroked Letti. "And he shall beat you."

"As usual," added Nikal.

"Nnn...nonsense!" intoned Aron with pretended indignation. "He lll...loses to me all the time, my lady."

"At Fifty-twos," said the prince knowingly.

"Indeed, yes! His Hiiigh...ness has forked over unquantifiable amounts of gold to me over long years." They all laughed. "Ah...ah...actually, I don't think this lll...little...that this little conversation is progressing in my favor, is it? I sh...shall, however," he added with a second bow in Dira's direction, "acknowledge that upon the challenge of ah...wooing lll...lovely ladies, His Highness has left me wallowing in mud."

She laughed. "Would that be because His Highness tells me you have vowed a temporary celibacy, General Aron?"

Aron, swordmaster, famed general, and Nikal's right-hand, flattened his lips and drew his eyebrows in close. Turning from the lady to the prince, he said, "I told you that in the strictest confidence, Your Highness, some years ago." His impediment disappeared not only in the heat of battle but also when he was annoyed or angry.

"You told it to me and at least a dozen others in a very drunken state, my friend. Everyone in the navy and the army knows your little 'secret,'" Nikal teased. "Forgive me for speaking of it to the Lady Dira."

"I will not," Aron replied with a pout.

"He speaks of you often, Aron, for he loves and trusts you, of course," said Dira consolingly. "You are his great friend. He likes to share these things with me. Besides, I think it's honorable! A man who as a boy had a little Vision from the Guardian, who told him to retain his passion until a promised Aura?"

Because he did feel a dash of guilt, Prince Nikal added, "It would be a better world if all were so inclined to honor a Discipline, as the General here does."

Aron was still annoyed. "He made it plain to me men should restrain their desires in favor of their true love, or when Auras occur."

"And you are very right!" said Nikal, with a sense of finality. "Would that that particular Discipline held sway among all."

"Yes," said Dira. "You have no skeptics here, Aron. There is no need to justify yourself to those present! Children should be born to happy parents. It is best that way. Your children are to be of great value to the Guardian! I'm sorry for teasing you. Now, General, are you going to come inside and have a bit of breakfast with us...your friends?"

An hour later, a full-bellied General Aron and Prince Nikal took their leave of one another.

"I will return tomorrow evening after sunset, Aron," said Nikal in a quiet voice. "My heart tells me to...how shall I put it? The war. It grows. The enemy pushes and has grown stronger despite all we have done. I...I do not know when I shall see her again."

"The Guardian Affirm you, Y...your Highness. You are not the only one who searches for words! I have pestered yyy...you many a time about the Lady Dira, and I realize I have, er, erred. Forgive me. Her ll...love for you is pure gold, Nikal." Aron was one of the few in all Nant who addressed the prince on such familiar terms. He mounted his horse. "Truly. Mm...may your extra day be...blessed. However, I *should* warn..."

"General, tomorrow evening we will set sail, so for now can you please dispense with the 'however's'? I know what I'm doing."

"I have my doubts. Birds and those, er, lovely buzzing bees. *Royal* bees, no less. Tsk, tsk. Even for the common man, *th...thumping thumpers make three*, you know, sir."

"Depart, you scoundrel," said Nikal, though he couldn't stop the grin on his face.

"Yes, *sir!*" Aron offered up his most cheeky wink and rode away.

When Nikal returned to the bedroom, to his great delight he found Dira standing at the side balcony looking over the lake. Banishing his concerns of Aron's news, he quickly removed his own garb so to mimic her own state of undress. From behind he reached around her, and she melted back into his embrace.

"You were expecting me?" he questioned.

"Whatever gave you that impression?" she responded, beaming.

He then picked her up lightly and carried her to the bed. They had most of two days remaining and a night between to make up for many lost months.

Would that life concentered on the joys of two lovers loving. Unfortunately, in the Imperfect Worlds, duties and sorrows too often interfere. Some are lucky, and for them such intrusions are fewer, though never absent, even among the luckiest. Yet for many, what few joys they have are dampened by the demands of the world, or by the evil choices of others who in their jealousy cannot allow them to experience what they themselves can never know. For their sake, it was good that these two did not know what the following weeks were to bring, for if they had, the enchantment—and the blessing—associated with these all too short days together may, out of fear, never have taken place. And the Kingdom of Nant—indeed all of Dumhoni—would have suffered from the denial of those delight-filled hours. But also, at the individual level, joys, no matter how few or how short, can help sustain one through the worst depression. This would prove the case for Nikal and Dira.

Chapter 2—A Prophetic Voice

Several days later, in the Nantian royal city of Sevarr, Royal Hawking and Rainwing of Green Isle greeted Nikal as he approached the Berugian Guest Tower in answer to their summons. This magnificent structure not far from King Monticu's palace was built by Etoppsi for their own use for their annual visits to attend the Meicalian Feast. It was standard for Etoppsi towers to have shelf-like platforms built out at various levels for the large creatures to take flight and land with ease. Massive staircases within led to various chambers.

Nikal had entered at ground level and bowed to the two striking creatures. Hawking was a member of the Berugian royal family, uncle to the current King of Berug, but to Nikal he was an old friend whom he had known since he was a boy. Advanced in age, Hawking still bore himself with an unmatched stateliness. Though his once tawny fur was now graying, his great wings still bore glistening black feathers, well-oiled. Rainwing was both a veteran of the Dragon Legion and a scholar. She was a handsomely carved feminine giant with silver fur and matching silver wings, a rare and stunning combination. The prince was immensely curious about her, for he overheard one of the Skyfront officers complain about her being unbonded. Nikal had sufficient knowledge of Etoppsi customs to realize how strange that was. Yet as she towered above him, he had no intention of ever asking her about it. He wasn't certain if it would be insulting or not, but he knew that if he were a Khestadone Human from the realms of the Khans, insulting an Etoppsis would surely be the last act of his life.

Unlike with the Khestadone, the Berugians were friends with the Nantians, so there was no reason to be intimidated. Yet Nikal smiled inwardly at the emotions he experienced as the two huge creatures stood tall before him.

"Prince Nikal," said Hawking. The stone floor vibrated when he spoke.

Nikal nodded. "It is good to speak to you as a friend, Old One, rather than as a Berugian delegate in a council meeting, and you as well, Rainwing of Green Isle!"

She returned the nod. Although it did not rumble earthquake-like as did Hawking's, her voice was still deeper—though smoother—than a Human man's. "We are friends, certainly, Nikal. The Meicalian Principles of honor and humility shine through in you."

"Despite all the bickering?" Nikal said, chuckling. Her statement struck him as odd. In fact, he thought himself purposeful and hard during the proceeding. It pained him that there had been doubts on the part of his brother and others to fulfill the Berugians' request. But he had brought them all around. In another week's time, a great many armorers and Nantian officers would travel on ship to Berug, the first in centuries, to aid in the equipping and training of their Etoppsi allies in ground combat. "I admit I wish I had been present when the meeting began. I was, eh, delayed."

A delay he was otherwise not in the least sorry about. Even now he drank in the mind image of Dira's face and body and could still feel the pressure of her skin against his own as they embraced naked in the cool waters of Lake Winnettt.

"Your speech was persuasive, and we thank you for it," replied Hawking. He then glanced at Rainwing before continuing. "Nikal, we have something of importance to discuss with you."

"Is there some further request regarding the special foods and supplies for the Human officers? I'm sure we can..."

Rainwing interrupted. "It has nothing to do with that. It is a matter, however, of great privacy. If you are prepared, the two of us would like to carry you—in flight—to a place away from the city where there is no chance we can be overheard."

Nikal raised an eyebrow.

"Is that well with you, Nikal?" asked Hawking.

Nikal looked up into his face. "You haven't taken me on a flight since Lekktor and I were boys!"

"Most Humans fear flight. Our offer to return to Berug with a few of your officers in tow was not received well, as you saw."

"Ah, yes," said Nikal. "Most of us prefer to remain close to the ground, ha! Though I would have done it. I remember that thrill all those years ago, Old One. It would be a joy to experience it again!"

With curiosity and excitement comingling, Nikal followed the pair as they wandered up through the tower. There were other Berugians that they passed, members of the delegation sent by Queen Silverwing. They nodded to Nikal and hailed Hawking, but only those who were civilian subjects of Berug acknowledged Rainwing. The all-male Skyfront officers ignored her.

Scaled to Etoppsi proportions, the stairs were three times as steep and wide as those in most Human houses, yet Nikal managed to mount them gracefully enough. It was like climbing a steep hill.

When they arrived at the lowest platform, Hawking said, "I could still carry you, Nikal, yet..."

"You are the Old One!" Nikal quipped. "I am perfectly content for Rainwing to carry me."

She grasped him strongly under his arms and around his middle and chest. Her hands were as big as serving platters and her arms as thick and hard as bedposts. It was a rather compromising position for two reasons: one, Nikal knew that if the female Etoppsis wished it, she was perfectly capable of squeezing the life out of him and crushing him like a basket of eggs, and secondly, though he refused to be embarrassed by it, he was quite rigidly held against her huge bare breasts.

Humans were often intimidated by the giant winged creatures, and at the same time mesmerized by their appearance and ability to fly. They also tended to have uncertain emotions regarding Etoppsi nakedness, if one could call it nakedness, and many Humans did. Their fur was short, sleek and tight, like that on a well-groomed horse, yet the glistening fur appeared to enhance their musculature and features rather than to camouflage them. It would have been different, perhaps, if Etoppsi were beasts of the fields or of the air, but they were not. Humans in the Northern world knew better. They were 'of the Mold', created in the same miracle in the depths of time as were the Humans and the Qeteral. They were sensuous, intelligent, creative beings. Their musky scent could even be of odd attraction to unwary Humans, and jokes were often made among the smaller race regarding them. They were powerful and obviously virile creatures. The Etoppsi may have been aware of their effect on the smaller race, but with regal bearing they ignored such foolishness.

Nikal, however, was not one to allow himself to be overwhelmed by them. Despite the momentary awkwardness, he took it in stride. Nikal simply took in Rainwing's aroma like a field of summer wildflowers, and with dignity ignored the physical proximity.

She took perhaps three broad steps with him and launched skyward. The platform fell away and Nikal experienced the rush of wind and the exhilaration of unsupported height. He knew there were no more than a dozen men in all Nant who had ever been allowed such a pleasure by a Berugian. Aron his friend was one. Lekktor, too, when the two of them were boys.

He looked down at the capital city with its white stone buildings as it slipped swiftly away. Suddenly Hawking was flying just below him. This to Nikal was a new sight. He had never before seen a winged Etoppsis in flight from above. Hawking flew with the grace of a gargantuan eagle, his powerful back muscles pumping his vast wings with ease.

Soon they were gliding on the high winds at magnificent speed. It was cold up here, yet Nikal bore it. The thrill vanquished all discomfort, and his back at least was warm against Rainwing's hot body.

To his left he could see the sea as it spread away to a far horizon. Close to shore in the capital port were the sails of a hundred ships. He knew his own ship was down there and wondered if Aron might at that moment be looking up at them. Rainwing then followed Hawking as they veered westward. Another ten minutes and they descended rapidly to a set of beautiful green hills which Nikal quickly realized were the Chalk Hills of Clees. They had traveled over twenty miles from the city.

Land approached him rapidly, but he squashed his fear. He knew better. And sure enough, Rainwing landed as lightly as Letti would on his shoulder and then removed her hold on him.

He began to warm again in the sun. They were on top of one of the Chalk Hills and a vast emerald panorama surrounded him. Wild goats in small flocks ran down the hills, startled apparently by the Etoppsi, but soon they settled down again to graze contentedly.

There was a rushing rivulet at the bottom of one side of the hill, but this was a nearly treeless part of the country. Green rolls dominated the landscape, dotted white here and there with goats, and they were alone. They walked and talked in the grass for a short while until Rainwing brought them back to their purpose.

"No one for now is to hear what we have to say to you. It is..." she paused and looked searchingly with her black eyes into Nikal's face. "Nikal, how would you respond to the proclamation of a Prophecy? A Prophecy that came to me last evening?"

Nikal stopped walking and stood with curious expression. "A Prophecy? You mean a genuine Meicalian Prophecy? Antonin once mentioned to me..." He paused, then looked up again into the female Etoppsis' face. "Rainwing, are you telling me that you are perhaps Gifted? Forgive me, but I was not aware that the Orders existed in Berug."

"They do not," she admitted, "as such. We have Bond Matrons and Ettopsi Physicians, and they are Gifted, but they do not undergo the sort of education and training that your Human Gifted undergo in the Valley of the Gifted. They provide their own training in Berug."

"Rainwing," offered Hawking, "is what some in Berug call a 'Follower of the Ancient Way.' Nowadays, it is only a handful of females who attempt to adhere to Monastic Disciplines, and they are looked upon with great skepticism. And Prophecy such as this is not known in Berug. It isn't only Human ears that we wished to avoid."

Nikal digested this piece of information pondering how to answer Rainwing's question. A stiff warm breeze blew across the hilltop.

"So, you are what Humans might call a Seeress? What or who does this Prophecy concern, Rainwing?"

"You," she said bluntly.

Nikal found himself shocked beyond anything he had experienced in a long while.

"The Taxiarch directed Rainwing to speak to you," Hawking clarified. "Perhaps this Prophecy does qualify her as a Seeress, as you say. Yet, it is the only Prophecy she has ever received. It was a Prophecy *within* a Vision. She saw Meical's Face."

Nikal was amazed. Yet, if he believed the old Sage Antonin, then who was he, Nikal, to deny the possibility. "I...don't know what to say, Rainwing. I certainly do not wish to deny the work of the Guardian."

"The Taxiarch works in you, I see that. Unlike Hawking, I have not met many Humans. Until I came here at Queen Silverwing's bidding I had never seen Humans before and was excited to come. I've always been curious about your race and have read your histories. But even among the few of you I have met I can tell you are different. You have a great sense of awareness...awareness of what is good in this world. Your words in the council meetings were telling. I would go so far as to say that you have been moved by the Taxiarch in a spiritual way, no? Perhaps, long ago, you were a different male than you are today? A different *man*—sorry, we simply use 'male' and 'female' in our society, and I keep forgetting that your race has specific names for your genders."

"He is very much a different *man* than he was ten, fifteen, years ago." Hawking said to Rainwing. "I have observed him at the Feast most every year since he was a young male topling, er, I mean since he was a *boy*. But anyway, once upon a time, Nikal was very self-possessed. He did indeed change. I remember quiet conversations with the previous Sage, Antonin. He and I were friends. Antonin had the highest regard for Nikal and spoke to me of Nikal's change of ways. He said that Nikal was the bright star in his family."

Nikal was surprised that others of a different country, not to mention a different race of being, were throwing truths at him that were so personal. Generally, he was a private man. It pleased him, though, to know that Antonin regarded him so highly—that he had spoken with positive regard about him to others such as Hawking was gratifying to know.

He nodded. "It is kind of you to say so, Hawking. As far as I am concerned, Sage Antonin was the best man I ever knew. I learned every good thing from him. I have no objection to hearing the Prophecy. Yet you say it must be kept a secret?"

"For the moment, we deem it wise. There will be, it seems likely once you hear it, others in your future to whom it will be appropriate to repeat. Most particularly, however, it should be kept secret from anyone in your family."

Nikal found this curious but nodded. "All right. I am listening."

Rainwing also nodded, as if satisfied with Nikal's receptiveness. "In the Vision, the Taxiarch instructed me to place my hand on your head when I repeat the Prophecy. I believe it will help you to remember."

Nikal swallowed hard, not because of fear, but rather because he was entering into a different world, one in which Meicalian History, Prophecy, and the Disciplines were physical entities, rather than as a way of life espoused by the Gifted and Monastics. He was sad that old Antonin retired years ago and returned to the Valley. Nikal was not as close to the current Sage; Ralle was a good man, but Nikal believed he was too passive. He did not push back against the dictates of the king and council as much as Nikal thought he should. Too many feared the men in power. Often, Nikal was alone in his desire to stand up for Meicalian Principles. Yet, he would convince himself that Ralle acted carefully to protect the Orders from further interference. In any event, he found he missed Antonin just now.

These thoughts transpired all in a moment. Suddenly, the prince felt for the second time that day Rainwing's massive hand, this time on his head. He noted there was no fur on the palms, and Rainwing's skin was as soft as any Human high-born woman's—as soft as Dira's, he thought. As she was a scholar and teacher, Nikal supposed she did not do hard work that might callous or roughen her hands, at least not since her days as a Dragon Legionnaire.

She exhibited the gentleness of a bird this time, rather than the muscular grip she employed during the flight. He half-imagined a sudden green light, and then Nikal's eyes closed on their own.

He then heard words in Rainwing's deep voice, and yet upon concentration, he thought that in concert with her own there was that of Another—a Voice of power and purpose, compelling and yet compassionate at the same time:

An island king has a son and a son;
In his father's heart the second is one.
The first is first in the heart of the mother;
To favor the first she betrays the other.
The second is warned by a twain with wings,
To him My chosen this message brings.

With the first the king will unwittingly side;
From the king the first the truth will hide.
The second is warned by one with shawl:
The choice before him could lead to his fall.
His pain will cause our hearts to break
Will he yet stand for his kingdom's sake?

The Staff of Terianh he then will wield,
For all the world with which to shield.
Vanaratu knows where it is hidden,
The second will seek, for it is bidden.
Eight will give of what they have
For the second to gain the Eagle Staff.

He mustn't deny the gifts of the others,
True family, new sisters, and genuine brothers.
One twin he trains who shares the Staff,
And Terianh's son will make them laugh,
A Sage who hears Vanaratu's call,
And he should heed the one with the shawl.

The island kingdom by a child is redeemed.
In truth the child was not as she seemed,
For the second was truly first all along,
And a friend thought lost will right the wrong.
Doom will fall on battlefield;
An enemy's fate should then be sealed.

When his eyes opened again, Rainwing had stopped speaking. Nikal still heard the other Voice, like an echo in his mind, as the words continued to write themselves in his memory.

When he spoke, his own voice in comparison sounded weak and distant to his own ears. "I...I am 'the second?'"

"You are. You are His 'chosen.' Though...it seems as though several have been chosen, not just yourself."

Nikal stumbled, unable to comprehend the magnitude of what he had heard.

"Let us sit, Nikal," Hawking said kindly and gestured to the ground.

As the three of them sat upon the soft turf, Nikal came to the conclusion it must be real. It must be genuine. Rainwing could not have made up all of it. There was no reason why she should be tempted to do so anyway. Besides, the second Voice still echoed in his mind.

Calling him.

He sat cross-legged and looked down for a minute, catching his breath. He was winded as if he had run a race. He looked up again. The others had spread their vast wings out in the sun, and Nikal couldn't remember ever seeing Etoppsi sitting on the ground before. They still managed to tower above him. He looked around. The sun was high and warm, distant birds flew in tiny flocks to and fro, a few goats approached their hill across the brook, and the wind continued to blow across the hills unabated.

"Was there more to this, eh, Vision that you had?"

"Meical made it clear to me that I am one of the eight mentioned in the Prophecy. The Taxiarch wishes me to be your friend. There were glimpses of things, maybe a face or two. Human faces."

Nikal looked steadily at her and took another long breath. "I will gladly accept the friendship, of course, but Rainwing, I find myself angry. The Guardian should be plainer with me. I don't like much of what I hear; it is as if I have no choices. Rather, I am subject now to some doom I won't be able to shake!"

"Yet it is clear you embody greatness, or the Guardian would not have directed such a Prophecy at you. Heroic deeds are not your fear, are they? It is the matter of your mother and brother that concerns you mostly, is it not?"

"Nikal, you are your father's favorite. I have always noted that. And is Prince Lekktor your mother's?" Hawking asked.

Nikal found himself standing again and looked into the old Etoppsis' golden eyes. "I've always thought these were subtleties, Hawking."

"There may be more intrigue than what can be seen on the surface."

"My mother has little voice, as you know. My father almost never sees her anymore. She appears at dinners."

"Yet you yourself treat her kindly."

"Well, certainly I do! So why and how would she betray me?" Nikal was visibly disturbed by the portents of the Prophecy.

"It is possible," said Hawking slowly, "she has already done so. Considering how much she is ignored, intrigue on her part should not come as a surprise. Human history is replete with tales of intrigue, and I think, from all my conversations with Antonin, that Nant, for many decades now, is quite ripe for it."

Rainwing nodded. "I believe Royal Hawking to be correct, Nikal. Have you ever shared with your mother any news or information that you consider secretive?"

"Something that she or Lekktor could use to hurt you?" pressed Hawking.

"Why would Lekktor wish to hurt me?" Nikal asked, still resistant.

Hawking looked at Nikal, and with his keen golden eyes he seemed especially stern. "You cannot be so blind, Nikal!"

Nikal blinked. He didn't want to respond. Finally, "I know he and I see things differently regarding the use of the military. You saw that in the meetings. Is that what you're talking about, Hawking? It has not been a serious problem between us, though."

"It has not been of issue in *your* mind. But every time your father sides with you...no, listen, Nikal!" Hawking emphasized as Nikal shook his head and turned away. "He always sides with you, and you know it to be true! And every time he does so, how do you think your brother views this? And if your mother favors Lekktor?"

"So, are you telling me I deserve what is coming to me? This...this betrayal?"

"No! No one of good heart deserves evil to come his way! And you must not think that Meical the Taxiarch desires any evil to come to you. It is wrong to think He tests His peoples in such ways. But, I have observed Lekktor over long years, just as I have you. Lekktor chose a different path long ago, before either of you had ever gained positions of power under your father. He is self-centered, and he is jealous of you."

Nikal shook his head again. "I just don't see..."

"Of course, you don't!" said Hawking. "Antonin taught you all too well. You tend to overlook the bad in others, unless he be a clear enemy like those whom you fight in the eastern war. The Principles teach forgiveness and wariness of harsh judgement, and you have adopted these as a part of your very nature. You are a good man, as Antonin knew the makeup of your heart, perhaps even before you yourself did."

Maybe it was truth, but it made Nikal uncomfortable.

"Meical has abandoned Lekktor," Rainwing said suddenly.

Nikal stared at her. "What do you mean? Why would Meical not care about Lekktor? This is strange talk!"

"It isn't so much that the Taxiarch does not care as it is that He sees He has no influence with Lekktor. I will qualify. Lekktor has abandoned Meical, and therefore Meical cannot influence him."

Nikal considered for a long moment. He knew that Lekktor cared little for Meicalian Principles or for any of the Disciplines. His brother was polite to the current Sage, Ralle, but as Nikal pondered this he knew that Lekktor had no real respect for Ralle's position. Lekktor dismissed his teachings and laughed at the work of the Matrimonials and the meditations of the Monastics and did not believe in Auras, for example, but of course his attitude was common among the high born. There was a line of thought among them that even the Gifts of the Healer pairs was a natural-born trait without connection to the Meicalian magic of Giftedness. "If Meical has abandoned him, maybe the Guardian has abandoned this whole country."

"Be not so cynical, Nikal. Nant is the hope of your Human world in its defense against the Enemy! And of ours, too! Your Orders still do good work among the common folk. From my observation, however, your country's leadership suffers terribly from pride."

"And you put no value in females," put in Rainwing. "Women, I mean."

"I care tremendously about women." Nikal said this almost as a whisper. He knew this view counted for little among most. Generally speaking, Rainwing was quite right.

"Rainwing did not mean you personally. You are the only one on your High Council, aside from Sage Ralle, who does care," said Hawking. "You are different than other Human males, at least among those in positions of authority, for you see what they do not, that females are of equal value. We, too, in Berug have our streak of chauvanistic pride in our military, so I am familiar with it, having served on the Sky Front long ago, but it is more than your view of females that makes you different. You, Nikal, value bravery and honesty and love in all people, males and females, and all the races. You carry out a naval policy geared to protecting even the land of the Qeteral, even though they owe you nothing and haven't been seen in a century. And of course, you have always supported the alliance with Berug. You are a powerful leader and general, and you are a great hero. All say so, but you don't seem to let it get to your head, because you don't crave power. You are thrust into your role because of duty and honor and a large measure of talent, and I think a desire to do some real good in the world. That last is a high Meicalian Principle. Lekktor, on the other hand, desires control. You need to open your eyes to his jealousy and be wary of it! Jealous people are angry people, and angry people are dangerous people. And that can be true among the other races."

Nikal did not speak for a minute. He wanted to argue further. He kept wanting to give Lekktor the benefit of the doubt. But as he considered the deepest thoughts in his heart, and scoured his memories, he realized Hawking and Rainwing might have a point. He really didn't have to go back that far. Just the previous morning in the presence of the king, Nikal overruled decisions he knew Lekktor had made regarding supplies to the East, and exactly as Hawking said, the king allowed Nikal's word to stand. The supply captains nodded appreciatively to Nikal and saluted him when they left, ignoring Lekktor altogether. His brother stood silently by. Lekktor had not argued his own points. Maybe his brother had concluded that preferences in opposition to those of Nikal's were futile to argue in front of their father? And at some point Lekktor removed himself from the audience chamber while Nikal and his father carried on conversation about the position of the Tirilorines. Was it possible that every time Nikal returned to the capital Lekktor believed his own position undermined?

He considered further. Nikal knew he never deliberately tried to step on his brother. His brother seemed simply to be persuaded by Nikal's point of view on matters. Yet in all actuality Nikal knew more than Lekktor did about such matters. It was Nikal's natural leadership skills and interests and talents that caused his father to place him in charge of the war in the east and gave Lekktor the responsibility of defending the island home kingdom. It suited Lekktor, for though he was talented with weaponry he was never the great warrior that Nikal was. Island defense did not require it, for the war had not reached this far. Did Lekktor resent Nikal's more powerful position? Nikal wondered. His brother had always deferred to and even complimented Nikal on such matters. They got along quite well and always had.

Or so Nikal had heretofore thought. Was Lekktor hiding his real feelings?

Nikal for his part had never dreamed of usurping Lekktor's position as the older brother. Lekktor was heir to the throne and Nikal had always shown him, and referred of him to others with, due accord. Nikal pictured his brother as king someday. He never really gave much thought to ever taking his brother's place. His brother would Bond someday and have a child who would be heir, and that was all there was to that. Nikal did not want to be king. He much preferred military training and leading men in battles. That was his forte. He never cared for maneuverings and politics. He did not believe he had deliberately done anything to make Lekktor jealous.

Yet he knew deep down that most people preferred his own leadership to that of his brother. People saluted and revered Nikal wherever he went. Maybe Lekktor did have good reason to be jealous of Nikal. Maybe he feared that, despite law and tradition, the people or the army would clamor for Nikal to be king when their father was gone?

It was folly. Nikal did not wish to be king. Yet, considering all, he looked at Hawking and finally nodded.

Hawking continued. "Rainwing and I only discussed the Prophecy a little this morning, for we did not want others in our delegation to hear us. Obviously, we do not understand much of it. Usually there is much in Prophecy that can never be understood until after events spoken of in it have taken place, and retrospection demonstrates its reality. We think, however, the timing of the Prophecy, in other words the fact that Rainwing received it last night, is important. Certain events may have taken place in recent days by which the Guardian has been able to make the Prophecy."

"Which is why I believe it possible that the portents of the first several lines may have already taken place," added Rainwing.

"Is there some information you have shared with your mother the queen that, by making use of the information, she or Lekktor could hurt you?" Hawking repeated.

Nikal thought, but nothing came to mind. He shook his head.

"Well," said Rainwing, "it is possible that she has learned something about you from other sources that could be used to hurt you. Something that will help Lekktor."

Nikal nodded. A thought momentarily tracked across his mind, and it seemed to involve Dira, but he dismissed it outright before allowing it to form a tangible image. He only said, "If you believe it has already taken place, then I don't see how I can do anything about it."

"True. Very true. You see, typically Prophecy still allows for the element of choice, Nikal. Despite what you said earlier, you can still choose to follow Meical's Calling or not."

"You mean I am not bound to it?"

"You are not," said Rainwing. "And yet, Nikal, Meical is making it known that you are the only person who can fulfill the need. However, you are correct that there is much in this Prophecy beyond your choice. There are friends who will come to you, for example. They will reveal themselves soon. I am one. Also, if the Guardian thought you could avoid this betrayal, we think He would have said so. He did not. For the moment let us set it aside. It will become clear eventually. Let us discuss other parts. Your Calling. You have been called to a great undertaking."

"The Staff of Terianh," said Hawking.

It was strange to Nikal to consider something as epic as the Staff and that it was somehow connected to him. "The Eagle Staff hasn't been seen in centuries as far as I know. But like every Human boy I've read the stories of Terianh the Great, how he used the Staff to defeat the last Ralsheen Emperor."

"And he used it to great effect throughout the war. Siriné had many minions and monsters, and temple priests to whom she had given over some of her magic."

"It is shocking—such a Calling. I don't know that I want such a weapon. Who am I to..."

"You are who you are, Nikal!" Hawking said, interrupting. "The great general of the Human world. The forces of the Alkhan have been held back in the east in large part due to your leadership."

Nikal looked away. "Maybe. He will soon launch a stronger attack and overrun Essemar if more help doesn't come to them soon. And Hralindi will quickly follow. You give me too much credit, I think."

"You don't take enough credit. You don't have the overwhelming pride typical of your male forebears. You are better than they."

"I wish you would stop. Stop telling me I am such a great man!"

"There may come a time when you will actually need reassurance." It was Rainwing who said this. "Quite frankly, Nikal, Meical Himself is proclaiming your greatness. You have the qualities He seeks. Will you accept this fact or not? For if not, there is really no need for us to explore the Prophecy any further. The Taxiarch will then be required to explore other options. Or, do you wish to help Him? I do. The freedom of the Three Peoples appears to be on the brink, and the Taxiarch calls us to fight!"

He stared at her. Maybe he did have choices, but ultimately it was down to this. Did he believe in all he had been taught? Did he trust old Antonin when he said years ago that Nikal had a high destiny? Did he trust Hawking's wisdom? Did he believe Meical was using Rainwing as an instrument for proclaiming a Prophecy to him?

And of course, he cared. He cared very much about all these things: the war and the future of the world. Without some great new thing, particularly in the light of the news that the Berugians had brought regarding the apparent maneuvers of the Alkhaness, much could be lost. If Tirilorin joined the war, it would be a great help, but Nikal wasn't certain it was enough. The eastern kingdoms had strong armies, but were on the edge, slowly decreasing in numbers at each engagement with the enemy. The Alkan's forces on the other hand, only seemed to increase, month by month, and he was using more and more of the trained wolves and bears. He was winning more battles and had overrun portions of Essemar's Southern Continental holdings and approached closer to the Great Arch connecting the two continents. If the Alkhaness chose to engage, too, all would be even more hard-pressed. Berug would be bogged down defending itself. Even Nant, though it seemed safe in its island home and with its powerful navy, might be threatened. Was the Eagle Staff of Terianh what was needed?

Obviously, Meical believed it could make a difference. The Guardian.

His inner turmoil, he realized, was that if he chose the path of the Prophecy, he believed there could be no return. He would be giving up a great deal. His dreams of a future with Dira most of all. How did his love for her factor into this? Even now he ached to be with her again. This last time they were together seemed fateful for some reason. If he could, he would abandon all and live with her forever at the lodge on Lake Winnett, raise up a family and let the rest of the world go by.

Yet from what Nikal was beginning to understand, the rest of the world might suffer terribly from such a choice. This was less about Mecial the Guardian as it was Meical the Taxiarch, he mused. The latter title used almost exclusively by the Etoppsi reflected Meical's role as supreme commander in the fight against the evils—evils not only of this world but according to Order belief, in the whole of the cosmology. Meical was the Great Warrior. The Berugian Sky Front was organized based on the ultimate authority of the Taxiarch. Yet the title was still used even in Human society upon occasion, in a military sense. So, the Taxiarch was Calling Nikal to represent His military authority? If the Berugians were right, he was the only one. Or...

"Who is this twin who shares the Staff?"

"We can only presume he has the same Calling as you," answered Hawking.

"You believe him to be male?" asked Rainwing, curious. "You did not say so, Hawking, when we discussed it before."

"I did not, but it has come to me why. For two reasons, yes. One, because such an instrument is designed to be used by Human males, the Staff is a symbolically male instrument, and secondly because Meical expects Nikal, a male, to train him with its use."

"Ah, that does make sense," she agreed. "I had not thought of that last. It is typical in the Orders for the genders to train their own."

"Yes," said Hawking. He turned back to Nikal. "This twin is possibly quite young. I think it reasonable to presume, that at least in the beginning, he will not have the leadership skills or perhaps the power you will have once you have taken possession of the Staff, hence *you* are his trainer."

He won't know any less than I do...about the Staff anyway, he said to himself, laughing grimly. He then realized something.

"This Prophecy isn't only about me."

Hawking replied. "The Guardian has likely called these others, the twin, his counterpart twin quite likely, the scion of Terianh and the rest. The world is in danger. The Enemies in the south grow stronger. Queen Silverwing senses that their magic has grown more powerful in recent months. Meical as Taxiarch has made His countermove. Will He move with you, Nikal?"

Though it left a bitter aftertaste, he nodded. *They may tell me I have choices, but it doesn't seem that way to me.*

Ultimately, Nikal knew he was not the man who could deny such a duty and calling. Hawking knew him too well. Antonin knew him too well. He even remembered something Dira said: *You could set it all aside and I would still love you, but it all makes you into the man you are. I would not want you to be any less than that...*

The Guardian walks with you.

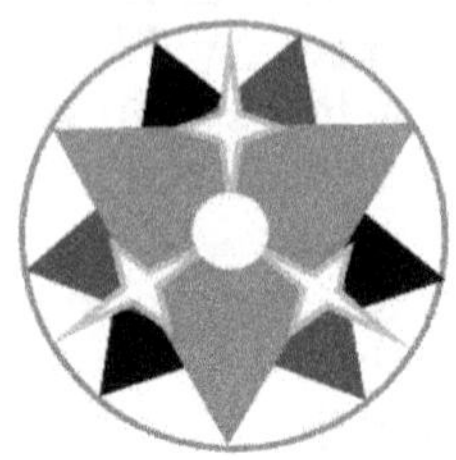

Chapter 3—False Brother

"I am willing to explore this...Calling." Nikal said finally, though he knew his reluctance was not very well-hidden.

"You will not be alone," said Rainwing, touching him lightly on his shoulder.

Nikal smiled faintly and sat on the ground again. "Good to know. Now, where in this world are we supposed to hunt Vanaratu? He is a World God! We don't even know what form he has taken upon himself."

Rainwing nodded. "The Sage spoken of in the message may know."

"Do you think the Sage is Ralle?"

"If he has not approached you then perhaps not. There is no way yet to know how to find Vanaratu. It is a great shock to me to know he still wanders This Side of the World, though there is a belief among the Orders from a book I read at the Institute that The Other Side of the World closed itself to a return after Siriné and Vanaratu left it in their pride eons ago. I dread the thought of meeting him. He disappeared at some point after Meical's Third Appearance, quite likely at Meical's command. Yet the Taxiarch desires to make use of him now. He was not of wicked heart as was his sister Siriné, and the Qeteral especially revered him, according to old records. I think, though, it best to start with what we can more easily discern."

"You mean Terianh's son," agreed Nikal. He considered. "We should go to Tirilorin and speak to Master Genehbro of the House of Terianh. He may know where the Staff is, or at least its history. Genehbro has a son, too. I have not met the son, but an old friend of mine, Swordmaster Jaden, has been training...ah! The line in the Prophecy could refer to Genehbro's son. Jaden taught me swordsmanship years ago; he's the best. This son of Genehbro will likely be superior with the sword. Yet he is young, no more than twenty years I should think, maybe less. Tiliruf! I believe I remember Jaden telling me his name was Tiliruf. He has not been in the wars, for I would know it if someone of his rank were among the Tirilorine mercenaries. He will be inexperienced. Well, we can put him to work soon enough for all that."

"Going to Tirilorin does seem a good place to begin as the Terianh reference is clearest and easiest to discern. Nikal, I am uncertain about the reference to the one with the shawl. What is a shawl? It is not a word used in Berug."

Nikal refrained from a chuckle. The Etoppsis would of course not know. They rarely used words that described clothing. It was another proof in his mind that Rainwing had not made up the Prophecy. "It is a drape of cloth that our females wear around their shoulders and head to protect them from the cold and the wind."

"Ah, so it is a female? A *woman?"*

"That pleases you?" He noted Rainwing's black eyes sparkle.

Hawking answered. "Rainwing is of the opinion females have more wisdom than males. She claims females see broadly, whereas males get caught in pride insisting upon looking at things the same way."

"I will not argue with her," said Nikal, echoing Hawking's look.

"Wisdom, of a certainty," agreed Hawking. "I never argue with females. It's much easier simply to agree with them on most matters."

"Does the reference mean something more to you, Nikal?" asked Rainwing, ignoring Hawking's sarcasm.

"I'm not sure, though long ago the Matrimonials in Nant wore shawls to designate their office, but the practice fell out of favor, though they may still don them in colder climes. I believe I did see some of them wear shawls in Eleni when I trained there years ago."

"Another part of the Prophecy that will likely become clearer in time," concluded Hawking. "And the more I think about the line referring to Vanaratu the more I believe it irrelevant to seek him. In all likelihood, he will find you if Meical is making use of him."

Nikal nodded. "What do the last several lines mean to you?"

The two Berugians looked at one another. Nikal could tell, however, that they were at a loss.

Rainwing replied. "They are much too uncertain. Yet to me they are hopeful words. They are quite likely, for you and for us all, the most important part of the Prophecy, for they seem to speak of a future should you and the others follow the Calling. But unless more is revealed as we travel our path, there can be no knowing what the 'child' refers to—usually a symbol of hope—or what 'redemption' Meical sees the need for, or how an enemy's fate will be sealed. If those whom He Calls fulfill their tasks, then it is to be hoped that the Enemy will be eliminated, or at least thwarted."

"I feel," offered Hawking, "that though suffering is possible, common enough in war of course, the last lines are to be held onto with great hope, just as Rainwing suggests."

They sat for a while in silence. Nikal gathered his thoughts. Even now he could still recall the echo of the Voice behind Rainwing's as she proclaimed the Prophecy. There was much just in the Voice. First of all, there was power in it, a sense of deep, ancient maneuverings. Nikal was inclined to think of it as magic. He was awestruck at the idea that he himself might have control of such power should he actually gain the Staff of Terianh. There was also something in the Voice's tone that Nikal could only describe as *need.* It was the Calling, perhaps, to action, but it contained a very personal edge. He knew Rainwing was right that it was directed at him. He felt it. He knew it.

There was more, but he couldn't quite comprehend it yet, but there was a measure of sadness or concern in the Voice as well. In time the phrase, *His pain will cause our hearts to break,* would gain more traction. In the end, with the help of others, Nikal would come to see that the Guardian was not remorselessly asking him to follow a sense of duty. For the moment, the pain foreseen in the Prophecy had not yet taken place.

It would soon, however. And it would cause Nikal in short order, not to deny the importance of the Prophecy, but to incline him more to his initial emotion. He would have a difficult time disconnecting from the anger, the result of feeling manipulated and used by Cosmic Powers, even if in his heart of hearts he believed those Powers to be operating with good intentions. It would take more than the memory of the Voice to allow him to reach past his cynicism. It would take friendship. It would take loyalty. It would take love.

A sudden bleating nearby startled Nikal. The little flock of wild goats he had noticed earlier had arrived at the top of the hill upon which they sat. The animals looked at the three of them curiously. Among them were several kids, running to and fro, and being prodded by their elders. They were a jittery group, and when the giant Hawking shifted to look at them, they scurried back down the side of the hill and out of sight.

"If we were in Berug, I just might have to capture one of the big ones for dinner!" Hawking's laugh shook the ground.

Though Nikal was struggling with the portents of the Prophecy, he nevertheless found himself grinning at this. After a moment he spoke.

"I will make arrangements to sail to Tirilorin."

"I suggest the three of us fly there," said Hawking. "Did you not say in the meeting that you did not know if Tirilorin would commit to the eastern war? Queen Silverwing gave me great latitude in my current position, and I think it is time I make a return to the old imperial city. It has been a few years since I have been that way. Genehbro was a younger man. Ten years. I think I recall his topling...*boy,* as a matter of fact, and yes he probably was around eight, nine years at the time."

Nikal thought on this. It made good sense to him. "If you speak at their Masters Assembly it may sway them. Tell them of the attack on your Great Wall by the Alkhaness, and they will be more attuned to the threat."

"Then let us plan it!"

They sat for another half hour in the grass and spoke among themselves as the noonday sun rode high. When they returned finally to the same platform at the guest tower, Nikal was hungry. He took his leave of the two Berugians and made his way to the palace to find some food, and for the rest of the day he pondered the Prophecy. It was the first lines that consumed his thoughts, and that night he slept little, wondering whether he should approach his mother or his brother, or even his father, and see if he could gain some clue as to what they may have done—what hurt they may have caused. Yet as he pondered this, he realized what he struggled with was not so much *what* they may have done as it was *why*.

When morning came, and as Nikal was dressing himself, Aron arrived at his bedchamber.

"Yyy...your mighty Highness," he said with a teasing bow.

"I'm not in the mood for frivolity, General."

Aron saw the look in Nikal's eye and wisely backed off. He nodded and spoke in a more business-like tone. "Ah...sorry, sir. I wahh...I was asked to summon you to the Council Chamber. The king your father has an announcement, and ah...all the nobles in the city are arriving even now."

"Could there be messages from Tirilorin, do you think?" asked the prince. "Do you think they have chosen to join the war?"

"I doubt that is ah...what it is about, sir. I would have h...heard something first. This has the air of one of your father's proclamations. You know, like the 'national celebration' when the Elantine ambassador and the Solantine ambassador arrived last year for trade talks."

"Ah, yes, he thought it was some grand portent that they were on the same ship together. Oh, well. It can't be helped. He is the king." Nikal attempted a smile, but Aron had come to know Nikal too well.

"Some...I say sss...something is troubling you, sir?"

"Yes. And I may share it with you at some point."

"I am yy...your friend, of course."

Nikal stood, having finished tying his boots, and put his hand on Aron's shoulders. "Yes, General, you are the best friend I've ever had."

"Thank you, sir."

The two left Nikal's chambers, but the prince was not in the mood even for small talk. He was anxious, trying to determine how much information he should give to his father, for he now agreed with the Etoppsi that he should not yet share the Prophecy with his family, but sufficient reason was needed for him to travel so quickly back to Tirilorin. He had come up with several explanations for the fact he was going to fly with Hawking and Rainwing to get there, but he was uncertain whether he wanted to leave just yet. His desire to uncover the truth behind the first lines of the Prophecy made him hesitant.

He knew his brooding could be sensed by his friend as they walked together. He would almost certainly have to share all with Aron, for he depended on Aron to manage. He would need his help on the search for the Staff of Terianh.

He made his decision. "As soon as this Council meeting is over, I will meet you at the garden by the Berugian Tower. I will explain several things to you then."

Aron nodded and veered off in another direction, whereas Nikal soon found himself at the large carven double doors to the Council Chamber.

These stood open. There were at least twenty others there already, and as he entered, he was approached by two, Dukes Sawnd and Midale.

"Your Highness!" said Duke Midale with a respectful short bow. "His Majesty keeps us in suspense! Do you know what this is about?"

Nikal shook his head. "I do not, I'm afraid. We shall find out, soon." It was hard for him to appear cheerful, but the men did not seem to notice. They sat on elaborate benches that faced the front of the room, where stood one large, magnificently carved, marble chair.

In the other remaining kingdoms of the former Anterianhi Empire, it was common for there to be two such chairs, one for the spouse of the reigning monarch, and sometimes other chairs of prominence for the adult princes and princesses, for all such persons were a vital part of the councils of those kingdoms.

This was not true in Nant. One chair for the king. All others sat on benches facing him. The queen was never present.

There were no women at all. In many regards, the Kingdom of Nant had a system as male-dominant as the Principality of Hesk. Perhaps the high-born of Nant treated their wives with more respect—less inclined than the rulers of Hesk to support lovers or use sex slaves in addition to their wives. Nevertheless, for all practical purposes commoner women in the kingdom had a great many more freedoms than their high-born counterparts.

In the case of Queen Gatha, King Monticu's estranged wife, almost no one ever saw her anymore. She had never in all her time as queen stepped foot in the Council Chamber. She might appear in the great throne room on high holidays such as the Meicalian Feast, and at the dining table when the king would deign to invite her.

Nikal's mind wandered to his mother. He could see in his mind the ice-hard gaze she bore at such events, forced as she was into the role of party décor. Nikal had always made a strong effort to treat her kindly and would visit her every time he returned to the capital from the campaign. He had visited her only three days previously, after the final Council meeting with the Berugian delegation.

The two had said little to one another of any consequence. He recalled now that short encounter. No, he had told her nothing of importance. Each had only inquired as to the health of the other. Maybe, Nikal thought, she was even quieter than she usually was. He knew she was much more open with Lekktor. Over the years there had been an occasion or two in which he had accidently interrupted the two in conversation. She would smile at Nikal, but never include him in her confidences. Rather, she would become quiet. Lekktor would carry on during these awkward moments. Lekktor, he knew, visited their mother quite often. She had her chambers in a remote part of the palace complex and with a forced sense of duty ordered the household from a self-confined distance.

Nikal realized that Hawking was right. The queen had great cause for possible intrigue against at least her husband. The king treated her poorly, there was no doubt about it, but Nikal for the life of him could not understand that she could in some way betray him, Nikal. He was as kindly to her as he knew how to be. It made perfect sense that Lekktor and she were closer, for his brother was in Sevarr often, but Nikal had never considered this to be all that important. He had never wondered why.

Maybe, he thought, he *should* be wondering why. He would add this to his growing list of worries.

He looked up, for the Chamber had grown suddenly quiet. All stood as the king entered, and with him walked two other men. And when Nikal saw who they were a horrible foreboding waxed in his chest, and a lump grew knot-hard in his throat. He would not have been able to speak just then if he had tried.

King Monticu sat down in his marble chair, and all the rest in the chamber followed suit, though Nikal with the greatest trepidation sat more slowly. Then the king motioned to the two men to stand on either side of him.

One of the men was Nikal's brother Lekktor. The other man was none other than Duke Rothee.

Dira's father.

Nikal was sitting as straight as a board, but being positioned near the back, the startled look on his face went unnoticed. Maybe, just maybe, Lekktor's eyes glanced his way, but Nikal couldn't be sure. Then suddenly his father looked towards him and smiled warmly, but it was only, Nikal realized, to ensure he was present. The king did not notice his favorite son's face had grown anxious and that he had broken into a sweat, for he quickly looked down again at a piece of parchment in his hands.

Then to Nikal's everlasting horror, to confirm his awful trepidation, unthinkable words proceeded from his own father's lips.

"I have called you all here today, my lords," began the king, "in order to proclaim to you great news! I have before me a contract signed and sealed that once I have summarized it for you, you will agree to join me in celebratory applause! The signatories stand here with me this morning, and I should hope you will all, after this announcement, offer them your most hearty congratulations!"

There were murmurings around the chamber that shuffled through Nikal's mind like cold water flowing through a cave. Why were people smiling and nodding? What were they murmuring to each other? Vaguely he was aware that Sawnd and Midale next to him were whispering.

"Ah, that is what this is about, is it?" said Midale quickly. "It is about time! His Highness Lekktor has put off choosing for long enough!"

Not far away sat Sage Ralle. Like Nikal, he was perfectly silent and was frowning. Before Nikal could process much of this, however, he heard his father's voice again over the mad beating of his heart.

"Yes!" he said. "His Grace the Duke Rothee has accepted His Highness Prince Lekktor's request for the hand of the duke's daughter the Lady Dira in Bonding! The contract of Bonding before me was signed two days ago in the afternoon. It is official and I have sealed it myself, and of course by the laws of our land it cannot be broken. The Lady Dira and His Highness Prince Lekktor are now legally Bondmates. The Lady Dira will arrive from the duke's estate in Noess in two more days, and on the fifth, I invite all of you to return to the Monastics Chapel for the customary Matrimonial rite."

Applause erupted, and all the men around him stood. Nikal, however, sat with a look on his face close to death. He stared at his brother standing beside his father's chair as he basked in, what was for Lekktor, rare applause. Nikal could hardly hear the clamorous sounds in the chamber, as his heart was now a vast drum, beating horribly. He did note that like himself, Sage Ralle had not stood either. Nikal looked at Lekktor again, who suddenly turned in his direction, and he watched with even more horror as a look developed in his brother's dark eyes and a sneer formed on his lips so vicious and conniving that Nikal believed he was looking in the face of one of the Alkhan's animal minions.

And Nikal knew. He had never spoken of Dira to his mother, never even mentioned that he had ever stayed in Noess, but somehow, she found out about the two of them.

And she told Lekktor.

Nikal could hardly comprehend the hate he now realized had all along been aimed at him, hate imbued through Lekktor's horrid sneer.

Nikal finally stood, and as the rest began to make their way to the front to offer their congratulations, he turned his back on the room full of lords and left.

Somehow, he got through it. Nikal was a man of the deepest emotion and greatest heart, but aside from the times he was with Dira, and old Antonin perhaps, he rarely allowed these traits to demonstrate themselves on the surface. It was not a matter of manly pride or any such nonsense, but rather because there were few with whom Nikal felt close or that seemed to understand that there was more to him than battle general and war hero. Within him existed a spiritual nature uncommon among the high-born in his country. His fame as a war hero also had an impact on him, causing him, aside from the heat of battle, to want to withdraw. He told the tale with grimmest determination.

Nikal knew Aron could read through the grimness. Aron was a rare breed of man. Quite likely it could be traced to the short Vision he had as a youngster. The two men, Nikal and Aron, shared Meicalian Principles and certain Disciplines, and it was what had drawn them together long ago. Otherwise, their surface natures were quite different. After Nikal had discoursed the proceeds of the Council meeting to him and of his love for Dira to the two Etoppsi, though Nikal himself seemed unable to express the full range of the emotions in his heart, Aron was not doing a good job fighting the tears that dripped from his gray eyes. He had seen the two, Dira and Nikal, together, and Aron alone was privy to the deep love those two shared for one another. He listened too as Rainwing, with Nikal's permission, repeated to him the Prophecy. Though clearly unnerved by it, Aron was attuned mostly to his friend.

"I swear to yyy...you upon my honor, sir, there is no one in this wide world who would have heard about Dira and you from me!"

"I did not suspect you, Aron, not at all. Have no fear. But now that you say that, I recall that Dira's mother knew of us. Dira told me so, and that her mother favored me."

"She mm..may have had a communication with the queen?"

"It would explain the source." Nikal realized his words sounded almost methodical and scientific, and the birds singing nearby in the gardens and the salt breeze off the nearby sea seemed surreal.

Hawking, though to a lesser degree perhaps than Aron, knew Nikal and the history of his spiritual maturation as well as anyone, for he had been close to old Antonin. Nikal could feel the empathy aimed his way from the giant creature.

Rainwing, too, though she had a blunt nature, looked at Nikal with sadness, though it was an Etoppsi trait to shed no tears.

"This is a bitter thing, and now we know the unfortunate truths of the first lines of the Taxiarch's message. The laws surrounding the pairings of your kind are strange to me."

"It is because these laws in Nant are highly unusual," explained Hawking. "In most other Human places, females are allowed to choose or to at least decline a pairing. These contractual Bondings among the high-born of Nant veer far from any Meicalian Disciplines, the ones designed for Humans, to establish monogamous pairings—happy ones, that is. And these derive out of the Principles of love, sacred to all the races. Tirilorin attempted contractual Bondings for a short period of time many years ago, but they abandoned them after the females of the city protested. But I remember when they were first imposed in Nant by your grandfather, Nikal. Antonin hotly opposed him on it, but the king had his way, and unfortunately the men on the Council at the time were equally inclined to the privilege. If privilege you call it. Even an Aura is denied. Yet I would think it might cut back on topling...I mean childbirths, considering how Auras impose their magic."

"Matrimonials are forbidden to mingle with the highborn, though they are summoned at the last to proclaim the nuptials. They are not even allowed to attend the Meicalian Feast in Sevarr but hold their own feast at the Convent. If the Aura is not seen, at least from what I understand what Antonin told me, then its magic cannot be worked. But, all this talk is not helpful. Dira is lost to me." He was grim as he said it, resigned to his fate. "If it is all the same to you two, I would like to leave for Tirilorin right away."

Rainwing was about to say something, but Hawking stopped her and spoke instead. "Meet us at the first platform in two hours. I will by then have messages prepared for one of my flyers to take back to Queen Silverwing, and we will bid farewell to our delegation."

As the two men walked together in the direction of the palace, Nikal listed for Aron several instructions.

After listening to these, Aron said, "Yy...your father will be unhappy thhh...that you do not remain for the ceremony."

"You and I both know that it is all a sham, and the rite is only for show. The deed is done, and there is no power in the universe that will make me even pretend to sanction what my brother has done to me...to Dira."

"Of course not, sir. I...ah...I am not suggesting you attend it. But the Prophecy mm...implies your father is ignorant. Do ah...you intend to inform him of the truth of the matter?"

"I don't know."

"How www...will he *ever* know?"

"I cannot decide, Aron, if it is important at this point for him to know. If he knew, what could he do? Nothing. It would become a great scandal if the truth were known! And Dira would be in the middle of it."

"I see it, and you...ah...you're right. Perhaps it is not wise to tell him, at least not now. It can ah...wait. However, Nikal, be aware that yyy...your brother has manipulated and used your father the king. Do ah...you really think it will be the last and only time?"

Nikal looked at Aron but did not answer. "You will give my father my excuses for having gone to Tirilorin after I have left with the Berugians. You understand?"

"Yy...yes, sir. Absolutely. The question is..."

"No, I don't know when I will return, and Letti cannot travel so far across open sea with messages, but you will carry on as though I have issued you a thousand orders, and my temporary absence will not be questioned by anyone. Gather the officers and specialists and armorers to send to Berug and have them set sail as soon as may be. Continue the recruitment, continue to send supplies and men east and gather what news you can. But I will return, Aron. Maybe I will be back before the military trainers set sail for Berug. But after the Bonding rite, for sure."

"I am going with you when you begin this hunt for the Staff of Terianh." Aron said this without flaw, determined as he obviously was and with a steely look.

It was the first time Nikal attempted a smile since early that morning. This time he put a hand on each of Aron's shoulders. "Yes, you are. Now, go. You have work to do, friend."

When Nikal arrived at his chambers, he paused for a moment and sighed deeply. Yet, knowing that it would kill him inside to dwell on the revelations of the day, he began to put a few items together to take with him. He retrieved a heavy woolen cloak. This time he would be better prepared for the great height at which the Etoppsi traveled.

"Climbing a mountain today, Brother?" said a conniving voice from the back of the room.

He whirled around. There stood the source of his heartbreak. But Nikal was much wiser now. *The man standing there hates you.*

"No words, Nikal? Surely you have something to say to me. After all the times you have countered my direction in this city, humiliating me in front of our father and all the rest?"

"I...I never knew I was hurting you."

"Perhaps not, yet you did. I am the older brother and heir to the throne of Nant, but I have dwelt always in your shadow. Always have you put me in my place, ridiculed my choices and set Father against me."

"I have never ridiculed you," Nikal replied steadily. "And Father has never..."

"Of course, he has! You think I'm a fool? He has always preferred you above me! Do you deny it?"

Nikal was silent for a moment. He had no desire to give Lekktor more excuses. "Like I said, Lekktor, I never knew I was hurting you. You should have come to me long ago if you felt this way! Long ago! We could have worked something out. We are brothers!"

"Would you have given up your position? No! And Father would not have allowed you to in any regard!"

"My position? Is that what you want, Lekktor? You want to be the one who goes off to battle in the east? Pardon me, but I never believed you wanted that."

"Battles! Wars!" Lekktor spat. "Who needs them? We have what we want here in Nant. It is a waste for us to go off and fight other people's wars! You play the hero, and because of it Father loves you!"

"I am not sure anymore that you understand what love is, Lekktor. Hearing you talk makes me see that there are even more differences between the two of us than I ever knew existed before. Nant is a great nation, and we fight the Alkhan because He threatens our friends, and we are committed! And now the Witch of Westrealm moves! Would you bring all our forces back to Nant?"

"Perhaps. Or I would go for a different strategy. Nant is great, as you say, but you would save the eastern kingdoms from their fate and allow them to continue as independent nations. Nant should rule, I say! The kingdoms of the world should follow our lead and pay us tribute in return for our protection. We could be a great empire!"

"You have expressed that view in Council. Most did not favor that position, and you changed your mind and accepted their take! I even remember you stating that the will of the Nantians was paramount. I remember you being quite eloquent about it!"

"At the time I believed my suggestion had perhaps gone a little too far."

"So, you only said the last to retain some support? Oh." A few things were beginning to make sense to him. Hawking was more right than Nikal had realized.

"You are growing wiser, Brother. However, I came here to find you, because I thought you might wish to discuss another little matter."

Nikal refused to respond. In fact, he began to gather more of his things for his journey and threw them on his bed.

"You love her, don't you?" Lekktor goaded.

Nikal paused. "You have never met her, have you? You have never laid eyes on Dira, have you, Lekktor?"

"She is the woman I have chosen. And it is my right, by law, to choose my Bondmate first...before you, that is. I hardly care what she looks like. She will bear my heirs, and like Father with Mother, I will otherwise see her rarely. There are plenty of other women at my call."

Though Dira was indeed the subject, Nikal was wary about expressing before Lekktor anything regarding his feelings for her. He did not want his brother to take more sadistic pleasure in his misery or use his own words to later taunt Dira. "You kept the truth from Father. You used the king for your own gain, and to hurt me."

"So, you will admit I hurt you?"

Nikal stopped the shuffling of his gear and turned around to glare fully at his brother. He never knew his brother was prone to such pettiness. He looked in his eyes but did not see madness there. Lekktor was in full control of his faculties. Nikal had one question, and he worded it carefully. "When did Mother suggest this to you?"

Lekktor grinned. "Not as uninformed as I thought you were, Brother. You're right. Not all, you see, favor you over me. Yes, I have sat on the idea for a while, waiting for the right time to implement it. You'll remember the other day I think when you overruled me on the supplies. How the captains fawned over you, praising your decisions. Father took your position on the matter...as he always does. For me, you see, it was the last straw."

The pettiness was beginning to really get to Nikal. He could hardly believe what he was hearing, and the confirmation that his mother was a major part of the scheme, though warned of it in the Prophecy, added to his pain. But the pain only clarified his thinking. "You would prefer it when military captains, as you say, 'fawn over' you?"

Though his cheeks reddened slightly, Lekktor suppressed a retort. "You know, old Duke Rothee was really delighted when I approached him that morning and proposed the match."

"Maybe you should leave now, Lekktor. I am busy." Nikal turned again to his packing.

"No! I will leave when you admit to me I have hurt you. I am, as you see, the oldest son and the heir. I am taking what is mine. I'm giving you a taste, Brother, of what your future will be. There will come a day when you will not be able to thwart me. You will not be able to overrule me, as there will be no one left who will favor you over me! I have taken away from you the woman you love. Love. What an old notion! Commoners and their stupid Matrimonials. Meicalian Principles and Disciplines, bah! Yet old notions played you for a fool, making you pin all your hopes in a *woman*, and that made it easy for me. Old Antonin played with your mind all those years ago."

"I am sorry you feel that way. Until today, Lekktor, I loved *you*. Until today, I was one who supported you. It is true that I did not agree with all your decisions, particularly regarding the use of the navy, but in other regards I had you on a pedestal. I would have served as your captain as readily as I serve now as Father's. Maybe I did not demonstrate that in such a way that you understood it. But now I have heard you speak, I realize that no matter what I might have done differently, it would not have altered what took place in the Council Chamber this morning."

Lekktor paused at this, but then seemed to cast aside his brother's sincerity. "It is good to know that by my own hand you have learned a lesson, Nikal. For the moment, anyway, I am content."

Nikal drew closer to his brother and looked at him darkly. "Really? You're telling me you don't intend to scheme again for a while? Content, are you? I, however, am *not* content. And I warn you, Lekktor, I never will be again."

As Nikal said these words with deadly seriousness, Lekktor's cynical smile faltered, and he swallowed hard.

Nikal aimed to turn away. Then, with the speed of a bolt of lightning and the power of a battering ram his heavy fist landed in the middle of Lekktor's face. The man staggered, then crumpled, falling to the floor with a thud, blood and puss pouring from his mouth and broken nose.

"You should have left my rooms when I suggested it. It is good to know that *by my own hand* you have learned a lesson, Lekktor."

As his brother lost consciousness, he took some comfort in the knowledge that Lekktor would never dare tell their father the truth, for the king would question him at length to get to the bottom of it. Nikal was quite sure Lekktor would not want that to happen. There were advantages, Nikal realized, to being his father's favorite.

"You are not king yet, dear brother of mine."

He finished packing his things then went to the balcony and called in a sharp whistle for Letti. In a moment, she had flown to him and landed on his shoulder.

"Go to Aron, little one!" he said, stroking her beak. "I will return."

She flew off again.

He grabbed his pack, his cloak and sword, and as he was leaving the palace, he ordered a servant to send a message to the queen that the Prince Lekktor wished her to attend to him in Nikal's bedchamber.

"...and tell Her Majesty she might wish to send for a pair of Meicalian Healers." Then, in answer to the servant's query he added, "No. His Highness my brother has injured himself, but no, there is no need to hurry. He'll live."

Nikal then made his way to the Berugian Guest Tower.

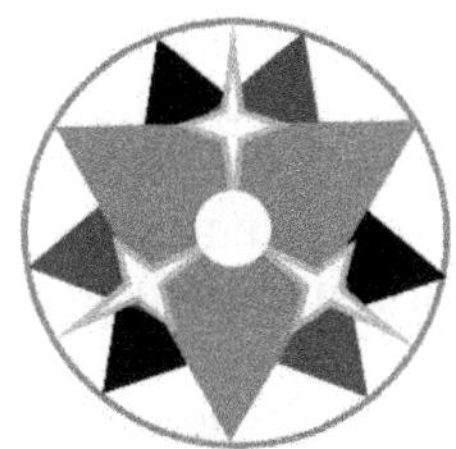

Chapter 4—Tirilorin

On the tenth day out from Guardian's Gate, Curdoz' company entered the southernmost of the two great harbors of Tirilorin. Captain Shond had sailed through the previous night, and now before them in the morning sun stood the former imperial capital in all its splendor.

No city in all the world compared. The Sage had visited the city over twenty years before, but the rest were stunned by the view. Even Kodi, who had experienced the city in reasonably vivid detail in his Vision was amazed at its vastness, for at this vantage the city spread in all directions as far as the eye could see. Aster and Ferostro were as villages in comparison, and according to Curdoz the larger part of the peoples of the Republic lived within its walls. There were villages and many hundreds of farms spreading outward from the walls eighty miles or more that supported the city's inhabitants, but its great wealth, Curdoz explained, relied on a vast trading network that spread from Solanto and Eleni in the north, to the island Kingdom of Nant, and all the way to the Eastern Kingdoms.

Established by Terianh the Great after the downfall of the Ralsheen, the city's emperors for nearly four hundred years ruled a land that in area outstretched the previous empire, encompassing nearly all of the Northern Continent in addition to Nant and many other islands. Only in the far north, where the Ice Tribes held sway, and in Ulakel, the land of the Qeteral, did they hold no dominion. Yet even the Qeteral acknowledged the emperor and maintained a communication until the Abdication.

Many circumstances led to that event. If Tirilorin had a disadvantage it was its location. Though perfect for maintaining overlordship of the western kingdoms, namely Solanto, Nant, and old Lintiri, in addition to the imperial domain of old Lorinth, the city's distance from the eastern realms made it nearly impossible for the emperors to hold much influence there. With the exception of Eleni, whose styles and customs were quite similar to the other western domains, those kingdoms further away were prone to disregard Terianh's successors. Eventually, Barant separated from the Empire after three wars and even expelled its Sage and Meicalian Orders, aligning themselves more closely with the Ice Tribes. The other two, Essemar and the desert kingdom of Hralindi, remained friendly and continued to believe in the High Guardian Meical and still had their Sages and Orders, sending their Gifted to the Valley.

But it was in the last war, when the small Kingdom of Lintiri was overrun by the Khestadone that the final blows fell to the Empire. Though the war was eventually won, and the enemy was forced to withdraw, the last emperor, Zarelio, could take no credit for the victory which came at substantial cost in lives. He remained in Tirilorin and did not join the fight, having sent the Solantine Grand Duke Baggaro to lead the armies in his stead. Hralindi and Essemar saw this move as cowardly, and when the war was over, those two kingdoms disavowed their association with the Empire, and Zarelio in his weakness could do nothing. Lintiri was no more, as most of its surviving inhabitants fled to Lorinth and Tirilorin, never to return, and even Eleni soon withdrew its ambassador from the emperor's court.

Finally, the merchants and rich men of Tirilorin, wanting more control over international trade and desiring to eliminate the tax burden that supported the imperial bureaucracy, persuaded Zarelio to abdicate in favor of an experiment in what came to be called republican government. Though Zarelio and his descendants were guaranteed a position on the new Republican Assembly and allowed to continue to dwell in the palace, the Assembly took over the government of the city, and the Imperial Domain of Lorinth was absorbed into the Assembly's jurisdiction. The name Lorinth was rarely used anymore.

It was the first such government in the history of the world, and though imperialism was no more, if anything, at least for Tirilorin, the move created greater efficiency and wealth. The city grew enormously, and the Outer Wall was built by Human hands within the last century. It was not quite as tall as the old Central City Wall, built by the Etoppsi centuries before with more massive stones, but it was nevertheless strong and imposing.

Upon disembarking, Sage Curdoz, Mother Idamé, and the twins went immediately to the harbormaster's office to request information. Curdoz thought it unwise to take Musca along until they learned more about the rules in the city regarding animals, so they left him with Captain Shond and the crew. When they arrived at the place, they found it was an attractive and clean building. Inside there were many people bustling about. The harbormaster was not there, but they quickly found his young assistant. He had trouble averting his eyes from the beautiful Lyndz, but when Kodi stepped up beside her and glared at the man, his smile faltered.

Curdoz introduced himself as the Sage of the Guardian of the Kingdom of Solanto; the assistant was amazed and sent immediately for his master.

When the man arrived, he was as surprised as was his assistant but greeted them with gracious words. "I am honored by your presence, Your Grace, as I know the rest of the City Masters will be also!" He was a heavyset, thickly bearded man, and stood with an important air.

Curdoz introduced the others to him and then asked, "So you yourself are one of the Masters?"

"Yes, Your Grace," he said with a little bow. "As Harbormaster of Southport, I am on the Assembly, and I welcome you to our city. My name is Candler Yamin, and I will escort you myself to the Central Offices if you wish it, to see High Master Naloro. Such esteemed guests! If I may ask, what brings you to our City? It must be important for a Sage to leave his own country, particularly when the world is as troubled as it now is. Are all things well in Solanto?"

Though trouble might be stirring in Solanto, Curdoz had no desire to bring up the subject with so many stray ears around them, so he skirted it. "Fine, fine. It's true, Master Yamin. There is a reason I and my companions here have come to Tirilorin. We are on a quest from the Guardian Meical Himself and have information of a critical nature to discuss with a certain few. We need assistance and guidance, and though I will certainly attend to your High Master, I must also meet with Master Genehbro, for I know him to be a great scholar."

Lyndz noticed that at the mention of the Guardian, Yamin lifted his eyebrows, and she remembered what Curdoz had told them about the skepticism of the Tirilorines towards Meicalian history.

Skeptic or not, Master Yamin was anxious to please. "Of course, Your Grace."

To a boy in the office, Yamin ordered him to have his carriage brought around, and then he spoke to the assistant for a few minutes on expectations for the next two hours for which he would be away. It was clear from his professional responses the assistant was as adept as the harbormaster himself at the operations of Southport Harbor. After a last stolen glance at Lyndz, the assistant went off to carry out his master's requests.

"I don't like that fellow," whispered Kodi.

"Just like home, of course you don't," chuckled Lyndz. "Are you going to scowl at every young man in Tirilorin who takes a liking to me?"

"Maybe."

"And shall I do the same to the women who look at you for more than two seconds?"

Kodi grinned and mumbled something inaudible.

"Speak up, Ko! I didn't hear that!"

He was spared having to clarify when Yamin came back over to them and spoke again. "Now, Your Grace, of the Masters only High Master

Naloro will likely be at the Offices. But if your errand is such that time is of the essence, I can send runners to any of the other Masters."

"I understand that my brother Sage in the Orders, Enric, is on the Republican Assembly? I think it best to meet with him first of all."

"Yes, by tradition, the Sage of Tirilorin is an Assembly member, just as myself. He is a good man, Enric, although we don't always see eye to eye. His residence is near to the Central Offices in Central City. Certainly seems fitting for you to visit him, of course. If you wish, I can take you to him rather than to High Master Naloro?"

"Yes, that would be greatly appreciated. I need to confer with Brother Enric about the Guardian Meical's quest, and then we will go to your High Master later in the afternoon. If you would send one other message to Master Genehbro telling him of my arrival and desire to meet with him perhaps tomorrow, then that would be sufficient."

Yamin nodded. "I'll send a message to the palace, yet Genehbro is visiting one of his estates outside the city. But he is scheduled to return in time for tomorrow afternoon's Assembly, so perhaps then the two of you shall meet. Let me check on the carriage. Do you have belongings to transport?"

"Yes, a few, although we will leave most of our things on my ship."

"Your ship and property will be fully secured, Your Grace. Thievery is rare in the city, yet I'll set guard upon it anyhow, and we have lodging for your ship's sailors. Do you have horses to stable?"

"We brought none, thank you. However, we do have a large dog on board. He belongs to Kodi and Lyndz. We didn't know if he..."

"Oh, he's quite welcome, Your Grace. Go and fetch him and your belongings. Do you need help with those? I will bring the carriage around to your dock."

"We'll manage, thank you, but your offer of the carriage is most welcome. May the Guardian Affirm you!" Curdoz said this last with the traditional raising of the forward palm.

"Um, yes, Your Grace. Ah, thank you." Yamin retreated promptly at that, leaving them alone. As the four companions were walking back to their ship, Lyndz asked Curdoz what he was doing continually bringing up the Guardian when he himself had told them about the doubts the Tirilorines had regarding what they called "religion."

He and Idamé both laughed, and it was she who responded. "It may be that most in the city doubt, but we don't, do we? It would not be wise for Curdoz, a Sage of the Guardian, to show doubt."

Curdoz added, "Their doubt may work to our advantage in some ways. Tirilorines are polite to a fault, and they will not question our sincerity or purpose. They doubt, yes, but they will be afraid to demonstrate actual disbelief to one of the Gifted, at least that is what I have learned through my correspondence with Sage Enric."

"But how do they treat Sage Enric if they are so doubtful?" asked Kodi.

"Again, they are polite. He's written me many a letter over the years, and he tells me that behind his back they continually disregard his teachings on the Prophecies and Histories. But by tradition the Orders operate freely. Most hold to the Principles in any regard, if less so to certain Disciplines. But the Republican Assembly is more a democratic institution than the King's Council in Solanto, and even the Sage has only one vote here. His position then is for the most part based on tradition, which the Tirilorines were, unlike their attitude toward other old traditions, unwilling to discard."

"They're superstitious," replied Lyndz.

The Sage looked at her, surprised again by Lyndz' ability to discern intricacies at her age and said so. "You are exactly right, Lyndz. Yet they would deny it. You can see that? Kodi, you need to pay attention to your sister more."

He laughed. "I do. But what are they superstitious of?"

Curdoz smiled at Lyndz. "You tell him."

"Well, they may be skeptical of Meicalian History and Prophecies, but they don't have any real way of disproving them, do they? If they are true, then they would look foolish to let it go."

"That's right," put in Mother Idamé. "Besides, they do have Meicalian Healers, and Matrimonials, and they can see the work they do, particularly the Healers. As long as the Healers claim their authority from the Guardian, and we can presume many of their healings are quite miraculous, and as Auras are proclaimed from time to time by the Matrimonials, they will have a hard time totally discarding the idea of Giftedness."

Back on board to retrieve their belongings, they found Musca anxious to leave the ship. "He needs to roam. He needs exercise," said Kodi.

"Yes, let's ask if he can run alongside instead of in the carriage," said Lyndz.

And so, they did. Master Yamin was perfectly amenable to that idea when Curdoz asked him. He was intrigued by Musca, as nearly all people were. "Fine, fine specimen, I say!" Besides, it was a tight fit for all of them, and it would have been even more so if Musca had to travel in the carriage, too. Therefore, he trotted proudly alongside as they traveled the well-paved streets towards Central City, and on their little journey many a head turned and pointed, and other city dogs barked at him. As typical, Musca ignored all of the attention.

Though tight, Yamin's carriage was sumptuous and well-padded, and was pulled by two massive charcoal mares. Everywhere they looked, the city of Tirilorin was a sight to behold. Never had they seen a city so perfectly manicured, and every building in the city was beautifully designed. Everywhere were pointed arches, towers and turrets. Even the areas where the working classes lived were quite nice, with wide streets as well-paved as in any other part of the city, kept clean by hundreds of workers, and small but beautifully painted houses decorated with window boxes and iron fences, and green parks where children played. Thousands of people visible upon the streets were going in and coming out of hundreds of shops and businesses. Though most people walked, there were nevertheless dozens of carriages and hundreds of wagons pulled by smart horses and mules. There were a hundred large stables in every part of the city, according to Master Yamin.

It took them at least half an hour to travel through this part of the city. All along, Master Yamin, the Sage, and Mother Idamé were deep in conversation.

"Your coming to us is rather opportune, Your Grace."

"In what way, Master Yamin?" asked Curdoz.

"Only a week ago we received a request from Hralindi and Essemar to send direct aid. They need more than the food supplies we send them. They request an army."

Kodi exclaimed, "Really? Is the war going that badly?"

"The Alkhan stalls near to the Great Arch and has taken possession of some of the towns and lands on the Southern Continent claimed by Essemar."

"What is the Great Arch?" asked Lyndz.

"It is a magnificent natural archway that connects a point of the Southern Continent with the Northern Continent. Under it the waters of the Central Passage empty into the Great Eastern Ocean, and by that all the world's waters are connected to each other. There is much ship traffic under the Arch. Essemar controls that region. If the Arch is taken, the enemy would not need ships in order to access the homelands of the Eastern Kingdoms. They are building more defenses in the vicinity of the Arch, but if the enemy were strong enough to take the Arch, it would nearly doom our eastern friends. The Arch is the key to the eastern half of the Northern Continent. But the stall by the enemy is surely for the purpose of making further preparations. The Assembly has been convening regularly and debating how we should respond. It would help to know how the situation stands in your kingdom, in Solanto. What is your king thinking on these matters?"

"Request for aid would be news, Master, though we are well aware of the war in the East," replied Curdoz. "But I'm afraid that what is happening in the rest of the world is for now a distraction for some, though not all. I am always encouraging friendship with the east, and the High Chancellor, Grand Duke Mannago is of like mind and is close to the king's ear."

"But there is a problem?"

"Yes, I'm afraid there is, and I was loath to leave Solanto. There is some internal dissension brewing. The ruler of the Principality of Hesk is the center of it. There is a situation unfolding. I'm afraid I left before I could determine the plot, but our king is unlikely to move to assist old allies until it is resolved. I'm afraid for now that your Assembly will have to leave Solanto out of your reckoning if you're looking for any serious help from us as well. At least until then."

"Ah, I am sorry to hear that, Your Grace. It does increase the burden on the rest of the former Empire to deal with the threat of the Twin Kingdoms."

"The Alkhaness has not engaged yet, has she?"

"Not precisely. However, news from the Nantian forts on the coast of the Southern Continent imply that her forces may be massing."

"You can rest assured that we are well aware of the threat they pose," offered Idamé.

"Mother Idamé is right. For it all speaks to our quest from the Guardian, Master Yamin. You could say that our leaving Solanto was a bit like following orders."

"Ah, you don't say." Yamin tried to hold back his skepticism. "A quest from the Guardian. Yes, of course. I suppose being Members of the Orders you... ah, never mind. I'm sure you have your reasons for looking at it so. I look forward to hearing more, of course. I'm sure the Masters will assist you as needed, Your Grace."

"Thank you, Master Yamin. That is encouraging to hear!" said Curdoz.

Finally, they came to Central City. This was obvious, as the Inner Wall stood stark and high, designating where this wealthy, older part of the city stood. The boulevard on which they rode pierced the Wall through fabulous wrought-iron gates. Imposing, these must be meant for show, Kodi realized, and not for defense. On the other side of the Wall stood houses of immense size and sundry colors reflecting different types of stone in their construction. The streets were even wider here, and in the distance upon its high hill was the old Imperial Palace. The twins and Idamé could hardly believe their eyes and could hardly wait for the opportunity to visit it. Pointed domes of gold and turquoise pierced the sky.

Compared to the bustle of the city outside the Wall, Central City seemed quieter, for there were fewer people out walking, and most of these appeared to be workers, servants, messengers, gardeners, and the like. There were more carriages and fancy coaches here, some small, designed for two occupants and pulled by one proud horse, and others larger like the one in which they themselves rode. The shops and markets they saw in this part of the city were fewer but larger and clearly contained more luxury goods. Numerous parks were filled with flowers and fountains and tall cypresses and other trees common to this more temperate clime.

These lovely parks and the beauty they exhibited finally found a way to pierce Lyndz' silence. "I wish every city were like this! This is the way a city ought to be. Spread out and spacious, with gardens and trees."

Kodi responded. "I know you love the gardens. I like the fountains and stonework. It'd be great to live here, but I'd miss the forests and the hills and the rivers after a while. But it's all really impressive. Nothing like it. Most of these houses are bigger than the manor they're building for Father back home in Felto! And did you see the Imperial Palace? I bet it's three times the size of the King's in Ferostro. And much taller. What do you think, Curdoz?"

"Yes. It was built by the Etoppsi long ago, as was the Great Library and the Inner Wall."

"The Etoppsi left their mark on many things here in Central City," added Master Yamin. "The largest fountains are all of Etoppsi design, and the water supply and aqueducts from the hills, the city's plumbing and sewer systems, all were conceived and constructed by the Etoppsi over four hundred years ago. There's nothing quite at the level in the Northern World, although they say that Berug, their country on the Southern Continent, is full of cities with parks and fountains like these, and hundreds of buildings bigger and taller than the old Imperial Palace. They say that there they build their great houses taller than the tallest watchtowers here in the North, for they prefer to take flight from high places."

"Have you ever seen an Etoppsis?" asked Lyndz. Kodi turned, too, to listen to the answer.

"I certainly have! They are as magnificent as anything you've ever heard tell of. They don't come here often like in the days of the Empire, but every ten years or so some will fly here, and there will be great celebration in the city. They are huge, you know, and er, they have very shapely bodies. They wear no garments, you see. They don't really think it's proper to wear clothes. They say that...well they still hold to old beliefs, and they say that the Creator made them the way they are, and that they were not meant for clothing. And they do have a fine fur coat, but, ahem," he coughed, "it doesn't hide much. They are a sight to behold, I'll say. Shapely like fine imperial statuary. They are a great people, and loyal friends to us in the Northern World, particularly the Nantians. They visit them quite regularly from what I hear."

It took another five minutes or so before Master Yamin's driver pulled left through a tall cypress hedge behind a low stone wall, divided by twin iron gates. They had arrived at the estate of the Sage of Tirilorin. His residence was smaller than some, still beautiful, with a formal, though colorful front garden. The driveway was in a curved, symmetrical pattern that wound through pretty trees, tall pines of a type with which Kodi wasn't familiar since these had lost all their lowest branches and opened high in broad canopies. Below them spread a shaded lawn of the brightest green interspersed with tiny, many-hued flowers of a type that Lyndz did not recognize. In the middle was a fountain carved in the exact likeness of a giant swan. Out of its bill poured a bright flow of crystal-clear water into a stone basin as large as a small pond. Surrounding this stonework were more of the tiny colorful flowers contained by stone pavers.

As the carriage pulled up to the front doors, they saw a man get up from a large cast-iron bench in a small patio inset to the right of the main entry. He appeared to have been taking in the late morning sunshine. They saw that he was a good deal older than Curdoz, with gray hair and long beard. When he stood, he was a little stooped, and yet he walked easily enough with no cane or staff. The carriage stopped, and promptly Yamin's driver climbed down and opened the carriage doors, whereupon all five of them popped out one by one. Musca had stopped at the fountain for a drink but pranced over to them when he saw Kodi stretching himself. The dog was cheered by the opportunity to run and move about after being on Curdoz' ship for so many days, and he licked Kodi's hand as was typical. The old man took in this scene with a warm expression on his face, as Yamin walked over to him. They greeted one another cordially.

"An unexpected pleasure, City Master Yamin!" spoke the old man. He had a voice that was a bit scratchy though strong, still.

"I should visit more often, City Master Enric! You have a lovely place."

Lyndz noted the use of the title. She presumed that 'Your Grace' was used by Yamin for Curdoz because he was an eminent figure from another country and it was a proper address, but that the Sage of Tirilorin was referred to with a respectful, though clearly republican designation.

"I have brought you some esteemed visitors from far off Solanto!" Yamin added.

Enric looked again at the visitors and walked over to them all. He noticed Curdoz' stole. "Why, I cannot believe my eyes! My dear Brother Curdoz of Solanto! No, I cannot believe it! What brings you here? The Affirmation of the Guardian be upon you, my good Brother!" The two Sages warmly embraced, and kissed each other's cheeks, the common greeting between Order Members.

"After all these many years we meet at last, Brother Enric! You yourself were visiting Brother Antonin in Nant when I came twenty years ago, and we missed each other! A hundred letters between us, I suppose. Haven't we shared much! It is great to get to see you at last!"

Kodi wondered at this. All along he had presumed that the two Sages must have known each other from the Valley of the Gifted, but apparently this wasn't so. Then he considered Enric's apparent age and it occurred to him that Enric had likely left the Valley of the Gifted some years before Curdoz had gone there to study for the Orders. And yet they apparently corresponded with one another regularly. He then wondered if there was a whole network of communications among the several Sages and tucked that question in the back of his mind for later.

"But there must be some great reason for you to have come here, my Brother. Ah! A Vision! Of course! You have had a Vision, Brother Curdoz! There could be no other reason for you to have left Solanto and come here when the world is troubled!"

Curdoz nodded. "Perceptive, Brother Enric. We have much to talk about. Let me introduce you to my companions." Whereupon he did so, and for each one, the older Sage looked intently into each of their faces with the same warmth and pronounced the Meicalian Affirmation. From Kodi he looked down at Musca. He appeared as much startled by the great silver dog as he was by Curdoz.

"But what is this!" Musca sat back respectfully and looked up at the old man. "Why! Could this be an Elentine Noble from my own home country? This is magnificent! I haven't seen one in fifty years! He belongs to you, young man? Kodi, is it?"

"Yes, sir. And my sister, too. My father purchased Musca here for us a few years ago."

"Really! I did not know there were any in Solanto. They are not common even in Eleni. Only the royal family and high noblemen are known to have them, and the silver coat is most rare. They are known to be ferocious in the battles with the Ice Tribes." He bent down, looking more closely and placed his hand on Musca's furry head. Musca remained still as Master Enric examined him. He looked over at Curdoz. "Brother Curdoz! This one has green eyes! I have never known of such a thing among dogs of any kind, have you? Musca is your name, is it? Why! You are no ordinary dog! Even for such a noble breed, you are not. There is something special about you!"

Curdoz replied, "I'm sure you're right, Brother Enric. In fact, Musca has already proven himself special."

"Sounds to me you have a tale or two to tell. You will all remain here with me. I have plenty of room for you all. Master Yamin, have your man unload. I will happily take them under wing from here."

Master Yamin had stepped back during all these welcomes and greetings, but now that he had completed his obligation of escorting his eminent visitors to their requested destination, he thought it well now to take his leave. They all thanked him for his kindness and the carriage ride, and he made one final comment, "I suppose, Master Enric, and Your Grace, Curdoz, I will see the two of you again, perhaps tomorrow afternoon at Assembly? Your presence among us leaves me curious, Your Grace, and I look forward to your tale. Is there anything else I can do for you, Your Grace? I'll send word to the High Master and Master Genehbro as you requested, and your ship's captain and crew will be well-taken care of, I promise you."

Curdoz assured him there was nothing more, but then pronounced the Affirmation again upon the harbormaster who after replying noncommittally boarded his carriage and rode out of the driveway. By that time, house servants had appeared, Monastics obviously in dark clothes, all respectful in their demeanor, and after receiving orders from their master, took all the guests' belongings inside. Sage Enric himself then followed, escorting his visitors.

It was nice though simple as befitted a high member of the Orders. Like Curdoz' estate on Island Saundry, nothing here was on the order of palatial in style, and yet it was still of high quality. In the large sitting room were many upholstered chairs in soft felts, all of solid colors. There were tables, again of good make and beautifully grained wood, but with straight, unadorned legs. Carpets, too, were plush but of no pattern. It was only on the walls that the visitor found paintings and the occasional tapestry that reflected great artistry.

On the largest wall in the main parlor, a mural of fabulous size and color was painted. Kodi recognized from his Vision the Valley of the Gifted, and without requesting permission strode over to it to get a closer look at the detail. Here it all was in a beautiful panorama with its green hills, waterways, white columned temples, and tree groves, surrounded by high mountains and numerous distant waterfalls. For several minutes he could not take his eyes from it. In addition to his concurrent wish to become a warrior, he had such a strong desire to go to that Valley, to bask in the light, to bathe in its waters, to run through the hills, to study in the great halls, to gather strength in his Gift. He didn't even know what his Gift was, besides Visions, and wondered if he would find the answers there. Curdoz had promised him that his Gift, and Lyndz' too, would manifest eventually whether or not they went there, and that a pilgrimage to the Valley would have to be put off. The quest was all-important, and the tradition of the pilgrimage and typical years of study could wait if it was even determined to be a part of their destiny. It did not bother Lyndz, because she had not experienced that feeling of inner strength and strong emotion that Kodi had. With the mural before him, he was again reminded of it, wishing to experience it all again, even in another Vision, although he began to wonder if he would have another. He turned around and saw the others were there too, looking around. For a moment he had forgotten them. Master Enric walked up to him.

"You recognize it, do you?"

"Yes, sir."

"From a Vision, I take it? That is why you are with Brother Curdoz, I presume."

"Yes, sir. If you don't mind my asking, sir, who painted this?"

Enric smiled. "I did it myself, as a matter of fact, soon after I came here. All from memory of course. Took me years. It remains on the mind, though."

Kodi understood and nodded.

"You are a great artist, sir!" Lyndz had now come over to them and began studying the mural herself.

"Thank you, young lady. Lyndz, is it? Are the two of you twins?"

"Yes, Master Enric. We are both nineteen," replied Lyndz.

"You certainly favor! And have you too had a Vision?"

"No, sir."

"You will," Enric stated matter-of-factly, to which Lyndz did not respond.

Curdoz was nearby, listening. "We all have much to discuss, Brother Enric. Mother Idamé is in need of some rest, and I'd like to talk to you privately for a while, if it is all the same to you."

"Certainly, Brother Curdoz. You should find your things in rooms upstairs and even a bite to eat. I was about to have a bit of lunch myself. I had a meeting scheduled with the Mother Superior in the afternoon, but she will understand if I put it off. I'll send word to her. I'll wait for you here. Go refresh yourselves."

They were then led by a cheery, female Monastic by the name of Hollina to rooms on a second floor where they each found their belongings. Curdoz and Idamé found themselves sharing a suite of rooms containing two bedrooms with a small sitting room between. Across a wide hall were more guestrooms where brother and sister were each bestowed. The Mother begged to be alone for a while, saying that she needed some reflection time and a long nap. Of all of them, she suffered the most from lack of sleep on the cabin hammocks in Curdoz' rolling ship and was eager to lie on a flat bed. She made arrangements, however, for Lyndz to return to her at two hours past noon.

"It is time to work more on discerning what your Gift is, Lyndz. We will likely be here many days, and this is the perfect opportunity. Sage Enric even has a temple setting in a back garden, he says. It will help us find the peace needed."

"I'll just wander around aimlessly then," said Kodi with a chuckle.

Idamé laughed. "Sage Curdoz, and perhaps even Sage Enric, will work with you, dear. It is tradition in the Orders that men work with men and that women work with women. Men understand other men better than we women do, and vice versa. But don't forget the general nature of all our Visions, Kodi. Lord Curdoz was meant to be your guide."

Frankly, it seemed to Kodi that Curdoz, being the leader of their company, was busy. After finding his rooms and washing his face, Curdoz had promptly headed back downstairs with his bread and cheese tray in hand and was now talking at length with the Sage of Tirilorin. Those two would likely depart at some point to meet the High Master of the City. Kodi wondered how much time Curdoz would really have for him. There was also the young man in Kodi's Vision who needed to be found. They did not yet know who he was, but it was almost certain he was wealthy. Most likely he lived right here in Central City. Kodi wanted to look for him and solve that mystery. He hoped Curdoz would at least take him with him when they went to see the High Master. Maybe upon asking around, possible clues as to who the man was would reveal themselves. Specifically, he wanted to go to the Palace front lawn and see the statue of Terianh the Great.

Lyndz did not act tired, though like the others she did relish the good cheese and fine white bread that the house servants had left in her rooms, for they had eaten none too well on Curdoz' tiny ship. Being a great observer of detail, she began a little stroll through Sage Enric's home taking in everything. Musca had been taken off to the kitchen for a treat, and Kodi decided since there was little else to do just now, he would join his sister. Lyndz made several observations, telling her brother that the ambience was the sort that their folks should create in their manor in Felto once it was time to occupy it. Kodi agreed. He knew that the simplicity of the furniture, the quality of the woodwork and art, would appeal to his mother and father. Nothing was gilt, nothing was overly decorated, and all was well-ordered and clean. After thoroughly exploring all the many rooms inside, carefully avoiding the Sages in conversation in the great parlor, they exited through a set of large rear doors and found themselves instantly in an enchanting garden.

The tall and unusual pines in the front entrance had cast shadows on the bright lawn, yet this rear garden was even shadier with numerous dense broadleaf trees and thick shrubs, ivies, groundcovers, large boulders of deliberate shapes like animal sculptures, and a little brook which ran and played through it all. It was all very green. Lyndz especially was mesmerized, a typical emotion for her when she visited any well-kept garden. There were many birds singing here, and together with the breezes, which from time to time moved in the upper reaches of the trees, they set into play an enchanting music. As they moved slowly through it on a winding path of crushed seashells beside the little brook, they eventually crossed this over a petite yellow bridge. Ahead of them, tucked into the shade of a dense planting of tall green trees, these more like the layered pines in the far north that Kodi knew, they found a marble temple. It was much like those in the mural on Enric's wall that Kodi so admired, although on a small scale as to fit well in its garden setting. There were comfortable benches of stone mounded with cushions and light blankets. On a small side table was a little stack of books. It was apparent that Enric, or some of the Monastics of the household, would spend time here in contemplation.

They stood on steps leading up to the floor of the temple taking in the beauty of it all. Kodi wondered if the old man had created this garden and its temple to remind him of the Valley as he had done by painting the mural. He couldn't help but to think upon the last part of his Vision. He reached down to the little brook and wet his hands.

Upon the cushioned benches both brother and sister lay down and contemplated the ceiling of the little temple with its painted clouds and flying birds. They concluded that Enric must have painted it as well. They discussed their journey, what each anticipated doing while in the city of Tirilorin, but eventually they fell silent as the distant sea breezes, slowed by all the cypresses and other trees, seeped into the garden and played lazily across them, while the birds sang, and the nearby brook continued playing its soft melody.

"Ah, there you are! I've been looking all over for you! Isn't this an enchanting place?"

The twins were awakened by a bright-eyed Idamé.

"I thought you were going to take a really long nap, Mother Idamé," said Kodi, yawning.

She laughed. "I'd say you yourself slept longer than you think you did! It's perhaps three hours passed noon!"

Kodi and Lyndz both sat up and stretched. "Really!" said Kodi. "I guess maybe I'm more tired than I thought."

"You've worked hard with Captain Shond and the crew the last couple weeks; it's not surprising," offered Lyndz. She too stretched and yawned. "Are you feeling better, Mother Idamé?"

"I feel fine. Well-rested. Though I do look forward to having the opportunity the next several days of getting to bed early. Not to mention having a decent bed to sleep in! This is a grand house, don't you think? And what a garden! I'll say. This temple is a lovely thing. It reminds me very much of the Valley."

They talked a little about the city and the house and garden, but Kodi knew that Idamé really wanted to spend time with Lyndz, so after a few minutes he volunteered to leave.

"Kodi, go check with Curdoz. He and Enric are still talking in the main parlor. They haven't left for the High Master's offices yet."

"I'll do that, then."

He wandered back inside and to his surprise, Curdoz intended Kodi to come with them. "We each have a job to do. You must find your friend in the Vision. Moving about the city, and even meeting people will be the best way for you to recognize him or to discover who he is. I need to speak with High Master Naloro."

They embarked in Sage Enric's small carriage.

"It isn't far. But I'm not as quick on my feet as I once was," the old man said.

Kodi asked if they were going to the Assembly Hall at the Palace.

"No," replied Enric. "High Master Naloro will be at the Central Offices, rather than the Hall of Government. The Assembly Hall is the name given to the Imperial Audience Chamber at the Palace after the Republic was established. It is where the Republican Assembly meets. But the Palace is still the home of the descendants of the emperor. Master Genehbro is the head of House Terianh and retains a voting position on the Assembly, although by law he is not allowed to be elected High Master. He is, even so, no doubt the wealthiest man in the city and has his hands in many enterprises. You will meet him tomorrow, I'm sure."

It took them only two or three short minutes, for the Central Offices were less than a few blocks distant from the Sage's home. When they stepped out of the carriage, Kodi's breath took. Before him stood imposingly a circular building containing at least thirty green marble arched pillars holding aloft a tall, pointed dome. It was not as large as some of the other structures in Central City, but it was taller than most and at least as ornate, for when an attendant opened wide the front door for them, Kodi thought he'd never seen as much gold in his life. Above were beams elaborately carved and gilded, extending upward to the center of the vast dome of gold leaf overhead. Lofty windows at the base of the dome lent it strong light causing it to glisten richly. It sprang heavenward where it finally came to a point far above. Hung from that distant point was the largest pendulum he had ever seen or imagined. It was immense. It hung a hundred feet or more from the apex to a few feet off the floor before him. It was ornately carved with a symmetrical sunburst pattern and was swinging in large arcs like a clock's might. Enric pointed out to his two guests that it was believed by scientists to be powered by the movement of the world's spin. There were golden handrails in a large circle around the center of the room around which one could walk and watch the movement of the pendulum without running into it.

There were many well-dressed, important-looking people moving about, and there were several offices in insets around the circular room. Opposite the entryway and balancing it architecturally was another set of high doors. These were open, and Enric led them around the central space and through them. There was a cleaning crew dusting and sweeping, and on ladders washing tall windows. Against the far right wall behind a large desk, sat a portly man listening intently to two women who sat in chairs before him. Kodi was surprised, for the women were talking about business. He knew that in Solanto there were many small businesses such as inns and shops operated by women, but these were talking about grand opportunities and trade, like merchants and noblemen in his home country. Perhaps it was more common here in a republic, he thought, for women to be in important positions.

"...and so, it's really a matter of common sense, you see, High Master," said one of the two, who from across the room looked to be tall and big-boned, in middle age. "We need to increase the traffic to Solanto, but winter winds and the ice flows are not favorable for trade by sea that time of year."

"The merchants would be willing to put down some of our own funds to rebuild the road from Tirilorin to Guardian's Gate," offered the other. She was quite young, Kodi noticed. "You could set up a toll like in imperial times. It would improve opportunities during those months when little is currently traded between us. Solanto is growing by leaps and bounds, the caravans through the passes from Eleni have increased greatly over the last several years, and the demand for commodities even in winter is on the rise."

"We simply cannot supply all by the current sea traffic," agreed the first woman.

"It is an intriguing concept, I must admit," said the High Master. "And we will consider it. However, is there no way simply to increase the ship traffic itself during the favorable seasons?"

"Well, in part that depends on what you will do if war comes, High Master. If it is determined that the Brigades should be sent to the east, then much of the ship traffic will naturally be diverted to troop supply."

"The Brigade generals think the Nantians would take over such a task."

"You're presuming that if Tirilorin decides to commit to the eastern wars that Nant will then commit its navy even more fully? We don't think so, High Master."

"Well, that is curious. How do you know this?"

"Our own contacts, High Master. Traders in Nant send word to us that the king is absolutely determined not to use more ships in the east, even if Tirilorin gets involved. Prince Lekktor is insistent upon retaining one half their navy for island defense and for patrolling the waters directly southwards towards Berug. A waste of resources in the view of our business contacts there, but Lekktor is an odd one by all accounts. In any regard they are, as a matter of fact, counting on Tirilorin to provide fully its own fleet and supplies. They will commit little more than they already do for their own troop transport. The Eastern Kingdoms cannot feed more than themselves and the Nantian soldiers. They want our help, but as you know, they wish us to provide everything for ourselves."

"True. It is just that we presumed that a formal military commitment by us would be sufficient for the Nantians to engage their navy more fully, but if you're certain otherwise, I can see why you want the road rebuilt. More ships can be built over time, but quite frankly a road would allow a certain continuity of trade, and that is important. The winter months, in any regard, like you say. We will need more information. If the king of Nant will not assist us, then that would require even more commitment on the part of the Republic if we go to war. It would be pressing to commit to rebuilding the road as well. It would seem secondary." He paused, but added, "Just how much would the business leaders of the city commit to such a project?"

"Perhaps up to half. But the tolls should compensate the government for its investment over a period of time."

"Hmm, I don't even know how long it might take and what commitment could be given to it. I'll bring it up to the Committee on Trade, but you should develop a written proposal that answers all the relevant questions. But quite frankly, if we go to war, then most of the young men who might otherwise engage in road building will feel the call to join the Brigades. I wonder if Solanto would share the labor of rebuilding the old road. There would be as much benefit to them as there would be for us."

"Perhaps in the future, but not at present, High Master Naloro!" interrupted Curdoz at this point. To now, the three at the desk had not noticed the visitors.

"On my word! Master Enric!" exclaimed the High Master, seeing him standing with the two strangers. Naloro and the two women all stood together. "Forgive me, Master Enric! I think that out of the corner of my eye I thought you were more of the cleaning crew! I am so very sorry! Forgive me!"

"There is no need to apologize, High Master," Enric offered, walking forward to shake the High Master's hand.

"And you have brought guests? Who is this that speaks for Solanto? Ah! But of course! I had received a message from Master Yamin. And the stole you wear! You must be his lordship Curdoz of Solanto! What a great honor! I was on the Assembly when you visited us twenty years ago, and we met then."

"I remember you. We were all much younger, were we not? I hope you did not mind my intrusion into your conversation, but..."

"Not at all!" spoke the big-boned woman. She strode forward and offered her hand. "How opportune that you should be here to offer input, Your Grace! I am Madam Enola Arlay. This is my business partner, Mistress Stri Itruvi."

The Sage kissed both their hands. "A pleasure. And what is your business, ladies?"

"We are importers and exporters mostly of luxury items, Your Grace."

"Would that include ambernut lumber?" Kodi spoke, and the two women and the High Master looked at him.

Curdoz drew back to introduce Kodi. "Ladies, and High Master, this is Kodi, heir to the Fothemry estate and titles from the Duchy of Tulesk. His father is Hess, the Count Fothemry."

"Why, I think I have heard of him, Your Grace! He is the man who re-opened the Tolosian Peninsula, is he not?" asked Madam Arlay.

"The very man," confirmed Curdoz.

"Astounding! And you are his son, Master Fothemry? Kodi, is it? It is a pleasure to meet you!" said Stri.

In fact, Itruvi, who could hardly be older than Princess Isatura of Solanto, developed quickly a strong gleam in her eye and a smile that Kodi was altogether too familiar with. She held out her hand, and Kodi forced himself to follow Curdoz' lead and kiss it. Reminded of Lyndz' comment at the harbormaster's office, he wished she were present to lend him her promised scowl.

"Er, thank you, Mistress," he said noncommittally and wished now he had kept his mouth shut and said nothing about ambernut.

"And you are correct, sir. What do you know of the ambernut trade?" She pressed with such obvious flirtation—her broad bosom even swung a little—that even Curdoz caught on.

The Sage smiled. "It is in his father's county in southeastern Tulesk where most of the ambernut comes from. It is the source of wealth for the county, and in part, of his own family."

Kodi nodded. "My father controls most of the ambernut trade. He delivers lumber to the port city of Ross. My grandfather, that is my mother's father, is a noted master ambernut cabinet maker and carver. Although he does only small things, now. He is old."

"Really! Why that is extraordinary, Master Kodi! We receive shipments from Ross, and you are right. To be sure, we do import ambernut. It is growing in popularity here among the wealthy families in Central City. It is one of those commodities that makes us so keen to rebuild the road. You see the lumber takes up cargo space on our ships that was previously used for..."

"But the ambernut trade is not why the Sage of Solanto comes to Tirilorin, is it?" interrupted the High Master. "As you know, ladies, Order Members do not typically involve themselves in trade matters."

"Ah, I've been known to involve myself in internal trade matters, but you are correct, High Master. Our purpose here," said Curdoz, "would probably not interest the business class of your city. For you see, Master Fothemry and I, and two others with us, have come to Tirilorin as part of an appointed quest."

There was silence for a moment or two.

"A quest, Your Grace?" asked Madam Arlay, curiously.

"Yes, Madam. A Quest dictated to us by the Guardian Meical Himself."

A much longer moment of silence reigned at this statement. The only sounds came from the cleaning crew, who were too busy on the far side of the large room to pay much mind. They were whispering among themselves about their tasks at hand, so as to disturb the guests of the High Master as little as possible.

Mistress Itruvi's mouth stood open in apparent shock. The High Master himself looked down at the plush carpet. After an awkward moment, Madam Arlay finally spoke. "Ah, of course, Your Grace. It is common among you, according to what Master Enric himself here tells us, to have Visions from, um, the Lord Meical. It is all rather, um, mystical, is it not? I've never quite understood it myself."

Master Enric and Curdoz exchanged a quick, knowing smile between them. "No and yes, Madam," responded Master Enric. "Visions are not all that common; aside from our initial Dreams that call us to join the Orders, they are otherwise quite rare, but to be sure, my Brother Curdoz and Master Fothemry too have each had one, which is why they have come to our city. Curdoz needs some assistance and some time to study certain matters in our Library."

Mistress Itruvi looked at Kodi with even more shock, causing him to chuckle inwardly. If his apparent connection to Meicalian Visions and Prophecies turned her off, it suited him fine. He had no problems with highly intelligent women, for his sister was one, but he thought Itruvi overly sophisticated in her manner and tone and too worldly. She wore three or four gold necklaces and several matching bracelets, even earrings, not to mention a heavy dose of makeup on her face, a rare custom in Solanto and one that Kodi never liked. In the matter of physical attraction, he far preferred women who were beautiful enough without needing to add to it with fakery.

In this last silence the High Master latched on to Enric's words. "But of course! We are happy to assist His Grace, for we are great friends of the Kingdom of Solanto! And he and his company may certainly access the Library! Master Genehbro will be pleased. Why, it will be a pleasure to host him!"

"That is a kind offer, High Master," said Curdoz. "Our immediate needs are being met by my Brother the Sage of Tirilorin, here. We will stay with him."

"Of course, and yet in the message from the Harbormaster, you may wish to address the Assembly tomorrow afternoon? That is perfectly acceptable. I'm sure we will all be glad to assist with your other needs, and we would be grateful of news from your kingdom, Lord Sage."

"I'm happy to offer the news in Assembly, High Master, although it is not all happy, which is why I was compelled to respond earlier to your suggestion that my country might be willing to help rebuild the old road. And frankly, I will at least make it clear for the benefit of the ladies here that I speak only for the immediate present. It is a noble idea, and I like it very much. I can see great benefit for the laborers and their families, the opportunities for the re-founding of the towns along the route. But certain events in the kingdom make me quite confident that the king will not commit to such a grand project in the immediate future. However, in another year or two once certain issues are resolved, perhaps then. I will personally endorse it, ladies."

At this last, Madam Arlay raised her eyebrows and nodded her appreciation, and unfortunately for Kodi, Itruvi seemed suddenly to warm up to him again and reapplied her flirtatious smile.

"A few hail travelers," continued Curdoz, "still take the old road on horse or foot from time to time, do they not? But yes, it is long ago impassable by wanes and wagons, which is what would be needed for increased trade."

"I am sorry to hear of troubles in your kingdom, Your Grace, but we do thank you for the endorsement, Lord Sage. And it gives us a good deal of time to think on proposals and logistics," replied Madam Arlay. She then turned on Kodi with a long and scrutinizing look, and just as suddenly raised an eyebrow high and turned to the High Master. "You know, High Master, I and some others might be willing to honor our Solantine guests with a dance! Central City hasn't experienced a grand dance in some years."

"Oh, yes! What a tremendous idea!" added Itruvi, beaming at Kodi. Her bosom jingled with the sound of her necklaces. "Master Fothemry I suspect cuts a fine figure! The merchantwomen of the city should definitely sponsor a grand dance!"

Kodi could do little other than hold his lips and teeth in positions that might resemble a pleased smile. He liked to dance, had done so often at the summer fairs in Felto, and was confident even with the elaborate steps likely at this affair, but he found himself repulsed by Itruvi's obvious attraction towards him.

Unfortunately, there was more.

"Yes," said Madam Arlay, "I have a daughter, Linova, who is a lovely dancer! I will introduce you, Master Fothemry."

Kodi came quite close to rolling his eyes, but he held steady and attempted to respond with all the forced politeness he could muster, which in this case was quite considerable. "Certainly, ladies. That is very kind of you. My twin sister Lyndz is an accomplished dancer. If you should host a dance while we are still here, we would very much enjoy ourselves, I'm sure." He nodded to them, but then turned to Curdoz with a blank expression.

Curdoz had come to know Kodi well enough by now to sense his young friend's annoyance, and yet he realized suddenly that he had indeed brought into the city a very handsome, very well-connected, and very eligible set of young adult twins, who had the added exotic attraction of being from a foreign country. He found it, however, much more amusing than Kodi and winked at him knowingly.

Kodi refused to alter his blank expression.

They continued to talk for several more minutes, and Naloro was delighted at the prospect of a dance, agreeing with Arlay that it would lift the spirits of the citizens as they contemplated the possibilities of war. Eventually, and to Kodi's relief, the two women took their leave. The High Master then ordered the cleaning crew out of the office and closed the doors for privacy. The four men sat in a circle of comfortable chairs in another section of the large room arranged for small conferences. The High Master himself poured for each of them a glass of port. Kodi sat quietly sipping his (he discovered he like port better than other wines), as did Master Enric, for most of the conversation was between the High Master and the Sage of Solanto.

"...and I know it is presumptive of me, High Master, but even if messages have by now been sent to Ferostro, I know the king will not commit at present to the eastern war, and yet all this news seems to speak to our Visions."

"The Visions? So, er, how many of these Visions have there been?" he asked with reluctant curiosity.

"In addition to Master Fothemry's and my own, Mother Idamé of the Matrimonial Order of Solanto has had one as well. She is here with us, along with Kodi's twin, the Lady Lyndz."

Enric spoke. "High Master, it is because of the combination of the Visions and their connection to one another that makes it so critical that we pay attention."

"Um, yes, Master Enric. It seems likely that though we have our, um, skeptics, it is the very fact that the Lord Sage of Solanto should leave his country and speak before our Assembly that may have weight rather than the, er, Visions." He turned to Curdoz. "I don't wish to presume it, particularly since you are a member of the Orders, but are you willing, Your Grace, to speak in favor of the engagement? For we need those to speak who have a broad view of the world."

"I am grateful that you take me so seriously. I will be glad to speak to the Assembly and encourage alliance with the Easterners, for I fully believe from the Visions that a stronger response to the enemy is required."

"I will admit that the majority of the Masters are in favor of mobilization already, but there are many still who prefer we hold out, unwilling to commit resources elsewhere."

Kodi finished his glass and set it down. "If you don't mind my asking, sir, why have you not voted then to go to war? I thought that on your Assembly you simply voted, and if most are in favor, then it becomes the law."

The High Master replied. "You're not wrong, Master Fothemry, but you see, war is a different matter. I haven't called a formal vote because I and some of the others believe that we should have full commitment from everyone, or virtually everyone, on the Assembly. We don't put our faith in and follow blindly the dictates of an emperor anymore, but instead we seek consensus when we can get it from the people. The Assembly represents the people, for many of its members are elected by the citizens of Tirilorin. Many of the positions are established by law to be filled by certain people like Master Enric here as the Sage, the Head of the House of Terianh Master Genehbro who still holds great respect among many, and some other city positions, um, such as the harbormaster, Master Yamin, whom you've met. But like I say, when it comes to war, I believe the whole of the people need to be committed. Most of the by-law Masters are willing, but several of the elected Masters are still skeptical. Now, it could be that Lord Curdoz' presence and speech will be the very thing needed to commit them. It could prove quite useful. But I must admit, Your Lordship," he said, turning from Kodi back to Curdoz, "your doubts as to Solanto's possible commitments are troubling. Do you mind telling me what might cause your king's hesitation to assist in the east if asked?"

Curdoz then took a few minutes to explain to the High Master the situation surrounding the Prince of Hesk and the King's Council that would shortly be taking place. "And though I expect word to be sent to me as soon as the Council is over, it could still be some weeks. However, though some are still hopeful, such as Father Marco of the Healing Order, others, including Grand Duke Mannago and myself, believe that the Prince is intending to pursue certain divisions and go against the king's former dictates on certain matters. King Carlomen will pursue internal unity before he commits resources to a foreign conflict."

He spoke further and reminded him also of the danger of the Ice Tribes, "...who are always a threat on our borders," he concluded.

When he was finished, Master Enric added, "High Master, you must see that Lord Curdoz and his company are, in a very real sense, acting as a substitute for the Kingdom of Solanto by following the Visions. He, Master Kodi here, and the two women, have been called to act by the Guardian, as a result of the moves by the Khestadone and the likelihood of the war's expansion. The far east is not the only threat."

The High Master sighed, for he had been quite consciously avoiding this for the last twenty minutes. "Ah, yes, the Visions. You wish to tell me of them, Lord Curdoz?"

"I will tell you the parts of our Visions that involve the Khestadone, High Master. The rest is only important to me and my company." He then spent the next half hour explaining to Naloro everything in the three Visions relating to the enemy. Kodi nodded from time to time as the Sage recounted it all. The High Master was attentive, and despite his underlying skepticism, the details of the Vision, the fact that it was three Visions which apparently corroborated, and the current state of affairs resulting from news from the south and east, all of this impressed him more than he had expected it would.

"That is remarkable, Lord Curdoz," he said when Curdoz finished. "You're convinced the Alkhaness will go to war, and side with her compatriot the Alkhan? He is terrible enough from what we hear. It is our hope that we would be able to help the Easterners defeat his threat and impose the old status quo, but you're saying that the war could become broader in scope? Berug and the fortresses of the Nantians have checked the Alkhaness before."

"But she grows stronger. Kodi and Idamé sensed her power in their Visions. We don't really know how, but she does. Her magic, that is. Now it could be that the Berugians or Nantians can, in the short term, contain her. But when she begins, she will focus on the trading cities and fortresses along the coasts, would she not? Master Yamin tells us that the Nantian fortresses on the Southern Continent believe she may be massing troops for just such a showdown."

"Yes, that is what we hear. Prince Nikal of Nant is a great man, perhaps the greatest captain among the western nations. He is the king's second son. He is responsible for the Nantian war effort in the east and for the defense of the coastal fortresses claimed by Nant. It was he who brought with him the war ambassadors from the eastern monarchs. By all accounts Nikal is the great hero of the eastern war, and until recently was able to hold the Alkhan's forces in check. However, the enemy has made advances of late, and Prince Nikal and the eastern rulers need more help. The prince then left for Nant to try to persuade his father to commit more troops, in addition to what we here in Tirilorin might provide. But you heard the ladies. Their contacts make that seem less certain. I *do* know that the Crown Prince of Nant, Nikal's older brother Lekktor, is the major force behind keeping the bulk of their navy as a shield for their island. And the ladies are right that it is a waste of their resources, for their island is under no immediate threat. Both the Alkhan and the Alkhaness would have to conquer the continental lands here in the west before they could even make a first move on Nant. Quite frankly, if Nant fully committed, I doubt that Tirilorin would have to go to the east, and we could continue to monitor against a move by the Alkhaness on our continental shores and the trading colonies. However, I admit, and have said thus to others, that it is hardly fair to presume that Nant bear the whole burden of aiding the Easterners. They have done so much already the last year while we bask in peace." The High Master thought for a minute. "I...I will press harder for mobilization, Your Lordship. You've convinced me even more fully. I'll have you speak first at the Assembly tomorrow. We could make real inroads for the pro-war side if I line up a range of good speeches. How long do you intend to remain in the city?"

"Two or three weeks, I imagine. From here we will go to Nant. It is part of our quest. It appears from our Visions that we are to engage a small Nantian fleet in order to search for the land of Ulakel and find the Qeteral."

Naloro almost choked on his port. "The Qeteral! Lord Curdoz! Why, no one has seen them in a hundred years! Oh well, I don't really need to know your other business I suppose, but really, even if you find them, they are not warriors."

"Ah, but that is not quite correct, High Master. They are great warriors when it comes to defending their own according to all the histories. Not even during the time of the Ralsheen were their lands overrun, and Siriné the world goddess tried very hard to do just that."

Kodi noted that Naloro pursed his lips at this. However, Curdoz continued. "It is just that they never leave their land to fight for others.

However, I don't think it is their fighting abilities for which we seek them. But until we find them, we are uncertain what the Guardian Meical wants with regard to them. They were friends with the emperors. Which is one reason I need to meet with Genehbro."

"They respected the emperors, certainly. Hmm. I can see why you'd want to talk to Master Genehbro. He'll be gracious, I'm sure, but I can assure you he has no communication with the Qeteral."

"I'm sure. And yet he might have some good information for us nonetheless."

"Yes, he might. He is visiting one of his estates in the country but is expected to return in time for the Assembly meeting."

When they began talking of expectations for tomorrow afternoon's Assembly meeting, the impatient Kodi signaled to Curdoz that he'd like to leave the room. Curdoz indicated in the affirmative and Kodi went out into the central room to wait. He looked all around again at the inside of the building but found himself mesmerized by the movement of the pendulum. Watching this for several minutes he realized that the arc in which the pendulum swung seemed to be pivoting ever so slowly. It was not swinging in the same arc that it was when they arrived. It had shifted. It made no sense to him. Of course, he couldn't understand that it had energy to swing in the first place. He had heard that there were those who theorized that the world twisted round and round and that it was the sun which stood in the firmament unmoving. When Enric had stated the fact without even a qualm of uncertainty, it made Kodi wonder. Yet even so, it was all very confusing that this apparent spin would cause the giant pendulum to move. It ought to just hang there, perfectly still, like curtains hanging in a window, or better yet the branch attached to the rope swing he and his friends had devised to jump out into one of the deeper swimming holes on the river. That might move from wind, of course, but there was no wind inside this building. Despite what he was told, he looked around, high and low, for some sort of weighted mechanism and coil spring that might give it the energy required, like on a clock, but it was in vain. There was no contraption of any kind in the great gilt hall.

With effort he put it out of his mind.

He began to focus his sights on the people. Dozens came in and out through the doors. All were mannerly, and their bearing and language implied they were all educated and professional. He wondered if he'd see the young man from his Vision, but no one he saw was of similar age to himself. Most were middle-aged or older men, but there were a number of women like Madam Arlay, and all were talking among themselves and to others behind desks on the inner wall of the great circular room. There were papers being signed and great ledger books being filled in by clerks. Many of the clerks were women, he noted. There were other doors, some closed and some opened, and as he walked slowly around the room, he attempted to peer into these to see what he could. All the offices, though smaller than the High Master's, were filled with ornate furniture. The cleaning crew was now in a different office still working diligently. All in all, it was a busy sort of place, and Kodi realized that the operations of such an immense city would require a great deal of effort by many people to operate efficiently.

He looked around at all the gilt trimming in the room. He understood how gilt was applied, with paper-thin sheets of gold hammered into place. He imagined it took a virtual army months and months to accomplish it here. He wondered how old this particular building was. Was it from early imperial times or was it added later? Did Etoppsi have to be involved in construction of the great dome? How would they have set the beams in place? It was all imposing and structurally interesting. Kodi had the mind of an engineer, and he was always pondering how things were constructed like bridges, walls, buildings, and how contraptions worked like lifts at building sites, drawbridges and gates, the sails of ships and the steering mechanisms, the pendulum here in the Central Offices. He had a sudden wish that he could meet an Etoppsis or whoever it was that built this building and find out step by step how it was accomplished. Maybe someday.

It wasn't long before the others emerged, and High Master Naloro walked with them out to Enric's waiting carriage. The High Master spoke again to Kodi.

"Master Fothemry, you have a certain charisma, and I couldn't help notice how taken with you the ladies were. Arlay spoke of her daughter, and the young Mistress Itruvi especially..."

"Maybe," Kodi said with a smile, "they'll be less eager to get to know me after they see me fumbling around on the dance-room floor!"

Naloro laughed. "If your sister is as attractive to the young men as you obviously are to the women, the two of you are likely to be the subject of a bit of gossip and social maneuvering here in Central City, I should warn you. Expect the invitations to start arriving, Master Enric, to your house!"

"Mistress Lyndz is indeed a beautiful young woman, but she and Kodi are quite capable of handling themselves," said Curdoz with a laugh and a wink at Kodi. "I have come to regard them as a self-aware and disciplined pair, considering their many charms."

Kodi grinned at Curdoz and found himself pleased with this positive observation on the Sage's part. Kodi hoped that Curdoz understood him better now than the time he had chastised him back in the monastery in Aster.

"Are you planning on joining the Meicalian Orders, then?" asked Naloro, perhaps misconstruing Curdoz' descriptors. "That would put a damper on Arlay's plans. We really could do with a grand dance. We need more gatherings of this sort for the young men and young women in Central City, especially if war is to come."

Kodi laughed gleefully so as to reassure the High Master. "If our being here is really that useful, sir, then have no worries. Lyndz my sister and I will dance all night! Though Lyndz will be far more at ease with her feet!"

"I'm so pleased, Master Fothemry!" The man shook Kodi's hand.

"What would be much more helpful," put in Curdoz, "for *us* anyway, High Master, is for Kodi to receive swordsmanship training while we are here."

"Considering his bearing, not to mention the pedigree, I might have presumed he was a knight already, or in training for it."

"Thank you, High Master, but no," said Kodi. "Not quite yet."

"He has been quite patient," responded Curdoz, placing his hand on Kodi's shoulder, "applying himself to needs at his home, High Master, with a household of women and an elderly grandfather, as his father Hess has been away so much. But he is eager now to pursue his strengths, and I intend for him to train for a part of the time we are here. He is a superior bowman already, and the king himself honored him with the gift of a beautifully worked quiver to go with the ambernut bow his grandfather crafted for him."

"Really!" said Naloro, looking at Kodi with additional interest. "I'll send word to General Stanlish of your presence, Master Fothemry. He leads the division of the Republican Brigades responsible for the wall guard. You'll be welcome to mingle with the Brigades while you're here and take part in any of their activities, and as for swordsmanship I know just the man! He is the preeminent swordmaster outside of Nant and trains many in the Brigades, at least the ones who can afford him. His name is Jaden. I will send word to him, as well. In fact, if you meet with Master Genehbro, you may well run into Jaden, for he is responsible for training Genehbro's son Tiliruf."

"Thank you very much, sir," said Kodi, but he was suddenly most interested in this last statement. "What does this *Tiliruf* look like, sir?"

"Tiliruf, hmm? Well, he is tall, of fair complexion, a young man like yourself."

Kodi looked at Curdoz with a raised eyebrow. "Does he have light, curly hair and wear fancy clothes?"

Naloro laughed, "Yes, he is a bit of a dandy in that regard, and rather a rascal in other ways, but he is friendly to everyone. He occasionally accompanies his father to the Assembly meetings. You've seen him, have you?"

"In a manner of speaking, maybe. Maybe so. I'd like to meet him."

"Well, watch your purse around his game table, and perhaps keep an eye out for your sister."

"Oh, really!" Kodi chuckled. "Why is that, sir?"

"Hmm? Perhaps I shouldn't say..."

Enric interrupted, laughing. “Be careful, High Master! Gossiping does not conform to Meicalian Disciplines! The escapades, particularly of our young men, tend to settle out, given time. Do you not agree, High Master? The wealthy sons of our city have, shall we say, ‘temptations’ that most do not? And in most cases, they allay themselves, given a few years of additional maturity.”

“I know it,” said Naloro, chuckling. “I do apologize. Tiliruf has good qualities. He is certainly quite likeable despite his, er…any faults he may have. In fact, from what I hear, he equals Jaden with the sword and has bested him more than once. He is near to being made a swordmaster himself. I’m sure you and he would get along quite splendidly, Master Fothemry, as energetic young men tend to do. If you—and your sister—are as disciplined as Lord Curdoz gives you credit for, then you can manage yourselves around Tiliruf should you come to know one another.”

As they rode away in Enric’s carriage, these words of the High Master left Kodi quite curious, but until he saw Genehbro’s son face to face, there was no reason to conclude yet that he was the young man in his Vision. Yet his physical description sounded promising.

Curdoz read his mind. “It would not surprise me at all, Kodi, if it is this Tiliruf.”

“Yes,” said Enric, who after his long conversation with Curdoz earlier in the afternoon was now fully aware of all three Visions. “A descendant of Terianh that the Guardian requires for reasons unknown. An opportunity!”

“For what, sir?” asked Kodi.

“Oh. You know. I have watched him. Watched him all his life. I’m not certain, of course, but think on it! Perhaps your quest will lead to something for the House of Terianh—a chance to rise from their self-imposed slumber of the last hundred years.”

As they approached Enric’s home, Kodi’s mind worked. He wondered if Enric could be right.

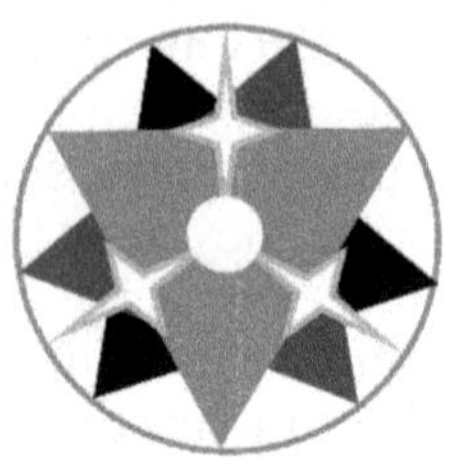

Chapter 5—The Assembly of the Republic

"Curdoz, I've finished the second one, finally! And Enric went through it for me carefully afterwards."

"Let's see it, then, Lyndz," replied Curdoz. "Read it to me. Like I've said before, sometimes reading aloud is helpful."

Lyndz had been working with the cipher code on the little book her grandfather had given Curdoz weeks ago. They had already deciphered the first one in the book which matched precisely the one in the pocket of the Ice Tribesman. It did take some shifting of the cipher for Lyndz to determine the layout of the second passage in the book.

"And very curious references," she said excitedly. "Especially...well, you'll see. Here it is!"

The Staff of Terianh he will wield,
For all the world with which to shield.
Vanaratu knows where the Staff is hidden.
He will seek, for it is bidden.
Eight will give of what they have
For him to gain the Eagle Staff.

He mustn't deny the gifts of the others,
New family, new sisters, and genuine brothers.
A twin he trains who shares the Staff,
Terianh's son who makes them laugh,
A Sage who hears Vanaratu's call,
And he should heed the one with the shawl.

"That's the whole of it, I believe."

"Let me see that!" said Curdoz, both eyebrows raised high, reaching for the parchment from Lyndz.

After perusing it himself for several minutes he looked seriously into Lyndz' face. "This...this has to be valuable to us, Lyndz! The Staff of

Terianh! Could such a powerful relic come into play for us? I wonder. Vanaratu, the world god, though. That really confuses. He hasn't been active in this world since Meical Himself was last here! Some believe he was banished somehow for disobedience. Rather like Siriné being imprisoned in the Serpent Sea. Of course, no one really knows what happened to him. Even the Qeteral have no records of him after that time."

"Terianh's son, though, Curdoz," said Enric. He had stepped into the parlor with a mug of chicory, strong and dark. "It must reference the House of Terianh. It could refer to Tiliruf, Genehbro's son. Our thoughts from yesterday I believe may prove true!"

"Do you think maybe 'twin' references me or Kodi?" asked Lyndz. To her it was the most interesting line of the whole piece.

"Definitely worth playing with that idea," replied Curdoz. "This could be a serious clue to a Calling. But the Staff of Terianh...well you see, Lyndz, very few magical talismans were ever made. None now. Yet those few were specific to gender. Males and females think and respond differently to given situations and such talismans would respond accordingly. A staff is considered to be masculine. Women almost never use them."

"So, you're saying that if it references a twin using the Staff it would mean Kodi if it meant either of us."

"Yes."

Enric nodded. "I believe Curdoz is right on that. But one with the shawl could *only* be a reference to one thing."

"A Matrimonial!" exclaimed Lyndz. "Of course! Oh, Curdoz! It can't be happenstance that it references a twin, a Sage, and a Matrimonial! And we're here in Tirilorin where the House of Terianh actually lives, if what Enric thinks is the other reference!"

"What are you three on about this morning?" asked Idamé walking in, who, like Enric, was carrying a steaming mug of chicory brew that a Monastic servant had just brought to her bedroom. Though sweetened heavily with cream and honey in her case.

And behind her was Kodi. "Great sleep. Great breakfast in my rooms! I wish I could take a warm bath every night before bed! Er...eh...er...you all look busy about something."

"You all *have* to listen to this!" said Lyndz. "It's from Great-grandmother's Prophecy book!" She took the translation back from Curdoz and read the whole thing aloud again.

At the final line, Idamé gasped and set down her chickory. "Oh, my! Oh, my! Curdoz..."

"That *has* to be us!" interrupted Kodi. "No way is it just coincidence! Twins, a Sage, a Shawl Lady, er, I mean a Matrimonial. Sorry Mother Idamé, er, that's what the ship's crew called you."

Idamé chuckled. "Oh, I remember, those silly boys. But Curdoz! The Staff of Terianh! I thought it was a legend!"

"It's not legend," said Kodi emphatically. "Terianh used it many times according to the book Theneri gave me. It was the Staff that made him a War Wizard and well...a member of the Orders."

Suddenly, Kodi realized what he was saying. He gasped and looked at Curdoz. A dozen thoughts shot through his head in a split second.

"We cannot know of a certainty what this Prophecy means any more than the first," said Curdoz, acknowledging Kodi's shock. "At least not yet. Let us learn what we can. Hopefully we will meet Genehbro today. He is the head of the House of Terianh and may have some thoughts on the matter."

"If I were you, Brother Curdoz," interjected Enric, "I'd approach it carefully. Like most, Genehbro is highly skeptical of the Guardian's History. The Staff is as much legend to Genehbro as it is to most everybody else."

Curdoz paced the parlor floor for at least a minute. Finally, he looked at the others. "For the time being, all we can do is continue to do what we are doing. If this Prophecy pertains to us, its elements will be revealed to us more definitively in time."

By the afternoon, when it was time for Curdoz and Enric to attend the Republican Assembly, Idamé and the twins were itching at the opportunity to see the Assembly Hall and the Imperial Palace. As Kodi had mentioned already, they had all had glorious baths the night before, and Curdoz had shaved his scruff, appearing now as neat and stately as ever in his finer clothing, carefully ironed by the Monastics that operated Enric's household. He wore a different stole than any the twins had seen before. Not only was it green to denote the color of the Meicalian Orders, but this one contained embroidered patterns of the white stag, the emblem of the Kingdom of Solanto. Mother Idamé had chosen a colorful light-weight linen shawl, for her woolen ones were heavy for the weather, now that she was off the sea and it was late spring in a southerly clime.

Hollina attended with Enric all the Assembly meetings and also the committees on which Enric worked. She took notes for the old man and otherwise kept his papers organized. She and Idamé had taken a friendly liking to each other, and so Hollina walked alongside the Matrimonial Mother and the twins after they all exited the carriage at the base of the grand staircase leading up to the front doors of the Palace. She was a great source of information, explaining to them the significance of every statue, relief carving, and any other grand element or intimate detail to which they pointed or inquired about.

There were some forty stairs and thus the 'journey' to the front doors was a decidedly long one for old Enric. He was using a carven cane today to assist with his balance, but only because of the sheer quantity of stairs required to maneuver, for otherwise he did not typically use such a support.

At the top of the stairs, they paused. Everywhere they looked was a remarkable view, and perhaps two hundred feet outward from the base of the staircase, on a wide green lawn and encircled by a pool of bubbling water, was the equestrian statue of Terianh the Great. Kodi was particularly eager to see this in waking life having only beheld it in his Vision. It was gold-plated and gleamed in the afternoon sunshine. He half expected to see the young man from his Vision sitting at the edge of the pool. There were many sightseers walking on the green lawn and peering upwards at the great statue.

"It is the largest statue in all the Republic," said Hollina, who spoke like a tour guide at a museum when she saw Kodi staring at it. "Over forty feet tall, it was crafted in bronze and steel by imperial sculptors, set in place by Etoppsi laborers, the parts welded together and then plated in gold—over three hundred years ago. As you can see, Terianh yields his Staff in his right hand and his sword in his left, for that was how he fought in the final battle against the last Ralsheen Emperor. His stallion was called B'ulstread, whose progeny are still bred by Master Genehbro and other wealthy families at their country estates."

Kodi was inspired, in particular now that the Prophecy from that morning was going around in his head. He wished to take a closer look but knew it would have to wait. He then looked high to the top of the tallest central tower to the great golden eagle statue. "How did they..." He pointed without finishing his question.

"The eagle statue? Made of alloy-hardened gold, Master Kodi, crafted by Qeteral artisans and presented to Terianh as a gift during the building of the Palace. Set in place, of course, by Etoppsi after the completion of the palace."

There were dozens more people milling around, climbing up and down the stairs, and Kodi wondered which were Republican City Masters and which were citizen observers. All were strikingly garbed, and Kodi was glad Curdoz suggested he and Lyndz wear their best. Kodi wore the clothes Curdoz had purchased for him in Ferostro. Lyndz wore her ivory dress and bore her emerald pendant and looked like a princess, her dark hair again in a lovely braid. Kodi noticed men, young and old, looking keenly at her and nodding as they walked past. Had he been aware, he might have noticed women, though more subtle and quicker in their glances, were eyeing him as well.

The front doors were taller than most houses, and these were swung wide as foot traffic in and out of the Hall was so great it was impossible to continually open and close them. The entry hall was splendid, and around the walls were at least two dozen marble statues of historical emperors. The one of Terianh was displayed most prominently. Hollina pointed out that the male line of Terianh endured without interruption, though twice a younger brother replaced an older who had no children. There had been no ruling empresses, only consorts. They would later see many paintings throughout the palace that depicted the emperors and their consorts.

She responded to one of Lyndz' observations. "You are quite right, young lady. It is only the Assembly Hall where the Masters gather that reflects Republican history, the decorations and the great Throne of the Emperors were long ago removed from there to accommodate the Assembly's needs and to symbolically at least do away with the trappings of imperial rule. The rest of the Palace still largely reflects the wealth and tastes of the old emperors."

Straight ahead they walked perhaps twenty paces to another set of high doors. These opened into the Assembly Hall of the Republic.

It was the largest enclosed space in which any of the Solantines had ever in their lives found themselves. It was so large that there were still large open surrounds before one even came to the grand portion of the room that was constructed and furnished for the Assembly Masters and citizen viewers. Several hundred people sat in the viewing galleries.

Enric looked around. "It has been a while," he noted, "since there have been so many citizens to view the proceedings. It appears, Brother Curdoz, that your arrival is now generally known. They are curious to hear what you have to say. But the crowd has been increasing lately anyway as the war is discussed."

"Do they disturb the Assembly?" Lyndz asked, pointing to the center of the vast room where there were arranged in concentric rows perhaps forty large, elegant wooden desks, each with two fancy chairs, one for a Master and the other for his or her assistant.

"Rarely. There are Brigadier soldiers stationed to remove anyone who interferes with the Assembly's proceedings. Proper decorum is nearly always maintained."

Enric and Curdoz left them to find Enric's desk in the middle of the Assembly, and Hollina lead Idamé and the twins to a set of seats reserved for special guests in the front row of one of the viewing sections and close to the speaker's podium on its dais. After she assured their comfort, she turned to make her own way to Enric's desk. But as she did so, Kodi gasped. "Who are they?"

He pointed, a bit rudely, though he quickly lowered his hand, to a group of four people sitting next to one another on the lowest level in the area designated for the High Master and his clerks. Even Lyndz looked and caught her breath.

They were the darkest skinned people—their skin tone was nearly black—that the twins had ever seen.

Hollina smiled. "You have never before encountered any of the Easterners, I see."

"I knew many in the Valley," offered Idamé

Hollina continued. "Two are from Hralindi, and two are from Essemar. Do not let the darkness of their skin put you off, dears. There is no reason in all of Dumhoni for it to do so. They are wartime ambassadors from those two kingdoms who came with Prince Nikal several days ago to press their kingdoms' needs in the war."

"Two are women!" noted Lyndz.

Hollina chuckled. "Yes, dear. They are. Though the women in their armies, as these are, keep their heads shaved. It is a cultural thing. Yet the Guardian approves of variety in culture, you see. Master Kodi, should you go to the east, as Sage Curdoz believes you will eventually, that is what you will see. But under the surface, they are no different than we light-skinned westerners."

Their shock was only due to the novelty. Lyndz and Kodi had been raised properly, and they had no especial qualms. They themselves were somewhat darker in coloring than everyone else in Felto. They understood to some degree what it was like to stand out in a village where everyone else had the ancient Elenite light complexion.

"They are very handsome," said Lyndz.

"I'm glad you think so, dear. They do hold themselves with great pride. Remember that upon a time, all of us were within the same empire. Those who study Human history say that the Easterners descend from those first Humans who shortly after the Molding dwelt in the South of the World, and dark skin protects one from the harsh sun found there. The ancient Nantians, and I am referring to a time even before the Ralsheen Empire, are assuredly a mix of the ancient northern Elenites and the ancestors of the Easterners. So, my dears, you yourselves share a common ancestry with them in ancient history."

Kodi knew from tales that Easterners were very dark, even if his first sight of them had caught him off guard. All in all, it hardly bothered him, and he was already comfortable with Hollina's explanations. Besides, he remembered Curdoz telling him that Hescians had a strong antipathy towards Easterners. He was determined to be nothing like Hescians. It made him happy to think that his own blood was a mix of many Human ethnicities and ancient minglings. He had definitely learned a great deal since leaving Felto about his ancestral past, from Curdoz, from Princess Isatura, from Hollina. The world was a much bigger place than he had once thought. "I'm glad. I didn't mean to act so. I hope to get to know them better. I hope they didn't see me pointing."

"I wouldn't worry about it, dear. There are many more Easterners in the city, mostly tradesmen and sailors; it's only chance you haven't seen any yet."

The twins shifted their observations to the chamber itself. High overhead were white ceilings held by impressive vaulting that took one's breath away. Inset high in the walls were lacy, leaded windows of clear glass. The room was bright, though there were many huge chandeliers, too, and each of the Masters' desks had elaborate oil lamps to provide additional light for those taking notes.

Other than architectural elements and detailing, there was no other sort of art or sculpture. Considering the vastness of the space it was stark compared to what they had seen so far in the city and in the entry hall of the Palace. More interestingly to Kodi and Lyndz, however, was the cavernous whisper on the air, echoing the communications going on throughout the room. It had an almost musical quality to it, and more than even the grandiosity of the space itself this ethereal sound created in the twins a feeling of serious-toned pageantry.

Soon the crowd quieted down, and the echoing silence reverberated throughout the chamber, and when High Master Naloro spoke, even though his voice seemed quiet, it was easily heard in every corner of the grand space.

"Ladies and Gentlemen of the Assembly, the business before us today is again the deliberations regarding the requests for military aid brought to us by His Highness Prince Nikal of Nant one week past and the delegations from the kingdoms of Essemar and Hralindi. To speak on the threat, I present to you His Grace, Lord Curdoz, Sage of the Orders of the Guardian from the Kingdom of Solanto. All rise, as our esteemed visitor makes his way to the podium."

All stood, both Masters and citizens.

Curdoz stepped up upon the dais, and from behind a large marble podium he began. Everyone sat down again. A formality of tone and seriousness came forth from his mouth that seemed strange to the twins who had grown to know him on such familiar terms over the last several weeks. "My gratitude to all. I wish to extend my sincerest thanks to High Master Naloro for allowing me to speak today before this esteemed Assembly and my warmest regards to my dear Brother in the Orders, City Master Enric, who is graciously hosting me and my comrades from the Kingdom of Solanto. Peace to all of you, and may the Eyes of the Guardian, Meical Beyond All Stars, watch over us in the days to come."

There was some shifting at this, for it had been a very, very long time since most of them had heard a Sage offer an Affirmation. Enric had not spoken at the Assembly in years.

"It has come to my attention that the war in the East is at a critical juncture and current efforts by the Eastern kingdoms and the Nantians have become insufficient in halting the advances of the Alkhan of Eastrealm Khestadon. I myself have little direct knowledge of the war at the front, but nevertheless have information of a critical nature to share..."

Then he spoke for some minutes describing elements of his Vision that reflected the conflict, how the power and the magic of the enemy had apparently grown, and the inevitability of the Alkhaness engaging in favor of her eastern cohort at some point in the near future.

"...the Alkhan of Eastrealm and the Alkhaness of Westrealm will always be a threat to us in the North and to the Etoppsi Kingdom of Berug. They have magic that has kept them alive for long centuries, and though it is uncertain their origins or from where they derive their power, that power is growing, inevitably growing, and great effort and sacrifice must be expended in order to counter them..."

As he continued, all were quiet, and like Enric had said, there were no interruptions, no echoing whispers of support or dissent, and though many a face both among the Masters and the observers turned to look at one another with raised eyebrows, a handful with skeptical frowns, none dared to demonstrate open disagreement. Most of the skepticism in those faces became most obvious when Curdoz reflected on his Visions or made the point that Meical the Guardian was aware of and directing countermoves against the enemy, and yet his masterly handling of the Histories to prove his points seemed to soften some of them. At the least they were taking in and processing every word. Some three dozen assistants charted out notes for the Masters to which they were employed, and messages were carried here and there by young pages in soft shoes.

"...and therefore, I bid the people of the Republic, represented by this noble Assembly, to make preparations and send to the east what help that can be mobilized, and also to send messages both to the kingdoms of Solanto and Eleni concerning such preparations in order for those two kingdoms to consider accordingly. Though I have stated already that my king will not commit in the immediate future and have explained to High Master Naloro in private why I believe that to be true, some support will inevitably come, and of the Elenites, too, although their ongoing conflict with the northern Ice Tribes should be looked upon by all as perhaps another chapter of this conflict, in this case against descendants of ancient Ralsheen remnants. I say remnants, but the Ice Tribes are perhaps a greater threat than they may seem, and I believe they continue to plot and scheme for advantage. The latest news from Eleni implies their current conflict is a stalemate at best. And as far as the Elenites are concerned they must too look to their eastern borders and the Barantines who have fought against them in the past. I have some fear for the future from the north and northeast, another reason why I believe Solanto will not commit to the eastern conflict. Should at some point in future the Barantines and the Ice Tribes combine in intrigue with the Khestadone Realms, it will be a great blow to the old Anterianhi peace. The burden in the south and east therefore is indeed with the Kingdom of Nant and with the Republic of Tirilorin. And of course, if the Alkhaness of Westrealm does commit her forces which I feel confident she will, based on my Vision, Berug of the Etoppsi will assuredly defend itself against her.

"Again, I wish to thank you for this opportunity to speak and wish I had more plain news of the war to offer you but will leave that up to those such as High Master Naloro and others who receive news from Nant and from the east. Those who wish to question or communicate with me may call upon me at the home of my Brother Enric. We are grateful for your hospitality while our company remains a little while in your great city."

All stood again when Curdoz finished, but as soon as he stepped down from the dais, there was suddenly a tremendous murmuring as the Masters and spectators began to talk openly among one another. Apparently, the High Master allowed several minutes of communication between speeches in order for the Masters to gather their thoughts and to gauge what their neighbors were thinking and to send up messages and questions to the High Master. He would take a few moments to look through these, perhaps to determine how the Masters were regarding the information presented.

There were other speeches, each from a Master issuing reports or otherwise reflecting on how the eastern conflict was affecting trade and the prosperity of the city. Some argued that it was the right thing to enter the conflict to support their allies, the Nantians and Easterners, who had borne the brunt of the war to date, others attempted to remind the Assembly that the fall of the eastern kingdoms would be a disaster of the highest order, and that the lack of participation so far by Tirilorin reflected poorly on the Republic's history. Still, there were some who spoke against the conflict.

"...for we must look to ourselves and the safety of our own peoples!" replied one that Naloro had introduced beforehand as 'the Elected Master Seroofa of North Port.' "It is not the place of our Republic to fight the wars of other countries. There is no solid reason to believe that the Khestadone are a threat to the Republic! Yes, should the Alkhaness engage then the threat to us would be more clear and closer to home, but so far, she has not. War will interfere with the prosperous trade that has made our city great..."

He went on like this for several minutes, but the twins could not help but to think that all of the man's arguments were narrow at best and at worst simply ignorant of the disaster should none but Tirilorin be left standing of the old Anterianhi alliance.

Though most of the Masters who spoke were men, there was one woman City Master, Madame Midianna of Guardian Hills, who spoke passionately.

"...and we should mobilize all our strength, including the merchant marine, to ensure a constant flow of men and supplies. Recent communications suggest that the Nantians will not commit additional ships for our benefit. We have made an error in our thinking to presume they will always be so forthcoming with their naval forces and transport. In addition, though I know it will be controversial, several women in my section of the city have approached me saying they would like to see a military company made up of women..."

Kodi and Lyndz looked quickly around to see how this extraordinary suggestion was being processed, and surely there were a great many more raised eyebrows and both nodding and shaking heads than when even Curdoz spoke of Visions and of the Guardian. But there was no outburst, the stationed Brigadiers throughout the room appearing suddenly more glowering. The room grew quieter and Midianna's voice grew stronger.

"...and these would be for the most part archers, though should any wish to receive training in swordsmanship, they should be encouraged to do so. It is a fact, is it not, that the Essemarians have many such companies in their army?" At this she looked to the black-skinned Easterners, who nodded. "And the women of Hralindi fight equally with their men in this war, do they not? Fantastic archery on horseback according to all our sources. It says a great deal for our Eastern friends that they are willing to mobilize all their talents in order to keep the Khestadone from taking their lands! We are not used to such a tradition in the western countries, nor does anyone deny the chivalric instinct, strength and heroism of our men, but all the tales say that during the Downfall of the Ralsheen, Terianh's army contained a number of women, their heroism and exploits told in many a book in our Great Library. As a free people we should consider allowing for a female company or even a brigade if there are so many volunteers.

"But again, I would like to speak to my support for the war. Can you not see that the overall situation is dire? It is wrong to believe that our Republic would endure in its present form should Essemar and Hralindi fall! Too many look to the past when those two detached themselves from the Anterianhi Empire a hundred years ago and seem to believe they are unimportant. Unimportant! As if in our times there is an ethic that suggests such a thing! Most of this feeling is based on the fact our trade with them is less lucrative than with the western kingdoms. Sad. It is sad, I tell you! There are those of us who disregard the teachings of the Orders of Meical and are skeptical that such a Being still exists to influence us in our time, and act as if economy and efficiency and trade are the only rule of the day by which our Republic gains greatness. Nevertheless, when we look to those older teachings, whether we acknowledge the Guardian or not, the Gifted and the Orders have it right when it comes to how we should all relate to one another. For myself, I am grateful that His Grace the Lord Curdoz spoke on these very subjects, for too long we have denied their impact upon our whole culture and way of life, at least here in the Republic. The point is that we have considered ourselves friends to, with the exception of the Barantines, the domains associated with the former Anterianhi Empire. When a friend asks for help, you help him! Essemar and Hralindi have requested our aid, and the Nantians to whom we are very close have made it plain—Prince Nikal made it plain when he was here—that without our help, the Alkhan will likely overrun the eastern kingdoms and soon. They have taken most of Essemar's lands on the Southern Continental coast leading to the Great Arch. It is the Masters on this Assembly who represent constituencies associated with wealthy tradesmen that resist, for they fear the immediate future and the diversion of the merchant marine, by which they gain their wealth, to the war effort. However, they seem not to see into a future where the eastern kingdoms are no more. If Essemar and Hralindi fall, the Barantines will surely make common cause with both the Khestadone and the Ice Tribes, as Lord Curdoz has suggested, and then Eleni will fall! After that, then what? Do we stand by when Eleni and then Solanto fall to their enemies? To pretend that somehow the Republic of Tirilorin and the Kingdom of Nant will continue to stand afterwards is folly, I tell you! And even if we did, what happens then to the trade and wealth that comes to our city? Most of it would be gone forever! Our merchant vessels would dry up on sand bars, our trade would diminish to a tithe of what it currently is, and tens of thousands of our citizens who rely on the wealth of our networks would fall into poverty. The greatness of our Republic, all that we have built together, would be gone. Our walls are strong, but do we want to see the combined armies of the Khestadone at our gates? Or do we find ourselves fleeing to Nant in the hopes that the sea and the Nantian navy will stop the advance of the Khestadone who will then have control of all the resources of the Northern Continent? Do we plea with the Berugians to hide us behind their Great Wall? Are we to become so diminished and begging of others? I say, woman that I am, that we fight now for the eastern kingdoms and do our utmost to stop the Khestadone advance. Some may be skeptical of the words of Lord Curdoz that the Guardian is at work and that He calls the Sage and us to action, but there is tremendous reason to do this whether one is skeptical or not. It is quite plain what our future will be should we do nothing! The right thing to do is to aid our friends. How would it be if the enemy were indeed at our gates, and none came to our aid..."

She went on for a little while longer like this urging action. It was a powerful speech, and when she finished, complete silence reigned for several moments as all stood until Midianna found her desk again. As soon as she sat, however, it appeared as though every person in that vast hall began to speak at once.

"I am stunned!" said Mother Idamé. "I see why she was elected to her position!"

"There were others who spoke for the war, but she was the first to openly side with Curdoz' view of the matter," offered Lyndz, "that is to say, with historical and moral considerations, not just those based on trade. Though she covered that too better than anyone else."

Kodi was impressed for other reasons. His whole mindset throughout his life had been developed in a world in which women were highly regarded and had many rights, and yet were still subject to rules favoring, and a culture dominated by, men. His coming to Tirilorin, however, had begun to make him see the value of women in high leadership roles. The manner in which Madame Arlay relayed her business propositions in the office of the High Master, and here in the Assembly the realization that the most powerful and moving speech came from Madame Midianna, a woman elected to her position due to obvious skills and talents, all was a revelation to him and made him see women in a new light.

It was a long time until the chamber grew quiet enough to continue. Interestingly, however, when Naloro came to the podium, he did not introduce any more speakers. Instead, he dismissed the Assembly with a few short words.

"The Assembly will meet again six days hence, at which time I will address the issues and the relevant questions presented to me."

"He ended it early!" said Kodi, as they all stood. "There were several others who wanted to speak!"

"It's brilliant!" replied Lyndz. "Don't you see? Master Naloro is in favor of the war, and he ended this meeting after the most effective of the pro-war speeches! The man knows what he's doing. Everyone will leave here today with the pro-war argument strong in their minds. Brilliant! In fact, I wonder if he deliberately intended to end with Madame Midianna. I bet he planned it with her right after he talked with Curdoz yesterday!"

Such maneuverings were bizarre to Kodi, who looked at his sister oddly.

"What is it?" Lyndz asked.

Kodi was startled by a thought that had finally wound its way through his highly intelligent, yet slower than his twin's, mind. It was as if his experiences with women the last couple days had opened his eyes. *I've been looking at her wrong. I've known she was smart. I've known what she's capable of. Yet I have feared for her anyway. But if her safety and success has anything to do with her mind, then what am I worried about?*

"I think you're just smarter than me, that's all. You're amazing, really, to think the way you do!"

Lyndz looked at her brother with a gleam in her eye, pleased by his compliment.

They made their way through the crowd of people and desks to where Curdoz, Enric, and Hollina stood. Several had gathered around them, for many were eager to meet the Sage of Solanto. Most said something favorable to him regarding his speech and his news. As it so happened, Madame Midianna's desk was quite close to Master Enric's, and the crowd around her was at least as large. The four Easterners were there, and many others were congratulating her on her masterful words, asking her questions and offering her support, even on the idea of a female company in the Brigades. To Kodi it was all very strange, and he had strong doubts that the lords that sat on the King's Council in Ferostro would react among one another after their Council meetings with such cordial affability. His impression based on his conversations with Curdoz and Brother Theneri was that the powerful lords of Solanto were always trying to gain some sort of advantage over everyone else, and the Sage, the King, and the Grand Duke worked hard over long years to ensure that everybody treated one another fairly and to keep the ambitions of the lords in check.

From these thoughts he found himself distracted suddenly.

Approaching the crowd gathered around Curdoz and Midianna were three men. The one leading was High Master Naloro. But the two tall men behind him attracted all of Kodi's attention. One was of middle age, handsome though bald, with sophisticated, almost regal bearing and the most expensive of clothes, and the other who looked very much like him in the face and yet was much younger, of the age of the twins, and who had on the top of his head a shock of thick curly blond locks. His smile was mischievous, if not quite roguish, which seemed to Kodi to say, like it had in his Vision, that he didn't have a care in all the world except to determine where and how he was to achieve his next round of fun.

Kodi was not at all startled when High Master Naloro spoke.

"Ah, Master Kodi Fothemry! I believe you mentioned yesterday you would be interested in getting to know this one! May I introduce Master Genehbro of the House of Terianh and his son, Tiliruf."

Immediately, Curdoz was at Kodi's side, for he had been observing from a few feet away Kodi's expression as the threesome approached. "Tis he, Kodi?" he whispered in his ear.

Kodi nodded. Lyndz too understood. Mother Idamé was a bit further away with Hollina and was unaware.

"Your Grace!" said Genehbro in a booming voice as he reached out and shook Curdoz' hands. "Twenty years it has been!"

The introductions took a few minutes, and Tiliruf was as affable and welcoming as his gregarious father. He gripped Kodi's hand and patted him on the shoulder.

"Solantines, eh? What a lark! Kodi, eh? Glad to know you, mate! And who is this lovely one beside you?"

He winked charmingly as he kissed her hand.

"Lyndz," she replied. "Also of the House of Fothemry."

"Ah, I see! Brother and sister are we? I could have guessed."

"Twins, actually," said Kodi.

"Delightful!" said Tiliruf with flair, kissing Lyndz' hand a second time and then glancing at Kodi with pretended disdain. "Wouldn't have it any other way! It's no fun if there's not a champion involved!"

Kodi hooted grandly at this.

Lyndz, however, was having none of it and withdrew her hand. "Oh, please! I don't need him to look after me!" She glared at her brother who was still chortling at her expense. In general she didn't really mind the joke, and Tiliruf was not being so uncouth as to continue to try to nettle her. They continued greetings and small talk, but it appeared that Tiliruf truly was intrigued by them and their coming on such a long journey.

"...and this mission the Lord Curdoz mentioned in his speech. You two are part of it, eh? Thrilling!"

Kodi in his socially sensitive manner knew instantly how to communicate with the man so as to spike his interest.

"You know it! Adventure, danger, fighting, undiscovered lands. Deadly secret, too." He winked.

"Really? You don't say! So, you're going to tell me all the details, eh?"

Lyndz apparently understood Kodi's game and played along.

"And why would we do that, Master Tiliruf?" she asked in such a tone as to appeal to his humor.

He cackled. "Ah, well, as to that, Lady Lyndz, I'm sure you could use my expert advice, for, you see, 'adventure' is my other name!"

"Don't believe him, Ko! Probably couldn't build a campfire!"

"Definitely not, sis. And couldn't wade across a puddle without getting his stockings wet and muddy, which would be a right shame considering," Kodi said this looking from head to toe at Tiliruf's satins, heavily damasked as they were with gold and silver threads, "they might rust."

He had determined the humorous side of Tiliruf's character with perfect accuracy. He was a give-and-take joker of the first rank. The young man guffawed royally. "Well, I can see we're going to have some fun together while you're here in the city, eh? And who knows? I just might have to follow you when you leave here and determine for myself what you're up to! But we can dispense, perhaps, with the 'Master' and the 'Lady' titles between us, don't you agree?"

"Absolutely," agreed Kodi with fervor. "I'm not a master, and Lyndz definitely isn't a..."

"Ko!" screeched Lyndz. But it was too late. Both young men howled extravagantly. Lyndz just shook her head. A lasting friendship had within a few moments been forged between them.

In the days to come, Lyndz would often find herself confronting some joke aimed with chauvinistic wit in her direction, but typically she was able to skewer either or both the men with her own style of cleverness, and all in all the three got along with one another as easily as puppies of different breeds.

Even so, this daughter of Hess and Elisa was aware that this was exactly the sort of young man her father especially would sometimes warn her about. She clearly remembered the words he had said to her the summer before on their outing together to Cumpero, when at the duke's court she was introduced to several young men of the baronial class. *There is a kind of man you must be especially wary of, my dear. For he is exceedingly intelligent, humorous, and as charming as Musca as a puppy. These are not unhappy traits, to be sure, taken at the surface. But sometimes they hide a very self-involved maneuverer. Be astute! As a friend he can be loyal and of great value, and I know such men who have traveled with me to Tolos. But as a Bondmate, he would be the worst sort possible. Such men are not faithful, my dear. Their minds and their bodies wander without shame. Trust me, my dear, for I have heard their tales on my journeys. They make for great laughter among the men, yet my private remonstrances rarely go anywhere with them.* Lyndz was quite determined that friendship was as far as her own relationship to the son of Genehbro would ever go.

The interchange between the young trio continued merrily just as it looked to be with the older crowd nearby. Genehbro was grandly insisting that Enric and all his guests were to remain for dinner, and then the invitation continued to grow to include Madame Midianna, her husband who acted as her assistant, the four eastern ambassadors, and High Master Naloro and his wife and entourage. Before they knew it, the noise of the crowd in the Assembly fell away as the twins, walking with Tiliruf, followed the rest of Genehbro's guests through a side doorway into another long grand hall and into the part of the great Palace occupied by the House of Terianh.

Kodi in particular was awestruck when he realized that here he was chatting and laughing with the descendants of Terianh the Great in the Palace from which for so many centuries a vast empire was ruled. As a country lad from a distant duchy, it was more than he ever expected for himself.

And so, it was done.

At some point during that evening, which consisted of large quantities of fine wines continuously poured into golden goblets by a dozen servants, and fabulous dinner prepared and served in palatial style by several dozen additional servants, certain conversations took place in little groups here and there involving the foursome from Solanto, and Tiliruf and his father. Before the evening had concluded, it had been announced that Tiliruf was to join the Sage of Solanto and his comrades on the quest to find the Qeteral and the hidden land of Ulakel.

Interestingly, Kodi never once felt inclined to make mention that such a conclusion was required by way of his Vision from Meical the Guardian. Tiliruf seemed oddly uninterested in the actual reasons behind the quest of the Solantines, but he was quite obviously excited by the fact of the mission itself. Intrigued by the novelty of the whole affair, in addition to the personalities involved, particularly Kodi whom he seemed to latch onto like a brother, he was simply insistent he wanted to be a part of it, and his father was content not to intervene.

Curdoz, of course, knew that Kodi's Vision required Tiliruf's participation and did nothing to discourage Tiliruf's eagerness. Yet in his mind he admitted the oddity at how rapidly it all transpired.

There was, however, one telling exchange as the evening wound down and the guests were preparing to leave.

Old Enric made a comment to Tiliruf regarding the work of the Guardian and wanted to offer him the common Meicalian Affirmation.

"Ah, Master Enric," replied Tiliruf. "You should know me well enough by now, eh? I don't go in for all that Guardian malarkey! But I thank you for your well-wishes!"

All four of the Solantines happened to hear this exchange, and there was an audible intake of breath coming from a shocked Mother Idamé. As Enric appeared not at all inclined to even gently chastise the young man, none of the others said anything.

However, like a grandfather might, Enric patted Tiliruf on the back and said, "Perhaps, young Tiliruf! We shall see, though, shan't we? Keep your mind open; there's a good man!"

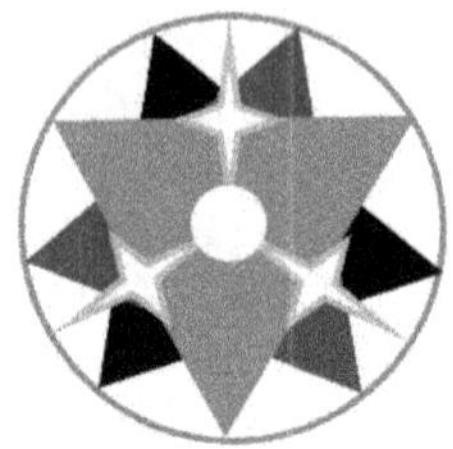

Chapter 6—Son of Emperors

The next day was spent by the twins entirely in Tiliruf's company, while the two Sages continued to discuss the Visions and the quest and also to meet with important people. Idamé took a day with her new friend Hollina on their own exploration of the sites of Central City.

Kodi and Lyndz had a great new companion in Tiliruf. He was as friendly and easy-going as any of their friends back home in Felto, and his humor was interesting and kept Kodi especially in stitches. The Tirliorine could be quite sarcastic at times. The sarcasm did not always appeal to Lyndz, though she fared well enough with it.

Kodi considered that Tiliruf was somewhat of a free spirit with few expectations placed upon him. Maybe, Kodi thought, he just didn't take himself and events very seriously. He was different than Kodi in several ways. Kodi had always reveled in races and trials of skill and strength, and competitions with the other young men and boys back in Felto. More importantly, though, he had been given a number of responsibilities. Kodi knew how to hunt, fish, trap, ride, work with wood and stone, care for horses, and a great many other activities besides. He ensured that his grandfather's daily needs were met, and then of course in the many long absences of his father, he provided most of the serious labor needed to operate his grandfather's household.

Tiliruf was strong from his exercises, fencing lessons, and horseback riding on his family's estates in the country, and he must have had some serious self-discipline when it came to his studies with his tutors. He was highly intelligent. Beyond these pursuits, however, Kodi wondered what else he might have much passion for. The Palace in which he lived in many ways operated little differently than it did a hundred years before in the days when Tiliruf's grandsires were ruling an empire. It was still stuffed with servants who took care of every little detail down to the setting out of Tiliruf's well-tailored clothes each morning. Different than what Kodi was used to, and yet he found this son of emperors easy to talk with and confide in. He was a great listener, and even though he often jested about himself or others, he took Kodi and Lyndz seriously enough, determined to take them under wing. He wanted the twins to have a positive experience in the city, and their first day was splendid as he showed them all the great buildings and monuments.

One private observation Lyndz had was how the young man appeared totally uninterested in his illustrious ancestry. Or rather his connection to it. Clearly, Tiliruf was scholarly in his historical knowledge, for he could effectively describe the various monuments, statues, public buildings, and works projects in the vast city that the twins would ask about and that represented the greatness of emperors past. They were amazed and awestruck at everything they came across. Tiliruf, on the other hand, seemed aloof to it. When the twins would remark upon the obvious accomplishments of these persons, he would make statements dismissive or sarcastic, such as, "Sure, if you say so, Lyndz, but he was the emperor that cut the navy in half, and the eastern kingdoms started ignoring imperial edicts and paying imperial taxes. He was an idiot." Or, "Yeah, Kodi, but Emperor Sanvelt couldn't keep his wife happy, eh? She had a dozen different men—soldiers, attendants and the like—that she called to her bedchambers pretty regular according to the legend, and I believe it. They say he got his stiffrod cut off in battle with the Barantines! His younger brother took the throne after he died." This last made Kodi laugh extravagantly and Lyndz turn scarlet, although she held her tongue. She had never been inclined to laugh at this sort of humor unless it came from her brother and then only if they happened to be alone.

In any event, whenever they might bring up his descent from these persons, they could detect his resistance. Even Terianh the Great, though he admired his militaristic accomplishments, he criticized for being too 'religious' and even faulted him hotly for not placing the imperial capital in a more central position in the empire, for he apparently thought it negatively affected the subsequent rule of Terianh's descendants. Kodi didn't know enough history or geography to comment otherwise, and Lyndz simply refused to argue with a young man that she hadn't known for very long, believing, like her mother, that it was uncouth to do so. That old-fashioned viewpoint, however, would be tested in subsequent days as they all grew to know one another better. For now, she held her tongue.

For his part, Tiliruf showed great interest in the twins. He would question them often and listen when they would make comparisons about life in the city to that in their remote northern duchy. He thought it was a great lark that they lived practically in the forest, and was quite interested in what it was like, the timber cutters, farms, animals wild and tame, the construction of the family manor, and even simple things like cooking on open fires, bathing in rivers, and camping. The weaving and sewing, quilting and cooking that Lyndz participated in with her mother and the other women in Felto, and the stone and woodwork, fishing and hunting that occupied Kodi's time, Tiliruf would go on about these as if they were amazing skills. He was complimentary of their grandfather and mother and acted as if their father's exploration and opening of Tolos, and even the development of the ambernut trade, was far more important and interesting than anything his own forebears were world-famous for.

The next morning, they again met him at the Palace. This time they spent an hour in the Palace Gardens at Lyndz' personal request.

These were located on the east side of the Palace which lent itself well to green shade gardens interspersed with rambling beds of colorful plantings. The color white was prominent, lending clarity and architectural interest, defining as it did the green. A network of eye-catching fountains wound its way down the various terraces, creating pools of crystal water and sprays across classic statuary. Tall cypresses created various garden rooms, most of which too contained fountains.

One of these which Lyndz especially liked contained a large statue of Meical the Guardian. A heavily muscled nude, with great wings spread behind him; she wondered if He must look like an Etoppsis. Sans wings, however, His features were Human. She stared for several minutes, mesmerized by the statue in its bubbling oval pool.

They descended through the terraces and crossed two broad quadrangles containing large spread-crowned oaks. On the shaded end of one of these, against the slope above, was a sensual little waterfall trickling musically and invitingly across a vertical carpet of fern and moss into a grotto, this containing a marble statue of a bathing woman. Like Lyndz in the Meical garden room, Kodi was particularly taken by this feature. It reminded him of the wet weather falls back home that in spring spilled from various gullies on their way to the Wolf River, and the statue of the nude woman seemed to plunge him into a private fantasy. Lyndz and Tiliruf had returned half-way across the quadrangle, talking to each other about the various kinds of plants and trees, before Kodi realized he was being left behind. He winked at the statue (which he pretended winked back) and ran to catch up with the others.

It was a great hour-long tour, and if anything, it proved that Tiliruf did at least appreciate the beauty and the work that the hundreds of gardeners put into making it such a grand place. Not only that, but Lyndz also found that, on the subject of gardens, she and Tiliruf had something in common. He knew as much about plants, their names and habits, as she did.

When the hour ended, Lyndz made it clear she wanted to spend time alone in the Great Library. This Tiliruf had taken them to the previous morning, and its vastness had captured Lyndz' soul and overwhelmed Kodi. It was perhaps four times again as large as the library in Aster that Brother Theneri supervised. Soaring beams and brown marble columns graced a vast space filled to a height of thirty feet or more with volumes. Here could be found the wealth of knowledge of the greatest Anterianhi historians, scientific theorists, mapmakers, and storytellers of the last five hundred years. They escorted her there and walked inside with her. She was more interested in this place than anything else Tiliruf had planned to show them later that day, so she politely begged off and remained there looking over the titles, pulling one, then another, off the shelves. Within minutes she had a large stack in her arms. Kodi explained to Tiliruf that his sister would be content reading books for the remainder of their stay in Tirilorin.

Kodi liked books well enough, but nothing on the level of his twin. He preferred rereading his favorite stories from his grandfather's bookshelves, particularly those that contained battles and wars and heroic feats by warriors, or of adventurers and explorers. Nor had he learned High Anterianhi as Lyndz had, which limited his choices to books in the common tongue. He was still in the middle of reading the book about Terianh the Great that Brother Theneri had so generously given him, and which he had subconsciously labeled his favorite book in the world. It contained details and battle tactics not covered by any of his grandfather's storybooks about the Conquest.

Terianh and the other heroes were characters Kodi admired and wished to emulate. But Lyndz devoured all her grandfather's books and also took in new information with a relish. So, the two men left her alone and walked back out the Library's great entryway.

Oddly, as soon as they came out into the sunlight again, Tiliruf developed upon his face a shocked expression. Kodi looked up and was surprised to see sitting on the edge of a stone fountain seven or eight women dressed in bright, mismatched colors. Interestingly, every single one of them was looking intently at Tiliruf and beaming. They beckoned him over.

"Ah, Kodi, sorry you have to see this," he said quietly, and yet he was now smirking.

"What? See what?" asked Kodi innocently at first, staring at the strangely-clad women. He could hardly help noticing that each was also displaying enormous amounts of bosom. The women now began to eye him too, giggling quite immodestly and pointing.

One or two of them might have been remotely pretty, but mostly he thought they all looked cheap, with their gaudy jewelry and garish makeup. Kodi rarely saw women in makeup except a few of those at court back in the King's Palace in Ferostro, though none of the ladies at court looked remotely like these women. Even Mistress Itruvi paled in comparison. He watched as Tiliruf stepped forward.

"Ruffy!" called one of them. "What a delightful surprise! You live here in Central City, do you? You never told me that! Perhaps we should be charging you more silver, hmm? Or even gold!"

"Hello ladies!" Tiliruf laughed expressively. "It's nice to see you, eh? But I'm sort of busy right now! I have a new friend here I'm showing..."

"Why, Ruffy! How sweet!" interrupted the same woman, apparently the leader, as the others were content to giggle. "He is a handsome specimen! Nantian, perhaps? I think you should introduce your handsome 'friend' to us! Perhaps we also can make him feel, hmm, 'at home' while he visits? He can be our 'friend' as well!"

Kodi now stepped up, looked sideways at Tiliruf, and smirked. "*Ruffy?*" he mouthed, having now caught on. Though he had never in Solanto seen such women, he had heard about them from some of the Cumpero supervisors on the manor site back in Felto. They implied they could be found in the cities and told bawdy, boastful stories about them for laughs. The sailors on Curdoz' ship were also well-acquainted with them.

Tiliruf whispered back. "Ah, well. Sorry. Didn't expect to see them here. They're usually in North Bend, another section of the city."

He then produced another exaggerated laugh as if to prove to the women he was the epitome of confidence. If he were embarrassed, it didn't especially show. He replied to their offer. "No, ladies, sorry. We'll have to catch you another time, eh?"

He then pulled Kodi by the arm and hustled him off down the lane and away from the fountain.

"Oh, we look forward to you catching us soon, Ruffy!" called the woman as the two young men sped away. The others cackled.

Kodi looked at Tiliruf. "I'm calling you Ruffy from now on."

"Um, no, mate, I guess I'd rather you didn't. Oh well, they uh..."

Kodi let out a howl of laughter. "Ruffy's like a coded name, isn't it? I just learned about codes. You know, it's not a very good one. Sounds like a puppy dog. In fact, I thought about that name instead for Musca! By the *Guardian*, Tiliruf!"

"Ah, well, they don't really represent the best of me, if you know what I mean. I guess, I mean, well they are kind of in the past. Not sure I want to be that person anymore. I'm a better man than that, eh? I'm going with you and Curdoz on this journey and I'm ready to move on."

"Right," laughed Kodi. "You don't have to explain."

Tiliruf looked at Kodi with relief in his eyes. "You understand, eh? I was afraid you might not."

"Don't bet on Lyndz."

"Shaft, Kodi! Don't tell her! Glad she was inside the Library! I've never seen them there. The Masters wouldn't be pleased they're hanging around Central City by the Library, eh? They stay in North Bend, usually."

"There's always those who we'd rather not know about our... *adventures*."

They came to the Inner Wall and walked through a different gate than the one Kodi had used before. "You've had 'em, too, have you? Spit 'em out, then. Let's go to a place I know and get an ale."

A continued tour of the city apparently postponed, Tiliruf steered Kodi in a new direction, and after a quarter hour or so they came to a street that sloped in the direction of Southport. They proceeded down this, and soon Kodi found himself following his new friend into a tavern.

It was a clean place built of brick and shaped timbers, yet even so it was clear it was not the sort of place to be frequented by the high-class citizens of Central City. Instead, there were many laborers of every type. The bartender was a burly man, in his fifties perhaps, and he had a look about him that showed he put up with no nonsense. It was noisy despite it being morning still. It intrigued Kodi that people were drinking this time of day. Back home many of the men went to the local inn and drank happily after a long day's work, and Kodi joined them sometimes. He concluded since this was a massive city there was probably drinking going on at all hours of the day and night. Though the bar was busy, there were still quite a few empty side tables. Walking towards one, Tiliruf nodded to the bartender and held up two fingers. Obviously Tiliruf thought nothing of drinking this early, and Kodi was interested enough in the idea not to suggest otherwise. He hadn't had a drink since sharing swigs with the crewmen on Curdoz' ship, refraining as he typically did until Idamé retired to the cabin in the evenings. And wine with Curdoz and his acquaintances didn't seem to really count. As all young men like Kodi and Tiliruf knew, there were real differences between drinking and...drinking.

Nodding, the bartender took two monstrous tankards down from a high shelf and began to fill them with a foamy brew from a huge oak barrel just behind him. The two young men had not been seated ten seconds before they were presented with two frothing dark ales. Kodi beamed.

It was beautiful.

Tiliruf handed the man a silver coin with a "Thanks, Zhock." Zhock the bartender grunted something and walked back to his busy bar.

"Nobody will recognize me here or bother us, not in this part of the city," said Tiliruf. "Really only Zhock knows who I am, although I suppose my clothes place me from Central City, eh?"

Kodi nodded and swallowed. It was as good as he had hoped. "Must be the stockings. Thanks, man. I love this." He swallowed again. Tiliruf stared.

"You're tame, Kodi." He winked and then proceeded to down half his tankard in one vast display of manly prowess.

Kodi laughed. "No. It's just that this is excellent. Savoring the first taste, you see, but I'm with you." The Solantine then proceeded to match the Tirilorine with a gargantuan gulp and then wiped the foam from his mouth on his sleeve.

"I'll buy that. It is good, eh? Zhock brings it in from some place east of the city. You need to get out and about more, mate." Intent upon staying well ahead, Tiliruf swallowed another huge mouthful.

"Maybe. Curdoz doesn't seem to mind, and the man sure likes his wine, but I promised to watch myself around Mother Idamé. And, with Lyndz and all, it isn't the sort of group that lends itself well to chugging ale, is it?" He again drank deeply. "Back home sometimes my mates and I would pitch in for a small barrel, strap it to a horse and take it to the river on summer nights to camp, build a fire, swim, and have a great ole time, or even climb up into the hills to camp for the view when the moons were bright. Thanks for bringing me back to a happy memory!" He lifted his tankard and knocked it against Tiliruf's.

Tiliruf laughed. "Sure, mate. Anytime." He'd almost finished his huge tankard and then proceeded to belch loudly. "We all need a drinking partner, eh? Best situation for talking about women or anything else, for that matter, and playing Fifty-twos. But we'll have to get a few more for gaming some other time."

"You have a reputation about that. I don't know if I want to sit at Fifty-twos with a rascally gambler!"

Tiliruf guffawed. "Ha! A rascally gambler? Yeah, well maybe so. What else have you heard?"

"Womanizer, though not in so many words."

"Well, yeah, not so much that as a 'customer,' eh? At least nowadays. I have my limits. I mean, sure, there was a time, you know, eh?" Tiliruf hesitated to say more and laughed. "But you were going to tell me your own tales, mate!"

Kodi found Tiliruf easy to open up to, and he could hardly be fully truthful about certain things with Lyndz. "Her name was Jonell. She's the daughter of the stablemaster in Felto. Close to four years ago, now. Early one morning when I went to saddle one of our horses to go out hunting, Jonell was in the stable. Nobody else was around."

Tiliruf sniggered. "She was expecting you, mate. You know she was. I bet she'd been watching you every day, eh? They're all alike."

Kodi had suspected this himself about Jonell at the time, but he set aside his friend's generalization about women as another sample of Tiliruf's cynicism. "Yeah, pretty sure she had been."

"She cornered you, eh?"

"You could say that. But I'd been wishing pretty hard for it, and I didn't stop her. She was older, seventeen or eighteen, and she was, er, shaped well. Really shaped well." He made a circling motion with his hands next to his chest in a demonstration. Tiliruf sniggered again, and Kodi took another, longer swig. He was perfectly content in making up tall tales about multiple encounters and extraordinary sexual prowess when in the presence of the workers and sailors, as that was an expected part of the manly communication 'game,' but he had never shared this one truth about himself with anyone.

Tiliruf had a funny way of drawing Kodi out. "She pretended she'd discovered a spanking young stallion in that stable!"

Kodi grinned big. "Yeah, you're reading my mind; she even called me that! *Young Stallion*, ha! And I turned horsey right quick. So, I think you can figure what happened for yourself."

"I, as a matter of fact, can do that, mate," he chortled. "So, you thumped her in a barn, eh? Interesting location. How was it?"

Kodi was no longer surprised by Tiliruf's straightforwardness. Nor did Kodi seem to mind anymore, because he was far away from Felto now, and there was no risk of damaging Jonell's reputation, and particularly with Tiliruf there seemed no reason for concern. "Tiliruf, I'll tell you something. We spent half the day together. After the stable we ran off to the forest to a secret place and had even more fun. Damned bucky, I was, considering how willing she was. I never did go hunting, about the only time I ever really lied to my mother. Well, you know, a big sort of lie. Used to fib a lot about drinking with my mates back then. Dad was gone at the time."

"And nothing happened to her later, eh? *Thumping thumpers make three,* as the old adage goes, eh? She didn't..."

"No, thank the Guardian. But I got scared about that after."

Tiliruf winked. "She knew what she was doing, eh? Those women who spoke to me at the fountain, they sure do. Couple weeks each month, you know, they're perfectly good for it. Got their time down."

"Well, it's a business to them, isn't it?"

"Yeah, well some push it, I hear, in order for the silver to keep coming. The Monastic's Orphanage is always taking in the produce."

"That's hideous, Tiliruf! How do you know none of 'em are..."

"Ah, they're always sure of themselves when they're with me, eh?"

"You really trust *them?*"

Tiliruf was silent and looked down. Kodi had begun to think it was impossible to actually embarrass Tiliruf, but maybe there was a point where a bit of an old Discipline punched through. He thought Tiliruf was being really foolish, with some chauvinistic male license thrown in, but considering his own encounter with Jonell, he wasn't going to say that. "Sorry, my friend. Sorry. I ain't going to judge you. I was extra lucky, Tiliruf, cause I'm pretty sure Jonell wasn't keeping up with it. In fact, I'm ashamed at my own stupidity, because I realized later she was trying to trap me into Bonding. And don't say I'm tame. I want it as much as any man. But I swear that day was the only time for me. Scared me, like I said. I'm the son of the count and cousin of a duke. I'm expected to have a care and find my life-mate before I get involved like that, otherwise it damages your family's reputation. I really wanted to know what it was like. An old buddy, Tanksen, and his friend Bluuter, you know, had a lot of experience and bragged a bit when we'd get together, and it kept setting off my imagination. So, I was kind of determined about it—just a dumb, fifteen-year-old boy and could hardly stop myself. I kind of appreciate that I had the experience, and I'd be lying to deny the fun of it at the time. But I never did tell Tanksen and Bluuter what *I* did, 'cause it felt kind of shameful to think of actually bringing up Jonell's name and hurting her own reputation in a roundabout sort of way. Wasn't long after, Bluuter was forced by one of his little scandals into Bonding a girl who turned out to be the worst henpeck. Tanksen has turned altogether into a real rake. At least one babe I know he admitted to me when he was half drunk was his, but he refuses to acknowledge it to her family, and hasn't slowed him down, either. He probably has one or two more. Probably going to be run out of town some day by a passle of angry fathers with pitchforks!"

"You're cracking me up, mate!"

"So I look back at what I did and what could have happened, and I'm not proud of it. I think about it, and I try not to think about it at the same time. I'm aiming for something better, and there's nobody at home that's right for me."

Tiliruf downed the last of his ale and looked at Kodi seriously. "If I use the word 'tame,' Kodi, you need to understand I'm jesting with you, eh? Really, it says a lot for you, mate. You're pretty noble. It kind of shows, really. I don't really stop myself thinking about it, so I guess you're just more disciplined than me. 'Discipline.' I hate hearing that word. Though what happened to your old buds Bluuter and Tanksen is why I switched from that womanizer phase to 'customer.' No woman's going to trap me. I don't really feel sorry about what I do, and I'm always looking forward to the next opportunity, if you know what I mean. But maybe I should give it up, eh? Going on this journey with you and the others. Time for me to grow up a little more, eh?"

Kodi couldn't quite tell if Tiliruf was being sincere or not. "Those women know you well, don't they? It's been going on a long time?"

Tiliruf winked. "Honestly, mate, I started meeting up with them when I was maybe fourteen. My father never asks me where I go, the servants don't tell him when I leave my rooms in the evening, and I wasn't stupid enough to tell anybody what I was doing."

Kodi chuckled. "Since fourteen? And you plan to change? Because of our quest?"

"Maybe. Probably should, eh?"

"Probably. But I swear, despite everything, it was the hardest thing I ever did not to try to get back with Jonell." Kodi paused. "Actually, if it weren't for my father, I know I would have."

"Your father found out, eh? Like I said, my father knows nothing. Well, nothing specific anyway."

"No, he didn't find out. But only a week or so after that happened between me and Jonell, he came home and we went fishing one morning at the river, and he started talking to me. He thought it was important to warn me about what could happen...you know, consequences. The, er, *making three* part. We'd talked about it before, and you'd think by that age it'd probably not make much difference, but I really listened this time.

Debating in my mind about Jonell. I hadn't yet pondered all that I said about Bluuter and Tanksen, as it was some time later before their real troubles came up. Father brought up a situation of his own telling me what he'd done when he was young, but guess what? It was my mother!"

"Ha! And they weren't Bonded, were they? So, what happened to them, eh? Was it a scandal?"

"Well, you're looking at what happened," Kodi said, grinning. "And Lyndz, of course. 'Cause in that case Thumping Thumpers made the two of them into *four*, not three, didn't they?"

Tiliruf laughed so loudly that others in the tavern looked in their direction.

Kodi continued. "No, it wasn't a scandal. Why would it be? That's the common way of it in our country, in Solanto, but by tradition it's quite all right if you love each other and intend to stay together. The point then is the commitment. Most aren't like Tanksen and Bluuter, obviously. The Matrimonial Troupes travel around the country and perform Bonding rites, but most of the couples have already been living together, and many even have children before the Matrimonials get back around to your town. Like with my parents. But they were madly in love. Father took charge of the *situation* like the best of men would. He went straight to my grandfather Yugan and confessed his love for my mother. Grandfather was impressed by his honesty and hard work ethic, and my grandmother, they tell me, was really charmed by him and his good looks, and so they gave them their full blessing. So, they settled down right away together on a farm not far from Felto."

"It's not a scandal in Solanto when couples mess around before they're Bonded? They don't try to hush it up?" Tiliruf was surprised. "That's not the way it is here, mate. People here are more strict about not living together before the Matrimonials do the rites. It's all foolish; nobody believes, well a few do, but I don't really believe that Guardian's 'blessings' tripe, because I think religion is a bunch of foolishness. Although the women pretend it's important to them. The rites, anyways."

Kodi pondered these remarks while Tiliruf went to the bar and ordered two more ales from Zhock. He wondered if illicit encounters were the norm in this city for young men, particularly rich ones like Tiliruf. Then there was the remark about the Guardian. It was a repeat, really, of what he'd said two days previously when they first met Tiliruf, but this time he clearly stated he didn't 'believe' what he called Meicalian 'religion.' *No,* Kodi said to himself. *It still isn't the right time to tell him.*

Tiliruf returned with their second ales and sat down. "So, you're saying that people in Solanto find their life-mates when they're what? Sixteen? Seventeen?"

"Pretty common. Though it's much more common a couple years older or so, but some are that young. Like my parents were, but nobody minds, really. Curdoz and Idamé say there aren't enough Matrimonials in

Solanto; they seem to blame it on the Mother Superior or something, I don't really understand. It's the common way to live together for months or even a year or so. But it was only a few months later that the Matrimonials came to Felto and Bonded my parents, then Lyndz and I came along pretty quick after." He winked, paused and drank deeply from the fresh tankard. He was beginning to feel the happy effects. The two knocked tankards again. The standard Tirilorine tankard was a bit bigger than in Solanto. "But what I was wanting to tell you was that when my dad talked to me that day at the river, he made me realize there are real differences in women, and that the best men need to be careful about whom they choose for a Bondmate. He was really being open and honest with me about why my mother was such a perfect match for him—he was really being 'sweet,' going on about my mother, talking about her beauty and her body and how she made him feel all bold and courageous, and how super smart she is." Kodi almost mentioned the fact that his parents had the Aura of Bonding seen above them by the Matrimonials, but he suspected Tiliruf would be skeptical of something like this, so he refrained from the detail. "He made me realize I wanted exactly the same as what he had. After he talked to me, I knew there was no way in the world I wanted to spend my life with Jonell. I had no real feelings for her.

"So, I grew up a lot that day. I swore to myself then and there while Father and I were fishing I'd never get myself in a situation like that again. I was lucky with Jonell. I'd see her in town over the months, and she'd come on to me, trying pretty hard to get me alone with her again, but I kept telling her I wasn't interested until she finally backed off. Mean, maybe, but I couldn't do anything about it. There wasn't anything I could say to make her feel better, I know. And I admit there were others, too, who'd try to get me alone like Jonell. I had to avoid them."

"Ah, they just want it like we men do."

"Well, maybe." Kodi didn't look at it quite the same way Tiliruf did, and he wondered suddenly if it was, as he had come to understand, because Tiliruf's mother had died not long after he was born. So, quite unlike Kodi, he was never around kind, loving women—just servants and in the last several years apparently, prostitutes. "Jonell and I made a mistake. She was wishing I'd Bond her, I think, so she'd feel, er, important."

"She thought you a great catch, eh? Pretty buck and the son of a nobleman."

"Yeah, maybe, but I want someone who's really amazing. My mother's like that. Lyndz is too, of course. But there's nobody else like that in Felto. Nobody. Maybe you think it's lame and corny, but I'm looking out for the one who really captures me, and I'm going to find her, and I refuse to *mess around* for the fun of it. It's not worth it to me."

"It's all right, mate. If that works for you. You are rather noble, like I said, and though I like to tease, as you can tell, I'm not teasing you right now, Kodi. Maybe there's an ideal we men should aim for, I don't know. Seems you're a really good man, and it's not going to hurt me to have a noble bloke like you for a friend, eh?" Tiliruf looked Kodi in the eye as he said this and raised his mug in another cheer to emphasize his sincerity. "A genuine nobleman! Not sure I've ever met one!"

"Ha, I guess I'm sometimes referred to as a viscount, which in Solanto is the first son of a count expected to inherit his titles. Thanks. But tell me a little more. I mean, really! Those women by the fountain? Are you really attracted to that? They're not good enough for somebody like you. Don't you know any decent women, Tiliruf? You're from a high family, yourself."

"Maybe. But the really decent ones aren't the kind that are going to let me into their bed that easily now, eh? And the less decent ones are schemers, Kodi, and I learned pretty damned quick to hate that. I agree like I said your ole Tanksen and Bluuter pals' ways are pretty bad, and yes, I did a bit of that until I decided instead to go the different route. Those women at the fountain give me exactly what I want when I want it. Nothing at all against your choice, mate, but this buck didn't want to give it up, and with them there are no expectations, no responsibilities, and no children! Ha!"

Kodi chuckled. So, there were decent women from high families, he realized, but Tiliruf was compelled rather to indulge a powerful, exploratory sex drive. The drive itself Kodi understood totally. Why should he be surprised that a rich young buck like Tiliruf, used to having everything he wanted, engaged prostitutes to satisfy his urges? Kodi knew if he allowed himself, he could very easily be drawn into that sort of indulgent experimentation. Yet his respect for women would not allow for it. He wondered suddenly what really drew women into prostitution in the first place.

"Umm, how many women like those at the library today are in the city, Tiliruf?"

"There are hundreds of them. Mostly in North Bend. Not the best part of town. Close to North Port where all the Nantian sailors and soldiers dock and provide 'em a lot of business, you know. Don't tell me they don't have them in Solanto!"

"Well, I know there are some, in the cities, but they're a lot more secretive than those ones from what I can figure. Those ones were brash, don't you think?"

"That's their job! That's how they snag the men, eh? The Assembly hates it, but they never do anything about it. They probably never will, either."

Kodi looked at his friend and leaned back, took a big swig, smiled broadly, and threw out his honest opinion. "You're hooked on it, Tiliruf. You're a rascal. You're not going to give it up, I can tell. I almost was after only one day."

Tiliruf grinned. “Well, you’re probably right, eh? You never know, though. Sometimes I even surprise myself! Anyway, who am I going to be able to get with on this quest to the Qeteral? Your sister?”

“If you try messing with Lyndz, she’ll give you the Teeth of Meical for it. You won’t know what hit you.”

“You’re scaring me, mate,” said Tiliruf sarcastically, and they laughed. In a few minutes they had finished their second round. “I can go for a third, mate, if you’re willing.”

Kodi’s head spun a little already, considering the size of these steins, and he was confident as to what the third one would do. “Sure. Trying to get me drunk, are you?”

“That’s the point I thought when we started!” His host admitted as their conversation and tone shifted away from the serious. “A bit, anyway. Nothing says we have to go home till tonight, mate! It’ll wear off long before we get you back to old Enric’s place. We’ll have one more, mate, then go down to the docks and you can show me Curdoz’ ship. The harbormaster will let us board it; he knows me. I know all the important people. There’s the beach, too, where everyone swims, about a half mile outside East Gate, eh? There’re different days for men and women, and today it’s all men. Some of my friends will be there, and you’ll get to meet them.”

Kodi was feeling good by now and could hardly refuse. “Never swam in the ocean!”

“Nothin’ like it, mate. The water’s warm here—the currents you know.”

They drank their third round and talked currents and shipping and other things that Kodi was not especially familiar with but was nevertheless interesting. Tiliruf told him a little about Nant, too, since that was Curdoz’ chosen destination for the travelers after they were to leave Tirilorin. But they didn’t stay on any of these topics long considering how they were feeling by now. Kodi was having trouble concentrating. He started looking around and found that almost everything seemed funnier than usual, and as they joked and their laughter increased, so also did the looks in their direction, mostly working men who thought it funny to see the young men imbibing as much as they were. Even Zhock grinned in their direction once or twice, oblivious to Tiliruf’s jokes about fat bartenders, which caused even more cackling on the part of the two. After another half hour, the two friends stumbled a little on their way out the door.

Gratefully, Kodi’s host hailed a trader in a wagon driving a load of dry goods towards a market in Southport, who cheerfully allowed the two to climb aboard. The man didn’t mind in the least as they continued to chatter and bray, clearly realizing they had been imbibing, and even laughed himself at some of Tiliruf’s outrageous jokes. After a while, the driver chimed in with his own, to which the two younger men responded with appropriate uproar. Kodi was kept in stitches as the two Tirilorines took turns spoofing the infamous rigidity of Nantian women, the gigantic sexual anatomy of Etoppsi males, the massive breasts of their females, and apocryphal tales of Qeteral virility.

"Tha's whacha need, Kodi mate," Tiliruf slurred. "Ya need ya a Qeteral woman! Ya can mate 'em all night in the moonlight, and they just want more! 'N all their babes is yours!"

"A'right, yeah, I kin manage that! Why don' ya get one for yerself, man?"

"Naw! I ain't ready for babes, no way, mate! Commitments—tha's the word, n't it? Or is it 'sponsibilities', Yeah, tha's right, babes 'n commitments 'n 'sponsibilities. Those'r fer noble blokes like yerself. 'Spose I could buy husbands for 'em, if it came right down to it."

"Yer a rotten scoundrel, Ruffy!"

"Don' call me, tha', mate!"

"I will, and y' ain' stoppin' me."

"How'm I s'pose'ta 'splain it ter Mudder Idamé 'n Lynzigirl?"

"'At's your problem, not mine, my man."

When they finally reached the driver's destination in Southport, the two thanked the driver who had suddenly turned all business now he was around his fellow market folk, so he just nodded and went about his work setting up his goods in a stall. There was plenty of food to be found here: cheese, salt ham, bread, and some early fruits such as strawberries. The seafood market was nearby, and the odor was not pleasant, so Tiliruf quickly bought them both plenty to eat for lunch. They found a hidden corner out of the wind and away from the smells and sat down to eat a solid meal. With full bellies, before long they were able to regain a little of their composure.

It was now early afternoon. When the two finished eating they began to walk towards the wharfs. Kodi's awe of the vastness of this city on this quarter-hour jaunt continued to increase. He was feeling really happy, too, and less unsteady, but he absolutely declined when Tiliruf produced a bottle of fine Nantian brandy he had just purchased from a vendor at the market. Tiliruf took a nip, but since it was clear his friend was unwilling to indulge further, he stuffed it away for some future opportunity. "A'right, mate, I'll save it for the journey, eh? Or have you over to my rooms for Fifty-twos."

"Good thinkin'," agreed Kodi. "Just have to make time away from the others. I don' think Curdoz'll care too much, 'specially if we're not plum fools all the time. He's less stern than I once thought he was. Well, I take that back. He can be stern about important things, but enjoying yourself from time to time don't seem to bother 'im."

"Damn good thing," said Tiliruf. "Then I'll be sure to acquire more before we go! I actually got plenty in my rooms. I'll have to introduce you to my solid silver liquor cabinet, eh?"

They then found themselves near the docks by the harbormaster's office. Seagulls cried loudly overhead.

Master Yamin was pleased to see both Tiliruf, whom he knew quite well, and Kodi, too. "So, Master Fothemry, how have you enjoyed your time here? Has Master Tiliruf been showing you the sights? Not getting you into too much trouble, is he?" He winked.

Kodi, aware of his still heavy-headed condition, made a concentrated effort to speak with clarity and not sound foolish. "He has been a good friend, thanks Master Yamin. We wanted to go on board Lord Curdoz' ship if you don't mind, and I wanted to show him around."

Yamin appeared not to notice anything odd. Or pretended not to through a smirky smile. "Go right ahead. Your Captain Shond and his men are here, cleaning and making repairs. It's a great little ship. Plenty good enough for these waters, if you don't count winter, but I'm of the opinion that if His Grace the Lord Curdoz chooses to sail beyond Nant on this journey of yours he'd better hire bigger and better."

"I think that is his plan, sir," replied Kodi. "But I think he expects to stay here a couple more weeks. I'm not sure when we leave exactly."

"Well, the Masters will help him as he requires. Great words he spoke the other day in the Hall. We wish you all well on your journeys. Anyway, go ahead aboard."

The crewmen and Captain Shond hailed '*Bookman*' cheerily, who returned their greeting and introduced them to Tiliruf. Tiliruf got a great kick out of it, for when the Solantine crewmen understood he was the last great-grandson of the last emperor they kept nodding to him, referring to him constantly as 'His Lordship' and wanting to shake his hand over and over. Several even bowed to him. Tiliruf was gracious and congenial, despite not really caring that much about his pedigree, yet did his best not to put on any airs, even to the point of adopting a bit of their own language patterns and gruff seamanlike manner. He was smooth, quicker than Kodi with funny jokes that appealed to the crew, and Kodi was quite impressed. He then showed his friend around Curdoz' beautifully built and well-apportioned little ship. Tiliruf admired much and proclaimed that someday he'd have a ship built like this for himself, only five times bigger. Kodi was again reminded that Tiliruf's father probably had enough gold to build his son his own personal navy if he wanted. Genehbro already had the largest merchant marine in the country according to what Kodi understood.

Afterwards, they made their way through the impressive eastern gates in the Outer Wall across the spit of land demarcating the bay and harbor, to an area of bright beach fronted in a wide strip of soft white sand. Seagulls floated and cried upon the ocean breezes, and the crashing waves created a feeling of energy and play. There were hundreds of men and boys here; perhaps the greater number were laborers, servants, along with Brigadiers enjoying one of their two free days of the eight-day calendar week, but there were still a number of the rich and merchant-class men from Central City and Guardian Hills. These latter parked their carriages nearby under large pavilions to shade the horses.

Apparently, these beach days were a long tradition in Tirilorin, dating back centuries, and yet because it was Tirilorin, it had developed itself into an important economic activity. There were food vendors everywhere, and drink vendors, and acrobats doing tricks for money for the children.

A great many fathers of all classes with their young sons were splashing in the surf and building forts and castles together with wet sand. Kodi was greatly intrigued by this, and perhaps for the first time in his young manhood he pondered what fun it could be to be a father. He and his own father spent much time together when Hess was at home, and despite their conflicts of the last couple years, they did enjoy being together. However, their activity consisted always of tasks; even the fishing was meant to supply food for the table. To actually play at something like what these fathers and their little boys were doing, which had no intrinsic value other than fun, was somewhat of a revelation to Kodi, and he liked what he saw. He paused momentarily, imagining what it would be like to be a father himself with his own little son shaping the sand and holding hands as they splashed in the waves.

There were old men too sitting on stools playing Kings and Castles at little tables with playing pieces carved from heavy stone or cast in lead so as not to blow over in the wind. Though most of the men on the beaches wore simple loose linen breeches, and the elders wore robes with hoods up to protect their eyes and wrinkling skin from the heat, all those out in the water were bare-skinned. It seemed appropriate to Kodi that here in this one place, no matter what social class or section of the city they hailed from, in their nakedness every man was equal to every other. It reminded him of times with his friends at the swimming holes on the Wolf River back home. He missed this sort of revelry and had begun to wonder lately if he'd ever experience it again on this journey, with the reserved, intellectual Sage, the mothering Matrimonial, and his sister whose company he genuninely liked but who nevertheless was not one with whom he engaged in athletic play. Kodi was grateful that Tiliruf was bringing him out to enjoy the male camaraderie he'd been missing for so long.

"Look at you, eh? Damn muscles!" Tiliruf exclaimed over the noisy seaside sounds, as the two stripped down. "You're like the classic Anterianhi bronze, Kodi! Paint you all shiny and set you on a plinth in the garden!"

No one could deny Kodi's rock-hard fitness. Yet the Tirilorine sported his own excellent physique. With his lighter complexion it was evident he exposed himself often to the sun; his face and body were half covered in freckles.

"That'd be right funny but make me sleepy just standing there! You're pretty damn impressive yourself, Ruffy! *Marble* statue for you instead of bronze! Just paint little brown dots on!" Kodi winked.

Tiliruf laughed and they slapped hands. Like boys they raced out to the surf.

Close by, two old men watched.

"Sport-blooded stallions," said the old Central City man to his Guardian Hills chess partner, nodding in the direction of the two young men just as they cut the water. "Or B'ulstread breed war horses."

"They know it, too. Look at 'em. Diving into the wave. The way they emerge and sling the water off their heads. Beautiful to watch. I'd give ten thousand golds if I could go back fifty years. Sixty years now, damn it all," the other chuckled. "To *feel* and look as damn good as they do."

"Me, too, mate. Old man envy. That's Genehbro's son, I think. Tiliruf. Some of the Brigadier set call him *a'Terianh*. Holding on to an old tradition."

"Imperial blood still shows. And the other looks like a young warrior prince out of Nant. The Brigadiers wish for old heroic times they never knew. Maybe we all do, mate."

The Central City man grinned. "Make a wager we see something special out of those two in future."

With a gleam in his old eyes, the Guardian Hills man looked up with his own grin. "Nope. Ain't gonna lose money on that one, old friend. I believe you. Your grandsons out here today?"

The other looked out far in the water. "Lukas and Colinn. My redheaded boys. Probably out there at the sandbar, where Tiliruf and the other young man are headed. That could be Colinn on the plank just now. Hard to tell."

"Yes. The red hair, I was forgetting. Saw them when I got here, some minutes before you. I know you're proud of them. They ain't boys anymore. Right studs, really, what I saw."

"Yes, you're right. They're fine men, I must say. They keep themselves occupied with work and clean fun and steer clear of North Bend, compared to some of their rascally chums. Adhere to good Disciplines, better than I did at their age. Make excellent husbands someday soon, I hope. And they do everything together. Joined the Brigade for fun. No money in it, not that they need it—what's mine is theirs. Don't blame them for joining it. Sometimes wish I had, back then. Great swordsmanship skills, too. Some of the best in the Brigade from what General Stanlish tells me." The Central City man's eyes grew a bit misty. "I worry, considering recent threats from the south and east. Tear me to pieces if something were to happen to them. Courage. Bravery. I know they have that. Just hope they have *luck* on top of it all."

"I agree, mate, it is worrisome. Have cheer in the moment, yes? Do they know you're here?"

The Central City man's eyes cleared. He smiled again and made a solid move on the gameboard. "Well. They may suspect it, mate. They know I like to keep tabs on them. Their father took over the business from me a long time ago and is always busy. I like being near them, and they know it. They'll get out of the water eventually, and when they see me, they'll come up and ruffle my head and give me good ole neck hugs. I think I live for that."

The Guardian Hills man smiled. "That's beautiful, really! When my lovely granddaughters kiss me, I feel I've done some real good in the world, eh? But we *are* old, aren't we, friend? Perhaps we should take on some of our grandchildren's energy and do a little more, you and I. Our lovely wives Dance the Stars now. Let's get together a little more often like we used to. Get out of old routines. Central City and Guardian Hills can be right stuffy, don't you think?"

"Go for an ale later? And some good old hard cheese and bread? Or fish 'n chips?"

"At an actual laborers' *pub?* Like in South Bend? Boy, we haven't done that in ages! Excellent thought!"

The Central City man looked at his old friend with a happy smile. Then he looked down and examined the board. "Er, did you just checkmate me, old man?"

"I think I did, old man. Ha! One up for Guardian Hills!"

"You damned thumping old pecker! Winner's buy! I'll choose the pub. Maybe young Zhock's place. You remember his father? The scowling mean-faced bastard? Died some time ago."

"Reckon Zhock ain't so young anymore, mate. Wonder if he *scowls* all bristly like his old dad! But their ale was the best anywhere, what I remember. Let's play another, mate. Maybe you'll beat me this time, and I won't have to buy both, ha!"

There were several young men of Kodi and Tiliruf's sort some way out in the water who appeared to be taking turns riding on what appeared to be flat, spearhead-shaped planks. They would try to stand up and balance short distances as they floated upon the bigger waves, which Kodi thought a great feat. As the two friends made their way out to this crowd, Kodi exclaimed upon the energetic motion of the waves and the saltiness on his tongue. He had never before swum in the ocean, nor in such warm water. Not counting his dip in the Lake in his Vision, he had never swum anywhere but the cool Wolf River in summertime. When they arrived at the distant sandbar, several of the young men hailed Tiliruf, who was friends with many of them. They took quickly to his charismatic Solantine friend, encouraging the northerner to take his turn on a plank. Kodi discovered that these were made of some lightweight buoyant wood with which, despite growing up in the timber trade, he was unfamiliar. Being around others close to his age always inspired Kodi's competitive nature. It was part of what he'd been missing. After only a few attempts he became adept at the trick, as he did at anything of physical skill he set his mind to. The others cheered and made complimentary remarks on how quickly he learned. Tiliruf enjoyed himself, too, and was even better than Kodi on the plank, but he'd obviously been practicing this for years. In any event, Kodi with his jovial good humor applied with his enjoyable Solantine accent became quite popular with this crowd, and they all had great fun showing off to one another as the afternoon progressed.

Later, Kodi and Tiliruf sat in the sand to dry themselves in the warm wind and the sun. They chatted cheerily with some of the other young men who likewise had had enough of the water. Kodi made good effort in remembering their names. There was Andir, Alin, and Bendrick from Central City, Calens and Spens from Guardian Hills, all whom Tiliruf knew well, and with whom he had played Fifty-twos from time to time. Most of these were sons of wealthy merchants. From Central City also were two soldiers from the Brigades, Lukas and Colinn, brothers three years apart with red hair, whom Tiliruf knew apparently from fencing lessons. They were as freckled as the blond-haired Tiliruf, if not more. Those two went off for a few minutes to chatter with a couple of old men playing Kings and Castles, and Kodi noticed them being affectionate with one of them.

"Our grandfather over there, Kodi!" said Colinn, explaining when they returned. "Had to go speak, of course!"

"Gotta show love to the old man, eh? Cheers him up," said Lukas. "Asked us who *you* are and told him. They recognized Tiliruf. He and his mate guess you two are going to be famous heroes someday, imagine that!"

"Love my old grandfather, too, Lukas! And miss him pretty bad. Tell 'em thanks for me when you next get the chance. Compliments from old men mean a lot! Makes me feel I'm doing something right, know what I mean?"

"Old *sagely* predictions crack me up," said Tiliruf with a laugh. "But it is kind of sweet! Don't know many old men, except old Sage Enric. He sometimes tries to play the grandfather role a bit to me, and I suppose that's not such a bad thing."

There was also a set of three, obviously of the labor class due to their speech, but they were made as much welcome in this little crowd as the rest. They enjoyed informing Kodi about which taverns in the city had the best ale, which included, not surprisingly, Zhock's place.

They latched onto the sociable Kodi like the leader he was and asked him about his background and his travels, and most were amazed when he said he came to the city with the Sage of Solanto, but he spoke nothing of the quest to the Qeteral or any of the rest of his business. He only said they were traveling on to Nant, and that they had stopped in

Tirilorin for a couple weeks so that Curdoz could meet Masters Enric and Genehbro. Tiliruf was astute enough not to elaborate too much on Kodi's tale, knowing that it was perhaps wise that particulars of the quest not be generally known. He did however bring up the presence of Kodi's sister Lyndz, for they all appreciated having a beautiful 'foreign woman' described to them. Kodi chortled at his friend's extravagant details, some of which he was glad Lyndz was not present to hear, but he kept out of it, nor did he, when pressed, make any promises to introduce his twin to any of them.

Kodi watched as the sun veered westward. It continued warm, and the water was sparkling and beautiful, and the wind made his skin feel good. Several hundred yards out, white-sailed ships passed slowly by, either on their way to or from Southport or Northport around the end of the spit. Many flew the Tirilorine Republican flag with its yellow-rayed sun, and there were several too from Nant flying the seagull. Considering all he had experienced the last few days, Kodi thought Tirilorin a magnificent city full of life, wealth, and good peaceful people, content with their way of life, pleasures, and profitable trade. Nevertheless, he knew some of those Nantian ships were warships, fitted with javelin throwers and fireball launchers stopping on their way to the eastern war, and containing well-trained archers and contingents of swordsmen, and Kodi couldn't help but to hope that the eastern conflict would never make its way here.

Nevertheless, much of the talk among the young men was naturally about the war and the recent deliberations of the Assembly. All of them, with the exception of Spens, who was decidedly pudgy and less inclined to physical exertion than the rest, spoke of their willingness to fight if the Assembly vote should end in favor of supporting the eastern kingdoms. The red-headed brother Brigadiers expressed the strongest war sentiment. They all listened closely to Tiliruf as he expressed his views, for he was the one most familiar with the workings and deliberations of the Assembly since his father was on it.

"The war is getting pretty bad, and I hope the Assembly votes to send support, and I'm beginning to think they will. I know my father will." When Kodi asked if he thought Tirilorin itself was threatened, Tiliruf expressed confidence. "The war will never get here as long as the Nantian navy patrols the seas. There's no way for the Khestadone to get large armies to this half of the Northern Continent. They have small navies, but they almost never leave the Khestadone Sea for fear of the Nantians. No need to worry about Tirilorin. The city is safe, anyway."

Kodi hoped so. Lukas and Colinn went on about the city's defenses and its great walls vowing that they were impossible to breach. So, though in essentials these two agreed with Tiliruf, their words implied they'd almost like to see the city under siege simply to prove to the world that the defenses were as superior as they claimed them to be. There was one admission among them, however, and that was the fact that Tirilorin's defenses had never been seriously tested in all its five-century lifespan. Not even during the last war when Lintiri was overrun, did the enemy's armies approach within a hundred miles of the city.

The sun having begun to sink now, they all dressed, and everyone expressed a desire to get together again the next week, particularly if Tiliruf and Kodi had not left the city by then. Kodi said leaving that soon was unlikely, so they all made arrangements to meet at a particular tavern near the gates for a few ales before coming again out to the beach. Tiliruf, with indulgent generosity, offered to buy everyone's food and drink when they got together, and all eagerly accepted. Finally, the two friends walked back together to the gates. Once inside, Tiliruf hired a city carriage to take them to Central City, a ride from this point of about a half hour. They arrived at dinner time, and they took their leave of one another after the carriage deposited Kodi at Sage Enric's home.

"Great day!" exclaimed Kodi. "Thanks for the ale and lunch and the swimming and everything else, Ruffy!"

"And I'll get some of the mates—we'll play Fifty-twos real soon, eh? Some of those from the beach like Calens and Spens."

"That'll be great, but don't expect me to bet much. I have gold and silver, but I don't reckon where I'm going to earn more of it anytime soon!"

"Ah, no, don't worry about that. You don't know Spens. He's pretty strict about it when he plays. He doesn't like losing money, 'cause he really doesn't have much, and his father won't give him any, so we all start with precisely two hundred coppers, and nobody loses more than that. I'll get all your coppers for you; that's nothin'. I play with some older merchants for gold, but they get pretty testy."

"Ah, so it's from them you get your reputation? They don't like it when you win?"

"Exactly, mate! I'll teach you a trick or two. Do you smoke? The pipe weed comes from Solanto."

"A bit." In fact, he quite wished to try it again without the reserve he experienced in Curdoz' presence back in Thorune. "But, er, I lost my pipe," he lied.

"Excellent. I have a dozen of 'em. Tusk ivory from the east, hand carved. And one belongs to you, mate."

That evening when they were alone with Curdoz and Idamé, the twins were talking about their time in the city the last couple days. As the conversation progressed, Lyndz at one point suggested that Tiliruf acted envious of their lives in Tulesk.

Kodi was shocked by this observation and said so. "What? Tiliruf lives here in this great city almost like a prince and has everything he wants." He would only speak in vague terms, for he was determined never in a Meicalian Age to discuss Tiliruf's more carnal exploits in front of the women.

Curdoz was listening, and he appeared to agree with Lyndz. "Though Tiliruf is surrounded by luxury, books, servants, tutoring and fencing lessons, and people that revere his family, he is in some ways less mature than you despite the similar age. He finds the two of you fascinating. Perhaps he longs to live a young man's life more typical of Kodi's than the one he currently leads. Everything you talk about he finds interesting."

"But he's so smart and outgoing. You didn't see him today. I'd think he'd be bored hunting and fishing and doing all the stuff I do."

"Hmm, but are you bored of those things?"

"No, no I love it; you know I do. Of course, I don't like being stuck doing one thing all the time."

"Well, you might be surprised that he might enjoy them as well. Most young men do. Life for a young man is not all about drinking, Fifty-Twos, and frolicking on the beach." This made Kodi wonder if Curdoz could read minds. "Those are meant to be pastimes. But I know what you mean. Tiliruf is gregarious and is around important people all the time, and you think of your life as quiet in comparison. What I observed the other night, and from what I've learned about him through Enric, is that he is ready to leave Tirilorin. In fact, he is so ready to begin a new life away from here that it concerns me somewhat."

"He's a grown man!" Kodi exclaimed.

Idamé interjected at this point. "Of course, Kodi. We're not saying he shouldn't go. Quite the opposite. He needs to move on. Curdoz and I see simply that he needs to mature in certain areas. He's been spoiled. But it will happen, I suppose, when we leave here. We have all grown as the weeks have gone by, haven't we? You twins have changed much since we left Tulesk all those weeks ago, and you are hardly the provincials that you were, for now you observe the world with greater confidence. You've come to realize you have a role to play in it. Tiliruf may not see that in himself, even though he may act cocksure."

Kodi laughed, "You have accused me sometimes of being the cocky one!"

"Yes, but that's almost universal among young men," she laughed. "But what I think Curdoz is saying is this. Tiliruf is, in a sense, burdened by his ancestry. You tell us he seems uninterested, but it's more likely that he feels he doesn't compare to them."

"And the republicanism of Tirilorin," added Curdoz, "seems to dismiss the former greatness anyway—an attitude that has worn off on him. Maybe he looks at Kodi for instance as someone his own age who has already experienced and achieved much, and is happy, and self-confident."

"So you're saying Tiliruf is not happy, or self-confident?" Kodi strongly doubted this and was confused by Curdoz' observation.

Curdoz sighed and said, "Maybe it's wrong of me to say he doesn't have a sense of confidence. But he's not entirely happy. I can read that in him, anyway. Even you should see it in his cynicism. He's missing something in his life. With our help, he might find what he needs. I hope so."

"When he appeared in my Vision, I was thinking that I was the one who was in need of a good friend. Somebody like me who was not from Felto, if you understand me. Of course, at the time I was feeling trapped there, and wanted to leave." Kodi looked at Lyndz as he said this, hoping she would not misunderstand. "When he tossed that apple away, I admired his free spirit and a sort of freedom of expression I didn't feel I had. But you're saying you think he's the one who's going to be learning from me?"

"You will learn from each other. And Lyndz will teach him a thing or two. I suspect while we travel together, his focus will be almost entirely upon you two. If anybody is going to teach him anything it will be the two of you. He will likely avoid me."

"Why?"

"Because of what I represent."

Kodi had to admit, "Oh, you mean Meicalian Principles and Disciplines."

"Yes, 'The Guardian and all that malarkey' as he puts it. And though, as with most in the city, his adherence to the Principles is satisfactory—though they would likely deny their origin—his adherence to any of the Disciplines is...limited. I've attempted several times to explain this to you. The Principles, which are high and broad and universal—as they attach us to the Life and the Energies of the Creator's Creation—make us generally good people. The Disciplines, which are specific and apply to our gender and social roles and our Callings and vocations, make us *better* people. I think it safe to presume Tiliruf has a good heart, but he is *self-motivated*, and I don't mean that in the positive way I might apply it to you. Perhaps the better term in his case is *self-involved*."

"Practically the whole city is like that," put in Lyndz. "He's not alone there."

"Yes, just so, Lyndz." the Sage then continued in one of his philosophical modes. "Our young friend comes by his attitude naturally. It comes ultimately from the collapse of imperial rule which had been established under Meical's dictates, and the subsequent institution of republicanism. These people care only for the present. Commerce, wealth. They have their great Library, but you will find that the history section is underused.

"But 'the present' without even symbolic connection to the good parts of history is not all it's cracked up to be. I am not opposed to 'elections' and 'assemblies', not by any means, and I have learned a good deal in the short time I have been here. The Republic is not a bad thing. And maybe, just maybe, it is a better thing than the tail end of imperial rule under a do-nothing Emperor Zarelio. Nevertheless, the empire had great symbolism and importance as it connected all the lands—the best word I can think of is 'spiritually'—in the ancient elimination of Ralsheen slavery and evil dictatorship, in addition to a strong connection to the Meicalian Orders and the Disciplines."

Kodi listened and thought it spoke to what he was thinking after the end of the Assembly the other day.

Curdoz continued. "So, I think it is a shame that the empire has been replaced and wish rather it had been 'reformed.' The 'dismissive' attitude has transferred naturally to Tiliruf. And in his case, it's more concentrated due to his resistance to his ancestral past. I worry Tiliruf's attitude could hinder his education on the journey. And I think he'll have a harder time of it than the rest of us." Curdoz looked at the others and smiled. "It took me a long time to make that point. I hope you understand me."

They all laughed.

"But Tiliruf does know his history, sir," Kodi put in.

Lyndz nodded. "He really does, Curdoz. Kodi's right. Tiliruf knows all about his ancestry and details of Anterianhi history. He just doesn't like thinking of himself as their descendant."

Curdoz looked up. "Hmm. Well, you know that really is a good sign, Lyndz. It is good that he knows imperial history. That's splendid, in fact. There's good information there, and maybe down the road he'll start pulling some of it out and using it to his advantage. As I say that, though, it makes me wonder if all of that is ingrained into him simply because his father feels obligated as the heir to the emperors' legacy to teach that to him at the very least, if nothing else. But even his father doesn't believe in the Guardian."

"But it was the Guardian that gave Terianh the empire in the first place!" Lyndz exclaimed.

"That is true, but they are skeptical nowadays nonetheless."

"I know it, but I still don't understand it."

"I'll admit I haven't delved too deeply in Tirilorin's history, the history, that is, since the Abdication of Genehbro's grandfather. Try Sage Enric. He might have some ideas on it, for he's been here for half that time anyway. He and I have not really discussed it. We're focused on other things."

Kodi realized he had a question he hadn't really asked Tiliruf. "Curdoz, why do you think he's chosen to go with us? Tiliruf that is. It's because of Meicalian Visions that we started this journey in the first place. It's why we're pursuing it. If he doesn't believe in it then why do you think he's going?"

"In part I have answered that already. He is ready to leave this place because he has accomplished all he is going to accomplish here. His father is healthy and active, and it will probably be decades before Tiliruf would inherit his father's position on the Assembly. And that's only if they allow the seat to remain an inherited position. Wouldn't surprise me in the least that by then they eliminated inherited positions, because it is not particularly 'democratic.' But even if the seat is held for him, what is he to do between now and then? He could perhaps go to Nant and apprentice himself to the royal family and learn to be a soldier and knight and fight in the eastern wars alongside their armies—to work up a reputation as a leader. I'm sure he has considered it, and there are a large number of Tirilorine mercenaries already in the fight. I think he has been waiting for some different opportunity, and now, with our arrival, it has. He is intrigued by the two of you. He's on a journey, like I said, looking to find himself and his place in the world, and he's hoping we will help him discover it. The rest of this 'malarkey' is incidental to him."

"Is that selfish?" asked Lyndz.

"Selfishness resides in everyone to a degree, rather on a continuum. Some are more selfish than others. But over time a great many of us learn better. There is much to be said for the fact that Tiliruf is willing to go. And he is *meant* to go with us, in the sense that Meical wants him to go, even though he doesn't know it yet. Unless Kodi has attempted to explain it to him, that is."

"No," Kodi admitted. "I haven't brought it up."

"Wise. At least until we are on the road, and he learns to know us all better. Anyway, the Guardian means for him to go with us. If we told Tiliruf this directly it might cause him to reconsider. I think you know what you're about, Kodi, not to expend much effort with him on Meicalian beliefs and Visions. He's already made the choice to go. He has a lot of growing to do, and the immaturity unnerves me. But at least he's going. Trust is critical, though. And loyalty. It pleases me that you and he are becoming good friends, Kodi. Have no qualms. Enjoy your exploration of the city, and your ale-drinking conversations, and your play at the beach! It makes a difference. Play Fifty-twos with his friends and don't worry about us. I'm glad for you to have a bit of enjoyment while you can. You need it when you're young. Your task is to become Tiliruf's confidante. The rest of us can worry about plans for the quest. But I am making a bit of a change in your fun, and it begins tomorrow morning, though you will still be spending all your time with Tiliruf."

"Training! Yah!" Kodi was thrilled.

"I've arranged it with Tiliruf's father. I met Jaden the Swordmaster today. Do you know he trained the princes of Nant? And I told him that you are already a superior marksman and that it's mostly sword play that you need. He's looking forward to meeting you. Third hour tomorrow morning at the Palace. Take your grandfather's bow. Tiliruf will be there, too."

"That's great!" Kodi replied.

"Don't expect to be a great swordsman right away. For some it takes years. But, knowing you, I don't think that will be your case at all."

"He'll learn fast, Curdoz," said Lyndz with perfect confidence, beaming at her brother. "It's just the way he is!"

Kodi came up behind his sister and wrapped his arms around her. "Thanks, Lyndz!"

"You taste like salt, and you still have sand all over you. Take a bath, Kodi!"

They took some time to discuss among themselves what Lyndz had learned in the Library about the Qeteral and their quest, and also the latest news regarding the war and the Twin Realms of Khestadon and how it might affect them. Kodi asked a final question.

"How much longer do we stay here, Curdoz?"

"We will stay two weeks, I think. From here we will take my ship to Nant. I have discussed it at length with Sage Enric, and he believes too that our Visions imply that Nant is to supply us a fleet for our venture to Ulakel, and perhaps a captain to lead us, someone who knows those waters, for the gulf that leads to Ulakel is filled with many rocky islands and can be treacherous. We need to find expertise for our expedition, but no one from Tirilorin has explored in that gulf for a century. The Nantians, however, still ply those waters. Genehbro mentioned to me that the Nantians still make attempts from time to time to seek out the Hidden People, though without success. The Qeteral have woven certain spells to conceal their land from Humans. As you know, they have inate forms of magic, unlike Humans and the Etoppsi."

"How are we supposed to get in, then?" asked Lyndz.

"I don't know the answer to that, yet."

"We can but go," offered Idamé. "If Meical wants us to find them, which He clearly does, they will be found."

Kodi made an observation. "I've thought about the Qeteral woman in my Vision. I believe she will be on the lookout for me. If she is someone important or of influence, then she may have some of her people watching for me. We'll find them."

Curdoz agreed. "That seems likely."

"But they do not like Humans much, from what I've been reading," offered Lyndz. "If there are a whole lot of us, I worry that they'll consider us a threat."

"That is what Genehbro says, as well. Only a small group of us will go. The remainder will have to remain with the ships or on shore close to whatever landing place we choose. But let's not think on it anymore and go down to the main parlor together and share some wine with Sage Enric before bed, shall we?"

Considering all, Kodi much preferred his twin's suggestion than wine. Thus, in another hour, and after the refreshing bath, Kodi was in his bed. Upon closing his eyes, he began to feel as if his body were shifting around, back in the ocean, floating on the waves again.

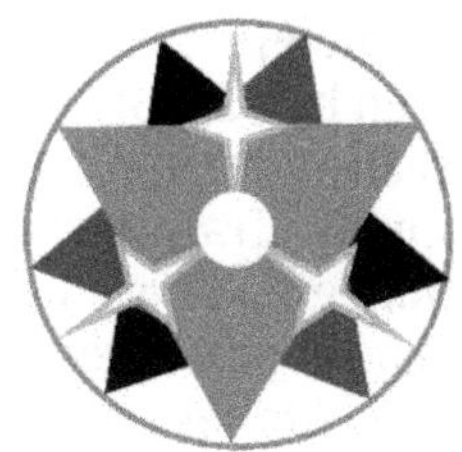

Chapter 7—Weaponry and Words

On their fifth day in Tirilorin, Lyndz returned once again to the Library accompanied this time by Idamé, for she too wanted to learn what she could about the Qeteral. The Sage walked with Kodi to the Imperial Palace, Curdoz to discuss ideas on the quest with Genehbro, and Kodi to spend another day with Tiliruf.

Today he was to start his training, and swordsmanship was the skill he desired most in order to achieve his goal of becoming a warrior and knight. When he and Tiliruf together approached Jaden in the vast back lawn of the palace, the famed swordmaster inspected Kodi like one might a horse at a fair.

"Excellent, excellent," the man said, walking around the Solantine. "Strong physique. You'd beat most any man in a wrestling contest. But wrestling is less efficient in a confrontation with an enemy perhaps than making good use of weaponry. I hear you are already quite accomplished with the bow? Let's see what you're capable of. Master Tiliruf here could use a bit of competition! He's superior at his swordplay, but he's been resistant to practicing his marksmanship. A bit impatient, you see."

Tiliruf winked at Kodi, indicating it was perfectly true.

"I don't see that mastering the bow is especially useful in my line of work. My favorite arrow always seems to find its mark," the Tirilorine said, looking downward at his mid-section with a cocky smile that made Kodi smirk and the swordmaster crack a smile. Apparently, Jaden was not unaware of Tiliruf's shenanigans. Probably Tiliruf expounded enough similar witticisms at other times. Kodi wondered if it was only Tiliruf's father that turned a blind eye to his son's escapades or to whom Tiliruf showed enough regard not to embarrass him with such blunt, self-slanderous cracks.

"There are arrows and then there are arrows. It's a matter of adopting a Discipline, Master Tiliruf," Jaden said as Tiliruf looked at Kodi with a wink and a nod. "You need to learn to choose your 'targets' with more care, but that is not for me to teach you. Come along, men. I'd like to see how well our Solantine neighbor shoots." He then led them to the far end of the broad lawn which had a glorious view of the city and the sea. There were servants here already who had set up targets at Jaden's orders, simple circular burlap-wrapped straw targets painted with concentric circles around a bright red bullseye. There were bows made of yew. Kodi, however, unwrapped his own and presented it to Jaden.

"Upon the Guardian! Ambernut heartwood, is it? I've never seen..."

"My grandfather made it for me long ago and gave it to me before I left home with Lord Curdoz."

"I want one," said Tiliruf, which for the son of probably the wealthiest man in the world, was perhaps the highest possible compliment.

"Sorry, friend. Can't help you there," Kodi said. "My grandfather still makes pretty things, but he'll never make another one of these."

Jaden handled it as if it were a thin glass goblet. "The most beautiful I have ever seen in my life! The detailed carving, unbelievable. Your grandfather is inspired. It is kingly, I tell you! Not even the princes of Nant have anything like it! And the quiver there?"

"King Carlomen presented it to me, sir."

Jaden was additionally impressed. "Remarkable gift, Master Kodi."

He handed the bow back and led them forward towards the targets.

Kodi had, of course, only used bows for contests and for hunting. He had never really thought of them much as weapons. All the Kingsmen in Solanto whom he had ever come across were always outfitted with swords. Felto being off the common route, he had never seen any soldier bowmen in Solanto, though logically he knew there must be some.

A servant was on hand to hand him arrows. Kodi wasn't used to such orderliness or being waited on like this, but he repressed his thoughts as he set his quiver aside, took an arrow from the attendant and fitted it on the string. He aimed carefully at the target a cool hundred feet distant. This was easy, he thought. He released.

It was a perfect bullseye. "Ah, very, very good, Kodi of Solanto! What I've heard about you from Lord Curdoz is true, then, and that bow and that quiver were well-given, I'd say! Let's see if Master Tiliruf has been practicing."

Tiliruf winked at Kodi, which the latter knew was an implication he had not. Tiliruf did, however, string one of the yew bows with sufficient grace and took another arrow from the servant. He aimed. Kodi could tell by the aim that his new friend would not find the target but said nothing.

Sure enough, when Tiliruf released, the arrow shot to the left of the burlap target, missing it altogether. Tiliruf laughed it off. "So you see, Kodi my mate, I'm not as perfect as everyone says I am."

"And precisely who says that? Library girls?"

Tiliruf burst with mirth. "They do like it when I show up, you know. Compared to most customers I make an effort to return what they give, eh?"

Kodi chuckled and nonchalantly shot another bullseye immediately afterward.

Master Jaden had them work at this for some time. He had them move back. He had them attach quivers to their backs and attempt rapid fire sequences. Tiliruf occasionally hit burlap but missed as often as not. Jaden marked that he was at least trying harder now that he had a friend to compete with, and he did make some minor improvement in form. In fact, Tiliruf appeared to be observing Kodi quite closely.

Kodi was expert. He'd been at this for years already, and hunting was an important part of his young life. He was also known to practice ritually. No matter what differences Jaden set up for the practice, all of Kodi's shots were on the bullseye or within an inch of it. Only when a quick stiff breeze off the distant sea hit them did his arrows stray even this far. However, under Jaden's direction he began to learn to anticipate and compensate. Kodi appreciated the compliments of both Jaden and Tiliruf, and it only encouraged him to want to perfect the skill.

"You are a superior marksman, Kodi of Solanto. All you need is a little more practice in the wind and performance speed so to increase your shooting rate. How do you manage while riding?"

Kodi replied truthfully. "Er, pretty good, sir."

"I believe it. There is little else for you to learn from me, for the sword is my highest specialty. You are as good as any man in our city's archery brigades. Better, actually. Tis only in actual battle where you are likely to realize new skills. The stresses of war will sharpen a man."

Kodi nodded in appreciation. To hear from such a master that he was superior, at least in the use of one weapon, was a serious boost to his sense of the warrior.

"All right, mate. Let's see how you are with a blade, eh?" said Tiliruf, who by now was eager to show off his own skills to his friend who had beaten him thus far.

"Enough of this," agreed Jaden, who then ordered the servants to remove all traces of the archery practice. The young men followed the swordmaster to another area of the field where there was body armor along with shields and practice swords of various sizes and makes all set orderly upon tables. There were two other men here, older students of Jaden's, already donning gear, and awaiting the order to spar with Tiliruf.

Tiliruf hailed them both by name. "Oy there, Hadon and Manwul! I hope you've practiced, or are you ready to be bested again?"

"You say so, Master Tiliruf!" said Manwul, a huge, ruggedly handsome man with the ethnic Nantian dark complexion and eyes. His hair was dark, with a well-trimmed beard.

"But indeed, we have!" added Hadon. He was large, but closer to Kodi's and Tiliruf's size, of northern complexion and blue eyes, but with black hair and trim beard, also very handsome.

They exhibited a demeanor and language style that would have caused them to stand out among common soldiers in Solanto, Kodi observed. He had noticed that most of the city's peoples, even the common folk, were more educated than those in Solanto, yet these were likely of the merchant class, almost an air of nobility had they been from one of the kingdoms. They were older than Tiliruf and Kodi by seven or eight years, yet they only began training with Jaden two years previously. He had plucked them from the Brigades after having noticed how talented they were and wanted to train them himself. Kodi learned too that they'd been inseparable friends since boyhood.

Without comment, Jaden allowed Tiliruf to prepare himself. He chose a simple mail coverlet and picked up a straight practice sword. He did not however choose a shield. He nodded to Manwul, who tossed away his own.

They began. Kodi thought their form beautiful. He admitted to Jaden when asked that he had had rare opportunity to witness swordsmen in training and knew little beyond what he had read of swords and weaponry in his grandfather's books. His father, Hess, like Kodi, was a skilled archer and carried a longknife on his journeys, but he did not possess a greatsword. Kodi watched carefully. Jaden pointed out several things to him: the need for balance, the grip on the sword, the movement of the feet. Swordplay without shields he said was different than with. It was faster and more fluid, though more dangerous, although it was important to learn both with and without.

"A man cannot always keep a shield upon him. You must gauge the situation. Tiliruf and Manwul are focusing mostly on technique just now."

The two continued for some time, and neither appeared to tire. Kodi was awed by Tiliruf's style and control, and Jaden called out compliments when the young man did everything right. Never did Tiliruf have to be corrected. After ten full minutes of this, Jaden directed Hadon to join in. Kodi was shocked by this at first, for he had never given much thought before to the possibility in a battle that a man might have to defend himself against more than one opponent at a time. In his mind's eye he had seen himself go up against one enemy, defeat him, then another, defeat him, and so on until he was the last one surrounded by a field of slain enemies. Never one to be concerned about self-pride, he laughed at himself and shared his ignorance with Jaden while they watched Tiliruf with inspiring skill hold his own against the two swordsmen.

"Many young men join the mercenaries with the same idea at first, Master Kodi. If they survive, they clearly learn otherwise. But you should only expect it in competitions rather than war. The Alkhan's armies have no such compunction to allow for any sense of fairness. It's all about killing. From time to time there may be a captain or champion among them who deigns to test himself against one of our own. Prince Nikal is one of those who finds himself challenged often. Yet the Warlock-king has wild bears and wolves that serve him as well, and they are vicious. I'm sorry we don't have any such for us to train with here; they might prove useful," he ended with a chuckle.

"Tiliruf is really good isn't he, Master Jaden?"

"The best I've ever had. He does at least take this seriously. I hear he is going with you and his lordship the Sage of Solanto on some sort of mission? I believe this will be a good thing. He needs such a task. And as you can see for yourself, he might prove useful should you enter dangerous places south or east."

Tiliruf continued to spar with the expert swordsmen. Though it was hard work against two, Tiliruf was the epitome of confidence and barely broke a sweat. Occasionally, he would spin around and toss his sword to the other hand. This too struck Kodi. "Is that, uh, necessary to learn?" he pointed. Kodi knew he was so dominantly right-handed he doubted he could ever learn such control with his left.

"No, but it can be useful if you wish to be the best of the best. Not all men have similar control with both hands as does Tiliruf. He is quite a natural at it, really, an inherited trait in the men of the House of Terianh. I will admit that I can teach Master Tiliruf very little more. He knows every technique I know. I have encouraged him to go to Nant. The best swordsmen in the world are there and he could train with their princes. I myself trained Prince Lekktor and Prince Nikal several years ago. They were quite young at the time. Nikal is superior with weaponry. The best. Master Tiliruf is a bit foolhardy. He needs more of the self-discipline that comes with army life. The Nantians could teach him that. Young Kodi, your swordsmen in your own country are accomplished? Although your wars with the Ice Tribes are long over. I'm surprised you haven't trained at home. You are the son of a nobleman, I understand."

"I was expecting to go soon, Master Jaden, to my cousin the Duke of Tulesk to train, and I was really looking forward to it. I have been needed at home, you see, for my father is often gone for long periods. Then Lord Curdoz came to fetch us. I regret I am so far behind, sir."

Jaden looked at him. "You will catch up. I see it in you! Have no fear that you are behind where you wish to be. Now, it is not my business, and you don't have to share it, but I'm curious about your party and Lord Curdoz the Sage."

"Our quest has come about because of Meicalian Visions that we experienced recently." Kodi wondered if Jaden would express skepticism like most of the others he had met in Tirilorin.

"Ah, the Lord Meical. I believe you," the swordmaster said to Kodi's surprise. "There are few in our city nowadays who believe in the oldest Anterianhi tales, let alone in the idea that Meical the Guardian still works in the World. I am one of the few and I revere Sage Enric. He is a wise one, and I always support what he says. Of course, I am not a City Master, so I hold little influence. But among the Brigades I try to squelch those who laugh at the few who profess their adherence to the Principles and a Discipline."

"Tiliruf does not believe."

Jaden snickered. "There is very little he does believe in. I am pleased, like I said, that he is going with you on this quest of yours. He must see much sincerity in you and your group to follow you. It says much for the Lord Curdoz and for you, Kodi, for Tiliruf has high regard for few people. He is capable of great things, if you ask my opinion. When he sets his mind to something, like his swordplay, he becomes expert at it. Perhaps your quest will open his mind somewhat."

"Lord Curdoz talks openly about the Guardian, but I haven't mentioned the Guardian to Tiliruf much. Sometimes I wonder if I should be more straightforward with him."

"Umm, there is some wisdom in your hesitation. Nevertheless, in time you might."

As they watched, Tiliruf suddenly tripped up Manwul who fell and signaled he was beaten, but then Hadon struck Tiliruf hard across his mail shirt from behind before the younger man could turn around fully. However, he did not fall, and if anything, the strike inspired him into a heat of passionate play in which both men engaged for another two long minutes. Finally, however, Hadon slowed a bit, and Tiliruf used it to his advantage. Tossing his sword to his left hand one last time he swooped in. Hadon unfortunately swung backward to correct an imbalance in his feet and Tiliruf plunged full on, knocking him down and stopping an inch from the man's chest. If it had been a real fight, Tiliruf would surely have skewered him.

They all applauded the match. "Fantastic, Tiliruf," said Hadon when he got his breath again. "You are beyond me."

"And me, as well, I must admit," confirmed Manwul.

It was Kodi's turn. Jaden helped him choose a mail coverlet like the one Tiliruf wore. Jaden insisted though that he use a shield, and pointed to one that was not especially weighty, broad at top and pointed at the bottom. Jaden himself, a hale man in late mid-life took upon himself the same gear. Kodi found a practice blade with a leather grip that fit his large hand perfectly.

Jaden said, “If you’re a novice, then we begin carefully. For this round, focus more upon your shield use.”

Tiliruf came up and showed his friend how to grip the sword properly and how high up to hold the shield at first. “It’s a good deal about confidence and energy, mate. It’s important that you don’t give up, no matter what Master Jaden does to you, eh?”

Kodi understood. To be successful in almost anything in life involved those two key ingredients, and like most young men he had them. Compared to most, he had them in greater quantities.

Jaden allowed Kodi to play against him without word for a few minutes. The weight of the mail and shield were not to be an issue for the muscular Kodi. Several times Jaden smacked Kodi’s shield hard to test his grip there. Kodi nearly dropped it the first time, for the blow was greater than he anticipated.

“Keep it up. It’s not just your hand, Kodi of Solanto. ‘Tis your whole arm that has to get into the movement with the shield. It becomes an extension of your arm and shoulder, which is why it has those straps.” Kodi thought he understood, held onto it higher and attempted broader blocking movements. He too struck out at Jaden many times, but every time the older man blocked quite easily. His speed was astonishing to Kodi.

“Just keep at it, mate,” called Tiliruf. “Try different angles.”

Striking hard and downwards had some minor effect, because Kodi had strong shoulder and back muscles, but only occasionally was he able to get in a blow upon Jaden’s shield. “That was good, Master Kodi, but you have to recover from each strike more rapidly.”

“Dance more on your feet, mate.”

Kodi stood back and indicated to Tiliruf to demonstrate. Tiliruf grabbed up his sword again and a shield this time and stood up to the swordmaster. Kodi watched him more closely as he moved this way and that with feet that did almost dance. “The foot movement is tiring at first, mate; it takes some getting used to, but it can help with the speed, and build on your energy,” said Tiliruf. He was good against Jaden though the older man appeared to hold his own. It was clear to Kodi that Jaden was still a master despite his age. Comparing his action with Tiliruf, he was virtually subdued in his efforts with Kodi.

Jaden made Tiliruf back out and called Kodi back. “Did you learn anything from that?”

“Maybe,” he said. Kodi came back with even more determination than before. For a couple minutes he did show more energy and was able to withdraw and strike again more rapidly. It was tiring, though, for unlike archery with its steely focus and concentration, this required rapid control of every muscle. He was sweating freely now but was determined to keep on as long as he could. “Am I allowed to try anything I want?”

“Go ahead, Kodi of Solanto.”

With that, Kodi attempted what looked like a wrestling move by swinging high, then plunging down low, turning to gain momentum, and bowling inward, shield and all, against Jaden. He successfully knocked him backward, but even as he stumbled, the older man swept upward, striking Kodi on the side of his head. If it had been a real sword instead of a practice weapon, he would have done damage. Kodi staggered and fell, but he wasn't too badly hurt. He had sustained worse blows in his life.

"Sorry about that Master Kodi, I didn't mean to hurt you! What you did was remarkable, because I wasn't expecting you to offer such an aggressive move, and I reacted instinctively. However, I can almost guarantee you will never succeed against me again with that move." He allowed Kodi a chance to sit back on the ground and rest, signalling a nearby servant to bring them all cool water.

The smarting on the side of his head having subsided quickly, Kodi after a few minutes was ready again, and Jaden obliged. They went on for some time, with both Jaden and Tiliruf calling out suggestions, and occasionally Kodi was able to get a decent strike on his opponent. Jaden, however, never fell again. He was superior to Kodi in all regards.

"But you have learned, Kodi of Solanto," assured the swordmaster when he called a halt, finally. "I congratulate you. You have everything in you that you need: energy, and endurance especially. Speed will come with practice. It was a successful beginning, and there is no one around who has ever knocked me down like that even if it was just once. Except Tiliruf perhaps. Once or twice."

"Master Jaden!" barked Tiliruf. "If I've knocked you down once, I've knocked you down fifty times."

"Ha! I don't think so, Master Tiliruf, but you surely need to go to Nant and train, as I have said before. All right, young Masters. As long as you are still here, Kodi, most mornings we will meet in this place. We can teach our Solantine friend much I think, before he departs, and Master Tiliruf needs to practice his archery with greater, what did you call it? Energy and confidence? Yes, I think so." He then arranged with the servants to set up the archery field again at nine the next morning. "Master Kodi, if you were here for a couple of months, we would try out many things. Spear casting, javelin throwing, and even go out to Genehbro's estate where he keeps some of the warhorses and work with them. But man-to-man swordplay, and archery, are perhaps the most useful for you since we only have two weeks; that is what we will emphasize."

Kodi remembered something that High Master Naloro had said. "I have gold. I hope it is enough to..."

"Never you mind about that, Master Kodi. 'Tis arranged. You can thank Master Genehbro, of course, but considering all, I would quite likely have worked with you anyway without compensation. You are a natural. You remind me of Prince Nikal of Nant. I'm eager to see you progress!"

Tiliruf promised to practice his archery in the evenings, and to work afterwards with Kodi on swordplay. Tiliruf did show more enthusiasm than he might have. Kodi, of course, needed no persuasion and readily agreed so long as Curdoz did not need him for anything else, and so far, he hadn't.

He had learned an important lesson that day. Learning to fight well with a sword was not something you could learn in one morning. Every time he thought back on their morning's exercise, he pictured in his mind the fluidity of Tiliruf and his speed and kept telling himself how Jaden had held back when he fought Kodi. And despite Jaden's words of confidence, he wondered if he would ever catch up to their expertise. He knew he wouldn't in the fortnight they had left in the city, but he was determined to do his best.

"I can keep training you, mate, after we leave here, eh? I'll have Father allow us into the old palace armories. You can pick out any sword that works best for you. Curdoz said he wanted you and me to carry some weapons, which makes me think there is the possibility of fighting at some point."

"And I can help you with your archery."

"It's a deal, mate."

"Sounds like a quest within a quest!"

Famished, the two friends strode arm over shoulder together back to the palace kitchens for a mid-day meal.

They didn't know that a pair of eyes was looking down on them.

"That young man who came with you, Lord Curdoz," said Tiliruf's father Genehbro, looking out the tower window. "Kodi of Tulesk. I like him. And his twin. Gorgeous girl. Regal. Tell me more about them. Tiliruf seems to have found a good friend in Kodi, and I can't tell you enough how that pleases me. He has been at his wits end for months, unable to make any important decisions for himself and his future. He no longer listens to my guidance, nor to anyone's, for that matter. Perhaps this Kodi will be of value to him. He seems a disciplined sort unlike some of Tiliruf's other friends. And you. I am glad Tiliruf will be going with you on this mission. There is nothing more for him here in Tirilorin."

Curdoz had been on a personal quest not dissimilar to Kodi's, albeit pursued in a manner much different, to learn what he could about the young man who was to join them on their quest to the Qeteral. He gleaned much information from Enric, from High Master Naloro, from the twins' observations, and from his own initial encounters with Tiliruf. Via his wisdom as a Sage, he was able to read much. Hearing Genehbro speak, Curdoz remembered there were familial patterns too that determined the younger man's character. He drew in his eyebrows, but suddenly recalled Genehbro's request.

"I have come to know Kodi quite well, and I can assure you he is the finest young man I have known. Solid, sturdy, determined. And genuine. And his twin sister is equally remarkable. Inspiring. Queenly, even as you say. Kodi has the most amazing knack of adapting to virtually any situation with extraordinary ease, and his twin can discern subtleties at a level far beyond what her youth would suggest. They are an extraordinary pair. The Guardian has Himself proven their worth through my Vision and through Kodi's own Vision as I have said before. Kodi aspires to greatness, but he is not self-involved, not too much so anyway. Occasionally a boyish silliness will exert itself, certainly, and a bit of impatience at tedium, as he is still young, and he takes risks that sometimes put him in danger. Although, his motives even then are for the benefit of others."

"Frankly Tiliruf could do with a bit of that sort of risk-taking."

Curdoz puckered his eyebrows again. "What were you going to say about Tiliruf and the Qeteral, before you spotted your son out the window?"

"Ah, yes, of course! I am thinking, Lord Curdoz, you may find that Tiliruf could be a key in your attempt to communicate with them. The Qeteral have always been distant with our kind. According to what is told in my House, the only reason they ever had contact with Humans in the past was because of their loyalty to the House of Terianh. I don't know that I believe in such tales, but the legends say that your Guardian ordered the Qeteral to craft Terianh's Staff—from a holly tree, for it was of white hue. They held Terianh himself in reverence and even gave him the title, 'Brother of Myghal.' Myghal, as you probably know is their name for Meical. They believed Terianh had a unique connection to your Guardian—that he could actually speak to the Guardian from afar, apart from what you call Visions. The Qeteral have odd notions. After my grandfather's abdication they refused any longer to have dealings with Humans. It is possible, therefore, that Tiliruf could be the one who is able to 'open the door', so to speak."

Curdoz predicted Genehbro's skepticism regarding Meicalian history—Enric had warned him—but he chose not to address it. The Staff he could bring up again another time. "Perhaps you could outfit him with symbols from your House, so they will recognize him?"

"Yes, I was thinking that. I'll hand over my sword, too. It is the Eagle Sword of Terianh, passed down through the ages."

Curdoz raised his eyebrows. The Master was still himself quite capable, and to give his son such an heirloom appeared premature. Curdoz was irked by the casualness of it.

Genehbro noticed the Sage's wonder but misunderstood it. "Ah, I know what you are thinking, Lord Curdoz. But you see, I have plenty of other swords at my disposal. The Eagle Sword has little meaning outside my House. It is an old relic to the people of Tirilorin. I wear it on High

Days, but I'm afraid there is not one person who would notice the difference should I wear another. Besides, you would be surprised. Tiliruf is already a much better swordsman than I. I was a Swordmaster, but when my father died, and I took his place on the Assembly, and with our business enterprises, I became too busy to keep up my skills. You should watch him. I suspect he is as good as many of my ancestors. As a swordsman, and as a protector, I have hope he will prove useful to you."

"Yes, I hope so. Which is why I requested he and Kodi carry weapons. It is to be hoped that we will not need them on the journey to Ulakel. It is afterwards I am concerned with."

"So, you believe the quest will ultimately take you to the war in the east?"

"Possibly. Or to the Southern Continent."

"The Twin Realms. I do not really wish my son to go there. It is dangerous. I hope you do not have to go that way."

"We can leave your son in Fort Danzilet if you wish it, after we leave the land of the Qeteral." Curdoz repressed an irked tone, but Genehbro's contradictory attitude towards his son was confusing. To suggest on the one hand Tiliruf act as a protector, and on the other to pretend somehow that he shouldn't be present when danger threatened was simply odd. Besides that, war was likely to be approved by the Assembly requiring action on the part of all. Why was Genehbro acting hesitant on his son's part? Did this incongruity coming from the father have an impact on the maturity, or lack thereof, of the son?

The Master considered for a minute before responding. He sighed deeply. "No, Your Grace. I release Tiliruf to you and to himself. He is a man by three years now, and he should go his own way. As you saw for yourself, he made his decision already without my input, and what that tells me is that I can no longer interfere."

Not wrong, yet Curdoz didn't quite like the man's choice of words here. It was almost like a surrender. "But you are the Head of your House, Master..."

"A failed House, Lord Curdoz. We are no longer emperors, if you haven't noticed."

He smiled as he said this, and Curdoz could tell that there were several conflicting emotions there: regret, resolve, and a casual lack of concern mixed in. If possible, Curdoz was even more disturbed. There was insecurity even in the father.

"You are still one of the Masters of the City and respected by most."

"I am only respected because of my wealth, Your Grace."

"Your House will always be highly regarded in other lands, too." Curdoz was aggravated that he somehow felt the need to boost the man's confidence. But he was more annoyed with himself for his lack of patience, finding himself half-inclined to launch into a slam like he did with poor Onri the Innkeeper back on the Hescian border.

"Perhaps. But I will say this to you in the highest confidence."

"Yes, Master Genehbro?"

"I am a Master on the Assembly, and I take my role seriously, because I know I can continue to contribute. But I refuse to Bond again, for my love for Róssela is everlasting, and I could never dishonor her memory by Bonding someone—pretending unfairly to love another—just for the sake of having more children." He hesitated. "There was an Aura anyway, they say."

"I did not know that. You could have no more children in any event unless there were a second Aura."

"So, as you see, Tiliruf is my one and only son, the last of my House. If there is to be greatness again in the House of Terianh, Tiliruf will have to prove he is an ember under the ashes ready to renew the flame. He can achieve next to nothing if he stays here in Tirilorin."

Finally, Curdoz thought, a bit of the man's wisdom was showing. "Master, have you ever considered telling your son that very thing in similar terms?" He thought he knew the answer.

"I have not. It seems unwise or maybe unfair to place that much upon the shoulders of one so young."

Curdoz debated only a moment. He was a Sage, after all. "Since you have trusted me with your confidence, I will take it as an opportunity to respond to you on that. Not long ago I too would have thought as you do, that such a burden, for that indeed is what it is, would be too much for anyone let alone those as young as the twins. But after having spent all these weeks with them, I have come to the realization that it may be an error to shield them. Kodi and Lyndz were not exactly sheltered, for they were actively a part of the communities in which they grew up with many responsibilities. And yet, for sundry reasons, their father had been holding them back, Kodi in particular. The Count experienced greatness of his own and has since been nearly chained to it by Duke Amerro who has continued his dependence upon the man in his goals to uncover the riches of the Tolosian Peninsula, to settle it and to claim it as part of an expanded duchy. I like the duke and consider him a friend and political ally, but he is overly ambitious. Anyway, thus, the Lord Hess has been absent from home often. And yet on those few occasions in which he is at home with his son he sees the same potential for greatness yet has been reluctant to allow him to leave home to pursue his goals. Hess has even been using his own absence as an excuse to require Kodi to remain at home to help the family. But that family is in no great need; they have great wealth and can hire out all their needs at will if need be. But Hess does not wish for the same chains that he himself bears to be attached to his own children. Greatness requires immense responsibility, and often requires us to set aside our own needs and desires in order to serve the higher needs of others.

"So, it was an error in judgment on Hess's part. He was not wrong about the twins' potential for greatness, but his belief that he could protect them from their future was a mistake. He should have let Kodi in particular follow his desire two or three years ago to train for knighthood with the duke. This is what Kodi has wanted and what he has needed. He is behind where he should be. He will become a great warrior. Perhaps one of the greatest of all warriors if I interpret our Visions correctly. And the Lady Elisa made it clear to me that had Hess been home when I arrived to fetch the twins, he would have withheld blessing from Lyndz so to discourage her from leaving with me. I admit I too had hesitations. I was wrong. I want the twins to learn in part through their own devices, but ultimately, I will not be withholding anything from them. My slowness is calculated, but it has nothing anymore to do with their age."

"I understand what you are saying, Lord Curdoz, but I am not sure if it is quite the same. I have not held my son back. I've even made effort to encourage him to leave. I and the Swordmaster too have attempted many times to encourage him to go to Nant and train with the princes."

"No, it is not exactly the same, true. But he has been held back from leaving even if the holding is of his own making."

"So, I should have ordered him to go?"

"In his case it might have been what was needed. He has had too much time on his hands. Your son has a reputation in this city, that is, how shall I put it?"

"Less than stellar? I am not blind to it."

"Yet you have never confronted him on it, have you? You may not be blind to it, but you turn a blind eye nevertheless. However, that may be less important than another thing. What I am saying is that you have not been fully honest with your son these years. You have not trusted him with your own hopes and fears. You have taught him his history, and he appears scholarly. But he is the last of your family, and you have not shown him the favor he deserves—not of your wealth and privilege, because you have not denied that, and he has abused it in order to spoil himself, but rather of your faith in him as your only son and in his innate abilities as the scion of the greatest House in the history of the world."

Looking intently at the Sage, Genehbro was silent for a while, and then he turned around and looked out the window again. Brilliant blue embraced the scene and the distant sea sparkled like diamonds. Ships sailed in and out of harbor. The city of Tirilorin, greatest on earth, his ancestors' city, was resplendent like jewels. "And now it is too late?" he asked sadly.

"One might think that Tiliruf's penchant for self-indulgence will be his certain undoing, and there is risk. Yet I think ultimately there is hope. Enric thinks so and has great faith in Tiliruf. Kodi has refrained from telling him so, due to Tiliruf's obvious cynicism regarding Meicalian teachings, but your son was one of four persons that appeared vividly in Kodi's Vision." Curdoz watched as Genehbro turned from the window and raised an eyebrow, but the Sage plunged on. "It was the principal reason the Guardian directed us here, I think. And Kodi recognized Tiliruf instantly when he saw him. We came here looking for the man in Kodi's Vision, your own son, Genehbro. There *must* be an ember under the ashes, just as you suggest, and you and all of us should derive hope from it. Why else would the Guardian choose him? Because he happens to be good with a blade? I don't think so.

"So, I'm telling you, no. It is not too late to talk to him and open yourself to him. You should tell him of your hopes and fears. It is a burden, yes, but it is his right to bear that burden. More importantly, though, it is the right thing for you to do to demonstrate your trust. After that, since you are *not* the emperor, and refuse to claim it, you would be released from any further responsibilities for the decisions that your son chooses to make."

"But what if I were the emperor?"

"Then I might say otherwise. A sovereign is responsible for the decisions of his heirs as long as he is still sovereign. But your grandfather relieved you of that."

"I detect cynicism in that statement, Lord Curdoz!"

Curdoz considered. "I beg your pardon, Master. I realize I am hiding an emotion from you that has been simmering within for a while."

"And what is that, may I ask?"

It cost Curdoz a little, for it breached decorum as a high official from another country. As such, he should respect the chosen form of government of the Tirilorines and the positions of the Masters, including this Master. But as a Sage of Meical the Guardian, he now felt compelled to say what he really believed.

"I am annoyed at the fact that your grandfather Zaralio abdicated. You see, if he had not, we would not be having this conversation, for you would be the emperor, and you would not have allowed your son to be so free in his spoiled exploits. I am right, am I not? You would have assured he was a high prince on fire rather than an ember slowly darkening under ashes!"

The bluntness shocked Genehbro, but after a moment he spoke. "You are wise, Lord Curdoz. I wish I had had you here these years."

"Enric is wise, and I can assure you he is fully aware. But you have kept him at a distance, unwilling to allow the taint of his 'religion' to diminish your importance politically. And again, if you were Emperor, that too would not have been the case."

Dumbstruck at the truths being cast at him, Genehbro was uncertain how to respond anymore. He sat down at his heavily carved, recently imported ambernut desk, leaned forward on his elbows, and placed his head between his hands. He was quiet for some time, but Curdoz believed it important to allow it all to sink into the man's mind.

Eventually, since the Master did not speak, Curdoz could sense the pain. He walked over to the desk and sat down before the Master and spoke with a quieter voice. "You are not responsible for your grandfather's poor choices, however. Nor was he the only emperor to make poor choices."

"But I am responsible for my choices and their consequences. I see that now. What a fool I have been, Lord Curdoz. In my fear of my House losing more face with the people I haven't been much of a leader. Or a father. I had lost faith in myself." He paused for a while, then added, "So, Master Enric is aware?"

"It isn't me, really, that you should be giving so much credit to for knowing these things, just for being the one willing to tell you of them, and that is only because you seemed in a way to request it. Enric watches you, and he watches Tiliruf, too. He could be your best friend and would be a superior advisor, as should be the case. You all foolishly lower his standing in my opinion by making him a City Master. In the Valley he is referred to as 'The High Lord Enric, Meicalian Sage of Imperial Tirilorin and the Domain of the Emperors.' He should be a constant presence in the House of Terianh, because you are the Head of that House, and if anyone can claim Enric's good counsel it is you. He is your greatest asset, but you unwittingly deny his worth.

"It is not too late. Enric's time is nearing its end, and he will be replaced soon. He will retire to the Valley in another year or so. But he is full of wisdom and knows your family and your history better than you do yourself. You should welcome him in your home every day, give him space here from which to supervise the Orders, and then provide likewise to the one who follows after him. The pox on what the other Masters or the people think! Most likely, if it appears you raise him and his standing in your home and confidences his reputation will be enhanced rather than yours to suffer. And if I am wrong, then it is nevertheless irrelevant. The point would be that you are doing the right thing and returning to a tradition, an excellent tradition that was established by your great ancestors and the Eight Great Sages after the Third Appearance of the Guardian and the Conquest."

The Master put his arms down and peered directly at the Sage. "I will do this, Lord Curdoz. It seems wisdom to me, and I need more of that. But what do I do for Tiliruf?"

"I remember your dear wife of course from my visit twenty years ago. She outshone the sun on this palace, a great woman. I, for one, honor your choice not to Bond again, and you will find that Enric feels the same. You should do as I suggested. We will be here many more days. You have time to have numerous conversations with Tiliruf. I believe, by the Guardian, that you were meant to have him as your one and only son. The

Aura is probably proof of that. There is a meaning and a potential there that even I cannot foresee. Open up to him, and it is to be hoped that he will latch on to your trust of him and that it will create a newfound respect for you and for his heritage, and...for himself."

Genehbro was listening.

"And one more thing," added Curdoz. "Don't simply 'hand over' the Eagle Sword of Terianh! It is one of the great heirlooms of history, and you planned to spoil him by simply giving it to him like a little bag of coins as he leaves on a journey!"

"Your insights amaze me, Your Grace. You are right. I am a fool! Yes. I will talk to Jaden. We will have a proper ceremony where we will proclaim Tiliruf a Swordmaster. I will show him high honor and present him with the great Sword."

"That is better. He needs to see the importance of these things as you present them to him over the years to come. It isn't your only heirloom, I know. But I fully support your desire to give it to him if he is the swordsman you and Jaden say he is. He needs to receive gifts *as he deserves them,* and not because you are a rich man with fine things. It reminds me of when we traveled through Ferostro. King Carlomen, bless his old heart, was willing to knight young Kodi if I wished it, and also due to his father's reputation. But I told him as I have told you, Kodi should only receive such honors when he has successfully met certain challenges. So instead, he presented Kodi with a beautifully engraved quiver, a very proper gift for one of his subjects with a reputation for superior marksmanship. But not only that, I feel I've grown to know Kodi well; though he wishes for it very much, he would have been confused and the honor lost on him if Carlomen had knighted him at that time. If you ask me as a man of the Kingdom of Solanto, too many men are knighted before they deserve it, and so it loses its value. But Kodi has a good sense of symbolism and sees it as a high, well-deserved honor, just as he should and just as it should be. His time will come, and the honor will be genuine. I expect more well-deserved honors to come his way in time. Let us think similarly, then, of Tiliruf."

Genehbro stood up then and came around the desk to the Sage. The Sage stood up, too, and looked into the man's face.

"Lord Sage, I admit to you my own hesitations regarding Meicalian teachings. Tiliruf comes by that innocently enough. There is much that makes one skeptical, for not all of us receive these 'Visions', and 'Giftedness' in the opinion of many is simply a natural trait. The Histories have become fables in our minds. But you have opened my eyes to possibilities, and though I might still wonder and may still on occasion express skepticism, I am at least willing to open my heart to the hope you proclaim for Tiliruf. Though it may not be in perfect faith, I am willing to proclaim again for the Guardian. Will you accept such proclamation?"

Curdoz smiled broadly, but said, “That is my Brother Enric’s privilege, of course. But when he does, it is certainly appropriate I be present. And don’t worry about perfect faith. I’m not so sure there is any such thing, and never does the Guardian hold that against the sincere individual. Just keep your senses and your heart open, Master Genehbro. Don’t expect Visions, but all around us the Great Work of the Celestial Powers can be found if one opens his eyes.”

“I can at least do that, I suppose,” said Genehbro as his face softened into a genuine smile.

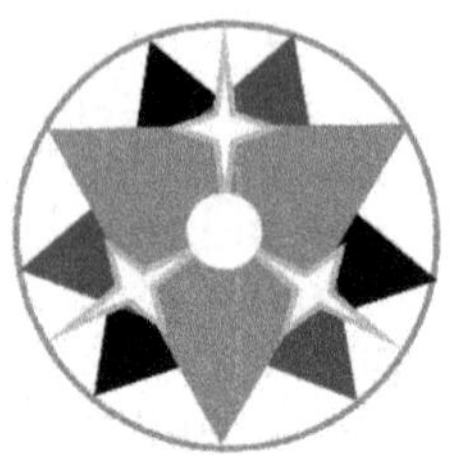

Chapter 8—Lyndz' Revelation

And so, a full eight-day Anterianhi week passed. Other than a rain squall that would on occasion come in off the ocean, the weather was fine for late spring.

Kodi advanced rapidly in his daily morning swordsmanship training with Jaden and the others, and his afternoons were made in easy effort getting to know better some of Tiliruf's friends and even to begin claiming them as his own. He visited Lukas and Colinn at the East Gate where they worked as a part of the Brigade detail assigned to its management and protection, and Kodi met a number of other Brigadiers, eating with them and learning what daily life was like for a common soldier. Andir and Bindrik invited him to visit their place of business where the two worked for their wealthy fathers, merchant partners. The two younger men were responsible for inventorying merchandise as it was unloaded into their fathers' warehouses in South Port. And yesterday the same crowd from the previous week met up as planned for an afternoon of food, ale, and sun-filled waters at the beach. Occasionally, Kodi would spend time with the two Sages, for they wanted him to meditate with them and try better to achieve 'emptying of the mind' and the Mode. Maybe it helped and maybe it didn't, but the discipline was probably useful, growing his patience.

Tiliruf spent most of his time with Kodi during the days, and often ate meals with all of them at Enric's invitation. However, though Kodi couldn't be certain, he doubted that Tiliruf's late nights had become totally free of North Bend excursions despite the latter's attempted promises during their conversation together at Zhock's tavern. A change of subject, a casual smirk or two, a crude reference, sleepy mid-morning yawns and a wink during training with Jaden—all these and other hints made Kodi wonder. Kodi's self-control and relative innocence in this area had little direct influence on Tiliruf. Nor could Kodi predict what it might take to encourage his friend to change his behavior, particularly when that friend thought what he was doing was perfectly natural, almost business-like, and who also had little thought towards a future that might include a devoted monogamous Bonding and a family. Tiliruf perhaps had certain goals relating to his abilities as a superior swordsman. But, being disciplined with what he sometimes joked was his 'other sword' or his 'arrow' was for now totally unimportant to him.

Even so, there could be no doubt that the friendship between the two young men was a meaningful one with strongly positive implications for both, where companionship, loyalty, deep understanding, and mutual respect increased daily, and Jaden, Enric, Genehbro, and Curdoz were pleased as they watched those two interrelate. Enric in private made reference to it to Curdoz one evening over wine.

"Tiliruf is growing again after a long stagnation. It is definitely for the better, and it has everything to do with Kodi having come here."

To which Curdoz replied, "I believe you, and I am glad for the friendship and Kodi's good influence, but Tiliruf has a long way to go to become the man the Guardian is hoping he will become."

"Yet it is a step," said Enric. "A big step in the right direction, and perhaps a real turning point. A turning point from idleness and apathy. And that is where Kodi is working magic."

"But he will need other turning points. You are right, though. There is much to be said for the friendship itself and for any effort on Tiliruf's part to think outward beyond himself. Nor do I discount Tiliruf's positive attributes, for his swordsmanship inspires Kodi, and the male camaraderie Tiliruf and his friends provide keeps Kodi energized and happy. It means much and will mean even more in future."

"Yes. Tiliruf may never achieve the individual heroism of his ancestor Terianh, but he might still achieve greatness particularly with great people at his side. That is my hope for him," concluded Enric.

"Then it is my duty to ensure he remains in proximity to such people," Curdoz said.

Several times Genehbro met with Enric who was overjoyed to accept the man's proclamation in favor of the Guardian, and they made plans regarding Enric's removing his administration of the Orders into the Palace. Idamé spent much time with Hollina who took her to visit the Matrimonial Convent, the Monastics Monastery, The Monastics Orphanage, the Hospital of the Healers, and other sites associated with the Orders in addition to many gardens, for she liked these nearly as much as Lyndz. Curdoz would often visit the library, sometimes with Lyndz, to read about the Qeteral or to study the old maps, but he was also busy communing with Enric or meeting with Assembly Masters. The next Assembly Meeting proved to be informative, and it appeared more progress had been made encouraging more of the reluctant Masters to change their thinking. However, High Master Naloro still did not yet feel assured of full consensus and delayed once more the final vote for mobilization.

Lyndz attended two or three small-affair teas, and though it was pleasant to meet some of the other women in the city, she afterwards refused any more invitations, for they interfered with what she enjoyed most, which was reading in the library and visiting the fabulous gardens in the city. Though Kodi's sessions with the Sages might have yielded minimal progress, the more patient Lyndz, on the other hand, was advancing. She might have, back in Solanto, been reluctant regarding her role, but her work with Deroge's book, her coming to terms with the Visions of the others, and her realization that there was more in the world than little Felto in remote Tulesk had opened her mind. The political and economic power and the abilities of many of the women of Central City inspired her. She was now beginning to have courageous thoughts and internal bursts of her own energy and wanted very much to discover her Gift. However, the realization that she was becoming less like her dutiful mother and more like her adventurous father had as yet not worked its way into her thinking.

"Something just happened, Mother Idamé!" said Lyndz, a look of minor shock appearing on her face.

"Try to describe it, dear." The Matrimonial opened her eyes.

The two women had been meditating in Enric's garden temple. It was a discipline they had been performing together at least once a day, and Lyndz took the exercise much more seriously than Kodi did with the Sages.

Musca was lying nearby, snoozing contentedly.

"It came into my mind the marble statue of the Guardian in the Palace garden. I saw it several days ago with Tiliruf and Kodi. You know the one I'm talking about?"

"Yes, Hollina and some Monastic Sisters took me there for a morning meditation," the Matrimonial said with a raised left eyebrow. "Are you sure you had emptied your mind? You weren't thinking of gardens like you often do?"

Lyndz was sure and said so. "I'm telling you, Mother Idamé, that I've become quite good at it."

"Yes, dear. I suppose I do believe you. That's good. But let's not presume we've had a breakthrough quite yet. Now, tell me, when you saw the statue did you feel emotion? In other words, were you admiring, say, how beautiful it is in its setting, with the fountain at the feet?"

"Not especially. I simply thought, 'well, this is interesting!' It was a bit more intellectual than what you're suggesting, Mother. No, no emotion. Don't get me wrong. I really did admire that garden room when Tiliruf took us into it, but there was no emotion in the depiction of the statue when it appeared in my mind."

"Anything else about it?"

Lyndz thought. She closed her eyes as if to retrieve the imprint on the back of her eyelids. "Well, yes! The wings were not there."

"That *is* odd," admitted Idamé, obviously intrigued. She shifted and sat up. "The wings are a distinctive feature on most Meical statues, including that one. Of course, there is no mention that Meical had wings in the Book of Histories. Though the Etoppsi insist that, like they, He has wings. Some of the philosophers in the Valley believe that each sees Meical in form according to his own race. Are you sure it was *that* statue in the garden?"

"Without wings, and yes, it was the same with the fountain and rocks—you know it has a different design than some of the others. The rocks that surround it are flat and layered rather than the larger cut blocks like the other fountains. And the dark green cypresses, and the little white flowers similar to the colored ones on Master Enric's front lawn. It was definitely the same."

Idamé raised her eyebrow again. "You know, it is a telling detail to me. If you had been thinking about it before, then you would have remembered it as you saw it with Tiliruf—with wings. The fact that you didn't makes me believe you really did achieve the Mode, even if it was only for a moment!"

"There did seem to be a green light, like a dome over the statue, come to think of it. It was lighter than the cypress trees, brighter."

The Matrimonial looked at her oddly. "A green light like a dome? What are you talking about, dear?"

"Well, you know, it was like what Kodi described that the librarian in Aster did, the Moment Master, what was his name? Theneri, wasn't it? I wish I had met him."

"Hmm, maybe I remember studying something like that in the Valley—that the Moment Master's magic moves outward from a green dome of light."

"That's what Kodi said, for sure. So the Healers and Matrimonials and the Sages and the rest don't experience that in the Mode?"

"Green light is associated with magic as a part of the Gift from Meical. But it is an outward expression once the magic is employed. With Matrimonials, when we see an Aura, the light above the couple is vivid green."

"But only Matrimonials see it, right?"

"Yes, it is different than the obvious green light you see coming from the hands of Healers when they touch someone. Anyone can see that. Aura magic is the oldest of all Gifted magic and works a little different than the other."

"And what about Seers?"

"Seers and Seeresses actually can place their hands on another to help the other recall the Prophecy more readily, and the receiver notices green in his eyes for a moment. Really, though I like to place Aura magic on a pedestal, frankly all the Gifts are quite different from each other." She paused, "Well, dear. I believe we've done enough for today. Let us not overdo it but return to this discussion later."

Lyndz stood. "I'm going to walk to the Library and see if there is a book about Moment Mastering."

"I'll go with you, dear. I'm not happy when you walk about the city alone."

"You're too sweet, Mother Idamé!" Lyndz replied, tapping the Matrimonial on the cheek. "Central City is safe enough. I've seen dozens of the ladies out and about without escort. There are even wealthy women of business, here, Mother, and they are not inhibited in their movements. I truly admire the freedoms women experience in this city."

"It's just that I promised your mother, dear, to watch after you."

"I know it, Mother Idamé, but really, it isn't necessary here. But I'm glad for the company of course. I think you like the Library as much as I do."

They were delayed in this plan, however, for as they entered from Enric's back garden into the house and made their way to the front, there was a messenger speaking with Sister Hollina in the entrance hall. He was handing her what appeared to be a decorated envelope.

"...so please present it to Master Enric, and he is to bring his Solantine guests. But Madam Arlay asked me to speak personally to the Matrimonial Mother and the young Mistress Lyndz, if that can be arranged, Sister Hollina. Are they present?"

Mother Idamé strode forward. "Well, yes we are, young man!" Hollina stepped aside to let her speak. "We've declined so many invitations already, you would think that..."

"This is different, Mother Idamé," interrupted Hollina. "This is something we've been expecting, and from what Brother Enric tells me, Master Kodi has already committed himself and his sister to this."

"Really?" asked Lyndz excitedly. "Is this about the dance?"

The messenger's eyes were glued to the beautiful Lyndz and spoke with a bit more excitement than was necessary. "Yes, mistress! And Madam Arlay had a special message for you and the Matrimonial Mother. She wished me to say to both of you that she is perfectly aware that you are on a journey, and that she would be appalled should you feel obliged to purchase new gowns from the clothiers just for this one affair. She wished me to invite both of you to come to her home for an afternoon tea, day after tomorrow, whereupon she wishes to present to you several dresses belonging to both her and her daughter. She is of the view that you should find something suitable in their wardrobes that you may borrow for the dance."

"How kind!" replied Lyndz. "And Mother Idamé, she'll have the proper Tirilorine fashions!"

"It is very sweet, and you should go, dear, but Matrimonials don't wear dance gowns."

The messenger looked at Idamé oddly, uncertain how to respond, but Hollina laughed. "Oh, dear Idamé! You shall of course wear a dance gown! This isn't like Solanto or Eleni. If an Order Member is invited to such an affair in Tirilorin, then it is perfectly acceptable for him or her to dress accordingly. You can still wear a shawl, of course. I promise you won't feel out of place, dear!" She then turned to the messenger, ignoring Idamé's continued protestations. "Tell Enola that her offer is extremely thoughtful and most appreciated and that both ladies will gladly attend her afternoon tea! Yes, tell Enola to lay out another teacup, for I'll bring them myself!"

The young man was pleased, and unwilling still to remove his eyes from Lyndz, bowed and stumbled his way backwards out the door. Whereupon he stood awkwardly, until Hollina rolled her eyes and shut it in his face.

"You'd think the men in this city had never in all their lives seen a young woman!" She then looked at Lyndz. "Yet you *are* quite lovely, dear. Perhaps at the Dance you'll take a liking to one of our city lads! But not the fawning sort like that one, please!"

Lyndz giggled as Idamé retrieved her shawl, and before long the two of them set forth for the Library.

Late that evening in Enric's parlor the company from Solanto sat about discussing the upcoming grand event. Tiliruf was there, too, having been invited again by Enric to dinner.

"Of course, we will all go, and so will you, Ida," said Curdoz matter-of-factly. "And not as a chaperone for Lyndz! And not just as a traditional Aura scout, either. Kodi will escort her through the introductions, and she can handle herself from there. I insist you enjoy yourself!"

The Matrimonial had continued in her uncertainty despite Hollina's reassurances that afternoon. "But I just don't know, Curdoz! It isn't seemly for a Matrimonial to be an actual participant in such a fancy affair! I think I'll just stand at the sides and keep my eye out..."

"And you will dance with every man who asks you," continued Curdoz. "It is all great fun, of course! You will go as my partner, and I at least intend to ask you to dance several times!"

This last set Idamé's cheeks pinking. She giggled like Lyndz could. "Oh Curdoz! You're too kind. All right, I give. Though I've surely forgotten the steps after all these years. I haven't been to a proper dance since I was a girl. So, Lyndz, you'll have to help me choose a dress from Madam Arlay."

"And I've got clothes that'll suit Kodi, eh?" Though Kodi was overall more muscular than Tiliruf, they were precisely the same height and not so different in size that Kodi couldn't try on his friend's clothes.

"I'm not wearing those ghastly gold and silver-threaded knee stockings like you do."

"You'll wear 'em, mate, and like 'em."

"They're fashionable in Central City, Kodi," said Lyndz, consolingly. "No one will think anything of it."

"Yes, probably not," said Enric. He had been sipping his wine and listening quietly to all the banter. "The point is, like Curdoz says, is that we all enjoy ourselves. And I should remind you that the ladies of Central City are sponsoring this with matchmaking in mind! Probably every young man and young lady in Central City will be there, quite a few from Guardian Hills, and a number of the Brigadier soldiers and officers recommended by the generals."

"Mistress Itruvi, too, I guess," said Kodi disgustingly as an aside, "Since she's helping sponsor the damned thing."

Tiliruf heard him and laughed. "You've met Stri, have you?"

"Our first day here. Never seen so much makeup on a woman in all my life, except for...," but Kodi remembered himself when he noticed Lyndz looking at him and trailed off.

Tiliruf laughed even louder.

"What have I missed?" said Lyndz, curiously.

"Nothing, sis. But really," Kodi said, "I'm not asking her to dance with me. So that's that."

"Not so simple, mate." said Tiliruf.

"Master Tiliruf is right, Master Kodi." Enric said, winking. "The rules are not the same here. You're thinking of the customs in the kingdoms. We are a republic! The expectations are different."

"Oh!" exclaimed Lyndz. "You mean we ladies are allowed to ask the men to dance, as well?"

Idamé gasped at this horror.

"Ah, no!" said Kodi, exasperated. "Lyndz, you've got to cut in and save me. You should have seen the way she came on to me the other day. Ask Curdoz. Or Master Enric; he was there, too. Itruvi will hound me all night!"

"Nah, she won't, mate!" said Tiliruf. "She's that way with every..."

"All right, Master Tiliruf!" interrupted Enric. "What have I told you before about gossip and reputation?"

Tiliruf desisted and winked at Kodi. "You ready to go, now, mate?"

Kodi stood.

"And where are you two headed, may I ask?" inquired Idamé. "It's already after dark!"

To Idamé anything 'after dark' was a questionable undertaking.

"It is a simple gathering of friends, Mother Idamé," said Tiliruf a bit too coolly and with an arrangement of word choices a hint too formal for his typical style, to which they had all by now grown accustomed.

Undaunted, she raised her left eyebrow menacingly.

Tiliruf was almost never embarrassed around anyone, but for some reason he found the Matrimonial Mother a tad too intimidating and knowing. His usual grin faltered slightly as he cleared his throat. "We have a date to play Fifty-twos with some friends of mine," he admitted. He turned rather to Sage Enric, with whom he felt safer, and winked. "And it's just coppers, eh, Master Enric? Nothing in it, you know, to damage a 'reputation.' We'll be at my rooms at the Palace, and Kodi's staying the night."

Before Idamé could question this arrangement, Curdoz chimed in. "Then we'll see you sometime tomorrow, Kodi. Take your bow, and don't forget your lessons with Jaden in the morning!"

Kodi nodded appreciatively at the Sage.

"That Mother Idamé makes me feel guilty even when I haven't done anything."

"Not going to hurt you. And knowing you, you could do with a bit of guilt. She already loves you like her own, I can tell. Anyway, I told you Curdoz doesn't mind us having a bit of fun as long as we're within certain boundaries. For instance, you keep the library girls away, will you? And don't try dragging me off to North Bend."

"So, you *are* tempted, eh?" Tiliruf said, slapping his friend on the back.

The streets of Central City were well-lit at night with many lantern posts, and the two young men were talking as they walked together towards the Palace. They were to meet up with a few of the fellows Kodi had met before at the beach.

Kodi chuckled. "I've told you what I'm aiming for. But you better never deliberately try messing me up, say, if I'm drunk."

"Wouldn't do that, mate. Not tonight anyway. Just us men. And I wouldn't have that lot at the Palace anyway. It might cause me to get a bad *reputation!*" he quipped. "'Course I could invite Stri Itruvi if you like! She's always wanted to get a closer look at my bedroom."

Kodi looked aghast at his friend. "You and she haven't..."

"I said she's *wanted* to, mate! Came close once, I must admit. Or twice. Er, well maybe it's a matter of your definition, if you know what I mean. She's got perpetually wet lips, a fantastic exploratory tongue, and some other useful, er, body parts that can allow a man to achieve great wonders. It wasn't *my* bedroom, and it's been a couple years, eh?" He looked at Kodi who was shaking his head and laughing. "What? I mean she's got some right attractive swingers, hasn't she? Always brushing 'em up against...what?"

Kodi could no longer control himself, hooting grandly at all these admissions, and particularly the justifying qualifiers and excuses.

Tiliruf grinned. He realized how crazy he must sound, even though from his point of view he was only trying to be honest and open with Kodi whom he'd come to trust and believed deserved his honesty. He hadn't quite told him everything during their conversation at Zhock's place, and he was even now leaving out and modifying certain pieces of his history with Stri. Though he was being more honest than he'd ever been before. "But you talked about that Jonell girl trying to trap you. That's Stri. I know her all too well. I don't mess with her type anymore, I swear, 'cause in fact there's several more of 'em like her. They're a calculating bunch, Kodi. Every last one just wants in on Father's wealth."

Tiliruf spat this last with a bitterness beyond his typical cynicism. It was the first time Kodi knew Tiliruf to express such resentment.

And he wasn't done. "I'm telling you, Kodi. There'll be a dozen of 'em of Stri's ilk that'll ask me to dance at Arlay's affair, maybe more, and not one of 'em will really care about me as...as me."

Kodi sympathized, but he also was wise enough to Tiliruf's ways by now to know that in part this was something he'd brought on himself.

"Sorry about that. But listen, Tiliruf! You've got to *want* the sort of relationship you're thinking about to receive it. The caring kind, that is. I don't think you're really wanting it, are you? I know I asked you the other day if there were good women in the city, but frankly I'm beginning to think that like me in Felto, there's no one from here that's really right for you."

"Never considered it."

"'Cause you don't really think about what it means to really love a woman that way."

"Sure I do. Or at least maybe I once did for an hour or two a couple years ago." He laughed at his own joke. "Mostly, I don't really believe in it, at least not for me. Love is for noble blokes like yourself. Anyway, mate," he said, cheering up again, "there's still a thing or two a woman's good for, eh? But like you I'm not letting any of 'em trap me into Bonding. Bonding's a waste of a perfectly good stiffrod, especially mine that prefers uncommitted sampling and exploration! I don't need Itruvi or any of her set for that."

Kodi chuckled. "The 'library girls' are good enough for Ruffy?"

"Precisely!" Tiliruf chortled as he punched Kodi in the arm. "No expectations, no responsibilities, and no children! They don't demand anything in return except silver, er, gold lately. Besides, they like it when I show up, eh? I give as good as I get, you know what I mean? Always give a little extra, I say."

Tiliruf had a magnificent set of rooms in a remote portion of the Palace. It was stuffed with valuable, hand-carved furnishings upholstered in velvet, paintings and large mirrors in gilt frames, huge windows with heavy satin draperies drawn for the night, bronze statues holding great lanterns, and imported Barantine carpets with fantastical creations woven into their plushness. Calen and Spens were already there, along with two whom Kodi had not yet met by the names of Cawlbert and Yakob. They were already into Tiliruf's large, heavily embellished silver cabinet of imported liquors, and they sat on fine upholstered chairs of velvet around a large ambernut and marble game table that Tiliruf had himself designed and had specially made for just this sort of entertaining. Smoke curled through the air, as all had ivory pipes lit. Tiliruf promptly handed one to Kodi.

Kodi then confessed his lie to Tiliruf, who laughed. "It's all right, mate! You just have to take it slow. Pull a little of the smoke from the pipe into your mouth and let it sit there a second or two and then breathe it in slowly. You might cough a few times, but it won't take long, and you'll get used to it. It's good mild tobacco from Solanto."

Kodi had watched Curdoz so many times that he thought he knew how to pack the ivory pipe Tiliruf handed him. Not too loose and not too tight. He even lit it easily enough with a matchstick, pulling into his cheeks and puffing repeatedly as he had often seen Curdoz and others back home do to get the fire going in the bowl. Finally, he drew on it, but perhaps remembering what it was like when he attempted it back in Thorune, he had a bit more caution and followed Tiliruf's instructions.

It worked much better this time. And after several more draws, he began to sense the change that the tobacco was effecting in his head. It was a most agreeable feeling, as if his brain just leaned back and relaxed, dispersing any anxieties. Though not quite as dramatic, it reminded him a little of when Danly and Xeno placed their hands on him and induced the Healing magic. He smiled. "So, this is what Curdoz is onto, is it? Ah, yeah, I see now. All right, Ruffy, pour me some of that special Nantian brandy you talk so much about!"

The men were full of fun and jokes as they enjoyed betting their coppers, drinking whatever they wished and smoking incessantly. Tiliruf had ordered the servants not to disturb them, and they had plenty of special treats to eat from the kitchens. And like a good host, he regularly refilled their tiny, gold cups with their choices from the silver cabinet.

Kodi had played Fifty-twos before, and there was little difference in the rules here than in faraway Solanto. He even won several rounds. However, after a couple hours of fun, the men started falling out one by one as they ran out of coppers until it was only Tiliruf and Spens who were left battling it out. The rest sat back and smoked their pipes, watching, cheering on each, and making deliberately misleading cracks about one players' card hand to try to goad or confuse the other. When Tiliruf at one point bet everything he had, Spens, surprisingly, took him up on it and bleated gloriously when he produced four nines and beat out the other man's threesome-and-a-pair.

The laughter didn't end with the end of the game, and neither did the drinking, and they all sat about on a different set of cushy chairs teasing each other or talking about women. Kodi's recreating the jokes and language styles of Captain Shond and the crew created much merriment, and they all teased Tiliruf mercilessly when they found out exactly why the Solantine kept calling their host *Ruffy*. But as Kodi found out, with the exception of Spens, who didn't work and who couldn't afford such decadence with the little allowance he received from his parsimonious father, the other three admitted to their own dalliances, confirming Kodi's suspicions: North Bend received much business from the rich young men of Central City. Tiliruf was not so different except perhaps for sheer level of self-indulgence. Yet unlike him, the others expressed hints of regret and made remarks wishing they'd find their Bondmate soon, so they wouldn't feel the urge to engage the addictive call of the brothels of North Bend.

This undertone wish for Bondmates led to talk about the upcoming Grand Dance, where it was expected that the social engagement would lead to a number of subsequent courtships and eventual Bondings.

"I'll dance w' Ssstri if she's that dessperate," slurred pudgy Spens, raising his tiny brandy cup in a cheer. In fact, they were all quite drunk by now. "I like her; she's rich! I don't care 'bout her makeup, like Kodi does. I'll lick it off her face, I will. If I could sssnatch her...hey, Kodi! That Matrimonial friend o' yours, you bring 'er over and I'll shhhtand by Itruvi, and she can tell us if there's an Aura!"

"She'll prob'ly be on the watch for 'em, for sure, but I ain't interrupting her fun. She'll be dancin' wi' Curdoz."

"Righ', mate," said Tiliruf sarcastically. "All the hopeful couples should jus' line up in long rows while the music's playin' and the Matrimonials can walk up 'n down, shuffle 'em about, and point out Auras! Or 'horrors' like Kodi's shipmates call 'em. Smart fellas, them. Ain't nobody gonna tell me who I have to Bond."

"Take a Matrimonial with ya nex' time ya go to North Bend," cracked Calens.

"Yep, I can see tha' now!" cackled Cawlbert. "Tiliruf in an Aura-Bonding with one o' his 'library girls'!"

They all bellowed boisterously at this.

"Ain' gonna happen, mate!"

"Auras are rare, anyways," said Yakob. "It'll be int'restin' if there's even jus' one seen at the Dance. I admit though, I always though' Auras were kind o' romantic."

Unfortunately, he said this last a bit too dreamily, for he was then teased jocularly by the others for the next several minutes.

The laughter and talk, the pipe-smoking and drinking, went on for another little while, but finally the playfulness of the night petered out as one by one the imbibers stumbled off to sundry sofas or guest beds attached to Tiliruf's apartments.

The following morning, despite Idamé's protestations again that she shouldn't be alone, Lyndz put her foot down. "I'm going there by myself, Mother Idamé. I just want to sit on a bench and meditate in the Palace garden."

The Matrimonial gave in, but then had a sudden thought. "At least take Musca with you, won't you, dear?"

Lyndz decided that yes, Musca would not interfere with her intended purpose and agreed to take him along.

Nor did she go empty-handed. Unlike the strict rules of the Aster Library, most books could be borrowed and returned to the Great Library of Tirilorin. So, with her she took the one and only book she and Idamé discovered there that dealt with the magic of Moment Mastering.

It was small, not much bigger than Deroge's Prophecies, and was written in High Anterianhi, which unlike the impatient Kodi, Lyndz had mastered long ago with her grandfather Yugan's help.

It was authored by a 'Brother Ernet' which surprised Curdoz, and when he explained, the others were just as surprised. As it turned out *Ernet* was the false name used by none other than Brother Theneri in his communications with the Sage, and the little book was in his very own handwriting.

The coincidence was not overlooked by Curdoz when Lyndz showed it to him the evening before. *Remarkable,* he had said. *Yet the more I think about it, it really shouldn't surprise me. Theneri has for years been sending copies of his works to the Valley. It makes perfect sense he would also send them here. He knows the value of separate collections. The Ralsheen had one massive library in their first capital, and it burned during the Conquest. Much ancient history and scholarship were lost.*

And why do you think he wrote it in the older language, Curdoz? She had asked.

I'm sure he expected only scholars to be able to read it, most of which would be Order Members. He would be pleased, I'm sure, to know you will read it. Considering its obscure content, quite possibly you are the only one who ever has!

This last implication continued to play in Lyndz' mind as she entered the secluded section of the garden that displayed the large, winged statue of Meical the Guardian. It was still fairly early, two hours past daybreak, and there was no one around. The sun had not yet risen above the crowns of the tall cypresses. It was shady here, dewy and cool, and the play of the bubbling fountain was peaceful. Several birds warbled in the shrubbery.

"Well, Musca," she said to the silver-haired beast beside her, "I don't know if I'm imagining things or not, but I've got to try this."

He looked at her with his knowing green eyes, and as if to watch for anyone who might disturb her, he went and sat sentinel-like in the open space where the one entryway cut its way in an archway through the tall living cypress hedge.

Lyndz sat upon a broad stone bench, one of three set into the hedge and which looked upon the fountain and statue in the center of the oval-shaped garden room.

The statue greatly appealed to her with its masculine physicality carved in white marble. The face was young and beardless. The hands were expressive and strong, reminding her strongly of both her father's and her brother's, but there was an erotic quality in its nudity which she'd never admitted. Yet the wings of course made the image celestial and otherworldly. It was a powerful piece of art, and she believed it to be the most carefully sculpted of all the statues in the garden.

She opened the book and began to reread a section she had examined the night before as she lay in bed:

Though I had had no training, I was of no more than fifteen years when I became adept at what the Order calls 'emptying of the mind.' I do not know how I learned it or why I even practiced it, it was so long ago, but I enjoyed privacy as a youth and would often sit at the top of a grassy hill in summertime near my home and contemplate. Eventually, something strange occurred. Whereas it is common for most who are Called to the Orders, both Gifted and Monastics, to have a Dream or Vision during their sleep in which the Lord Meical appears or speaks to them and invites them to the Valley, with me it was different.

I shall never forget it. Upon an occasion in which I sat on that same hill and emptied my mind, an image broke through. I had been to the famed library in Aster with my mother many times before, so I was quite familiar with the setting. Since we came from a well-to-do merchant's family, we were allowed to make use of the library. The image that came to me was of the central room of the Aster library; overhead painted into the dome was Zadrem's famous Condemnation scene. That of Meical the Guardian was enclosed in green light. That light I of course learned later is associated with magic originating from the Guardian. It is a bright, pure, spring-time green. And I also learned, that though the Gifted can achieve the Mode through meditative exercise, to see an encompassing green light within the Mode is unique to Moment-Masters such as myself, an obscure reference I found in a source when I went to study in the Valley. Of course, at the time this waking Vision appeared to me, I did not know that was to be my destiny.

The other figures in the painting, those of the Condemned World Gods, melted away from the scape leaving only the Guardian and the green light which grew larger. Quite interestingly the painted wings were gone, His expression became less stern, and to me He looked warmer and more Human than the celestial imagery with which He is often depicted in high art. I was moved, for He seemed with knowing eyes to understand me, even to love me. And suddenly, He spoke to me from the image for the first time...

Lyndz closed the book and set it beside her. She looked on the statue again for a few moments, and then closed her eyes.

"You're a natural, Master Kodi, no doubt about it!" exclaimed the swordmaster. Kodi's daily swordplay under Jaden's direction had been almost transformative. "I've rarely seen anything like it! You are as intuitive as Prince Nikal when I began training him years ago. As I said, I knew it wouldn't take you long. You are not at Tiliruf's level, which, quite frankly, would be genius if you were, but already you are quite capable of defending yourself. I'm pleased, very pleased! You will definitely be a swordmaster someday, and probably sooner rather than later."

Kodi was sitting on the ground, winded after a heated bout with Hadon in which he performed brilliantly against the far more experienced man, having knocked his sword from his grasp and pinned him to the ground. Kodi grinned enormously at the compliments, but he was worn out and sweating furiously in his heavy hauberk in a hot mid-morning sun. With amazing resolve, he had repressed his hangover, though Tiliruf had ensured he was well-watered and well-fed at breakfast after a hot bath. The headache returned now, and he begged Tiliruf for more water.

"You...you're good to say so, sir. Sorry," he panted. "Sorry, Master Jaden, I don't think I can go more just now, though."

"Kept you up half the night, did he?" Jaden said, chuckling. "I'm not surprised. Not getting your friend in trouble, I hope, Master Tiliruf?"

He gave Tiliruf a comically reproving look.

Tiliruf was, of course, more used to drinking strong liquors than his Solantine friend and cheerfully knelt down and helped Kodi consume a large canteen of cool water. "Master Jaden, you're just like that Mother Idamé that came with the Lord Curdoz! Why is everybody convinced I'm going to turn Kodi into some kind of rascally rapscallion!"

"Because just maybe you're one yourself," intoned Manwul, who threw down his shield. He had been dueling Tiliruf until a few minutes ago.

The others chuckled, Tiliruf likewise. "Well, maybe I am, but Kodi's not. What's drinks and coppers and the occasional pipe-smoking, eh?"

"Nothing, of course," Manwul assured him, and yet his tone turned somewhat dark. "It's that we've come to like Master Kodi, but drinks and coppers is tame entertainment for the likes of you, so if you try tarnishing him with any of your heavy gambling and North Bend shenanigans, you'll have us to answer to!"

Hadon stood beside Manwul, crossed his arms, and nodded his complete agreement.

"I'm NOT going to do anything to...to *tarnish* KODI!" shouted Tiliruf who suddenly felt backed into a corner. "I swear!"

"It's all good, it's all good!" said Kodi still trying to catch his breath and to stand up. He felt badly that they were laying into Tiliruf without cause, and yet he couldn't help the upsurge in pride that these disciplined swordsmen whom he had come to admire so well were taking up for him. "Don't worry, friends!"

"We trust *you*, Kodi," assured Hadon, brushing past Tiliruf. He pulled Kodi up onto his feet.

"You liked me fine, until you met Kodi!" observed Tiliruf.

"Rest assured we still like you!" said Hadon. "It's just that we know what you're like, and Kodi's a better man than you!"

"All right, all right!" interjected Jaden sternly. "Sorry I made my little quip, gentlemen! I only meant to tease, of course! These friendships are all good, and I think we can all tell that Master Tiliruf and Master Kodi have a good one going, and from what I see, each gains only good from the other."

Tiliruf nodded appreciatively. Yet he was still somewhat put out and couldn't quite let it go without saying one more thing. "I'm telling all of you now, that, like you, I have great respect for Kodi! He's... well he's become like a brother to me in a few short days. I...I know he's a better man than me, and I'm not...I swear it on my mother's grave...I'm not going to lead him astray from his goals or do anything to bring him harm!"

Manwul and Hadon both were surprised and sufficiently chastised by this sudden seriousness on Tiliruf's part. They knew it was probably the only time the man had ever sworn anything on his mother's grave.

Manwul reached out and performed the soldier's grip with Tiliruf. "I ask your pardon, Tiliruf. I spoke accusingly."

"I, too," agreed Hadon, repeating the same grip with Tiliruf. "I should see it as Master Jaden does."

Tiliruf nodded as Kodi came and put his hand on his shoulder.

"We are *all* friends even if none of us are flawless," added Jaden. "I well remember a couple of scalawag Brigadiers, who not so many years ago were pleasure-seeking *fools*, am I right? You spent half your lives carousing in North Bend!"

Manwul and Hadon both looked down sheepishly.

"You're right, sir," said Hadon.

"And how they have become good men since that time."

"We owe it to you, sir," said Manwul.

"No, not really. I only discovered your talents and gave you a focus through specialized training. You owe it to your own friendship with each other, the Discipline you adopted together, and learning better and holding each other since then to a standard. You will allow the same privilege for these younger two to build each other, for I tell you it will happen—is already happening. Now, the rest of you walk over to the archery field. I'd like to speak with Master Kodi for a moment."

The others did as they were told, walking together and talking away. The three were on friendly terms again as if the previous exchange had never taken place.

To Kodi it had all been a revelation.

"You have an effect on people, Master Kodi," said Jaden, promptly addressing Kodi's startled look. The two walked together slowly towards the archery field, staying out of earshot of the others ahead. "Don't get me wrong. It seems you inspire loyalty. You were the leader among those at home, weren't you? Your friends—the other boys and young men? They would follow your lead, wouldn't they?"

Kodi smiled and nodded. "I suppose my father is like that, too."

"Not surprising. It is happening here. Do you not see it?"

"But...well, maybe not Tiliruf, but the others are a bit older than I."

"And as you see, it doesn't matter. Already, they admire you. There's a quality about you; it's a quality that many leaders of history have, Master Kodi. It's a friendliness and generous spirit, or at least it is related to that. And an eager discipline and an unassuming self-confidence that is infectious. The common soldier is drawn to it. I know I keep comparing you to Prince Nikal of Nant, but you truly are like him in some ways. Although, the prince is somewhat more reserved. Unlike you, who are quite sociable, the prince prefers to be alone or in the company of one or two. But when he is required to lead...he does."

"I hope I get to meet him someday, then, sir." Kodi paused for a second. "I thought Manwul and Tiliruf were about to come to blows!"

"If something of the sort should happen again, I want you to act like a captain and order them to desist. You watch, and I guarantee the men will stand straight and listen to you. If men will offer you their loyalty, then you must learn to control them by setting boundaries. Jealousy occurs among friendships, too. It is not only associated with romances. But good men respond well to boundaries once you set them, though they need to be reminded of them sometimes in stern words."

"You think the men would follow my orders like that?"

"You prefer to draw people in and then persuade them or even better to come to some consensus. That's best in much of our living, but army life and war, as you must realize, requires otherwise. If you were to give the order, Manwul and Hadon would quite likely follow you on your quest with Lord Curdoz." Jaden smiled at the surprise on Kodi's face. "I heard of your visit to the unit at East Gate."

"High Master Naloro gave me permission. Tiliruf has some friends there, Lukas and Colinn. I met them at the beach. They asked me to visit them on duty, so I did."

"Yes. The red-haired brothers; they were also students of mine. Their father is a good friend. Those two would follow you, too. What I understand from the captain there, you were greatly admired. He said to me, *That Master Fothemry from Solanto is very popular with the men. They were drawn to him like moths on a lantern, him and his friendly ways. Good moral fiber there; disciplined, smart, confident. Respectful. Natural leader if you ask me. Engineer's mind, too. He understood the entirety of the gate's mechanisms in half a minute.*"

Kodi looked down, a bit embarrassed. "Well, I, uh..."

"And have you studied battle tactics?"

Kodi looked at him, surprised. "Some. Mostly Terianh the Great."

"Excellent, excellent. Baggaro would be of great benefit to you, as well."

Kodi looked puzzled. "Baggaro? I think I've heard his name before."

"Well, you certainly should have. He was a great general. He's from..."

But Jaden didn't finish, for he was interrupted.

"Kodi! Ko!" called a frantic female voice from behind them. She was running towards them across the lawn, Musca at her side.

"Lyndz?" said Kodi, shocked, and to Jaden he explained, "It's my twin sister! Er, and our dog."

"Kodi! You're here, just like I saw you! You really are! Oh, Ko!" She ran to him, and despite how sweaty he was and the hauberk he wore, she embraced him anxiously.

"What is it, Lyndz? Is something wrong?"

It was then that Tiliruf and the others came racing back as well. "Is there a problem, Lyndz?" he asked.

"No!" she replied breathlessly. "No! Nothing's wrong! Oh, Ko! He just spoke to me! He finally spoke to me!"

"What? You mean...?" Kodi's eyes grew wide.

"Yes! Meical! The Guardian! Just now! In the garden!"

"Really! Lyndz, you had a Vision?"

"Meical the Guardian!" exclaimed Tiliruf, his momentary concern turning suddenly to mocking skepticism. "You sure you hadn't been smoking too much on Curdoz' pipe?"

Kodi didn't even have to take up for her, for Lyndz herself, obviously on fire, blasted him. "Just because you don't accept the Guardian, dolt, doesn't mean all the rest of us don't!"

"Dolt!" said Tiliruf with amused shock. "Did you just call me a dolt? That's one of your better ones, Lyndz."

"Be silent, Tiliruf!" ordered Jaden hotly. He then nodded to Hadon and Manwul, who, shockingly, lifted Tiliruf bodily and carried him kicking back to the archery field. Jaden then nodded to the twins. "I am glad to meet you, Lady Lyndz! I am Jaden. Your brother here is a great young man, and likewise I can tell you are a great lady. And a very beautiful one I might add. I shall leave the two of you alone. May the Guardian Affirm you in all your endeavors! Master Kodi, I'll have your bow and quiver delivered safely to Sage Enric's home. Go with your sister."

He bowed to Lyndz, patted the Elentine Noble on the head. "Best breed in the world!" he said.

"Oh, Ko!" she said again, as Jaden walked away. "You've got to come with me!"

"Well, sure, but where?"

"Back to the garden! I've got to show you! And I left the book there, anyway!"

Kodi was beat, but he managed to remove the heavy hauberk and set it alongside the other gear used for their training.

"What book? The one Theneri wrote? Lyndz!" He looked at her with the question on his tongue, for he suddenly remembered something she said a few minutes ago. Had he not experienced it with Theneri, he would not have realized.

"Yes! Yes!" Lyndz was too excited, and yet Kodi could also tell that she was struggling with other emotions. He reached out and held her hand as they walked in the direction of the head of the lawn path that led to the gardens, Musca leading. "I'm a Moment Master, Ko! I figured it out with that book!"

She then launched into her whole story beginning with the moment during her meditation the day before when the image of the statue broke into her mind.

"...so you see, it was the Meicalian green light *within* the Mode that was the biggest clue! It only happens with Moment Masters! But I wouldn't have known it probably for a long time if you hadn't had your experience with Theneri and told me about it. Which is why I thought to try to locate a book on the subject. That was lucky, too. More than luck, if you ask me."

"But you were awake? That's really different than for everyone else."

"Being in the Mode is a bit like it, like sleep that is, at least that's what Idamé says."

Until now, Kodi had never really understood this. He had attempted 'emptying of the mind' several times with both Enric and Curdoz, the state of mind that can help the Gifted enter the Mode, but, due to his energetic nature he struggled with the patience needed for it, and he never could understand its value. Neither of the Sages acted particularly concerned about it, either, saying it would come to him eventually if he was Gifted, which they all believed he was. But if Lyndz could achieve the Mode with the exercise, he could, too. Maybe, just maybe, although Curdoz had never suggested it, he could speak again to Meical. He was determined to try harder at the exercise in future.

He realized, however, that he was becoming a bit self-absorbed when it was his sister he should be focusing on.

"Are you all right, Lyndz?" he asked kindly, squeezing her hand.

"I...I am, but...but like you told me in Felto it was very emotional. The connection...the kind friendship...as though I was being enfolded. But I'll be more prepared next time."

They traveled through the Palace gardens and finally to their destination. The stone statue of the Guardian stood rigid as always, unchanged certainly in Kodi's eyes. Lyndz went promptly to the bench and retrieved the undisturbed book. She then proceeded to explain to Kodi precisely what happened: how she had sat and emptied her mind and waited for the image to break through as it had the day before.

"...but it became real, Kodi! I at least *thought* I opened my eyes, and the statue itself *became* Meical! The wings vanished, the marble turned to skin, and like Theneri said in the book, there was all this green light, and He became very Human-like. He reminded me so much of you! He was strong and handsome, and He was like you in some ways—very brotherly and warm. But like Father, too. He...er...spoke to me."

"He seems to use different ways. I only heard His Voice in my Vision. I never saw His face. Are you going to tell me what He said?"

Suddenly, she looked embarrassed. "I must keep exactly what He said to myself."

"You mean...you mean He told you what He expects...what He expects you to do?"

A tear fell, and she sat on the bench.

Kodi looked at her. This was unusual. Meical had not declared any such specific warnings to him, and he had told his family and the Sage and the Matrimonial pretty much the whole tale. He and Curdoz had discussed the details of it several times. And yet, it occurred to him that Curdoz had admitted that he himself had not divulged the entirety of his own Vision. In addition, Kodi certainly believed it wise not to discuss his Vision with random people. In all likelihood, his mother would speak to his father of it, and Curdoz had discussed portions of it with the trusty Enric, his fellow Sage. But otherwise, it was not likely to travel to anyone else without Kodi himself permitting it.

He nodded his acceptance. He would not press his sister. He sat beside her, reached around her shoulders and drew him to her. "I don't have to know. I'll stand up for you if the others push you. I don't think they will, though. Well, Curdoz won't. I don't know about Idamé."

For her own part, Lyndz was overwhelmed by this first encounter with the Guardian, and was grateful for Kodi's reassuring presence, understanding, and refusal to try to weed out of her the entirety of her encounter. It was unfortunate that she had to keep him in the dark, but the Guardian had been quite specific.

The words came to her again as she leaned back into her brother's embrace.

"...if the men were to know, in order to protect you, they will try to stop you. That instinct was engraved upon the Masculine Energy by the Creator, and the best of men act upon it. And your brother is one of the best of men, as is Curdoz, my Servant. But they have other tasks, and it is the Feminine Energy that is needed. I have chosen you for this purpose, for the Gift has come to you. Therefore, the men must not know what you are about until you have undertaken the separation. I deem it will be some time yet, but by that time, you will have gained more endurance, knowledge, and skill. Only with Idamé should you share this, and with the other female who will soon come to you to lend her friendship and protection. Other women may wish to share the secret and the danger. You may share with them, as you see fit to trust them. I foresee them teaching you good skills." He smiled. "Musca will go with you. Keep him close to you once you leave the land of Ulakel. And even now as I speak to you, I foresee another possibility. One man may be desirous, at the last moment, of going with you. If so, do not stop him, for his desire will be based on a choice for which I do not wish to interfere..."

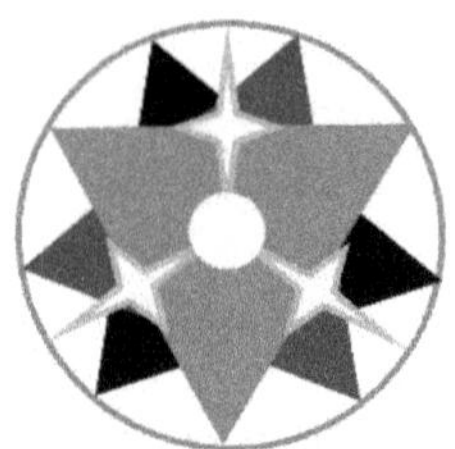

Chapter 9—Dresses and Swords

There was both excitement and angst among all of them that afternoon. On the one hand all were happy for Lyndz that she had like the rest of them now connected to the Guardian through a Vision and in the process discovered her rare and potentially powerful Gift. Yet on the other hand it was plainer now that she too, in addition to Kodi, would be involved in some significant danger ahead. Idamé admitted that she had all along held out hope that Lyndz would not have to face real perils and, being the only one privy to the Guardian's message to Lyndz—Lyndz had taken her aside and as Meical directed, secretly told her—she was full of worry and yet was required to hide it from the others to maintain the secret. The men found the Matrimonial oddly quiet through the remainder of the evening.

Curdoz was troubled, in part because he was uncertain how to help Lyndz without clearer information. Yet he was also concerned that Meical's secrecy on this had a motive behind it. As a Sage he discerned much and didn't like the portents: the Guardian did not want the rest of them to know what He communicated with Lyndz, for the Guardian did not intend the rest of them to be involved in whatever it was. The Sage deduced that at some point in the future Lyndz at least would be required to pursue a quest separate from the rest of them. He did not know yet that Idamé or others were to share Lyndz' burden, but even if he had, it probably would not have made him any less uneasy. All he could do was to remind her and the others that Moment Masters had a Gift that could be of value to an enemy, and like with that of Theneri's, it was best to keep the knowledge of her particular Gift as private as possible.

Kodi shared Curdoz' unease, and though it took him longer to reach the same conclusions as the Sage, it all shuffled around inside his head the rest of that day, and by the time he went to bed that night he too had realized that whatever it was Meical wanted Lyndz to do, the Guardian did not intend for Kodi to assist his sister. He had recently concluded that his twin was exceedingly capable and that he had been underestimating her potential. Yet, it occurred to him now that a future separation would likely take place. It upset him. He really wanted to question Lyndz, yet he had promised not to and knew it would be unfair to do so. Lyndz had no intention of stopping Kodi from whatever was his Calling, and so likewise he knew he had to do the same in her case. He had to trust Lyndz, and he had to trust Meical. It irked him, as a man, compounded by his deep love and sense of protection for his sister, that he might not be present to champion her as needed. He had trouble sleeping that night—rare for him.

The following afternoon found Lyndz, Idamé, and Hollina exiting the driveway in Enric's small carriage at the same time that Master Genehbro, accompanied by his son, entered the driveway in one of Genehbro's much larger and fancier coaches. He was coming to escort the Sage of Tirilorin to his new offices in the Palace.

Though Enric was of course still planning to dwell in his own home, he was moving his administration into a space in the same Palace tower as Genehbro's offices. It was in fact the same set of rooms that Sage Royllen had occupied a hundred years previously when he had attended as a witness the signing of the Abdication documents of the last emperor, Genehbro's grandfather, Zaralio. From this location as in days of old, Enric would manage the day-to-day affairs of the Orders of the Guardian in the Republic and be near in order to advise Genehbro. Though the latter was not emperor, his position both as a Master on the Assembly and as the wealthiest and most prosperous businessman in the country made him very important, and Enric would from now on be in on the discussions and planning related to Genehbro's management. It promised to be a position of significant influence. There had already been some rumor regarding this in the city, for Genehbro's proclamation and the new arrangement had become known, Genehbro himself having made the knowledge public. Not all the rumor was good, for the majority of Tirilorines, though they may have had respect for Enric as a kind, generous, and elderly gentleman, otherwise did not believe in the reality let alone the role of the Guardian Meical and believed those who joined the Orders to be odd and archaic. To combine Order Disciplines with Genehbro's business operations, which had an enormous impact due to their vast size on the overall economy of the country, in addition to influencing his votes on the Assembly, was looked upon with skepticism. Yet with newfound wisdom in his conversations with Curdoz, Genehbro no longer concerned himself with what anyone else thought.

Enric, though aging, had, with Genehbro's proclamation, been renewed in focus and determination. He was a keen administrator already, and the added responsibilities seemed not to trouble him. Rather, they energized the old man. Only that morning he had spoken to Curdoz of this.

"I believe, Brother Curdoz, that even as war is coming and the world is to experience much conflict, there is great hope in this other situation. Genehbro's change of heart, in addition to your own coming to

me as a part of your quest, and perhaps even Lyndz' own revelations of yesterday, have made me realize again how much the Guardian is at work in the world and in this city. I never believed He had abandoned us, of course, and yet I had begun to think most everyone else believed He had. My desire to retire and move back to the Valley has been due less to my age than to my belief that there was little more I could offer to encourage the people in this country to look beyond themselves and see that there is something greater and higher to be striven for than trade goods and wealth. Yet if Genehbro can see the higher and the better, then so can others. Driving out the self-possession and the cynicism of free peoples is just as important as fighting wars against evil enemies."

Kodi had overheard these words and he was pondering them now as he watched Genehbro and Tiliruf emerge from the coach. He had been standing there, as he had seen off Lyndz and the other women as they left for Madam Arlay's tea. He had made every effort to remain close to Lyndz since the revelation of the previous day, for she was still full of emotion from her contact with the Guardian and had only absented himself to attend his morning lessons with Jaden. When Kodi looked at Tiliruf walking beside his father, he thought his friend subdued. There was an unnatural crinkle between his eyebrows.

When Tiliruf saw Kodi, however, he attempted a smile.

"Hello, mate."

Genehbro with typical exuberance walked straight up to Kodi and shook his hand. "Good to see you again, Master Fothemry!"

"And you, sir. I've been meaning to thank you, sir, for your kindness in hiring Swordmaster Jaden to train me."

"Ah, yes! No need to, though. Considering Lord Curdoz' words to me recently I believe we are all in this business together, eh? I am grateful you have come to our city and been such a good friend to my son, here. He and I have had some long conversations the last several days, and I find you a worthy man based on his loyalty to you as a friend, and also from my observations and what Jaden has told me. And others, I might add. Anyway, Jaden tells me you have achieved much in only a week's time! Even bested Hadon yesterday, I hear! I'm here to fetch Master Enric, and yet I am wanting you to come with us as well. Tiliruf here tells me he has promised you the opportunity to scour the old armories for a sword to fit you? You should come now and do so, yes! There are some good blades there, eh? Imperial swords I believe are the best, though the Nantians set much store on their own modern steel. Whatever you choose, we shall have it sharpened and polished and find a new scabbard for it, eh?"

"I look forward to it, sir! Yes, I will come!" He chuckled to himself, for he now realized where Tiliruf had learned at least one element of his common speech pattern. *"Eh?"* did not seem to be used by many others in the city of Tirilorin.

Genehbro then marched past Kodi and entered into Enric's front door, leaving him alone with Tiliruf.

"What's the matter, Ruffy? Why so down?" He looked at his friend, who promptly collapsed on a step and invited Kodi to sit beside him.

"Ah, mate. Father and I have been, well, like he said, having some long conversations lately. This morning's went on and on. Which is why I wasn't there to practice with you and Jaden today. Been a real eye opener. Er, yeah, but I don't know if I can really talk much about it just yet. Still running around in my head, eh? But, yeah, I don't know. Well, I...well, if I do start talking about it, mate, then just sort of let me talk it out, all right? I'm sure I'll open up about it sometime. Maybe over a drink or two. Or three."

"I'm here for you, brother."

"Thanks, mate. Sorry if I seem sort of gloomy."

"It definitely isn't like you."

"No, I reckon it isn't. But yeah, mate! You come, all right? Jaden's going to meet you and me in the old armory. He wants to help you pick out a sword. He thinks it's important for some reason you find one 'of historic significance.' Oh, er, and by the way, er..." Tiliruf added with atypical modesty. "They're going to have this big ceremony in a day or two and Jaden's going to declare me a Swordmaster."

"Really! Congratulations! That's amazing, Tiliruf! Swordmaster! Ah, I'm envious. Couldn't happen to a better man, though."

"Er, yeah, it could. Hadon. Manwul. Only Jaden's so picky. But oh well, thanks, mate. I suppose I really am excited about it."

"Neither are as good as you with a blade, and you know it. Quit putting yourself down. I know it was hard what they said yesterday morning, but you know I don't care..."

"It's not just them," Tiliruf interrupted. "Some things Father said, too, I guess is bothering me more than that, but anyway."

"You didn't let me finish. I don't care what others might say. Some things are more important than others, and I care about friendship and brotherhood, and as far as I'm concerned, you're the best friend I've ever had, and you and I are going to try to stick close, you hear me?"

"Yeah, mate, I hear you." Tiliruf finally achieved his more natural smile and put his hand on Kodi's shoulder. "Well, it's tradition for others of Jaden's students to stand by in the ceremony, so you're to be there, and Hadon and Manwul and Lukas and Colinn."

"I'm honored!"

"And you have to wear a sword, so you definitely should pick one out today, so we can have it sharpened and polished in time. Oh, and by the way, is Lyndz angry with me? About yesterday?"

"She hasn't mentioned it. You're the last thing on her mind right now, I can tell you that."

"I, uh, made a promise to Father today I would keep my mouth shut when others talk about religion. We had a heated discussion on that. It had never been an issue between us before. He's changed, for sure. Since Curdoz came. Anyway, I guess I owe her an apology."

"I'm going to be blunt with you, friend. Meical the Guardian is real, and all of us—Curdoz, Lyndz, Mother Idamé and me, too—have seen or talked to Him in our Visions."

"You, too? Well, maybe I'd been wondering about that. A little. I heard what Curdoz said at the Assembly."

"So, you really were paying attention. You want to know everything?"

"No," Tiliruf said bluntly. "No, I guess I don't. I don't think I want to know too much, quite frankly."

"'Cause maybe you're a tall chicken that wears gold and silver-threaded knee stockings."

Tiliruf grinned at his friend's jibe. "'Cause maybe I want to live a free life without thinking there's Somebody Out There DIRECTING all my actions and choices."

"'Cause you're a chicken. And you need to quit thinking of it as 'religion.' Meical isn't about religion. He's about caring about what's good in the world. Fighting the bad and affirming the good. Curdoz has taught me a lot. Religion was for the old times, during the Ralsheen and before, and everybody was turning it into great nonsense, and the worship of Siriné corrupted it altogether. I don't think acknowledging the Guardian as a Messenger qualifies as a 'religion.' Religion is full of doctrines and worship and time-consuming expectations, and even the meditations of the Monastic Order barely qualify. Do you really have a problem with the work of Healers and the Bonding rites of Matrimonials? I don't. They're Gifts! And practical and have a lot of meaning. And the Monastics are hard-working people and do a ton of good. I admit there's one or two things I don't like, like the Vow. I know everybody jokes about it here, and we do in Solanto, too. The Principles are universal, and they're all about being good to each other. But when it comes to Meicalian Disciplines you adopt the Disciplines that work for you. Those in the Orders respond to Meical when He Calls them in a Vision. Your choices are still your own. The Vow is less important than some other things. There's not a Power in the universe, Tiliruf, that can stop you holding your arm in front of you and choosing whether to move it to the right or to the left. I believe the Guardian to be wise, and so I've *chosen* to trust Him, see? I also think of him as a friend and a brother. What I've found is that He seems to want the same that I want. He's Called me, and I know in part what I'm supposed to do. Or try my best to do. And the real point is that I *want* to do it and not that He's making me do it."

Tiliruf had by now grown as close to Kodi as he never had anyone before, so unlike with Lyndz yesterday, he tried to set aside his skepticism.

"I believe that you believe it anyway, though it's still beyond me. And what are you supposed to do, mate?"

"Eliminate the Alkhan of Eastrealm Khestadon." Though Kodi had in the past in his conversations with Lyndz expressed the idea that in some way he was meant to counter the Alkhan, this was the first time he had stated aloud what he believed his heart had been telling him specifically he might have to do in the end. Maybe his musings since Lyndz' own Vision yesterday had sharpened his thinking on it.

"You! You're going to hunt down the Alkhan and kill him?"

"Yep."

"And just how're you going to kill a centuries-old evil sorcerer-king?"

"Don't know. Haven't figured that part out, yet. And there's some other adventure, too, that has to do with the Qeteral that I'm committed to. But you say you don't want to hear about my Vision, so I won't trouble you with it. You still want to come along?" Kodi asked this in a nonchalant manner and in such a way as to test his new friend's true resolve.

Tiliruf sat there staring at Kodi with open mouth. Finally, however, he responded. "Yeah, mate. I suppose if you get right down to it I wasn't so unaware. Guessed at some things. Ignored some things. Yeah, I really do. Somebody needs to watch your back, eh? And, er, I really am ready to leave home, and you know, having a friend or two to learn with seems good to me."

"Good enough for me. Who wouldn't want a genuine Swordmaster at their side? Yet, what if you find you are called elsewhere?"

"I'll do what I want, mate. You just said I could move my hand left or right and it's up to me what I choose."

"That's right."

"I choose not to be a chicken, then."

"Good one. All I meant by it is that you never know when something important separates us and we feel the need to follow another path. Based on what little I know from Lyndz yesterday, I'm kind of concerned about that. It doesn't matter, you know, so long as you do what you believe is right, one choice at a time."

Again, Tiliruf stared at Kodi. "You sound like old Enric. I guess I shouldn't be surprised. I feel like I've had truisms tossed at me like balls by about a dozen different people ever since you got here."

"Maybe Somebody Out There's trying to tell you something?"

"No, mate, stop! Ah, great. That's what I *don't* need is some ethereal spirit thing watching over my shoulder night and day!"

"Ruffy, even if Meical was capable of doing that, I don't think that's how it'd work. Not the constant judgment like what I think you're thinking on. That's another part of the old religions that doesn't work. That'd be enough to drive a man mad with preoccupation, constant second guessing, and guilt. If anything, the Orders is about building up people, not condemning folks for every blunder or less than ideal choice. But you know, I'm talking about more than I know. Personally, I don't like being alone. If Meical is standing at my shoulder or if somehow He's inside my head, then I'm fine with it. More importantly, though, is that we keep our family and friends close, even if it's just in our thoughts. It's our relationships with each other that are more important than anything else. Of course, that's the Principles."

"More truisms?"

"I'm telling you what I think."

"I think you're cracked, but I don't really care, eh? Because what I know about you is plenty good enough for friendship...and brotherhood, like you said."

"Actually, you said it first yesterday."

"I did?"

"Sure. You said *he's become like a brother to me in a few short days*. Really meant a lot, too, when you said it. I won't forget it. 'Course I was fightin' the remnants of a bloody hangover."

"Guess I'm full of truisms, too, eh?"

"Except most of yours are funny and have to do with...shenanigans."

"'Bout the only kind I know, mate."

They both laughed and stood, belatedly following Genehbro into the house.

It appeared this gathering of Madam Arlay's was more a grand garden party than it was a private afternoon tea. A number of prominent women had come at Arlay's invitation, and it included much talk, not only of the upcoming dance but also of the recent Assembly deliberations. The two dark-skinned women from Hralindi and Essemar were present. Madam Midianna was there giving greater detail of her ideas for a female Brigade. She had a number of rapt listeners gathered round her on Arlay's rear verandah when the hostess emerged through the rear door escorting Lyndz, Idamé, and Hollina.

All stood then and gathered around the Solantine ladies, eager to get to know them, Lyndz in particular, as her reputation for beauty and intelligence had made its way through the gossip circles of the city. All were as polite as they could be to Idamé as well, and a number of the older ladies, including a Matrimonial or two whom Hollina knew, leaned into her to hear what she was willing to tell of news in Solanto. Matrimonials were the one Order, due to the high regard most women still had for the Bonding rites, that was immune to the general skepticism typical of most Tirilorines to the Meicalian Orders. As long as they did not mention Visions, the Vow, or Order Disciplines, Matrimonials held up well among the circle of influential women of Tirilorin.

Lyndz now had the opportunity to encounter the infamous Stri Itruvi, and she instantly could see why Kodi, who preferred natural beauty, would be repelled by the showy, gussied-up, bosomy businesswoman. Nevertheless, she found Stri to be exceedingly knowledgeable about a vast array of topics—Lyndz was certain she had seen her once or twice in the Library—and one of the few who had studied up on the role of women in other societies. She had even had extensive conversations with the Eastern ambassador women since their arrival. Inspired by their tales, Itruvi offered her own gold to outfit a female Tirilorine Brigade unit in appropriate attire suitable for war, in addition to refitting two of her trading vessels as transport ships to be placed at their disposal.

All this talk was fascinating to Lyndz who had never in her life been around a large set of women of similar tastes and ideas as her own. And they were educated beyond most of the women she knew in Solanto. Her time in the Convent of the Matrimonials in Ferostro was the only other time she had been around a group of educated women, and yet they were, with the exception of Idamé, intent upon a narrow subject range and their duty as Order Members. Her only commonality with them had been botany and gardening.

She did believe some of Arlay's friends worldly, and yet despite this she could see underneath that they had above all a desire to maintain the beauty and the glory of the city of Tirilorin. On the other hand, though the words of Meical were running through her head regarding the idea there may be other women who might wish to share in Lyndz' quest, she could tell that none of these could possibly be to whom the Guardian was referring. She found herself wondering who, then, He could mean. She also wondered who the specific female was to come to her soon to be her friend. Again, it was none of these.

After tea and refreshments, Arlay and her lovely daughter Linova, with whom Lyndz got along quite well, took her, Hollina, and Idamé to their private quarters to peruse several dresses they had kindly laid out for the Solantines to consider. Linova suggested either the white or the light green one would go well with Lyndz' beautiful emerald pendant. Lyndz agreed they would be lovely, and yet her eye was drawn to one of a rose tone. Arlay and Hollina too replied undeniably it would go well with her dark olive skin, and Idamé agreed it would be stunning. Linova helped her to try it on in her mirrored dressing room, and the effect was so perfect the other ladies oohed and aahed for long minutes. Linova had a darker rose sash which could be easily traded out with Lyndz' green one so to still be able to wear the gold buckle from Princess Isatura.

Idamé was much harder to please, which at first Lyndz and Hollina believed was because the Matrimonial was resistant still to wearing a fancy gown in the first place. As it turned out through much goading on Hollina's part the real reason she was being difficult was because she thought every single one of Arlay's offerings were as beautiful as all the others, and so it was hard to choose. In other words, in her heart, the typically self-denying Matrimonial wished she could wear each and every one! All the ladies laughed at this astonishing admission which caused Idamé to pink up enormously. Finally, however, she chose a lilac gown which when she tried it on fit her quite well. She proclaimed she had a mostly purple shawl that would complement it, too.

A mile or so away from Arlay's mansion where the women were on a mission to choose dance gowns, in the armory of the imperial Palace three men were on a mission, too.

"Emperor Gandeen's second son Paduren used this imperial-made blade in the First Barantine War. That was a fine show of imperial might. Barant was forced to remain within the Empire and pay tribute. Unfortunately, the Second Barantine War did not go so well at first. If Paduren had been there too it would have proved a different situation. His brother who was emperor by that time, Sanvelt, was one of the Empire's worst generals."

"What happened?"

"He lost and got his stiffrod cut off, remember me telling you that?" quipped Tiliruf.

"That's a concocted legend, Tiliruf," said Jaden, rolling his eyes.

"Was that the time?" asked Kodi, chuckling. "I gathered that it went badly. I mean why didn't Sanvelt send a better general?"

"They did a year later," said Jaden. "By that time the imperial council had removed Sanvelt's military authority and given it to his younger brother Paduren. Paduren conquered Barant and restored imperial authority there. But it was the last time. Paduren succeeded to the imperial throne because Sanvelt had no children of his own..."

"Because he got his stiffrod cut off; I keep telling you that, and you don't believe me. It takes that good *thrusting* action we chaps like so much, eh? *Mmph!*" Tiliruf grunted and made some rather illustrative hip movements. "And if you don't have anything to *thrust* with, Master Jaden, it doesn't happen! *Mmph!* You don't make baby emperors by lickin' the empress's nipples! No matter how much she might like it. *Mmm...MMPH!*"

Jaden, having over long years proven his patience with all his young male students' racy remarks, innuendo, and crude displays—he didn't care as long as they demonstrated proper decorum in front of ladies—rolled his eyes again, though he couldn't stop a brief chuckle, especially since Tiliruf now had Kodi shaking with laughter. When the latter finally quieted down, the swordmaster continued. "So Paduren became emperor. He was the last of the great emperors of Anterianhi history. In the Third Barantine War, about fifty years later, after Paduren was long gone, Barant won its separation from the Empire and disavowed the Guardian Meical, kicking out their Sage and the Orders. The Ice Tribes with whom they traded tried to get them to build a temple to Siriné, but from what I understand to this day the Barantines acknowledge no other authority than their king. They still trade their famous carpets with Hralindi, which is why the merchants here can still get them sometimes. Other than the minimal carpet trade, they have little to do with the countries of the former Empire. They only have regular dealings with the Ice Tribes. They still skirmish often with the Elenites over territory. Until this new war with the Alkhan, warriors and princes from the other countries who wished to hone their skills in battle would travel to Eleni and fight for their king. Such as myself. And Prince Nikal and his older brother Crown Prince Lekktor. Their mother, Queen Gatha, is from Eleni. Anyway, Paduren's is a famed sword, Kodi."

Kodi performed a few moves with it. "I do like it, sir. What else would you like to show me? It's mighty good that Master Genehbro is being so generous."

"He likes you, mate."

"He knows good blood when he sees it," added Jaden. "Well, Master Kodi, there is this one over here. Quite frankly it should be in Solanto. King Carlomen would probably give a pretty penny if he knew we had it here. Or one of his nobles should they like collecting."

"Who did it belong to?" Kodi took the blade from the Swordmaster. Though it was slightly longer than some, it was light in his right hand. It would need a new leather grip, for the old one was dry-rotted and crumbling. The two edges were smooth, and it wouldn't take much to have it sharpened and polished. Like many here in the armory, it was well-preserved with regular oiling. There was hardly any rust on it. It was long, a cutting blade, but with a tapered point as well, good for a final thrust. It was not unlike blades Kodi typically chose for his bouts with Manwul and Hadon.

"I mentioned General Bagarro to you the other day."

"Bagarro was from Solanto?" asked Kodi, surprised. He still felt there was something about that name that seemed familiar to him. "You never did tell me who he was."

"You don't know about Bagarro, mate?"

Kodi stared at him. "Unlike you, I didn't grow up beside a fifty-thousand volume library! Grandfather had more books than anybody in the county, but I haven't read about him. Master Jaden, what am I missing? Like I told you I feel I've heard his name somewhere."

"I would have thought he would be well known in Solanto."

"Er, Tulesk is relatively remote."

"He was a nobleman from Solanto. The last emperor, Zarelio, chose Bagarro to lead the imperial army against the Alkhan in the last war. Bagarro's forces defeated him and kicked the enemy out of Lintiri after it was overrun."

"I've got a book on Bagarro, mate. I'll bring it with us. You can read it."

"I will. Master Jaden, did he actually fight the Alkhan?"

"He intended to. Unfortunately, at the last Bagarro was killed by a hoard of the warlock-king's great slave bears that he had hidden behind a veil of invisibility. According to the tale, this blade killed several of those monsters, and Bagarro fought ferociously. In the end he was overcome. There were too many. The troops went after the Alkhan in anger, but he fled in his ship. Almost the entirety of his army had been annihilated, though. He never bothered the realms of the Northern Continent again until this most recent war. Bagarro is considered to be the last great hero of the Empire before the Abdication."

Like he had done with all the other swords Jaden showed him, Kodi made several moves with this one as well. Something itched in the back of his mind.

"I like it, sir. So, it was made in Solanto?"

"It was assuredly made there, yes. 'Twould be most fitting, I think, for another Solantine to have it."

Kodi nodded. He continued to swing it back and forth with great vigor, thrusting, parrying.

It felt right to him.

"Looks like he's made his choice, Master Jaden," offered Tiliruf.

"Very good, then, Master Kodi. Hand it back and I'll have it restored."

"Thank you, sir." Kodi let it go reluctantly. Jaden left them, and the two marched back to Tiliruf's rooms. Kodi was staying the afternoon, for Genehbro had invited everyone to dinner to celebrate Enric moving his administration into the Palace.

"... and you can try on some of my clothes for the Dance, eh? Got something in mind. The trousers are a little big in the waist for me; they ought to fit you well."

"Only if you insist."

"'Course I do. Got to get you spiffed up for the damsels. And I bought you a pair of brand-new knee stockings!"

"Curse you!" Kodi jested.

"I thought I was your brother, eh? You shouldn't curse your brother; that's got to be in the Principles somewhere, eh?"

They did find a suit of clothes perfect for Kodi for the Dance, though he refused to try on the knee stockings saying that the day of the Dance was soon enough. Afterwards, with a couple of Tiliruf's bows, the two friends went out for some archery practice until dinner was called.

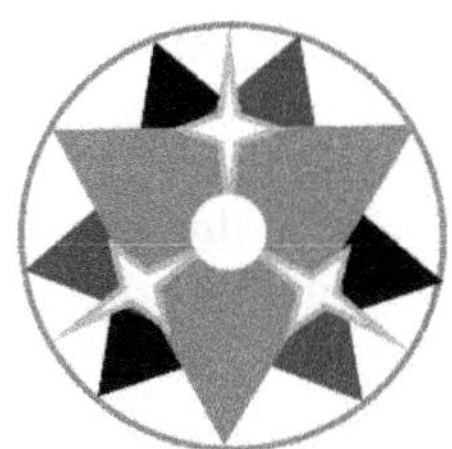

Chapter 10—Important Visitors

The small dinner to which Genehbro invited Enric, Hollina, the Solantine travelers, and Jaden and his wife took place on the back verandah by the lawn upon which Jaden held his classes and which looked out over the distant sea. Small only in the number around the table, otherwise, much wine was poured, and a tremendous quantity of food was consumed, with the dinner discussion on all topics. Now, Jaden was let in on the circle of those who were familiar with the quest to the Qeteral and some of the more general implications of the Visions, to which he was both utterly astonished and yet not in the least surprised.

"The Guardian knows what He is about, choosing people such as yourselves," he said to Lyndz by whom he was sitting. "As I said the other day, I wish you well in all your endeavors."

It was about halfway through dessert when the keen-eyed Kodi, looking off beyond the sea southward, exclaimed, "What is that? They have gigantic eagles here in the south?"

All looked in the direction he was pointing.

Jaden stood from the table and walked to the edge of the stonework. "Genehbro!" he called. "Send a runner to Naloro!"

Genehbro had also stood. He walked over to where Jaden was standing. "It has been ten years!" He called quickly to one of the servants who came running. "Have Rithean ride swiftly to Master Naloro and bring him here straightaway! They will land here on the lawn of the Palace...they always do."

The servant hurried off.

"One is carrying something, Father! See that, eh? Is it...is it a man?"

"What are they, Tiliruf?" asked Kodi again. "Curdoz?"

Curdoz looked at Kodi. "Not *what*, Kodi, but *who*. And never forget that. You are about to have your wish granted that you made when we approached Guardian's Gate."

"Etoppsi!" Lyndz cried out. "They are Etoppsi?"

"Remarkable, noble people," said Lady Ludley, Jaden's wife.

Kodi gasped. All were standing at the stone-work balcony now watching as the two gigantic flyers, one carrying what they could all now see was a man, approached the city.

"One is male, and the smaller one carrying the man is female," said Jaden. There was still plenty of bright light in the west as the sun was only beginning to set. "Genehbro! Could that be Hawking?"

"I remember him coming when I was a boy!" said Tiliruf.

"If it is, he's over a hundred years old now. This is beyond belief. I say it may have to do with the war. It could be the Alkhaness has moved against Berug!"

"We will find out soon," offered Enric. "They're close, now. I think Jaden is right. I think that is Hawking!"

"Who is Hawking?" asked Lyndz and Kodi at the same time.

"Royal Hawking is his title and name, uncle to the King of Berug, brother to the former," said Enric loud enough for all to hear. "A good man...male, I should say. They call themselves 'males' and 'females;' they don't tend to use Human and Qeteral expressions for the two genders, though they do use the terms 'daughter', 'son', 'mother' and 'father', and they call children 'toplings.' I do not know who the female is." He turned to the twins. "And do not be embarrassed by them my friends! As you may have heard, they have tight fur and wear no garments. They think Humans are fools if we bring it up or stare at them wrongly, though they are usually quite patient with our kind. They can be rather formal in their speech. But they are good people. Hawking is an old friend of Genehbro's, and a bit more down to earth than some I have met in the past. They travel to Nant often, but seldom come here. Ten years ago was the last time. It was Hawking then, as well, like Tiliruf says."

"It is he," said Genehbro with finality. "Tis his coloring. Tawny with shiny black wings. He is very old. There is much gray, now. He appears healthy! He was always a tough old bird."

Within a moment the Etoppsi had arrived gracefully on the back lawn like gargantuan eagles landing on the edge of an eyrie, and the dinner party made its way quickly down the verandah stairs onto the green to greet the giants. The Human walking now with them appeared small in comparison. The twins were admiring of their shapely muscular fitness. They could not of course help but notice anatomical variances in comparison to Humans. The female's breasts were huge, unmoving like tight muscle, and nipples could not be seen due to her fur. In contrast to the tawny male, she was a stunning silver-gray, both fur and wings. Her hips and buttocks were pronounced, though not out of proportion to her overall size. Based on Tiliruf's joke the other day, Kodi half expected the male's sexual anatomy to appear obvious as it did on Human men. Instead, it looked to be withdrawn in a tight but large buldging *pouch* camouflaged by longer, darker fur. His shoulders and chest were massive. His abdomen rippled in large waves as he walked. The sensual quality of their bodies enhanced by their sleekness reminded one of virile horses.

"Well, of course they don't wear clothes!" Lyndz whispered to Kodi. "They're above them. Beyond them. Like gods."

The observation was precisely what Kodi thought. He remembered what Curdoz said to him in Aster, *Clothes are unworthy of their race.*

The sheer size of the giant creatures along with their exotic, almost fierce faces and vast wings folded behind made it difficult for them not to stare. Along with the twins, Idamé was the only other present who had never before seen such creatures, and she too was mesmerized.

"It's Prince Nikal!" said Jaden. "Fascinating! He was only here two weeks ago! Yes, Genehbro, it must be as you say—the war. He would not have come back so soon otherwise. Not in such a fashion as this!"

"Brave man, eh?" said Tiliruf as an aside to Kodi. "You'd never get me to fly with one of those!"

"I don't know," replied Kodi. "I think it'd be incredible!"

"Like I said this morning, you're cracked, mate. And still cracking."

Genehbro stood forward. "Hawking! What a grand surprise!"

"My old friend, Genehbro!"

Kodi thought it thundered and looked up in the sky for a storm cloud, for the ground seemed to tremble when the giant Etoppsi male spoke.

The two friends bowed to one another. Shaking hands between the two races would have been a one-sided affair, as the hands of the larger were as big as large platters. It would have been like a man shaking hands with a house cat. Despite their size, their hands were not unlike Human hands, the tips of their fingers and palms were not fur-covered, though were nearly black in color. Standing close now, the twins noticed an intoxicating scent exuding from the Ettopsi, a pleasant sort of musky aroma.

"Introductions are in order, I think," boomed Hawking again. He turned to the female. "This is Rainwing of Green Isle. She is the Geography Professor at the Institute, a great scholar, and a veteran of the Dragon Legion."

Rainwing bowed to the others. "I am glad to make your acquaintance."

Her voice did not shake the earth, and yet it was still deep and round.

"Some of you know His Highness, Prince Nikal."

Several heads nodded.

"Yet there are some I do not know. New faces." Lyndz thought the prince's tone was grim and yet not deliberately impolite. It was more a curious detachment as if he were reading the minds of all present, gauging the character of each. His eye rested momentarily on Curdoz' stole, and then upon Idamé's shawl. He raised an eyebrow. "Rainwing, here are surely at least one or two from your Prophecy."

Lyndz gasped, though no one noticed. It suddenly occurred to her what Enric had just said about the genders, and Meical's specific words to her in the Vision. The *female*. Of course! She stared at the massive Rainwing. And when she looked again at Prince Nikal, taking in his strong, manly bearing, and hearing him mention a Prophecy, she then had a revelation. Yet for the moment it seemed unwise to proclaim it without further news.

Nikal looked at Jaden. "Tell me, Jaden, old friend. Is one of these your student Tiliruf? Genehbro, I did not speak to you when I was here before. You were out of the city. You have a son Tiliruf, do you not?"

"I do, Your Highness. This is he."

Tiliruf bowed quite graciously. "Glad to know you, Your Highness. Tiliruf at your service."

"Several times here over the years, yet we've never met. But I remember Jaden saying something of you in one of his letters to me."

"Yes, Prince," said Jaden, who having known Nikal most of his life typically called him this, dispensing with the more formal *Your Highness*. "And yet the day after tomorrow this one will no longer be a student of mine."

Nikal understood and looked at Tiliruf with additional interest. "You are that good? Few have ever achieved such a measure under this master's tutelage."

"Your Highness, if you are still here in two days, then I would be greatly honored of your presence at the ceremony."

Nikal nodded without smiling. "I will attend." He then looked at Genehbro and then to Enric who was standing beside him. "Master Enric, I need to know, *by the Guardian*, if all here are...friendly."

Lyndz rightly understood this to mean 'trustworthy.'

"Feel free to speak your mind," assured Enric. "At least until Naloro gets here. What is this Prophecy you speak of?"

"I will let Rainwing repeat it in a moment, since it came to her from the Guardian." He looked at Curdoz and bowed. "My lord Sage. Your stole bears the white stag of Solanto."

"I am Curdoz, Your Highness."

"You may please call me Nikal. It seems I am in need of your assistance, Lord Curdoz."

The Sage nodded a second time and winked. "Then please call me Curdoz."

"Rainwing, you wished to know what a shawl is!" he said a bit louder. He bowed to Idamé and politely kissed her hand. "They must still wear them in Solanto, of course. May I have your name, Mother...?"

"Idamé, Your Highness."

"The Guardian is at work, then, even in our first meeting here, Nikal!" stated Rainwing eagerly. "The Prophecy is being fulfilled even now!"

"The Prophecy spoke of a 'twin.'"

This time Lyndz' gasp was much more apparent.

Now Curdoz' eyebrow was raised. In a flash barely slower than Lyndz' he saw it all. The Prophecy from Deroge's book that Lyndz had deciphered. The Sage was suddenly moved to speak it aloud:

The Staff of Terianh he will wield,
For all the world with which to shield.
Vanaratu knows where the Staff is hidden.
He will seek, for it is bidden.
Eight will give of what they have
For him to gain the Eagle Staff.

It was then, however, that Rainwing took up the next verse.

He mustn't deny the gifts of the others,
New family, new sisters, and genuine brothers.
One twin he trains who shares the Staff,
Terianh's son who makes them laugh,
A Sage who hears Vanaratu's call,
And he should heed the one with the shawl.

"They know it, Curdoz!" exclaimed Lyndz, unable now to keep silent.

"Then 'twin' does refer to you or me!" said Kodi to his sister, equally amazed by what he was hearing. "And Terianh's son..." he then looked at Tiliruf. "*'Who makes them laugh.'* Am I an idiot or what? Of course!"

Tiliruf's eyes popped wide. "What the Guardian's craggy Teeth are you talking about, mate?"

Nikal forced a smile and looked at Kodi. "You should have picked that one up quick enough, Master..."

Kodi bowed and spoke eagerly to the prince. "Kodi, Your Highness. Kodi of the House of Fothemry of Solanto. And this is my twin sister, Lyndz."

Nikal kissed Lyndz' hand as well. "You appear as a Nantian princess out of old tales."

"As they have Escarantine heritage, Nikal," said Curdoz.

Nikal's eyes moved from one twin to the other. "Which, centuries ago, originated in my country. Yes, that would explain it." But then he focused on Kodi. "That particular reference is of you, for I must train you. And as the wise Hawking here makes clear, in the Meicalian Orders, males train males, females train females. War Wizards are of the Order of the Guardian. The Staff is for you and me, I suppose. Yet you are young, as Hawking guessed."

Tiliruf stared wide-eyed at Kodi now as if he'd never before seen him, the words being bandied about coalescing slowly in a resistant mind. "You? The Staff of Terianh!"

"Young, yet of his full manhood, responsible, disciplined, and worthy, Prince," put in Jaden, ignoring Tiliruf's astonishment. "A master archer having trained all his young life, and a natural with a blade with only one week's schooling, under my direction. A leader among others. He has made an impression among the men in the city."

"Impressive," Nikal stated with bare emotion. He then looked at Lyndz again. "Yet I would grant you are one of the eight friends, My Lady."

"Of a certainty," stated Rainwing with a broad smile. Though she was mildly frightening to look at by Humans unfamiliar with her race, in some ways she acted friendlier than the Human Nikal. "I am not so unsure now her face did not flash across my mind in the Vision! I am almost certain it did. And...Mother Idamé is it, *the one with the shawl?* I believe the three of us females will become good friends. Do you not think so, Lyndz?"

Lyndz nodded. "Yes! But who exactly are all of the eight?"

"It should be discussed later," said Enric suddenly. "Here comes High Master Naloro. He knows somewhat of what Curdoz has shared, but he is a Meicalian skeptic and not a part of our circle. Yet, in my opinion, he will need to know soon, perhaps even tonight, whether he believes it all or not."

Kodi looked at Tiliruf who still had astonishment painted in big eyes and open mouth all over his freckled face, and winked. His friend wanted very much to say something just then, and it was all the man could do to restrain himself. And it was all Kodi could do to refrain from laughing, despite the enormous portent of the truth behind the Prophecy Lyndz had deciphered from Deroge's little book, confirmed by Prince Nikal, and the idea of himself having possession of the Eagle Staff of Terianh the Great.

Naloro was there. He bowed low to the Berugians, and when he saw Prince Nikal with them, he started.

"Your Highness!" he exclaimed. "Was that you we saw in flight with the Berugians? I think everyone in the city had his eyes to the sky and is aware of the arrival of our southern friends."

Nikal nodded. "High Master, Royal Hawking and Rainwing of Green Isle have tidings from Queen Silverwing of Berug. I came along...in order to lend my assistance."

Naloro looked at Hawking who plunged right in with his thunderous voice. "High Master, forces loyal to the Alkhaness of Eastrealm captured our southernmost tower on the Great Wall. Within the

Infested Jungle itself, I might add, a feat only possible, in Queen Silverwing's opinion, by dark magic in the employ of the enemy. King Eagleron has led a force to retake the tower, and Queen Silverwing has undertaken the task of putting our realm on a war footing."

"So it's true, then!" said Naloro looking at Curdoz. "You were right! It was only a matter of time before the Alkhaness made a move."

"Rainwing and I left Berug on the orders of Queen Silverwing, and I do not know how King Eagleron has fared. I would presume he has retaken the tower by now. However, we do not know yet whether this is an odd and isolated event designed to test our defenses, or if it is a prelude to a greater event to come. Queen Silverwing is acting under the latter presumption."

"So, you are preparing for war."

Rainwing spoke. "High Master, the King and the Queen both are convinced that the magic of the Alkhaness has been strengthening. The Queen and I are close, and I can tell you that she at least is of the opinion that open war with Westrealm Khestadon is inevitable and that it is going to come very, very soon. You must look to your trading posts and their protection, and the Nantians their fortresses between here and the eastern Human kingdoms. Fort Danzilet would assuredly be a high prize. She will assuredly attack these first in order to have full control of the coasts of the western half of the Southern Continent. She has always claimed those lands for herself despite your footholds and forts there."

Naloro looked at Hawking. "Your coming to us will be the catalyst that makes the difference. I have worked it and worked it, for I'm sure His Highness has told you I favor mobilization and engagement in the east. But it has been slow-going for we are required to build consensus on such a grave matter. I think we have it now. I will send word to all the Masters that the war vote will be called at an emergency Assembly to take place tomorrow. You must speak to them, Royal Hawking." He then nodded to Nikal. "I can assure you we are almost there, Your Highness. I am sorry it has taken even this long. Things should move much faster after tomorrow."

Genehbro came and stood by Naloro. "We have everything in place. Except for one final piece." It was then that both Naloro and Genehbro looked at Swordmaster Jaden.

And then Nikal came and stood by his old trainer and put his hand on his shoulder. Now everyone was looking at Jaden, for the rest of them had no idea what was going on in this cryptic exchange.

"You...you want me to command the Brigades?" He then looked at the prince with shock. "You put them up to this when you were here last time, didn't you, old friend?"

"They know your worth, as well as I."

"Indeed," added Genehbro. "And as Master Enric has demanded of me, all of my resources are at your personal disposal, Jaden. My entire fleet is yours and all the treasure of the House of Terianh. Others will follow my lead. The city will stand tall in the conflict to come."

"You are to be proclaimed War Marshal of the Republic. The generals will respect you, Jaden," stated Naloro.

"Damn it all," whispered Tiliruf in Kodi's ear as the whole party walked across the lawn back towards the stairs to the verandah and the rear entrance of the Palace. "Did you hear that? I'm poor as Spens now Father's pouring it all into the army."

"I doubt it," Kodi whispered back. "All you have to do is melt down that liquor cabinet in your bedroom into about five thousand silver pieces. Besides, who cares?"

"Then where am I going to store the bottles, mate? In my pockets? And what about gold, eh? How does a man function without gold?"

"Melt down that outrageous mirror stand by your bathtub, towhead, as if you have time now to stand naked and stare at your muscles and your rod in a mirror every day."

Tiliruf side-eyed him and grinned. "What's wrong with that, eh? That fellow likes to be stared at; he's a right damn specimen! And what about that ship I was going to have built, like Curdoz', but bigger and fitted out in ambernut?"

Kodi stopped walking and looked at him. "You were really going to do that? Like we don't have a mission or two ahead of us and battles to fight?"

"Got to come back to something fun, eh, eventually. I'd actually begun sketching out the specifications, you know."

Kodi crossed his arms and stared. "And you think *I'm* the one who's cracked!"

Tiliruf paused. "The whole world's cracked, mate, if the Staff of Terianh is real."

"You admitted this morning to me the Alkhan is a sorcerer who uses magic; I presume you believe the same of the Alkhaness. You'd better hope the Staff of Terianh is real, because our side's going to need something, for in the end it's not just about who's got the bigger, better armies! The enemy's more magically powerful now than in Bagarro's time! And apparently picked up more magic lately. You heard what Rainwing said." Then, as if to himself he continued, "It's all making more sense to me now. I knew it! War Wizard! I just knew it! And I bet Curdoz...and Theneri and Father Marco and Enric...I bet they all knew it, or at least suspected. That's exactly why Theneri gave me that book. Not to mention Meical Himself. They just all wanted me to learn it for myself. Lyndz suspected Curdoz knew more than he was telling. To piece it together slowly I guess so it wouldn't seem so overwhelming all at once. She and I talked out all this back in Ferostro. We talked about it, but it's hard to believe when it comes right down to it. War Wizard! I think maybe I always knew it from the moment I woke up from that Vision."

Tiliruf, thankfully, had finally come to a point where his skepticism of Meicalian everything was now trumped by his respect for his new best friend. He had the grace now to at least pretend to see things from Kodi's perspective. He'd even begun to think Kodi's perspective might be the right one. At least in some ways. "Listen, mate. If that Staff is real, and if you...and Prince Nikal, are going to be War Wizards...you're going to be the most powerful men in the world! When the Alkhan finds out, he will come after you, Kodi! He will want to kill you!"

"I 'spect he will, but not if I kill him first. Still with me?"

Tiliruf swallowed hard as he looked with the most serious expression he'd ever tried at his friend. "Wish you'd quit asking me that. I am, mate. I know a good thing when I see it and don't need Sages or invisible Guardians and convoluted Prophecies to explain it to me. I want to fight on the right side. I don't know what I believe anymore, but it's all—whatever it is—going to center around you and the others; I see it now. I want to be there in the thick of it. I didn't go to all this damned trouble these years to become a Swordmaster for no shafting good reason."

"Pretty muscle boy in the gold mirror really does want to be a hero...eh?"

Tiliruf burst out laughing, amused by Kodi's insight and wit. "Among other things. I'm a man, aren't I! And I like being one. What makes you think I'm that much different than you on that, mate? As if you didn't use my mirror when you took that extra long bath yesterday morn."

"Just practicing my charming smile." Kodi chuckled. "Besides, I like the luxuries of all these fancy baths since I left home. They're amazing. I really like being in water. Had a brandy hangover, too, remember? Anyway, makes me feel good. Clean. Reminds me of...oh, never mind. Ruffy, if I really thought you and I differed that much at the core of things, I don't think we'd be great friends so quick, do you? But you're more than just any man, Tiliruf, don't you understand? Your dad's a great man, but you're the *point,* don't you see? The last son of Terianh the Great! Live into that! It means something, I'm telling you!"

"Sounds like I don't really have to say much to you about what Father's been talking at me about the last week. You seem to already be pretty close to the mark." Tiliruf paused, reflecting, and Kodi did not interrupt him. "Maybe I am what you say, mate. I like the bloke in the mirror, you're right, because I'm familiar with him, and I feel pretty good sharing that one's skin. But there is something I look at maybe more often than the mirror. Think about it sometimes when I look in that mirror. Wishing...wishing for..."

He shook his head and went silent.

Kodi thought he'd go a bit out on a limb, hoping Tiliruf wouldn't overreact. "I know what else it is you look at."

"No, you don't. I never...I've never mentioned it."

"Walk with me, brother. I'll show you."

The others had already entered the rear of the Palace. Though he was anxious to hear more from the newly arrived guests and to see more of the Etoppsi, Kodi decided the company could do without their presence at least for a while. Nor did he wish to go through the Palace, though it might have been quicker. Instead, he led Tiliruf to the side path to the grand gardens on the east side and then through its upper terraces. All was shadowed now the sun was sinking beyond the Palace. He passed the garden room containing the statue of Meical the Guardian and smiled as he did so. It was now an important place in his sister's life.

Yet his focus now was on his friend, a Voice in Kodi's head telling him this was important. Tiliruf, uncharacteristically quiet and curious, was willing to let Kodi answer the unspoken question in his own way. Kodi climbed the stairs that led to the level at the front of the Palace upon which were the carriage driveway and the vast front green lawn. He paused and stared ahead momentarily to let Tiliruf catch up. When he did, Kodi traipsed straight across to the large round, fountain pool within which stood the enormous golden statue of Tiliruf's first illustrious ancestor, founder of the Anterianhi Empire, Terianh the Great. In his right hand was the Staff. In his left, his sword. No one else was around. The sun in the west was setting much faster now, and a thin though bright crescent Solvermoon was high in the east. Golden Orohmoon stood smaller, though full, lower in the sky. It would appear brighter once the sun had fully set.

He pointed up at the statue.

"How did you know?" Tiliruf was perplexed...at first. "Ah, no, don't tell me."

Kodi said nothing and waited. Finally, Tiliruf sighed and spoke again. "Yeah. I come out here most mornings, and a lot of evenings about this same time, actually..."

"And...you eat an apple," said Kodi winking.

Tiliruf caught his breath. After staring into Kodi's face he said, "Eh, maybe I do, sometimes."

Again, Kodi waited.

Tiliruf sighed finally. "He liked apples. Actually, he loved apples. Terianh came from Eleni. Wasn't called that then; it was a province of the Ralsheen Empire. Anyway, he was a slave boy and worked in an apple orchard alongside his mother before he was conscripted into the Ralsheen army. Eventually he looked back on it as decent work and missed it, especially the time with his mother. He never knew his father. Terianh would steal and eat right away all the apples he could during the harvest. We have a huge apple orchard on the closest of Father's estates about five miles east of the city. I like going there. It's also where the horses are, the breed that descends from B'ulstread."

Tiliruf pointed up at the horse, then sat on the short stone wall enclosing the fountain pool and was silent.

Kodi kept quiet too for a time. He took the opportunity to study carefully the great equestrian statue, for it was the first time he'd gotten such a close look. The burnished gold reflected deep orange in the setting sun. Mostly, he peered at the Staff. It was perfectly straight, notably long, and thick in Terianh's grasp. At the head of the staff was a round sphere like a moon clutched in the talons of an eagle with outspread wings. It appeared precisely the same as the much larger eagle statue on the pinnacle of the tallest Palace tower. It too clutched a correspondingly larger round globe. He had not paid much attention to the globe before, his focus being on the Eagle.

"That tower was built by the Etoppsi to suggest the Staff, wasn't it? I wonder where it is. What do you know about it, Tiliruf?"

"Made of holly by the Qeteral. Disappeared after the Conquest. Terianh's last entry about it was this: *It cannot be retrieved by an enemy.* That is all I know."

"I wonder what makes it magical."

"You'll have to ask the Qeteral that one, mate. Ah, look!" Tiliruf indicated the front of the Palace where a man was descending the long flight of marble stairs. "It's Prince Nikal!"

"We shouldn't have been away so long. Hope Curdoz isn't annoyed we left them. Probably talking all sorts of matters we should be in on."

"Yes, but they could have sent a servant to fetch us, eh? I bet you he wants to talk to us. Or you, *War Wizard.* He acted rather forbidding when he got here, you think, eh? Don't remember Father ever telling me he was like that. And Jaden thinks the world of him and talks about him all the time. Tonight's the first time I've actually met him. We didn't cross paths when he was here before. Hmm. Things happen to people. He's been a commander in the war in the east. It's got to weigh on him."

"I saw what you saw. Something tells me it's something else. Something more personal."

They stood and waited. In another minute the prince from Nant stood before them, eyeing them closely.

Kodi bowed, followed hesitantly by Tiliruf. "Your Highness."

"Though I am sure I will always defer to his wisdom, Sage Curdoz agrees fully that our quests are combined as one, and that for the time being I should lead the company. I have had much information tossed at me the last half hour and know now of your quest to the Qeteral, but our first mission when we leave here will be to hunt for the Staff of Terianh. There will be no need of bowing to me, ever. I am not a king, and I never want to be a king. You will call me Nikal or 'sir' except in the most formal settings. I am taking it upon myself to further your training for war, and time we have for such will be limited. Jaden...that is, War Marshal Jaden, is suddenly a very busy man." He then looked at Tiliruf. "I honor your skill as a Swordmaster, yet you will need more. When I speak, you will follow my direction and do exactly as I tell you. You will need greater discipline in the fights before you."

Tiliruf stood there still as a statue, mouth wide in astonishment, yet he did not dare to counter the stern prince. Though submitting in such a way to another man was about as awful to him as the idea of taking the Vow of Chastity and joining the Monastics, he swallowed hard and nodded acquiescence.

"Good. And yet," with this, Nikal attempted a smile. These seemed difficult for him. "You may speak your mind when we are not in the middle of something dangerous. Apparently, the Guardian thinks you capable of humorous wit."

He frowned again as if humor were the last thing he ever wanted to hear from Tiliruf. Nor at that moment did Tiliruf appear in the least likely to display any.

Nikal turned then to Kodi and said, "You appear solid, body and mind. I look in your eyes and see depth. When before I said you were 'young' I only meant it in contrast, I suppose, to me, and it was a reflection upon a discussion I had had before with Rainwing and Hawking. You and Tiliruf here are at an age common to the men in our army and navy. I even have officers at nineteen. And Master Jaden says you are tough and a natural at everything. High praise, Kodi. Have you ever wrestled a giant bear?" He winked when Kodi cracked a smile and shook his head unnecessarily. "What kind of rider are you?"

"Pretty good, sir. I've been around horses all my life."

"My own warhorse, Tindalle, was given to me by my father, purchased from Master Genehbro some years ago." He glanced up at the statue of B'ulstread and his rider, then back at Kodi and Tiliruf. "It is late, I know, yet the three of us are going to travel this evening by coach to Genehbro's estate in the country. The ride will give the three of us a chance to talk. Beginning early tomorrow we have work to do."

"What about the Assembly tomorrow, sir?" asked Kodi.

"We will not be needed. Hawking and Rainwing will likely overawe the reluctant Masters and bend them quickly. We will return the second evening in time for Master Tiliruf's ceremony. I have been made aware that the day after that is the occasion of some grand city Dance to which everyone has committed." Nikal sighed heavily as if this was to him the most useless frivolity. "We will therefore delay our departure till the following day. We will travel on one of my naval transport ships in harbor here. I must return to Nant, where we will arrive after a few days. I made a promise to retrieve General Aron who will be traveling with us as the final of the eight friends on the search for the Staff. Curdoz tells me his own ship is too small for all of us—Rainwing too will be traveling with us—he will send it back to Solanto. Old Hawking will be flying home to Berug. Where is this bow of yours Jaden speaks of?" When Kodi explained it was at Enric's home where they were staying, Nikal continued. "We will retrieve it as we leave here. Tiliruf, I presume all is set up for the Brigadier cavalry to train with the B'ulstreads?

"Yes, sir. Everything. Jaden, Manwul, Hadon and I train there regularly. I can assure you, sir, Jaden has done his work well by me. He has only had a week with Kodi, though. Sir, is my father allowing Kodi his own warhorse?"

"Eventually, I think, we will battle the Alkhan in the East where cavalry is one of our key elements. Until now he has directed his forces from the safety of his citadel in the mountains. Yet I think he will show himself should we acquire the Staff, for such a talisman can hardly remain secret. I suspect he will sense its magic the first time we use it. It is difficult to see that far ahead, though. The Guardian has said nothing to me beyond the one Prophecy...to Rainwing." He said this with some cynicism, Kodi noticed. "We must be prepared for all contingencies. Yes, Kodi is to have his pick among the best-trained colts unclaimed by others of the B'ulstread breed. Your father will be transporting large numbers of horses to the east. Those claimed by the two of you will travel with the others to Fort Danzilet, which is where I keep Tindalle. It will be some weeks I believe before we will meet up with them again. They will not likely be needed until we reach the far east, yet we will train more with them in Danzilet unless Curdoz deems we are behind on your quest to the Qeteral."

Tiliruf looked at Kodi, who was obviously elated at the idea of having a warhorse of his own.

"Like I said, mate. Father likes you. And you won't believe how well-trained they are. Father's trainers are good. You'll find B'ulstread's breed as docile as geldings until they feel like showing off, eh? Of course, they like to do that pretty regular. Anyways, you'll see; they think like people. They'll take to you in a heartbeat. In fact, you know, mate? I think I got one in the back of my mind that'll suit you perfect. Not quite three years old. Dash more spirited than some. He'll either knock you down or lick your face off, one of the two. Probably the latter in your case, Master 'Natural-at-Everything.' And then he'll be loyal to you like Musca the dog. You'll get to see the apple orchard, eh? Of course, it's not harvest time and the blossoming is long gone. Still."

"Musca...the dog?" queried the prince.

"Belongs to Lyndz and me, sir," said Kodi. "Elentine Noble. He..."

"Say no more!" said Nikal with a smile, the first fully genuine one he had used. "I'm familiar with the breed. I fought with Jaden years ago in Eleni. He is with you on this journey? We will take him with us tonight."

"He will be glad to get out to the country, sir. I think he misses hunting on his own."

"Very good. Tiliruf, send messages to this Manwul and Hadon to meet us there by second hour tomorrow. They could prove most helpful, particularly if they are Jaden's students as well. And if there are other Brigadiers training there the next two days, all the better. Very well, then, men. I'll have Genehbro order a coach here in front in half an hour. We will pause at Enric's home to retrieve Kodi's bow and things and then be on our way."

Hawking would have been much too large, yet he was to stay in specially designed Berugian quarters in the Palace as Genehbro's guest. As it was, Rainwing had to stoop to enter all of Enric's doors and carefully watch always the location of her folded wings so as not to knock over the furniture or bump into the chandeliers. The Monastic servants had to clear much of the furniture out of the largest guestroom and arrange two bed mattresses lengthwise on the floor for her comfort. Yet she wanted this time separate from the Republic crowd now gathered at the Palace around Hawking so to confer privately with Lyndz and Idamé. Enric thus did his utmost to make her feel welcome.

Lyndz wasted no time in opening herself to her strange new friend as the three sat that evening in the parlor between Lyndz' and Kodi's bedrooms. Kodi and Musca had left earlier with the prince and Tiliruf. Curdoz and Enric had retired to conversation and a bottle of fine Escarantine wine in the little temple in Enric's garden. The two Sages wanted to go through everything they had ever read or studied, and to review every tale and rumor, regarding the World God Vanaratu.

Rainwing sat upon a sturdy oak center table. Considering their wings, Etoppsi never sat upon furniture with backs, and most Human-sized furniture would not accommodate their bulk.

The three were also drinking wine, although the silver goblet-shaped vase which the Monastic servants poured for Rainwing's large hand held the same quantity as two decanters.

"So, the Prophecy came to you, Rainwing, yet we had it too in the book I was telling you about."

The Etoppsis did her best to keep the volume of her voice low, succeeding reasonably, though it still was rumbly and caused the floor to vibrate slightly. "Clearly that portion of the Prophecy has an earlier source with this Seeress great-grandmother of yours, and you must tell me more! But there were additional lines when it came to me both before and after the verses we recited aloud. However, the other was of such a personal nature involving Prince Nikal I cannot repeat it without his express permission. Suffice it to say that the prince is under a certain amount of strain. Unfortunately, deeply personal events have transpired since the revealing of the Prophecy that have tested him sorely."

"Poor man," said Idamé. "I can imagine how the burden of the Prophecy would affect him."

"It is worse than that. All in all, the idea of wielding the Staff of Terianh is not the main source of the burden in his heart. Though he is resistance to trust and affection at this time, we must do our best to fulfill our role in the Prophecy as his friends. He will need us. However, let us steer away from that for the moment and discuss this Vision of yours, Lyndz!"

For the next quarter hour, Lyndz recalled aloud every detail.

When she was done, Idamé spoke first. "I must admit I am fearful, actually I'm petrified, of this task! When Lyndz told me of it the first time, my only thought was how small and unprepared we are! How to approach the citadel of the Alkhaness and gain entry without being captured and tortured is beyond me. This is a job for courageous men in disguise! How do we make ourselves invisible?"

Rainwing took a large swallow from her vase, set it down and folded her arms. "I deem you to be more courageous than you think you are, Mother Idamé!" The floor surely vibrated with her vehemence. "And the Guardian has Called you and proclaimed you a part of this great venture to save our world from the enemy! I know now I saw your face in my Prophecy Vision, as I did Lyndz'. You are as capable as any *male!* Now, moving about that country at night will likely be required, particularly in my case. If I can fight dragons, I can protect you. I see myself in such a role, and it could be a primary reason the Guardian has Called me to be a part of your group, particularly considering His words to Lyndz. We could fly there in less than a week of nights, of course. I know precisely what bearing to make. But I do not think that is the manner Meical wants us to use to get there. He made it plain to you that the time will present itself."

"And that there will be others who will go with us."

"Other females and perhaps one male? It is all very curious. I don't think this is something we can plan much in advance. It is like my time in the Dragon Legion. The beasts appear in the plains or the rare Winged kind in the sky, and we go after them immediately, or they will destroy the orchards and sheep ranches and the towns. We can but prepare ourselves and consider possibilities. Yet we have at least had experience and know how dragons behave." Rainwing paused, reached over for another swallow of wine and continued. "Mmm, this Nantian vintage is good. I got used to it while we stayed there. They make a good brandy, too, that we import to Berug. Describe how your Gift works, Lyndz. I have studied the Orders of the Gifted all my life, for everything about the workings of Meical the Guardian interests me profoundly. I have heard of Moment Masters and am aware that they are rare, but I know nothing about their magic and what they can do with it."

Lyndz retrieved and handed Theneri's book to Rainwing, yet it was so small in her hands she had a hard time with the pages. "Our books in Berug are perhaps as large as the top of that table beside your chair!" Rainwing pointed with a laugh. Nevertheless, she did manage to turn the pages, and bringing it close to her face she declared, "Yes, I can read this. I learned High Anterianhi on purpose so I could read some of the older works by the Orders. We have our own great library, you know, at the Institute. If you have read it through, already, then I would like to borrow it."

"It is thorough," replied Lyndz. "Theneri is extremely detailed on what the magic is capable of. From what Kodi and Curdoz tell me, he uses the Gift for spying on Filiddor."

"Spying! On whom did you say?"

Idamé explained, "Prince Filiddor rules a principality virtually independent of Solanto and is an ambitious and powerful ruler. Curdoz has Theneri keep an eye on him."

Lyndz then spent several minutes describing the Gift to Rainwing.

"...but I've only practiced the magic a couple of times since I had my Vision. Entering into the Moment is eerie. I don't like being there. Textures are strange, the seeming weightlessness of objects is strange, the lifelessness of people is frightening. Even the Mode itself becomes an instant and only a means of entry back and forth between the Moment and normal time, so it is not calming like it normally might be. Theneri clearly enjoys the experience for he finds it all intellectually fascinating. But I find it too quiet and lonely. It is almost like entering into a realm of death, a lifeless tomb. Also, I have a difficult time with the ethicality of observing others without their knowledge. I think that last would not be an issue for me if it is enemies I am observing. I'm not that squeamish. I will use the Gift for our advantage."

"I think the disquiet will wear off as you use it more, dear," said Idamé reassuringly. "And, when possible, once you retreat from the world of the Moment back into the Mode, see if you can force the Mode to revert to normal time and then relax in it for a while. I think that might help to dispel the discomfort."

"This page," said Rainwing excitedly, "says that Moment Masters can carry others into the Mode with them?"

"Yes!" said Lyndz. "It is unique to Moment Masters to be able to do that. Theneri did it with Kodi a couple of times, because he was able to use Kodi and send him into the Moment. Theneri is extremely old and cannot enter the Moment anymore..."

"At least not without help from a Healer with powerful Mind Support," Idamé clarified. "We're presuming Xeno is with him and is now able to help Theneri to overcome his deficiency."

"Sounds to me your group has had some adventures already!" said Rainwing. "You'll have to tell me more about that, too! This ability, though, that Moment Masters have to carry others into the Mode is a powerful thing. Why could you not carry me or another with you to aid you in the Moment? Then it wouldn't be so lonely or frightening with company. If this Theneri could use your twin in such a way..."

"There is great danger to the other," said Idamé, interrupting. "Theneri was reluctant to use Kodi, and they only did it because they felt it necessary. Kodi could have been lost in the Moment if Theneri had lost his grasp of the Mode. It would have been his end. His body would have disappeared."

"And Theneri speculates in his book it could even happen to the Master, too," said Lyndz. "If I should lose the Mode while outside the Dome of Meicalian light, I too could disappear. It's speculative, but I tend to believe him. Thankfully, losing the Mode is virtually impossible unless someone forcefully interrupts you, and since the Mode is only a couple of seconds for the Moment Master, that can't realistically happen..."

"Because there is no time for anyone to interrupt you! Of course," said Idamé. "I bet you that is why the Mode is abbreviated for Moment Masters. The Guardian probably built that into the magic as a safeguard."

Lyndz raised her eyebrow at this observation. "Even Theneri omits that in his book, but I bet you're right, Mother Idamé!"

"Female thinking," said Rainwing with a wink. The others laughed. "It's true, though. I'm sure this Theneri is brilliant, nevertheless, I bet you there is even more to this magic he has never considered. In my mind it has potential to be used as a weapon. Particularly defense."

"Really? How?"

"If you were fast enough...if you could train your mind to skip the Emptying of the Mind exercise and enter into the Mode instantaneously, observe your enemy's position, you could use it to..."

"Anticipate!" interrupted Lyndz. "Of course! Like in a fight! I see it, I see it, Rainwing! That's brilliant!"

Idamé didn't like it, for she didn't want Lyndz in any fight and said so. Nevertheless, Lyndz was at least able to convince the Matrimonial that practicing such anticipatory tricks could be of value in a pinch. "You know I don't want to become a fighting warrior like Kodi does! But, I'm going to use everything I have to combat the Alkhaness! She has magic of her own, and you can bet I'm not going to hold back. At the least this Gift would be cumbersome in such a situation, so I have a difficult time picturing me using it that way. But the Guardian gave me this, he expects me to do my best with it. There may be ways...ways that it could work for me."

Lyndz was so on fire from these new thoughts that she set her wine goblet down, got up and started pacing about the room. Which was more difficult than otherwise it might have been considering how much space the Etoppsi female took up. But Rainwing's enthusiasm had a way of transferring to Lyndz, and she just couldn't keep still.

"Fighting is a good thing when it is necessary. Yes, there is risk, but there are usually worse risks from inaction! Nevertheless, I think subtlety is the key," said the self-assured Berugian. "The Alkhaness is a thinker and a schemer, according to Queen Silverwing. She's less hot-headed than the Alkhan who is impatient for conquest. Now, don't get me wrong. She wants to control all the world as much as he; it's just that she is not likely to move until she has all her pieces in place."

There was silence for a time when Idamé stood, too. She was tense, and the good wine, strong though it was, was not settling her nerves. "It is all terrifying to me, and we may be jumping to conclusions, but I remember a number of details about that fortress. Visions stay with you, you know. There are surely ways to get inside. Women can go in disguise, too, I suppose. There are cooks, laundresses, laborers." She then looked at Rainwing. "Forgive me, though, but I cannot picture in my mind anything..."

"No. Admittedly, no. And I can't vanish at will like the Qeteral. If it were not for my wings, I could perhaps pull off the guise of the largest of her champion guards. It is believed the Alkhaness surrounds herself with the most massive Human males she can find, and they serve her as bodyguards and champions. Even so, I would be many inches or so taller than their very tallest, I'm sure. However, my role may become better known. Darkness will hide me and I can move as fast as a shadow. And there is likely nothing in all her realm that can stop me once I am out of range of arrows, as my wings can provide us quick escape. I can carry many Humans. Nikal is a large male in your eyes? I could have carried four his size. I am strong for a female Etoppsis, which is one reason I passed the tests to join the Dragon Legion years ago."

"I think it is you who have had the adventures!" said Idamé. "You must tell us all about your people and the country of Berug!"

Indeed, the conversation turned to Rainwing and her life in Berug. They talked together till long after midnight, sharing and learning, drinking more wine and laughing, and eventually going to their beds. Due to Rainwing's strong energy and confidence, even Idamé went to sleep quickly, comfortable in the thought that perhaps even she could attempt the struggles and dangers ahead, so long as she was not alone.

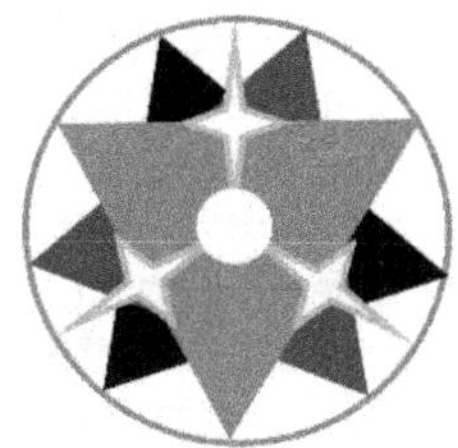

Chapter 11—Facing Change

The following day was an eventful one. The Republican Assembly met in emergency session, Hawking and Rainwing laid out the dangers, and High Master Naloro called for the final vote. It was unanimous. The Republic of Tirilorin would, along with Nant, aid Essemar and Hralindi in their war with the Alkhan and prepare for war with the Alkhaness as well. Naloro installed Jaden as War Marshal in charge of the Republican Grand Brigade, and by mid-afternoon some fifty stations throughout the city were already signing men up in droves. In time, stations in the surrounding provincial towns would recruit many thousands more. A sense of duty to old allies seemed to grip the country with the vote, though it may have been latent before. The wealthy merchants, worried about interruptions in trade and the confiscation of their ships for the transport and supply of the armies, realized that they had better adjust to the inevitable, support the war effort, or risk being ostracized by the masses.

"We have enjoyed the blessings of peace for many years," proclaimed Naloro. "It is time for sacrifice!"

The women were not left out. The Assembly vote to allow them to form up their own units was not unanimous, yet it was a sufficient majority. Madam Midianna was made responsible for female recruitment, and Jaden had officers in mind to lead them. To appease the more conservative element, it was agreed that only strong young women from the provincial farms or those with labor or riding skills be permitted to join. Should any ladies of the leisure classes wish to join, they would be required to undergo strenuous exercise routines for at least two months beforehand to prove their commitment to hardship and to build endurance. It was not really different from what was required of some of the male recruits, particularly some of the softer sons of the rich families of Central City. And yet a goodly number of these were not inclined to join.

And Jaden did not particularly want them. "Not all men are suited," he said simply. Yet he did issue an edict requiring all young men who did not join the Brigades to attend four days a week the new Programs that he was initiating in the city requiring regular exercise under the stern guidance of some of the older, retired officers, and he made warning: "There may come a time when more recruits are needed than are willing to volunteer at this early stage. You are to prepare your minds and your bodies should you be called to the city's defense!"

Spens was not at all pleased with the idea of being required to join one of the Programs and complained bitterly. He quickly realized his mistake. Though they all liked him very much and thought him both fun and funny to be around, none of his friends had the least sympathy for him on this, for every last one of them who were not already members of the Brigades went readily to the recruiting stations in Central City. Andir and Bendrick blasted him for his laziness. "You get your fat rump to the Programs!" said Andir. "Or you'll be the first one the Alkhan skewers like a pig if he gets this far! Think of your mother and your sisters, you little thumper, should he knock at the gates!"

Though his mind was in a continuous grumble, Spens never again said a word aloud in protest. And, in time, after some concerted effort in the Programs, he began to trim down and even began to feel more self-confident, strong and manly. Eventually, he even chose to join a unit assigned to the guard at the Hall of Government and learned defense techniques with the sword. In such a position it was unlikely he would ever be required to fight, but his friends were impressed with his newfound courage and willingness and demonstrated their pride in his efforts. This only encouraged him more.

Curdoz, taking with him Lyndz and Idamé, drove in Enric's carriage to South Port to retrieve the rest of their belongings, and to break the news to Captain Shond that his services would no longer be needed and ordered him to return to Solanto with a packet of letters for the Grand Duke. All the crew in their usual tipsy state were fighting emotion with the realization they wouldn't be seeing the beautiful Lyndz again perhaps for some time to come, if ever, and some cried drunken tears when Idamé kissed them on their cheeks and bid them all farewell.

On Genehbro's estate east of the city, the men were engaged all day long on horseback maneuvers. Despite Nikal's gray mood he expressed well-deserved praise for all of them, Kodi proving himself an excellent rider on the very horse Tiliruf had suggested for him—a B'ulstread colt by the name of Scadyne—and naturally capable in all their exercises even in heavy armor particularly under proper instruction. Nikal found Manwul and Hadon so exceptionally skilled he asked them if they would be willing to join their party when they returned to Tirilorin—though he did not mention the quest for the Terianh Staff specifically—on their way back to the east and the war.

He made it clear to them what their tasks would be. "In battle you will fight alongside Master Tiliruf. You will be his knights and protectors."

"I don't need extra protection!" objected Tiliruf, pulling up his horse beside them and removing his helm. He had momentarily forgotten his promise to the prince the evening before. However, Nikal stared him down menacingly, and he wilted. "Sorry! Sorry, sir! Yet you did say I could speak my mind."

"You will need protection!" Nikal said sternly. "You don't think you would be a great prize to the Alkhan or the Alkhaness? In battle you will be representing the House of Terianh, and you and your father are the last of that great House! You are no longer emperors, but they would proudly capture and then torture you, body and soul, and then send your head to your father on a platter! This is no old-fashioned knightly tournament! You wish to fight alongside Kodi and me, and I will allow it, but you will also have these two beside you at all times. And I may employ others besides. I have a large contingent of knights around me in battle lending their protection, and a great many have died in this war doing just that." He then looked at Manwul and Hadon. "You two will be his bodyguard in battle and in camp. Your purpose will be to preserve the House of Terianh and to ensure this one doesn't do something stupid."

Tiliruf turned ferociously red. Kodi had never seen him before so angry and embarrassed. Nikal was being patient in his explanation, but that last statement was humiliating, and Kodi wondered why Nikal was being particularly harsh with Tiliruf. Tiliruf had outshone everyone with his skills today. Kodi wanted to say something to reassure his friend, but now was obviously not the time.

It was Manwul however who stepped in and turned it all around. He proclaimed, "It will be my great honor to be at Tiliruf's side, to fight for and to protect the House of Terianh!"

Then, both he and Hadon dismounted and genuflected before Tiliruf as he still sat on his horse.

If anything, Tiliruf's face turned slightly redder.

Say the right thing! Kodi thought. *It's not the time for one of your jests! They're offering their lives to you, don't you see?*

Apparently, he did. There was no doubt that during the last two weeks under Kodi's influence some change had worked itself in the last offspring of Terianh. He looked first at Nikal, and realizing the prince was not going to interfere or embarrass him further, he too dismounted.

He nodded to the two men. "I...I never meant to imply I would not want you at my side. Of course, I am most honored to fight with you. Thank you, Manwul. Thank you, Hadon. I know I could have no greater protection, but more than that I know I will value your company when we go east. Together we will watch after our friend Kodi!"

With that the three of them engaged in the soldier's grip and placed their hands on one another's shoulders in a show of Tirilorine solidarity.

Then, Nikal indicated he wanted to speak to Kodi alone, and the two of them rode off to the distant apple orchard.

When they reached the rows of trees and were alone, Nikal spoke. "Kodi, I see now that Jaden's faith in you is well-placed. Not to mention the Guardian's. There is much I can teach you, but you have all the basics you require, and can already handle most of what comes at you. Curdoz expressed concern to me you were behind, and no doubt the struggles ahead will sharpen your skills, but I can reassure him...and you."

"Thank you, sir." Kodi was elated at the prince's praise. He had reached a new milestone in a very short period of time.

"I want you to know, however, that regarding the Staff of Terianh, I am as ignorant of its powers and capabilities as you. The histories tell somewhat of its magic, but I don't know how to control it any more than I can fly like Rainwing. Of course, we've got to find it first, haven't we?"

"I have only had the one Vision, and Meical did not tell me about the Staff nor how to use it. The book I'm reading is detailed and tells how Terianh made use of it, which is helpful, but how to access the magic, I don't have a clue. But for my part I have no qualms about it, sir. We will find it, and we will learn."

"You have a compelling confidence that I like quite much. I should myself brush up on the old tales and might take a look into that book of yours. Kodi, I want to know all about your Vision sometime if you're willing to tell me, but at the moment I would only like to know what it showed you of Tiliruf, for I presume from what little I got from Curdoz last evening that it did."

Kodi explained to him what he saw. And he admitted he thought it limited. "...and so, all I knew was that I was to seek him out and to gain his friendship, and that of course he was meant to come with us."

Nikal acted pleased. "He was sitting under that statue of Terianh the Great?"

Kodi hoped if he shared with the prince a bit of what Tiliruf had told him the evening before, that maybe it would help Nikal not think so harshly of Tiliruf. And so, he did.

Nikal listened intently. When Kodi was done, the prince said, "That is good, I must grant you. There's a spark there, then. Very good. I'm sure it appears to you I'm being hard on the man."

"You offer praise where it is deserved, sir. He will have to get used to that. He has me as his friend. I will watch after him."

"That's a diplomatic way of saying you think I've been a right beast towards him." Kodi looked up at the prince with a bit of a guilty smirk on his face. Nikal continued. "I think he is loyal to *you*, yes, which is an important start. But I want him to be loyal to himself, to his House, and to his country. You saw the manner Hadon and Manwul offered their services to him just now. He resists it, but he is a symbol of ancient greatness to some. He can grow it into something, or he can squander it."

"Curdoz says Tiliruf is on a quest to find himself. I guess I'm hoping it will come to him eventually."

"Hoping? It will not come *naturally*, if that is what you mean. Not without constant prodding. He's nothing like you on that, for your goals are clear, and I imagine they have been so for some time. So, you think I should try a different tack?"

Kodi thought long and hard as they rode between rows of apple trees. Finally, he sighed. "No, sir. He submitted to you last night, which was really something for him. I...I think it's a 'reaching out,' if you know what I mean. He needs you as you are, so no I don't think you're being too hard on him. Just don't expect me to be like that to him, even if I should end up being in a position of authority someday. I realize now I prod him too, but in my own way."

"I respect your honesty. I would not expect you to be anything to him other than the friend that you are. I will say this, the potential for Tiliruf to rise to prominence is there. Jaden thinks so and would never have worked with him these years if he didn't—it wouldn't have mattered how much gold Genehbro offered him, he would not have wasted his time. And Tiliruf *is* talented. By the Guardian I admit he was superior today. But because of that I do worry he might do something imprudent or rash. The self-involved streak is plain to see. I foresee the potential for darkness in Tiliruf's future. I think he will be tested. Sounds to me like Curdoz is thinking similarly. Sages see things often that only Meical Himself sees. But Meical also sees the potential or Tiliruf would not have appeared in your Vision at all, let alone sitting under the very statue of Terianh the Great. Nor mentioned in Rainwing's Prophecy. But I warn you, there may come a time when I'm not there, and someone will have to put their foot down and be hard. It may be that in that time, you will be the only one who will be able to save Tiliruf from himself."

Kodi swallowed hard. He could not understand all of what the prince meant, but, looking into his eyes and seeing the depth and the seriousness there and considering the man's long experience, he was not going to dispute him. "I am committed, then, sir."

"Good."

"Sir? Pardon me for asking, but I can't help but wonder if there is something disturbing you. I am committed to you, too, you see. This quest and that Prophecy bind us together, you and me."

Nikal's face visibly softened, and he brought his horse to a standstill. "You have good intentions, Kodi, but though I am troubled, it is a situation I am not prepared to disclose just now. But..." he looked over at the young man and smiled, "thank you for your concern. Jaden says you are the most genuine and open young man he has known. He is right."

"He often compares me to you, sir."

"Mmm. I think he may be wrong on that."

"Say rather that Jaden sees the good in people, sir. I am sure I am honored to be compared to you by him."

Nikal looked into Kodi's friendly face. "Graciousness and even wisdom in a young man." He paused. "I was certainly not as you at your years, and if anything, at least in my teen years, I was more indulging and selfish than Tiliruf. Yet I did have a change in heart. In truth, though, you're more like my friend General Aron than you are me. He is the naturally noble one. You will meet him soon, I think."

Suddenly, Musca appeared in front of them carrying two large rabbits in his maw. The horses shifted but settled quickly. "Speaking of Nobles, I was wondering where he'd got to," said Nikal. "I like that fellow. Slept beside me last night as if he were mine."

"He understands people I think, sometimes. Maybe he thought you lonely and in need of a friend, Nikal," Kodi said boldly.

Nikal smiled at Kodi's use of his given name. "Perhaps. Something about him, I don't know what, that says 'one of these days I'll be the most famous dog in all of history!' Takes after his real master, I guess."

Kodi laughed. "I intend to do my part, that's true, sir."

"I know, and I hope the joy that drives your will, Kodi, is never tested. Or taken from you." Nikal looked grim again for a moment as if in deep thought, but when he realized Kodi was watching him, he smiled again. "Well then, if I acknowledge some wisdom in you, I'd best listen to it. Especially when it comes to Tiliruf, for I see now the Guardian put you with him on deliberate purpose. I will make this promise then to you. I will not be severe with Tiliruf except when he needs it, though I'll expect you and Manwul and Hadon to keep him in check. Some of my words were out of line back there, were they not? I will make an attempt to be a bit more at ease around all of you unless we are in the middle of something. Rainwing keeps reminding me we are all in this business together. If I fail to remember that on occasion, do not hold it against me. Despite Jaden's praise of me, I have many flaws."

"I refuse to expect perfection from me or you or Tiliruf or anyone. In fact, the ones who think they're perfect or expect perfection from others are best avoided..."

"...for they can never be pleased." Nikal laughed. It was the first time Kodi had ever heard him laugh. "Let us go to our supper, then. Afterwards there will still be two hours remaining of daylight. We can get in some good swordplay before bed!"

"You will challenge Tiliruf, then, if you wish for a contest, Nikal."

Nikal eyed Kodi, impressed with his bold wording and undaunted grin.

And so it was that after dinner, Kodi, Manwul, Hadon, among some few Brigadiers who had been there that day training with the B'ulstreads, got to witness the most glorious clash between two Swordmasters. Nikal and Tiliruf were as two lightning storms crashing, and neither appeared to weary. Perhaps Nikal was more innovative due to long experience, but Tiliruf's speed was uncanny. Kodi nor Manwul or Hadon had ever seen him work so hard. Everyone was in utter awe at the artful display. The daylight began to fade, and after an hour of heated play Manwul intervened and called them to a halt, declaring it a draw.

All applauded. The two men bowed respectfully to one another, Tiliruf with the biggest grin on his hot face and Nikal with a look not at all displeased. His gloom temporarily subdued, he nodded to Kodi who smiled back at him.

The prince said loudly so all could hear, "Jaden has done well by you, just as you say, Master Tiliruf! I look forward to the ceremony tomorrow evening!"

They all trained hard the next morning as well, and soon after the lunch hour, they gathered up Musca and boarded the coach for the return jaunt to the city. They deposited the silver Noble at Enric's and arrived at the Palace by mid-afternoon.

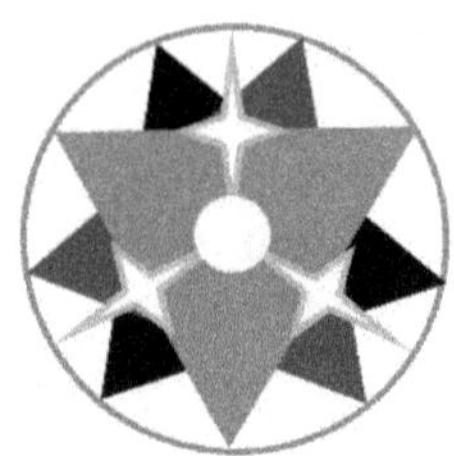

Chapter 12—Swordmaster

"Gazing in my gold mirror, eh?" joked Tiliruf through the door. "I don't believe that rubbish about 'practicing your smile!'"

He barged in to find his friend half immersed in the elegantly carved, red marble bath.

Kodi leaned back and stretched, a curious smirk on his face. "Told you I liked the water, didn't I? What's the matter?"

"Package for you, mate. And somebody wants to see you." He threw a large linen towel at Kodi.

"Male or female? How much clothes have I got to put on?" asked Kodi, reluctantly getting out of the water.

"Wouldn't make any difference to me; just march right on out to the parlor."

"I ain't you. Male or female?"

"It's Jaden, you innocent virginal lump o' pretty brown flesh!"

"I'm not innocent and virginal. Told you all about..."

"...Jonell, yeah, I know. The stablemaster's 'really shaped well' daughter. If you ask me, you start out all fresh at *four years!* You sure you still know how to work that thing, eh?" He pointed. "Oh!"

Kodi stood straight to dry his backside and grinned at himself in the privately famous, tall, gold-framed mirror. "Quite sure. I *am* a 'pretty brown,' aren't I?"

"Damn, Kodi, you're right well *cocked!* Just *finished up* something, eh?"

"Felt sorta horsey after shavin', yeah." He winked at Tiliruf through the mirror. "Bit o' innocent *tension release* for the healthy buck. Might wanna drain the tub before you take your turn."

"Ha! Yeah, wouldn't want to come out all *sticky* and covered in black razor stubble." They both heehawed. "Reckon you do still know the *theory,* then. That's definitely *healthy,* mate, what I'm seein'. Measures favorably to my own high standard. We must be related after all, *brother!*

Women crave that *particular* look, Kodi, you shouldn't be so stingy with it. They get all misty-eyed and expectant."

Kodi chuckled. "Lyndz caught me this way once or twice like you did, bustin' in. Wouldn't say *she* was misty-eyed. More like shock and quick retreat, ha! You get what you get when you don't knock. I reckon she mighta learned somethin' useful, though. Old worn-out anatomy book on Grandpa's shelf didn't provide very *noteworthy* illustrations."

"You're funnier'n horseshit, mate!"

"But only one lucky woman's gonna experience this look regular, then I'll make up for lost time and catch up to *Ruffy*."

"I've always found the *theory* should be *applied* often, mate, true. So, I'm an inspiration, eh?"

"Dash o' envy for some of your female play, ain't gonna lie. Now quit your gawking, buddy, and give me half a moment." He turned around and snapped the towel good-naturedly at Tiliruf, forcing him towards the door.

"Calm down, mate. And calm *it* down. And hurry up about it. Jaden's a busy man."

"Hard to calm down when we keep talkin' up the related subject matter!"

He emerged as quickly as he—reasonably—could, the towel knotted tightly around his waist. He nodded respectfully to the patient swordmaster.

Jaden took in Kodi's figure and blinked. "Don't show that much skin at the Dance tomorrow night, Master Kodi, or you'll have all the young ladies of Central City in an unrecoverable swoon, I think."

Kodi grinned.

Tiliruf chortled mischievously. "They can all line up and wait their turn hopelessly, 'cause this one's holding out, Master Jaden, for some perfect sweet damsel that certainly don't exist anywhere in these parts. The ladies of Central City'll have to get their fancies—and fannies—tickled by some other, less-finicky chap. The only woman here he's even looked at for more than two seconds is that lay-about marble nude in the back fountain with the water pouring all over her! He'd get in and swim around with her if the gardeners would let him. He says all the rest of 'em 'round here either got too much money, too much flattery, or too much makeup. So, he just ponders busty statues in the bathtub. Seems to work well for him, anyways."

"Is all this true, Master Kodi?" Jaden asked with pretended seriousness.

"Maybe."

"Smart man. I like that statue. She's a sensuous one, isn't she?" Jaden concluded with a wink. Tiliruf burst with glee. "Anyway, brought you something."

With that, Jaden withdrew a cloth and handed over to Kodi a beautiful new silver and steal scabbard with gold inlays, the newly leathered hilt of Bagarro's sword protruding from one end.

Kodi looked at it longingly and pulled the sword out of the sheath, stood back and swung it this way and that like a master. Its newly polished steal gleamed in the late afternoon sunshine pouring in from Tiliruf's open windows. "Thank you, Master Jaden, sir!"

"Of course, when I present a new sword to a man, he tends to wear something a bit more formal," joked Jaden.

"I'd have been prepared if I'd known, sir. Sorry about that!"

"Didn't even have time to write a message," said Jaden, unconcerned. "Never been so busy in all my days! But I was determined to bring it to you myself so you could wear it tonight. Some might say it is premature to give you a sword with a history like that. You'll have to prove them wrong. Tonight, at the ceremony, you'll stand in a line by age, which makes Manwul first, and you last. Manwul, Hadon, the red-haired brothers, and the two of you are the only students and former students I have that still live here in the city. All the others are with the Tirilorine mercenaries in the Nantian army. Of course, I'm recalling them. I need more officers for our own army."

"It has been a great honor to have you as my trainer, sir, even if it has only been for a short while."

"The honor I think has been mine, young Kodi. Your training I leave in most competent hands: the prince and Tiliruf. I expect you to practice with them every day without fail!"

"Yes, sir!"

Jaden then looked at Tiliruf. "And I understand you will be returning, maybe in a few weeks, only to take away my remaining students! Of course, I don't have time for training anymore. I had it in mind to make Hadon and Manwul into high-level officers..."

"It wasn't my idea, Master Jaden," said Tiliruf with a dash of annoyance. "The prince seems to think I need watching after."

"Prince Nikal is the great man of our age, and anyone including you would be a fool not to abide by his wisdom when it comes to war! The point is this. All of you men must watch after each other! Now buck up, Tiliruf, and make me proud! Be grateful to have the best of men with which to march into your future!"

"Just pride fightin' with me, I suppose, sir. I know that's what Enric would say. Sorry. You're absolutely right. I'm learning, eh? You, Father, Enric. And Kodi here's a good one, too. The prince makes me hot, but I'll listen to him."

Tiliruf appeared immensely humble and out of character saying all this in front of Jaden.

The Swordmaster smiled. "See you in two hours. And get on some proper clothes, Kodi, will you now?" He turned around and left the room.

Tiliruf folded his arms and watched Kodi in the bath towel as he continued to swing his new sword around in the center of the room. "You really should go exactly like that tomorrow night; the ladies'll have *two* swords to gape at!"

"Yep, they would, now shut up with the wisecracks and get me what you think I ought to wear tonight. And *don't* call the servants in here, I can dress myself, thanks!"

One might call it a private affair, though there were at least a hundred people present.

In the front of the Hall of Gifts, a spectacularly imposing chamber of inlay amber panels and mirrors, used upon a time by emperors to receive and present gifts to dignitaries, the six students stood to the left: Manwul closest to the center of the dais, followed by Hadon, Lukas, Colinn, Tiliruf, and lastly Kodi. They were all dressed quite splendidly, and only Tiliruf did not have a sword or belt. On the right stood Jaden, then Genehbro, Prince Nikal as the only fully-fledged Swordmaster graduate of Jaden's, and then, in accordance with an old tradition to which Jaden adhered, the Sage of Tirilorin.

In addition to the Solantines and all of Tiliruf's invited young friends, the audience included a sizeable contingent of Assembly Masters, including High Master Naloro, Harbor Master Yamin, and Madam Midianna. Father Garule, the Head of the Order of Meicalian Healers in Tirilorin, and Mother Superior Nastrumé of the Matrimonial Order were also there along with their functionaries. It was the first time these eminent Order figures had been invited to an official function at the Palace in many years. Yet with the Sage of Tirilorin reinstated as a high official on Genehbro's staff, they were to be seen and heard from a great deal more often. Also seated were all the highest-level servants of the Palace whom Genehbro personally invited, and then in the rear sitting on marble blocks were the massive Royal Hawking and Rainwing of Green Isle. Behind them, peering through several open doorways were at least three or four dozen additional Palace servants who wished to get a glimpse of the spectacle. With the two Etoppsi in their way, however, these didn't get to see very much.

When through a side door, two smartly dressed servants bore between them a large velvet cushion, Tiliruf gasped. His eyes were wide with uttermost astonishment. Upon the cushion lay a great longsword, ancient and beautiful, and beside it a scabbard of silver and gold, not unlike Kodi's new one though even more elaborately detailed.

"Is something wrong?" Kodi whispered as quietly as he could.

"It's...it's Father's! It's Terianh's!"

Prince Nikal stepped forward and, leaving the scabbard in place, took the great blade from the cushion, turned around and held it up before Genehbro. "The great Eagle Sword of your House, Genehbro a'Terianh!"

Genehbro took the sword from the prince and lifted it high. Then he held it out for Enric to bless.

Enric stood forward and placed his left hand on the hilt and lifted his right hand into the air. The other Order Members in the room too raised their right hand.

Battles behind us,
Battles before us,
Taxiarch Meical on High!
Leader in the fight
For Truth and Light!

Within the man to whom You grant this blade,
May truth never fade.

He lowered his right hand and removed his left from the hilt, and all the Order Members lowered their hands as well.

Then, Genehbro stepped out in front, followed by Jaden. Genehbro then turned to Tiliruf.

"Come, my son."

Tiliruf, still amazed beyond belief, stepped away from the line of Jaden's students. He knelt before his father.

"Rise, my son."

Tiliruf stood.

"Tiliruf a'Terianh, I present to you the sword of our great ancestor. You shall wield it in the battles before you, representing your father, your country, and the House of Terianh. Marshal Jaden, Swordmaster, do now the honors."

With that Jaden took the sword and inserted it into its scabbard. This he took and attached it to a belt of elaborate make, then came and wrapped it around Tiliruf's waist. He drew it tight and clasped it with a silver and gold buckle similar in look to the new scabbard. Only the blade itself was from Terianh. All else had been newly minted for Tiliruf. When he was finished, Jaden placed his hands on Tiliruf's shoulders and smiled proudly. Tiliruf's face still showed amazement. Then Jaden stood back and said, "Tiliruf a'Terianh, I proclaim you Swordmaster, the latest of a long line of Swordmasters stretching back through your father Genehbro to the days of your ancestor, Terianh the Great! Wield your new sword, the ancient Eagle Sword, with the pride of all Tirilorines!"

"Draw your blade!" commanded Genehbro.

Then with a ring, Tiliruf drew with serious purpose the blade from its scabbard and held it aloft. "Tirilorin!" he called in a loud and proud voice.

And in echo all of Jaden's students, Nikal as well, drew their swords in one resounding flourish. "Tirilorin!" they cried.

Then all the men in the room who had ever served in or were currently serving in the Republican Brigade stood and cheered magnificently, followed by a standing ovation by the remainder of the crowd and loud praises. Suddenly, everyone was milling around at the conclusion, the first around Tiliruf being all his male comrades. They congratulated him and pounded him proudly on the back, but then these were forced out of the way by Assembly Masters and other folk who wanted to shake his hand and wish him well.

Eventually, the greater crowd dispersed through the doorways leaving behind the smaller crowd of closest friends. And now Tiliruf approached his father Genehbro and looked him in the eye.

"Father! I...I didn't know!"

"That would be because he didn't tell you, Swordmaster!" said Jaden standing there beside Genehbro.

"Yet you knew it, eh?"

"As did about a dozen others."

Tiliruf looked at his father. "I am proud, sir. Yet it is not in the tradition of..."

"I know the tradition, son. Yet the tradition should give way to that which is more relevant. You are the one stepping forward into war in a dangerous time, whereas I remain behind to my duty in the city. This is the better and the new tradition. Now go celebrate with your friends. I expect you at breakfast at second hour. The Dance is tomorrow night, so don't overdo, eh?"

Genehbro and Jaden walked away with Enric and Curdoz.

Prince Nikal was suddenly there. He was not smiling, yet he was definitely not frowning. Tiliruf nodded respectfully. "Thank you, sir, for participating. It was a great honor to see you standing there with the others."

"The honor is mine to take part in a ceremony of the House of Terianh. Congratulations, Tiliruf." He nodded and then walked away and disappeared.

"I still don't think he cares much for me," Tiliruf whispered to Kodi who was standing close by his friend.

"He actually cares a lot. Found out he does have something on his mind, though he won't tell me what it is."

"If you say so, mate."

In great contrast to the prince, Idamé appeared, dabbing her eyes on the tip of her shawl. "Tiliruf, I'm so proud of you!" She leaned forward, embraced and kissed him most sweetly, a display of motherly affection that came remarkably close to making Tiliruf squeeze out a most rare tear.

"Mother Idamé! That's...that's really...well, I don't know what to say! I'm really glad you're here!" And then quite shockingly, he grabbed her up again and gave her another huge hug. She walked away wiping even more tears with her shawl. Tiliruf watched her as she left the room with Hollina.

"Told you she already loves you like her own."

"Yeah, you did, mate. I didn't believe you. Guess I was wrong on that one, eh?"

"Ko!" It was Lyndz, who walked up to her brother. "Oh, Tiliruf! That was grand! You look dashing! What a lovely display and ceremony!"

"So, I'm 'dashing' now and not a 'dolt' anymore, eh?"

"Well, maybe slightly less so."

"Er, thanks. Dance with me tomorrow night, then?"

"Oh, I suppose so," she sighed as if exhausted.

"You 'suppose!'"

"Yes, I suppose. I've had a slew of handsome men approach me the last ten minutes. You're in a line behind Colinn, Manwul, Lukas, Hadon, Jaden..."

"Jaden! He's Bonded over thirty years!"

"Yes, but he says his wife doesn't like to dance, and then there's Calens, Alin, Andir, Bendrik..."

"Bendrik's Bonding next week!" Tiliruf exclaimed.

She ignored him. "Yakob, Cawlbert, and what's the chubby one?"

"Spens," said Tiliruf and Kodi at the same time.

"Right. Spens. He's funny. And, well anyway, not to mention Ko here whom I'm going to dance with first of course since he's escorting me, and I'm sure I'll do a jig with Curdoz and Enric if they ask."

"You're going to put me at the tail end of all those!"

"Oh! And your father, too. He seems to really like me. Then there are the ones I'm planning to ask!" She winked ruthlessly, patted his cheek, and walked away to find Rainwing, which of course was not difficult.

The confounded Tiliruf looked at Kodi. "She's playing games with me, that one is! Can't you do something about her? I'm being degraded! I was a new Swordmaster five minutes ago, with the most famous sword in the world here at my side, and now I'm...well, I'm..."

"Number seventeen, I think," concluded Kodi, counting on his fingers.

Tiliruf's face showed the same shock as when the Sword of Terianh appeared on its velvet cushion. "I've never been 'number seventeen!' What's the world coming to?"

"I decided shortly after we got here, I wasn't going to stop her doing whatever she wants. She's a right to as much fun as I'm having. Besides, Manwul and Hadon are decent blokes, and so are Lukas and Colinn. I suppose they deserve a dance with her. Yakob and Cawlbert and Spens and Calens won't last half a minute with her. They'll say something crude and find themselves dancing with air. So there, that'll get you trimmed down to around thirteen. Then of course, if any of 'em touch her wrong...well," Kodi cracked his knuckles, "that's a different matter."

"Oh," said Tiliruf, slightly mollified. "Well, thirteen's better than seventeen, eh? Come along then, the others are probably at my rooms by now. I locked the liquor cabinet—taking most of the contents with me when we leave here—but I've procured a large barrel from Zhock; ought to be there by now. And a spread from the kitchens on the balcony. You heard Father. Guess I'd better end the party after a couple hours and send everybody home. Except you, mate. You can stay again if you want."

"Heck, yeah. You've got all my clothes for tomorrow, too. And I'm in a mood for a late-night smoke after everybody leaves."

"You got it, mate."

Chapter 13—The Grand Dance

There had been no question as to the location of the Grand Dance, for Madam Arlay had approached Master Genehbro within two days of expounding her idea in High Master Naloro's office, after she had received commitments from a dozen others to sponsor the event with her. Considering it was so seldom used for its intended purpose, Genehbro was delighted to allow the merchantwomen of Tirilorin to host the affair in the magnificent ballroom of the Palace. Aside from the Assembly, it was the largest chamber, easily accommodating the enormous crowd Arlay expected. All Genehbro had to do was to have the glass windows and mirrors cleaned and all the chandeliers polished and outfitted with fresh candles. Arlay and her associates did the rest. Considering the grandiosity of the entire affair and all the logistics involved, with invitations, musicians, food, decorations and all the rest, it said much for Arlay's organization skills to manage such a feat in two weeks time. No wonder, Lyndz thought, she was so successful in business.

It was largely a Central City affair, though all the Assembly Masters representing other parts of the city and the province, in addition to wealthy estate owners from beyond the walls were invited, too. Otherwise, the only set of persons invited that were not of the privileged classes were a chosen set of thirty Brigadier soldiers and officers hand-picked by the generals at Arlay's request. It must be noted, however, that news of the event spread throughout the city so that the day of the Grand Dance evolved into a general holiday, and a great many gatherings, parties and dances took place all round the city at the same time as the much larger affair at the Palace.

As Enric had reminded the twins, Arlay had two goals. One, she wanted a display of grandiosity and pomp to cheer all as talk of war was in the works. Now with the declaration of war by the Assembly, such a scheme carried even more importance than before. It was a chance to celebrate before the inevitable great sacrifices took place. Her second reason was to bring together many of the unbonded young people in order to promote couplings and courtships. She believed quite rightly that such pairings would prove of great benefit to those going off to war as it would boost morale.

She might possibly have had a third reason, suspected by Kodi, and that was to get her lovely daughter Linova into the arms of the handsome Solantine nobleman's son. He had not forgotten her little statement to that effect back in Naloro's office, and just as with Stri Itruvi, he had put up his 'be wary' shield. By the end of the evening, thus, this little hope on Arlay's part was dashed. He only danced with the girl once. Yet there were other prospects, and Linova enjoyed herself quite much, and in the days to come in the immediate aftermath of the Dance a line of courtiers began to call upon Arlay's mansion, and it wasn't long before the likeable and intelligent girl had a great many suitable Kodi substitutes.

There was, in part, more to the affair than a Dance.

A certain few, though 'few' in this case meant perhaps a hundred or more, including the Solantine guests of Enric, were invited to a special archery event in which those who believed themselves sufficiently skilled were allowed a bit of a chance to show off. This took place in the late afternoon prior to the official introductions before the main event; the Dance was not to take place until after sundown. These gathered on the back verandah in the westering sunlight, the same where Genehbro held his dinner only a few nights previously when the Berugians arrived. Here, refreshments were served, and since this had a perfect view of the green lawn, all could see the men and handful of well-practiced women, shoot at targets and applaud their efforts.

One young man outshone everyone, and this one man had a bow so stunningly beautiful that it and the handsome one who bore it became the subject of much chatter, particularly of the female sort, well into the evening.

Kodi, outfitted in some of Tiliruf's finest—a rich blue and white-trimmed trapping complete with the new though dreaded gold and silver-threaded stockings—though he knew all eyes were on him, was determined to make all those in the crowd whom he cared about proud of his determination and skill. His ego might not have minded the two or three dozen young unbonded ladies—Central City's most eligible—that seemed to watch him the closest, tittering with unveiled admiration. But as he was competing, his thoughts were mostly on Lyndz, Idamé, Curdoz, Enric, Genehbro, Hollina, Jaden, and Tiliruf. These were assuredly the ones applauding the loudest and calling out to him unreservedly from the stonework balcony.

With the exception of Tiliruf, who was of course next to him, putting on his own show.

Though he could not, nor would he ever, compare to Kodi with a bow, he had nevertheless begun to practice more often and had made improvement since their first day together under Jaden's eye on this same lawn over a week ago. He was now hitting the burlap targets nearly all the time. He also received applause on occasion after a particularly good shot, to which, unlike Kodi, he would turn to the crowd and bow with great swagger in his beautifully tailored, gold-embroidered, green suit. This would be the occasion of much tittering amongst the young ladies, though it was clear they liked what they saw.

In fact, all the twenty or so young men on the green were eagerly eyed by the ladies on the balcony, and when it was time for the half-dozen women who wished to participate to debut their skills—notably the dark-skinned ambassador from Essemar was one of these—all of the male archers stood back and watched and applauded. Though in their case it made little difference whether a given young lady hit the burlap or not, for the men, with typical chauvinism, were more attuned to their "form" and "style" than their skill. Yet missing the target was rare, for these few women were all-in-all as good as the men. The Essemarian scored highest of the women, and as word spread quickly round the verandah, it was understood she had recently served as an archery commander in the eastern army. It was interesting to watch her handle the bow in the long silk sari she wore.

Yet Kodi won the contest easily with his typically perfect score. He simply never missed the bullseye, occasionally splitting his own arrows. It was a good thing he was such a friendly sort, otherwise his display could easily have produced a good deal of jealousy among the men. Instead, the competitors simply marveled.

There was mingling afterwards, and the half-dozen female competitors found themselves quickly paired with eligible young bucks who found their sportiness quite attractive. Among others, Manwul was off on a walk around the lawn, arm in arm with one of the loveliest of these, as was his friend Hadon with another. Apparently these two, approaching their late twenties, were determined now to find Bondmates if they could before they joined with Prince Nikal's company upon their return from the journey to seek the Eagle Staff. Too, Colinn and his older brother Lukas had joined up for goblets of wine punch at the edge of the balcony with a couple of the lasses who had been particularly admiring of their handsome red hair, physiques and skills.

Kodi, though he grinned often and spoke in friendly tone to all the various damsels who approached him, it wasn't long before he would begin avoiding these little flirtatious crowds and pull himself closer to his twin sister, to whom he would converse with exaggerated effect, with the hopes the others would take the hint he wasn't interested and flirt elsewhere. Lyndz knew precisely what Kodi was using her for, and though she didn't mind, she would quietly tease him for it and then whisper suggestions about specific ladies in the crowd he should be more open-minded towards.

"She's lovely!" she pointed with a nod. "And smart. Her name is Consessa. I met her at Arlay's tea. I *know* what you like, Ko. She's got the perfect figure. And smart, like I said."

"No," he said adamantly. "There's more to it in...in what I...what I want. She...she...she..."

"She *what*, Ko? You're so particular, I swear."

"She *draws* her eyebrows on with one of those damned whatever they are. She looks like a clown. A woman needs to have her own...her own nice eyebrows. Like you."

Lyndz looked at him a bit crazily at first, but then smiled sweetly as she considered the compliment towards her behind his words.

She winked. "You're right, of course. You might prefer a dark-haired woman, then."

"Maybe."

"There's Milmana over there. She's got the Nantian look and dark hair. She doesn't draw on her eyebrows! She's perfect for you."

Kodi grinned and kissed his sister's hand. "Pretty face, but her ears are too big. She looks like a bat!"

The laughter of twins is surely a Cosmic theme.

At the introductions prior to the Dance, two loud announcers, one at the main entryway and the other situated at the entrance between the hall and the part of the Palace from where the archery tournament crowd were coming in from the rear, would rapidly take cards and call out the titles and names of each and every person who entered. The entrance hall was the perfect place for mingling and viewing the entrants as they stepped down when their names were called, and ample hors d'oeuvres and wine punch were served by eighty or more servants milling around with silver trays.

"...the Ambassadors from the Realm of Essemar, Cee Amirah Sturla Keen and Cee Ameer Karsoon Mir. The Ambassadors from the Realm of Hralindi, Cee Amirah Lenma Otrune and Cee Ameer Yammo Oklar..." The Easterners' silk saris trailed behind them as they descended the stairs.

"...Matrimonial Servant of the Guardian, Mother Idamé, escorted by His Lordship Curdoz, High Sage of the Kingdom of Solanto. Monastic Servant of the Guardian, Sister Hollina, escorted by Assembly Master Enric, High Sage of the Republic of Tirilorin..."

The crowd had quieted down to get a good look at all these eminent persons. Idamé stepped down the stairs with Curdoz, and she was as lovely as perhaps she had ever been, in Arlay's lavender dress and her own purple shawl. She wore no jewelry, but the shawl was clasped at her bosom with a plain silver circular pin. Hollina was in a light-yellow gown. The two Sages were like old dandies in well-ironed attire, Curdoz, newly shaven, hair combed, in his green stole bearing the stag of Solanto, and the bearded Enric in his, bearing the rayed sun of the Republic.

The crowd remained quiet, correctly presuming other key persons would be close behind.

"...The Lady Lyndz, escorted by her brother Kodi, Viscount Fothemry, of the Kingdom of Solanto..."

The oohs and aahs were pronounced as the handsome, olive-toned, dark-haired twins made their way down the stairs. And if the strapping Kodi was particularly fine-looking wearing Tiliruf's clothes, Lyndz was the delight of everyone's eyes in Linova's rose dress, the emerald pendant sparkling upon her bosom, and the rose sash secured around her waist by the bright gold buckle from Princess Isatura. Her hair was not braided this time, but fell in waves around her face, and her smile lit the room. Most thought her the most stunning woman they had ever seen, a princess out of old tales, just as Nikal had said.

"...Of the Great High House of Terianh, Assembly Master Genehbro and Swordmaster Tiliruf his son. High Lady Ludly, escorted by her husband Swordmaster Jaden, War Marshall of the Republic..."

There were so many to introduce that there was never a pause until this last, creating as it did a great murmur in the crowd erupting then into general applause, for no doubt Jaden in his newly proclaimed role was the man of the hour. And every man in the crowd with a sword at his side drew it high and shouted, "Tirilorin!" in his honor.

The introductions otherwise continued most efficiently, so by the end of an hour the by now well-fed multitude had heard called some five hundred names. And when at the end there was a great monstrous shadow in the front doorway, no name card was really needed by the chamberlain.

"Professoress at the Berugian Institute, Rainwing of the House of Green Isle, escorted by His Highness Royal Hawking of the Most Ancient House of Berug."

And since there was now not a square foot of space remaining in the entry hall for these large-scaled guests, the doors to the hallway leading to the ballroom burst asunder in order to allow the crowd to move on. There would be plenty of room there for one and all, including the Berugian guests.

On the way, every man with a sword was required to deposit his swordbelt, scabbard and blade on linen-clothed long tables lining this hall, for it was considered uncouth, not to mention unwieldy, to have a sword at your side during a dance. Kodi and Tiliruf were both reluctant and complaining as they lay down their newly acquired weapons, each looking at the other with disappointment.

"Just one sword left to us then, mate! Swing it wide and high, eh?" Tiliruf whispered to his friend who snickered and shook his head.

"You haven't told me about your new sword yet, Ko!" said the unhearing Lyndz, who took her brother's arm again as they walked down the hall towards the ballroom.

"I will, though. But it's such a great tale I want to save for later. You and I need to talk, for sure. Sorry I've been holed up so much with Tiliruf."

"Don't be. I've been reading books and practicing my Gift and getting to know Rainwing. You've needed a friend like Tiliruf, and I didn't know it before, but I needed one, too. Rainwing is as great as having a big sister!"

"Very, very big sister!" he replied with a laugh.

There was great cheer as they spilled into the dance hall like sands pouring out the neck of an hourglass, and the musicians were playing a joyful tune in greeting. Yet it would be another ten minutes until the first dance was to officially begin.

"But where is Prince Nikal?" asked Idamé, coming in behind the twins on Curdoz' arm. "Did he arrive before us?"

Kodi was fairly sure he knew the answer.

"He would not come," said Jaden, "though Madam Arlay sent messages assuring him of an invitation. I must admit, I have never seen my friend so troubled, and yet he would not open himself to me. He remains in his rooms. The only thing he would assure me was that his troubles have nothing to do with anything since his arrival but reflect some situation at home. I have heard no rumors of anything of especial ill coming out of Nant, only war news, and it is all the typical sort. Take heed of that Prophecy, however. All of you are meant to become his friends."

"Yet maybe not his confidantes," said Curdoz. "At least not right away. I see the trouble in his mind. I am convinced Rainwing and Hawking know what it is, but they too are silent on the matter. Troubling. And yet perhaps in time he will find in us the trust he requires."

"Rainwing does know," said Lyndz. "But you're right, she said it is private and would not clarify."

The huge dance floor was delineated from the surrounding area by an alteration in the marble parquetry. The dance floor was of course perfectly empty, but hundreds of little chairs at tiny tables filled the observation area all round it. Servants continued to serve refreshments. Great glass-paned side doors were open to a long verandah upon which could be found more tables and chairs and buffet tables loaded with delectable treats.

In the middle of the great chamber was an inset balcony upon which sat and played the musicians. At one end of the length of the room was a broad dais, and whereas in olden times the imperial family would sit to watch the revelry, those seats were removed long ago. Instead, here sat all the dozen or so wealthy merchantwomen who hosted the event, with their families in chairs around larger tables. These of course included

Arlay with Linova, and also Itruvi, who, Kodi noticed with disgust, every time he glanced in her direction, was looking directly at him and smiling most provocatively.

Balancing the dais on the other end of the room the two Berugians were provided heavy, cushioned benches upon which to sit. They of course did not dance the Human dances, and they would have crushed a great many folk if they had attempted such maneuvers, yet they were spoken to and greeted by many important people, and occasionally Hawking's voice would boom a bit too loudly in laughter and cause heads to turn. They did, however, add to the memory of the evening just by their presence. Yet they did not stay but perhaps two hours. Hawking, due to his advanced age, needed his rest, for his plan was to begin his long flight home tomorrow, and Rainwing, having become bored by the revelry and the music which seemed to hum with redundancy to ears unused to such instrumentals, took the opportunity to exit with him.

A trumpet blew, and when the first dance began, those with opposite gender escorts were presumed to accompany him or her. But after the first dance, with the exception of Bonded couples, it was expected that there would be, not quite a free-for-all, at least a relaxed sort of mingling. In other words, it was not against any sort of etiquette for any unbonded individual, male or female, to ask another such individual to dance. Of course, as the evening went on, a fairly large number of 'couplings' took place as many of the lads and lasses found themselves mutually attracted, this resulting in less mixing and more deliberate pairings.

It wasn't long before the first Aura of the evening occurred, and though there may have been a dozen Matrimonials in the crowd, low and behold, who would be the first to see it but Mother Idamé.

She was in the middle of a fashionable and lively dance with Curdoz when she saw it just beyond them and shrieked, gathering quickly to her all the Matrimonials in the room.

And who would she point to other than someone the friends had all come to honor and like quite well.

Everyone around them was in a flutter when the dozen Matrimonials with Idamé leading them descended upon the reposing Manwul, though he was no longer with the woman with whom he had stridden arm in arm around the back lawn. Instead, he and his comrade Hadon had agreed to swap partners to see if the realigned pairing might produce even more harmony. Sure enough, the instant Manwul kissed the hand of Hadon's walking partner and sat in a little chair beside her so as to get to know her, the Aura appeared above their heads. Since Idamé spotted it first, Mother Superior Nastrumé allowed her to proclaim it to the unsuspecting couple.

Arlay, like a great hawk, had her eyes open for just such a possibility, and when she saw from her perch on the dais the Matrimonials gathering around the couple, she lifted her hand, causing a pause in the music, and all eyes turned to see what had caused it.

Idamé smiled as cheerily as she did when Lyndz and Kodi saw her eyeing Yugan their grandfather and Ansy the cook all those long weeks ago.

"The Guardian Himself Affirms your pairing, my dears!" she said aloud, to their utter astonishment.

Though such a situation might have mortified someone like skeptical Tiliruf, within a few seconds the countenances of these two relaxed to the inevitable, and the ruggedly handsome Manwul looked at the sporty, rosy-cheeked lass at his side, whose name was Steffia, and winked most roguishly. Steffia responded with a rather suggestive, and eagerly receptive look that caused one or two of the virginal Sisters at Idamé's side to pink up, though everyone else around the couple laughed heartily.

The two then stood from their chairs; Manwul promptly bowed and went to his knees and kissed for only the second time the hand of who was now his officially betrothed. The two walked eye-to-eye and hand-in-hand out to the dance floor and a great cheer went up. The music began again, and the new couple danced splendidly, all eyes upon them for many minutes.

"They haven't known each other half a minute!" stated Tiliruf in shock. "Now if that's not the most scandalous thing I ever saw!"

Kodi looked at Tiliruf and chuckled. "I don't think so. I think it's fantastic! That good man deserves a mate; I'm proud for him. He's waited long enough." Kodi then reminded him in a little whisper in his ear. "The scandalous thing is a highborn Swordmaster who insists on getting his thumper thumped by a gaggle of women he has to pay."

Tiliruf's smirk was pronounced when he too reminded Kodi, "No expectations, no responsibilities, and no children!"

Kodi laughed, as did Tiliruf, but then the latter immediately advanced upon an unsuspecting Linova, and though she did complete a dance with him, Tiliruf never asked her again, nor she him. He moved on to the next woman immediately afterwards. Despite his jest to Kodi earlier regarding swinging swords, Tiliruf had no intentions whatsoever of indulging his hormonal flows with any of these eligible females. He truly had sworn them off a couple years ago in favor of the detached freedoms associated with his 'library girls.' Nevertheless, he loved to flirt outrageously for sheer fun and delighted when it was reciprocated. His reputation, however, was such that though the women liked to be seen with him—he was after all the richest young buck in the world, handsome, and from a most famous House of heroes—few fooled themselves into believing they had any chance. He was known to be callous towards the idea of Bonding, and he moved from woman to woman with each dance as if they were delicious treats off the hors d'oeuvre trays.

When Kodi found himself momentarily without anyone to talk to, Stri Itruvi pounced, fleeced out as she was in layers of shiny satin, three gold necklaces, earrings and, to his disgust, heavy makeup. Having been caught suddenly without excuses, he felt forced to accompany her onto the dance floor. Unfortunately for him, it was a specifically formal dance this time requiring a number of coordinated moves with many partners moving in and out. He could not expect Lyndz to cut in and rescue him without risking an interruption in the flow of the piece. Besides, he could see his sister down the dance row opposite Andir.

The innocent small talk lasted all of thirty seconds when she plunged in.

"Absolutely adore the way you *release* your *arrows* with such virile poise, Master Fothemry!" she stated with the most obvious innuendo he'd had cast at him by a female since his experience with Jonell jumping on him from the hayloft and proclaiming him her 'stallion' in the horse barn nearly four years before. He unwittingly grinned, finding it quite funny even if it was shocking. With Tiliruf's help he had already categorized this woman in his mind as 'clown' and had decided her methods were meant to be laughed at. When they came close again in the movement three seconds later, she mistook the meaning behind his smile and said, "You must come sit with me at one of the upper tables, Master Fothemry, or if you'd prefer," she winked, "we can have a go in the palace garden if you like! 'Archery practice!'"

She was as full of these sorts of laced quips as Tiliruf. Forced away again by the movement, Kodi knew he had exactly four seconds to think of a fitting reply. He could either repel the 'woman' or engage the 'clown.'

He decided upon the latter. "I'm sure you say that to all the bucks, Mistress Stri."

"Only the ones that intrigue me, dear."

Again, they were brushed apart. There was a spin, a sidestep, another spin, and they were together again.

"What do you find so intriguing about me...*dear?*" He winked back. He allowed girls to flirt with him back home, though they were nothing compared to Stri. If she insisted on such a game, he'd play it for the sheer fun of it. At least for another minute or two. Maybe something Tilirufian was rubbing off on him. He knew precisely how he was going to end it; it had come to him in a brilliant flash. High Master Naloro's words had come back to him. It could wait, though. He wanted to know if...

"Ambernut, Kodi, *Viscount* Fothemry!"

He knew it. As the only son of Hess Fothemry, in her mind Kodi was the key to eventual control of the lucrative Tulescian ambernut trade.

"And of course, I must say you're the most stunning piece of masculine flesh this side of the Imperial Divide! It doesn't hurt your prospects, dear," she added with a seductive gleam in her eye.

A whisk away, a turn on a heel, and a return.

"Why, thank you for the compliment! Eh, what's in it for me...*dear?*"

"Everlasting satisfaction," she stated with a lick of her lips and a most suggestive nod towards his mid-section. She might as well have pointed like Tiliruf did yesterday afternoon at the bath.

"Ah, that's too easy, Mistress Itruvi! How could a *virile* young lad like me pass up the opportunity? But tell me, what's the difference should I make more regular trips to North Bend?"

"You, my dear, have never been to North Bend."

She was having his movements watched! No, indeed, he had never before met a woman like Stri Itruvi.

And never hoped to again. The music created another separation, though only for a few seconds. "Keeping an eye on me, are you? I'm flattered." He said this with his most fetching grin. He was of such a mind to actually allow her to walk with him out to the dark garden and break it to her at a key 'moment' and teach her a dirty lesson. But such a thought checked him—leading on women was not Kodi's style. Despite the fun of this little game, he was not Tiliruf and never would be.

He dropped the smile and looked at her with serious purpose. "The only reason I haven't been to North Bend is because I have my mind set on higher things."

"I can give you anything you want, Master Fothemry!" she twittered, batting her eyes.

"No. I'm afraid you can't know what I want by having me watched from a distance."

Realizing finally this might not end the way she'd hoped, Itruvi became a dash desperate.

"Then show me what it is you like, Kodi," she stated, using the familiar. "I will be glad to learn a lesson or two. From you, my dear, it would be most...pleasurable! Come out to the garden! We can talk about it, why don't we?"

"No. I will be joining the Meicalian Orders soon. I had a Vision from the Guardian Meical, and I have no intention of disappointing Him."

Though taking the Vow was not in the cards for Kodi, Stri need not know it. Shock appeared on her overly painted face. As the music took her away, she missed a step and had to correct. "But...but you're training to be a *warrior!* You're not going to the Valley of the Gifted! That makes no sense!"

"It's true, though. That's what my Brother Meical Called me to do in a Vision a couple of months ago. A Vision confirmed by Lord Curdoz, and Master Enric, too. Sorry, Stri. I'm not the man for you. Now let me be. And as far as the ambernut trade is concerned, all you have to do is, like my father says, offer the most gold."

The music having finally concluded, Kodi bowed properly, then walked away.

Never again did he need worry himself about Stri Itruvi.

He sat at a little table, quickly downed another glass of wine punch with Tiliruf, and told him the tale.

"Ah, mate! I guess I was wrong! She really was after you, just like you said! Well, she'll recover quick enough, that one will. I know from personal experience." He then winked at Kodi and smirked. "'Course you should have at least let her treat you in the garden, mate! She's got the wettest tongue in Central City!"

Kodi laughed, "Yeah, so you've admitted before."

"Did I? I s'pose I did. Been a couple years, though, like I said. I swear."

"Just library girls now. Ruffy has his standards."

"Exactly!" Tiliruf winked again. "You finally understand, mate!"

"No expectations, no responsibilities, and no children!" they both repeated at the same time, cackling and slapping each other on the back.

Tiliruf was quite right about Stri. The next time Kodi looked around for her, the bosomy vamp was dancing with another young man, obviously a rich, Central City son of someone. Her eyes sparkled, and this man appeared much more receptive to her advances.

"Well, good for her," Kodi said aloud to no one in particular. "Poor bloke."

Kodi asked no one other than Lyndz to dance, and she only did so twice, for she was much too busy with not seventeen, but more like thirty-seven young gallants throughout the evening. Kodi, however, was asked by nearly as many female hopefuls, and for the most part he had a good time dancing with them all, and though many of them did toy with him a bit, he found none of them remotely like Stri. None certainly asked him for a personal archery demonstration in the dark garden. This was a good thing, for he had begun to worry that maybe Stri was the rule rather than the exception. By the end of the evening, his faith in the young women of Central City was restored. Yes, some of them were worldly for his tastes, but most were like Linova, intelligent and fun.

Yet as with Linova, after dancing with her, he barely looked twice at any of them. Despite the purpose of the event, no one caught Kodi's fancy. Thankfully, he didn't expect it and was not disappointed. In the back of his mind, he sensed he was being led into a future that promised something in this arena, and he was willing to delay. However, it would have been wrong to presume the evening and the various couplings did not have any effect at all on Kodi's senses. To see the new and intense happiness on the faces of those such as Manwul and Steffia moved him. His mind wandered, and when his thoughts brushed upon the statue of the nude bather in the garden fountain, he caught himself and grinned.

Love was in the air, or perhaps mystical movements of Meicalian cosmological providence, for remarkably, and unexpectedly, not just one Aura, but three presented themselves during the evening, and most extraordinarily, another one of Tiliruf's friends was the subject of one of these.

Alin, a fellow quieter in nature than most of the swaggerers Tiliruf tended to surround himself with, had asked a diminutive and sweet-cheeked wallflower by the name of Mandí to dance about half-way through the evening, and the instant he brought her onto the dance floor, the green light appeared above them. It was the Mother Superior herself who announced it this time, and the pair were as shocked as Manwul and Steffia had been. Unlike those two, however, these each looked at the other with modest, humble expressions and embarrassed grins. The parents of the young lady bowled through the crowd and shook Alin's hand, proclaiming good-natured pride and joy, dispersing the shyness of the moment.

Towards the end of the evening the third Aura appeared above one of the young Brigadiers in uniform and the charming daughter of one of the Republic Masters. As Tiliruf later found out through his circles, the soldier had been secretly in love with the girl for a long time, for they lived near one another in the section of the city her father represented. However, the soldier had always considered the great beauty 'out of reach.' Nevertheless, her father expressed delight in the match, for the lad, though from a humble family, was most gentlemanly in all regards, considered brave and capable by the general who recommended him, and the daughter was obviously quite smitten.

Poor Spens had few dance partners, for he asked few, none asked him, and he claimed he didn't particularly like dancing anyway. Late in the night, however, he did, with some amount of bravura and under the influence of great quantities of wine punch, approach his rich, fantasy girl Stri. Calens, Yakob and Cawlbert, who were responsible for stoking their friend into this most hopeless of encounters, nevertheless laughed uproariously when the proud woman looked at his pudgy form and squawked, "*You* want to dance with *me?* I think you'd tip right over. Aren't you that chap that that mad Tiliruf lets win at coppers? Coppers! I haven't held a *copper* in my hand since I was two years old!" She turned on him haughtily and whisked away.

Thankfully, Spens was sufficiently drunk so that this magnificent abuse did not have much long-term effect.

Altogether, the evening was as successful as it could possibly have been, and a great many non-Aura matches occurred. The Matrimonials appointed to the city found their services in great demand over the next few weeks as Central City saw the Bondings of several dozen young couples. And the multiple concurrent parties in the other parts of the city produced five times as many more pairings. The joys of the moment might give way to sacrifice and war, but it was to be hoped that shared love would bring hope in the many separations that were shortly to follow.

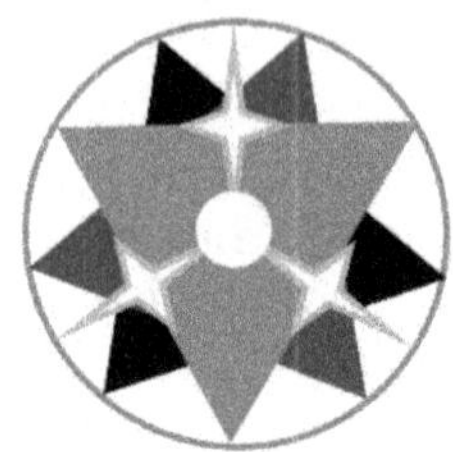

Chapter 14—Rainwing's Semantics

The following morning, the fourth hour found a line of three carriages making their way through the streets of the city to North Port where a Nantian transport vessel was waiting to carry Prince Nikal and his party to Nant. None of the Solantines had been to this part of the city. South Port, where Curdoz' ship had docked, was reserved for merchant and civilian transport vessels, whereas North Port was the docking site for navy ships and where new Tirilorine ships were constructed and launched. It was bustling, for merchant vessels were, under Jaden's orders, swiftly being converted to transport and naval ships for the Republic.

When they arrived, they found Hawking and Rainwing, having flown down from the palace, already waiting at the docks. Enric had come with the group to offer his blessings and bid them farewell. Genehbro too wanted to offer last minute advice to his son with whom he had never before parted for very long, and so the two of them had ridden alone together. Though father and son said little to anyone else about it, it appeared they had over the last couple of weeks grown to have a better understanding of one another.

There were others who came along also with the wish to say farewell, although most were under the impression that once the Staff of Terianh was found, the travelers would be returning to Tirilorin on their way east. It was presumed that such a future stay would be brief, however, probably no more than two or three days before setting sail again.

Prince Nikal was in a no-nonsense mood when he required the party to wait at the docks while he inspected the vessel and its crew. He had issued strict orders to the ship's captain to make available and arrange the cabins for the comfort of the passengers, with particular attention to the one in which the females would be traveling. He knew Rainwing could just squeeze herself into it for sleeping on padding on the floor, and Idamé, who had come to detest the hammocks in Curdoz' tiny ship, was to have an alcove with a clean mattress upon which she could lie flat, Lyndz as well. In any event, Nikal wished to ensure all was in perfect order before he would allow any of the party on board. When he returned, he found the farewells taking place amongst various little groups.

Hadon and Tiliruf were a little way away from the others chatting and laughing when Kodi stepped out of the carriage in which he was riding with the other Solantines and Musca. When Kodi saw Hadon he automatically looked around for Manwul, and upon walking over to them and asking where he was, the two men chortled.

"Have a guess, mate!" said Tiliruf.

Kodi looked confused.

Hadon explained. "He and Steffia, they and their folks met with the Mother Superior this morning as soon as they opened the gates at the Convent. The Aura of course allowed them to be Bonded in short order without counselling, and you know Master Genehbro thinks most highly of Manwul, and so he had his best coach sent to carry them off to the guest house on his estate out in the country. He's letting them stay there until Prince Nikal gets back and takes us away. Manwul and I share a house, and he woke me up at the crack of dawn to go with him to the Convent. Never seen him so happy! Bouncy like a rogue stallion, I tell you!"

"He'll have her de-flowered in the coach before they ever get there, eh?"

"He won't," said Hadon quite firmly. "The man's frisky, and so is Steffia—you saw how she looked at him last night! But over the years since our wilder days Manwul's become a romancer of the first rank, and he'll do it all proper especially this their first day together. He'll take her off on a horseback ride, pick flowers in a meadow, come back to the house and have the servants bring them a fine dinner and light candles. They'll take a grand bath together, then I reckon, Tiliruf, you can allow your mind to wander as to what happens after dark!"

"You all want to waste too much time, sounds to me. And what about you, Hadon, eh? You couldn't find yourself a golden egg in all that pack of hens last night? We saw you dance a couple times with that ambassador woman from Essemar. Exotic thing, eh? With that dark skin."

"You could say that. And maybe a pairing would appear odd, though it is said that some of the Nantian soldiers find life-mates in the east."

Kodi said, "I don't see what difference it'd make, if you like her, Hadon. Why don't you approach her again and get to know her?"

"I may. Yet I did find out her husband was killed less than a year ago in an eastern battle. So should I do so, it might appear insensitive. And I know she has no children."

Kodi looked at him and smiled. "Sounds like you're already gathering information about her, Hadon, through the gossip circles!"

"Aha!" said Tiliruf.

Hadon grinned but said no more about it. "Well, Kodi, I wish you well, and Tiliruf, I'll be prepared to do my duty upon your return!"

The three put their arms on each other's shoulders in a gesture of camaraderie, and then Hadon walked back to the carriage to await Jaden and the others. Kodi and Tiliruf walked over to the other men who were busy going through some additional ideas and plans.

"Presuming it will only be a few weeks," Jaden was saying, "by the time you return, Prince, I'll have a fleet and ten thousands prepared to follow you to Fort Danzilet. General Skaggins will command that legion under your authority. It would be my preference you station them nearby to contest the Alkhaness should she make a move on the trading colonies. However, if all remains quiet, then send them east to the main front to aid the Essemarians if you wish. I'll have another legion ready soon thereafter, and I'll be with them. You sure they'll never be able to bring their fleet out of the Khestadone Sea? That is my greatest fear, for if they do, I'll be forced to think much closer to home."

"All I can tell you is that as things stand now it would be impossible. We have it firmly bottled up. But you heard Rainwing and Hawking speak of Queen Silverwing's fears. If the Alkhaness chooses to engage and comes herself and wields some dark magic, I am uncertain. We discussed all of this already, but as I said before, you must prepare for all possibilities. I will need a legion from Tirilorin in the east, preferably two, or we'll never break the Alkhan's current advance. He will break through to the Arch by fall unless the Easterners have another trick up their sleeve which I doubt. I worry if they perceive a weakness, the Barantines themselves might take advantage and swear homage to the Alkhan so as to gain control over some of those lands. If that happens, it's all over for the Easterners if we ourselves cannot come up with new armies. Reconquest could take years if they entrench, and that's only if we're lucky enough to eliminate the Alkhan first. Hopefully we'll keep the situation from deteriorating that badly. I have great hopes with your legions, and your actions should induce my own country to commit further, but I have other fears. The Staff of Terianh should give us hope, should we gain it, but as Lord Curdoz suggested and as I told Kodi the other day, the first time we use it, the Alkhan and Alkhaness will know it. They'll sense the power of the magic. When that happens, I think they will press us hard. That's what I would do to keep us from gaining ground against them. War is coming for us in the west as well as the east."

Jaden considered for a moment. "I am confident in our numbers, yet I should know much more how the recruitment goes by your return. I may be able to increase that first force by another few thousands with some effort, especially if you're delayed a week or two. That'll give you a little more leeway."

"Yes, it might. I wish I could confirm when we will return. We're sailing blind at the moment. I must retrieve General Aron, but afterwards we don't know what direction to head for."

Curdoz shifted. "That isn't quite true. Lyndz and I have something to share after we set sail."

"You mean on finding the Eagle Staff?"

"Yes, I think so."

Kodi was listening to all of this and was compelled to add something. "I'm telling you the Alkhaness *will* engage, sirs. Why wait for her to make the first move? Have you considered challenging Westrealm before she invades you?"

Curdoz agreed. "Kodi is not wrong. My own Vision was more explicit than Kodi's, as I told Naloro. She will engage, and there is not a single hope that she will not."

"I admit I am expecting Berug to make the first move against her," said Jaden.

"And we might," thundered Hawking. "Yet we have no ground forces, and from the air it is insufficient for an offensive assault. The Nantians are going to be helping us on that as we have discussed before, but the training under the Nantian officers will not even begin for two more weeks. Do not count on us for an offensive move for some time."

Nikal looked at Kodi. "Your idea is not bad, and part of the plan is to build up the defensive force at Ft. Danzilet. It *should* keep her from lending aid to her cohort in the east. But I emphasize *should*."

"It makes sense to me that we're the ones who open a second front on our own terms instead of them," Kodi concluded.

"And yet it does stretch us," said Nikal. He looked at Jaden again. "Soldiers, Jaden. Soldiers, war material, and food supplies. And ships. Build it, build it, build it. That's the most we can consider just now."

"Then let us be off," said Curdoz. "We will reckon again when we return. By then, should we have the Staff in hand, we will have a better understanding."

Jaden looked at Kodi. "You're a bright one, Master Kodi. Master Tiliruf, did you bring that book you promised for Kodi to read?"

"Yes, sir. It's in my trunk."

"Keep up your reading, Master Kodi!" Jaden nodded and walked away with Genehbro.

"Sister Hollina!" said Idamé, giving her new friend a warm embrace and kissing her on the cheek. "You've made our time here as perfect as it could be! Experiencing Tirilorin in a time of peace and plenty has been a memory that I'll cherish! I love Solanto and miss it, but I can say that Tirilorin has been a home away from home. Thank you, dear!"

"Of course, dear. Now you ladies watch after one another! That goes for you, too, Rainwing!"

"'Ladies!'" the Etoppsis tssked. "The word has such a delicate feel, I don't like it. We are *females!* It describes our minds and defines our *energy!* I suppose your 'ladies' word might work for your Human ones who do nothing but simper as they watch the males display their prowess or drink tea out of those minute delicate cups in the afternoon."

"But we like our tea, dear," said Idamé, patiently. "It makes us civilized."

Lyndz laughed. "And what about the word 'women,' Rainwing? It's not so bad, is it?"

"I've observed your use of that strange word, as well. It isn't as repulsive to me as 'ladies.' It seems to at least 'gather' the females into a useful 'collective.' It's all right, I suppose. But oddly in contrast the singular form, 'woman,' is too 'separating' if you know what I mean. As if she stands apart."

"But I would think you would like that," observed Lyndz. "You are brave and independent. You've never acquired a Bondmate which you say is universally expected among Etoppsi. It seems you like living your own life and doing as you will."

"In part, yet you misunderstand still. Independent is probably not a good way to describe me. Anyway, we use only the word *female*, for we believe that *along with* our males we are in balance with nature."

"So, the natural order is critical to Etoppsi culture."

"At a universal and mystical level, though, Lyndz. Mystical feminine and masculine *energies* that we as females and males absorb from, and impart upon, our environment. The Guardian Himself mentioned it in your Vision. But the reason I have never chosen a Bondmate is that I have not found one that appeals to me and who understands me. Too, I like the self-discipline of chastity in the Orders. If I could bring back the Monastic Order to Berug as it existed a hundred years ago, I would do it, for I believe it would give others like me an institutionally approved way to express ourselves."

"Would any of your males choose to join it?" asked Hollina skeptically.

"No doubt it would be unusual, though maybe, if he were open to the *Guardian* Meical speaking in his mind of contemplation and service, then perhaps, rather than just the presumed militaristic Disciplines of the *Taxiarch* Meical which currently define the common expression of masculinity in Berug. Though that is important too, even though they wrongly claim it for males only. I have admiration for the Skyfront Feathers, though they scorn the few females such as myself who have chosen the Old Way, but they only do so because of the prejudiced attitudes of their *male* officers. The Feathers don't start out being prejudiced. They learn it. I do not care much for the male officers of the Sky Front. If females were allowed units in the Sky Front, maybe it would not be so bad. The Dragon Legion does it right, though, for all who wish to, male or female, may join, presuming they qualify for the physical demands, and the attitudes of their officers reflect the Disciplines better. But yes, it would be rare for a male to join the Monastic Orders even if it existed, and there were very few even in the old times. Our males..." she laughed. "Well, our young males are so hotly desirous of mating, and the courtship rituals and Bonding expectations so ingrained, that for them there is no alternative. I am spurned by many, yes, but at least people will talk to me. My students at the Institute, except for most Skyfront officers, seem to like me and engage me often; I have friends. But, yes, a male who made the same choice as I would be a virtual outcast. I don't deny the value of the traditions of the mating dances and Bonding, nor of Taxiarchan Disciplines; I just believe that individual differences are paramount and should not be so disparaged. So, Lyndz. Don't call me *independent*, but you can certainly call me *individual*. Surely, Hollina, Idamé, you get some criticism for having taken the Vow and joined the Orders?"

"I definitely used to," said Idamé.

"I definitely do still," agreed Hollina. "This is all fascinating, Rainwing, to say the least. I've never considered much the subtleties of words and of female roles. You've given me much to think on. Human men do claim an advantage, based entirely upon the simple fact they are male, which is not necessarily deserved. Most may be physically stronger, and they can often be more forceful in their personalities, though not always. But, they are not smarter. And you're saying that it's the same in Etoppsi culture, though mostly just in the military."

"Yes, exactly that. It appears in your Human society males dominate at many more levels. Though Tirilorin is apparently not so bad, especially with leaders like your Madam Midianna and Madam Arlay. I like them, by the way. The Kingdom of Nant is a horrid place for a female Human; I dread going back there. They have nothing beyond obeisance to their Bondmates and no way to express themselves freely."

"And the Principality of Hesk in Solanto," said Idamé. "It is much the same."

They paused in their discussion as Kodi walked up to them.

"Just what are you ladies talking about?" he asked innocently. "Nikal says it's time to board."

"Ah! There it is again!" Rainwing's wing feathers ruffled, and the other three laughed.

"What?" asked Kodi. "What did I say?"

"You called us *ladies!*" said Lyndz.

"Er, but you *are* ladies last I looked. Whatever is wrong with that?"

"Nothing's wrong with it, dear," said Idamé patting him on the cheeks and winking at the others. Lyndz and Hollina continued to laugh, and Kodi put on a perplexed frown as Idamé turned to Rainwing. "As you see, dear, it is mostly used for its perceived politeness! You shouldn't read too much into it, I think."

"*Too* polite," said Rainwing unconvinced. "I still do not like it."

A last goodbye and a few more waves and Hollina, Enric, Jaden, Genehbro, and Hadon entered the carriages for the ride back to Central City. The Solantines, the Berugians, Musca the dog, Tiliruf and Nikal then boarded the ship, in preparation for the quest of the Staff of Terianh.

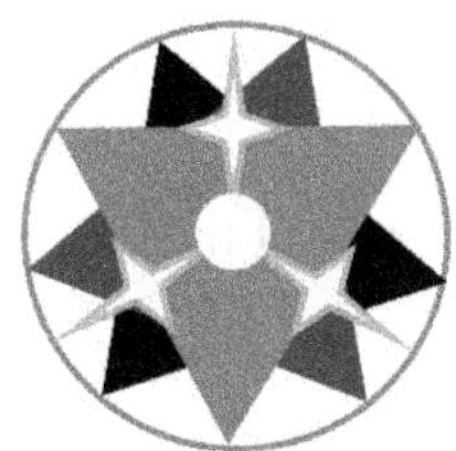

Chapter 15—Troubled Minds

You betrayed the trust of the Guardian.
Repentance offered, forgiveness given,
Yet reparation required.
Long slow age for a lonely god under the wave.
The Wisdom of Meical will seek you.
To return what was hidden and guide those in need
Will give hope to all,
And absolution will be yours.
Will you go beyond that, Worldbuilder?
To right your wrong
You must lose all that you have.
The Guardian knows your heart of hearts,
And you will never be lonely again.

After Lyndz read it aloud, the group retained their silence for a moment. They had been sailing an hour. Tirilorin could still be seen glittering far behind them in the sunshine. The winds were favorable, and they were making good time.

She had finished deciphering it two evenings previously, after Tiliruf's swordmaster ceremony. But they had been so busy the following day with dressing and preparation, the archery tournament and the dance, in addition to packing, that they had not really had time as a group to gather together and discuss it. Only Idamé and Curdoz, along with Enric, had seen Lyndz' parchment with the translation. The cipher had to be reformulated for this one, too, but Lyndz had finally worked it out.

"So, you and Enric believe it speaks of Vanaratu?" asked Rainwing. "Certainly, there is the reference to a Worldbuilder, but do you mind explaining to the rest of us what you see?"

"There is no proof, of course," began Curdoz. "Yet there was speculation soon after the establishment of the Anterianhi Empire, that Vanaratu was not allowed to return to Other Side of the World by Meical, but rather that He was banished. The Qeteral say that he was a great lover of the song of the sea, in fact that water features of all kinds—waterfalls, lakes, rivers—were close to his heart. And so, they tell a tale that he disappeared into the sea at Meical's command. The earliest Order members had little else to go on but this tale of the Qeteral, for Meical did not tell them what happened to either Siriné or Vanaratu. There is good evidence that Siriné was transformed and trapped within the great sea that now bears her name. It was called the Serpent Sea before. She is now but a twirling torment, a great storm that bounces from shore to shore. Few have been that way, and none since the rise of the Khestadone, who guard the straights to those southern waters. But there has been no clear sign of the whereabouts of Vanaratu. Yet the sea elements persist. What we do know is that Vanaratu was not a wicked being and that Meical would not have given him the same punishment He gave to Siriné. The Derogian Prophecy fits. So, should we believe it references Vanaratu, and if we believe the Deroge book came into our timely possession for our benefit through the workings of Meical, then it confirms our course. The Wisdom of Meical is symbolic of the Sage Order and *could* reference any Sage of the Guardian, er..."

Curdoz faltered, a dash embarrassed.

"But it's you," said Kodi, "specifically. It's your name; you told me so. That *Curdoz* was the name given you in your first Vision by Meical and that it means..."

"*Wisdom*," said Rainwing, finishing his thought. "I learned High Anterianhi when I was a topling! And of course, Curdoz, you are obviously the Sage in the other Prophecy, too."

"So," said Lyndz, "what is hidden that Vanaratu will help Curdoz find is..."

"The Eagle Staff," concluded Prince Nikal, but with nary a hint of the excitement displayed by the others in the conversation. He then walked away from the group and made himself busy among the ship's crew.

Tiliruf was not excited either but said nothing. He had for all practical purposes submitted himself to Nikal and Curdoz' quest, and though he doubted, he decided to stay out of it. At least for now, anyway, for holding his tongue was not really his strength.

Almost an hour later, Royal Hawking began to offer his goodbyes.

"I will go with you if you wish it," offered Rainwing. "I can see you safely to Sevarr and stay in the guest tower after you and the delegation leave, and then await Nikal."

"No. It is unnecessary. Although I appreciate your willingness to accompany this old Etoppsis!" He looked at his young friend and smiled at her. The two pressed the ends of their huge fingers together as the common Etoppsi sign of dear friendship. "I will manage fine. You have not spent any time yet with Kodi and Tiliruf. It is important for you to get to know them." Then to Nikal who was standing by, Hawking said, "I will let Aron know your current expectations, deliver these letters from Jaden and Naloro to the king, and return promptly to Berug with the delegation. We will have left Sevarr by the time you arrive. Queen Silverwing needs to know the developments in Tirilorin."

Nikal nodded. "Tell Aron it will be six days from now. I will not be docking in Noess on the way. In four days, he can send out my grayhawk Letti with messages for me. She will find me. Tell him we will stay in Sevarr two nights...possibly only one. I must speak to my father about the Staff quest, but as you know I have no desire to remain in the capital any longer than I can help. Aron knows that."

Hawking then took his leave of the others and bowed one last time. They waved at the giant as he stood on the aft deck and spread his vast wings. The brisk winds lifted him effortlessly, and upon reaching perhaps two hundred feet, he tilted and steered southwards, pumping and lifting himself to mountain-top heights. For a half hour they could still make out his position until he became a speck against the southern sun and disappeared.

"What is it like to fly, Nikal, sir?" asked Tiliruf after Hawking departed, making a determined effort to be friendly and to try to get on the prince's good side. He had reason to believe their relationship so far had been prickly.

"Exhilarating, assuredly, yet cold at the heights," the prince responded. Then he frowned, turned away, and as if to himself he said, "Yet not as cold as the hearts of some men."

Thankfully, Tiliruf didn't hear this last, or he might have misinterpreted its meaning.

Kodi was standing next to the prince and heard it, yet he kept it to himself. He knew it had nothing to do with Tiliruf. "Then let us warm up, Nikal."

The prince smiled at this. There could be little doubt he was warming to Kodi more swiftly than the others, even Rainwing. Kodi appeared to instinctively know how to help manage the man's emotions. As far as he was concerned, physical activity was for him a panacea for dealing with anything and suspected the same might be true for Nikal.

"Yes! We will. It is to become a part of your daily routine in any regard, whether it be with me or with Tiliruf. And when Aron joins us, him, too. The others must stand aside, or they may watch from the aftcastle."

Nikal then sent for appropriate armor, and he and Kodi engaged in spirited swordplay on the main deck for some time.

This was a new venture for Kodi to maintain balance as the ship rolled upon the waves. Thankfully, it was a much bigger ship than Curdoz' and the swinging movement was not quite as pronounced.

The prince may not have worked as hard as he did when he went up against Tiliruf, nevertheless, Kodi's performance was quite good.

"Assuredly you will be a swordmaster someday, Kodi, should you keep working at it," said the prince.

Some of the sailors who stood by applauded the match, and likewise several soldiers in transport, taking leave from the eastern war.

Lyndz was amazed, for she had not been to watch any of the sessions with Jaden. To see her brother wielding a blade with such skill was a new sight for her. She came down when they were done, followed by Curdoz. Idamé, typical for her, had retreated to the bed in the cabin as soon as Hawking took flight, and Musca had gone with her. Rainwing was so large that she had two or three places on deck and on the aftcastle where she would sit resolutely on a bench she would carry around with her, but she did not move around often. She was worried she would get in the way of the sailors as they worked. She remained on the aft in the spot she had staked out for herself, keeping her wings tight against her body, and watching the sailors work. She found it almost as fascinating as Kodi his first day on Curdoz' ship, though for different reasons. Etoppsi considered ships to be strange contraptions.

Tiliruf helped Kodi remove his hauberk. Attentive soldiers brought both combatants water to drink.

"It's amazing to watch you, Ko! You're not the same brother I knew back in Felto."

"Sure I am. Just harder and tougher, I hope."

"You still haven't told us yet about the sword Jaden helped you choose."

Kodi asked Tiliruf to retrieve his new good sword from the cabin, so he could show it to Lyndz and the others, while he took a minute to catch his breath and drank more water.

Tiliruf returned with the sword.

"Tis a very good blade, Kodi," said Nikal. "Solantine work, is it?"

"Well..." began Kodi. He went on to explain the hour in the old Palace armory, and the final choice.

"Baggaro's sword!" said Lyndz with astonishment. "Baggaro! Kodi, you didn't remember who he is? He's our ancestor! Our great-great-grandfather! Don't you remember Mannago showing us on his family charts? He was Grand Duke of Escarant!"

"Like I said, 'tis a very good blade," repeated Nikal, laughing heartily for once. "And to go with very good blood. And you too, Lady Lyndz. Jaden detected something quite potent about the two of you, something he could not put his finger on. By the Guardian! And yet why should I be surprised."

Kodi stood there dumbfounded, looking at his sword with much renewed interest and with a crazy sort of grin on his face. "But...but he's a great war hero!" Then he caught Curdoz looking at them with a guilty expression. "You mean we're descendants from this man? Curdoz, did you know about Baggaro and not tell us?"

"A war hero?" said Lyndz. "Mannago didn't mention..."

"It explains much to me, and like I said, no surprise," interrupted Nikal. "So, you've been play-acting a couple of country larks from a distant northern forest? When, in actuality, you have the blood of legends running through your veins."

Lyndz appeared even more mystified.

Kodi then explained to his twin what Jaden had told him about the story of Baggaro. "...so, you see, he defeated the Alkhan's armies in the last war!"

The implications of it all now dawned on her. Appearing as shocked as her twin, she too looked at Curdoz.

"I reckon I did know." The Sage responded about as humble and boy-like as when he spoke to Uncle Normene on his death bed.

"Why didn't you tell me?" asked Kodi.

"I didn't want you to know then," Curdoz replied bluntly. "But I assure you I have my reasons. If I explain them, will you forgive me? Ah! And I gave Genehbro such a difficult way of it, and here I am guilty myself."

Tiliruf thought all this back-and-forth quite humorous, though he was oblivious to this last reference regarding a key conversation Curdoz had had with his father about him. He was standing back laughing continually at the amusing encounter. When Nikal turned and gave him a stern look, however, he desisted.

Kodi and Lyndz stood there, arms folded, looking at the Sage.

"Well, I didn't know it when I met you, and that's the truth. I knew you were cousins to Duke Amerro and probably with Mannago, but I paid it little heed. It was in conversation with Mannago that I understood, and I requested he say nothing. I did not want the possible motive of revenge added to Kodi's set of emotions. Revenge does not reflect the Principles nor any Discipline I know. I wanted Kodi's thoughts and methods to remain clean, focused on making the right choices at the right time. Should he carry a vengeful grudge in his heart knowing the wicked manner in which the Alkhan killed his great-great-grandfather, he might act upon old family honor, impulsively, and he might make an error. And I didn't know about the sword, of course, until now. That's the truth. I think we must presume, considering the little Voice in the back of Kodi's head at the time he chose that sword, as he's admitted to us, that the Guardian means for him to understand now the connection."

"So, this is the 'being young' reasoning you've used before."

"I have fought that impulse with enough grace, have I not? You are your own man, and Lyndz is her own woman. I know that, but you must understand how one such as myself must look upon your relative youth. Yet, too, we each have our supposed strengths and gifts. We were put together on a purpose, and I was acting according to my wisdom at the time. Besides, I'm not so sure the timing was right back then. I didn't want Mannago encouraging a vengeance motive for the House of Escarant, for he was inclined to. Kodi's a naturally eager fellow. I didn't know if he'd latch upon such motive, and we were all dealing with much—with the ramifications of our various Visions and leaving home as we were. Finding out this way has, if you ask me, been better."

"All right, then, I guess I will have to forgive you," said Kodi after a long pause, pretending to do so grudgingly and giving Curdoz a look like Idamé might give Tiliruf.

"Well, of course we will!" said Lyndz, going over and giving Curdoz a huge hug. "You were acting as a father might! What's wrong with that?"

Curdoz laughed. "Well, I suppose the only thing wrong with it is that it is not always required." But then he looked at the twins and spoke more seriously. "I have come to know of course that vengeance is not a *natural* trait for either of you. Yet you must, you hear me, you *must* have a care, for one never knows how a bad or intense situation may affect one's attitude. A goading insult, a cruel action, a hard death, a destroyed friendship—in other words emotional pain—these things can breed vengeful thoughts. And such thoughts can destroy cool-headedness and good decision-making."

"Yet sometimes a return punch in anger can be effective," said Nikal, sternly. "Nevertheless, the Sage speaks rightly, particularly with regard to the Alkhan, for he is evil and can engineer hatred for the very reasons Lord Curdoz suggests—to catch you off guard. If the Alkhan knew you to be a descendent of Baggaro, he would taunt you and try to entrap you. So, I do not wish to dispute. You must both trust your heart and use your head."

The rest of the afternoon was spent in this way. Curdoz and Kodi retreated to the cabin they were to share with the prince and Tiliruf. Curdoz had begun a journal upon leaving Island Saundry, though he had neglected it mostly during their stay in Tirilorin. He wanted to take the relatively free time he had now to try to catch up on it. He had much to write, doubted he would get it all down, and half wished for a Monastic Scribe to take down faster dictation. Kodi, who had finally finished the Terianh book and loaned it to Nikal was eager to begin the book Tiliruf had brought about Baggaro. Especially so, now he understood his connection to this imperial hero. So those two were back-to-back on the floor by the porthole for light, Kodi with the book in his hand and the Sage with a wooden lap desk he carried with him on journeys that was hinged upon a case and within which he carried parchment, pen and ink. Musca snoozed at their feet. Lyndz sat in the sunshine chatting with Rainwing, for the latter was rarely likely to remain in their cramped cabin while she was awake. Besides, napping helped Idamé adjust to being at sea, and there was no point in disturbing her. The two 'females' talked mostly about similarities and differences among Human and Etoppsi cultures, and the Nantian sailors were well-disciplined to mind their own business and paid them little mind as they themselves went about their work. Nikal took Tiliruf below decks where there were assorted iron weights and bars and other equipment used for heavy lifting and pushing exercises. Some of the other men were there making use of it.

This was standard on every Nantian naval vessel so as to keep the soldiers and sailors in prime muscular fitness. It was a new thing for Tiliruf, for though Jaden had all his students perform certain exercises, they did not specifically use weighted equipment for the express purpose of building muscle. Yet the discipline was heavily promoted in the Nantian military, and by and large the soldiers and sailors of Nant were brawnier than their counterparts in other countries.

Tiliruf did not see the importance of this, for he was quite fit and muscular by Tirilorine standards, and no one could complain about his physical skills. Yet he did as he was told and as the weeks went by under Nikal's eye, he gained in strength and build until he compared quite favorably even to Kodi, who had deliberately built muscle through similar workouts and all his stonework back home, and also to Nikal who was himself a paragon. And though the effort and aches and pains associated with hard workouts annoyed the spoiled rich man greatly, when Tiliruf realized that the increase in strength allowed him even more forcefulness, physical control, balance, and stamina during his swordplay, he finally understood its value. Nor did he mind how his muscles grew, and in time the effort became more natural to him, and he began to push himself at these weight maneuvers without being told.

Yet here in the beginning he was grudging, and when he offered instead a round of swordplay on deck like the prince had done with Kodi, to his disappointment Nikal scowled a bit and told him no.

Nikal could be a severe taskmaster at times, but he was otherwise quite patient with Tiliruf. He would demonstrate the exercises he wanted Tiliruf to perform, and he would assist him so that he would not hurt himself. Nevertheless, whenever Tiliruf was alone with Nikal, that is 'alone' in the sense that Kodi was not present, for there were always the other men—sailors and soldiers—around them all the time, it tended to make Tiliruf gloomy. Nikal was never in the mood for light-hearted conversation or joking. Tiliruf was always much cheerier whenever Kodi was present taking part with them and at those times acted as if he minded these new disciplines much less. It was a long time before Tiliruf realized just how much Nikal really cared, and that his success, not only in his swordsmanship but in everything else he did, was at the forefront of the prince's efforts with him. Once he finally did realize it his loyalty to and reverence for the prince grew markedly, and in many ways this respect for

Nikal had a greater effect on him than perhaps even his friendship with Kodi. Though Nikal was no more than ten years older than they, and for Kodi he was like an older brother, for Tiliruf anyway he became a sort of father figure. He provided a set of boundaries and discipline that Genehbro had never attempted with his son. The self-indulgent younger man would occasionally burst these boundaries, yet nevertheless, over a long period of time, he grew.

A squall on the second day out from Tirilorin undermined any activity above deck, and the consequent higher waves and wind terrified poor Idamé who remained on her mattress in her alcove. Curdoz had some minor healing magic, nothing on the level of a Gifted Healer, yet he did what he could to ease his sweet friend's mind, placing his hand on her head yet eventually forcing her, as he had done to Kodi back in Aster, into forgetful sleep.

As the Matrimonial drifted off, Lyndz having watched the green light as it emanated from the Sage's hands asked him a question. "You have said once or twice that the magic of Sages is...'muted' from what it used to be."

Curdoz nodded as he watched Idamé sleep. "The first eight Sages, those chosen by Meical at the time of Terianh the Great, and who are referred to often in the Book of Histories and Prophecies, were much more powerful, magically. They themselves were not allowed to use their magic to cause physical harm or death to the Ralsheen enemy, but they nevertheless had great powers. They were fully-fledged Healers, all of them, but they also had the ability to read people's minds, which they used to uncover Ralsheen spies in Terianh's camp. They also had destructive powers which they used to blast away the palaces of the Ralsheen high nobility, the slave markets, and also in order to destroy the old temples to the goddess Siriné. The Valley-trained viewpoint teaches that the Guardian was determined to put a damper upon cult-like aspects of religion. It wasn't simply a means to eliminate the false worship of Siriné, but also the fact that Meical did not wish to replace it with anything else. Many refer to the Orders of the Guardian, with its teaching of the Principles and Disciplines, as a religion, but in our view, they do not fit the mold of religion. Even prior to Siriné's corruptive influence there were temples to Meical and the Creator. The eight Sages believed that Meical wanted religion to be replaced with the Principles and Disciplines without focus on the idea of *worship*. Worship often brings out the worst in Humans, for through it they are prone to extreme forms of thinking, latching on to the false idea that Meical or the gods or the Creator or Siriné are wanting them to focus on religion and worship and the adherence to strict, made-up rules, at the expense of loving and caring of all. The old religions supported priests and priestesses who began to demand tribute and sacrifice, supposedly to gain the favor of the one they worshipped, and they could work their followers into a zeal to antagonize or even fight against those who did not conform. This was taken to its worst extreme under the Siriné cult of the late Ralsheen era, but it was also a problem during the time the World Gods still lived amongst the Three Peoples in the deeps of time prior to the Condemnation and the establishment of the Other Side of the World and of the Teeth of Meical by which the World Gods would be required to live separately from the Three Peoples. But even after the Condemnation there was a long era in which many worshipped Meical Himself, believing Him to be an avatar of the Creator. Temples were built to promote the worship of Meical. Strange rules and conditions began to be enacted, few of which had anything to do with what we know today as the Principles and the Disciplines. Meical claimed He Himself was a Messenger and Guardian sent by the Creator, rather than an incarnation. We revere Him, yes. But it is wrong to worship Him.

"The eight Great Sages were determined to eliminate religion per se. With their magic they went about the northern world and destroyed all the worship temples. Not even the ruins of such temples exist today. The buildings in the Valley of the Gifted, some are called temples, yet these are not foci for worship but rather places of study and contemplation. Though we Sages and others still have some priestly functions, we are forbidden to set up worship sites and surround ourselves with followers. It is even rare that we allow the Book of Histories and Prophecies to be read by others not associated with the Orders, for there are those who would likely create religion around the Book itself. That almost happened, but those who set too much store by the Book were eventually made to understand their error. The Principles we teach, yes, because these we believe to be universal, as they promote goodness and love of all, rather than the division and separation common to religion, and the Disciplines are various means by which Order Members and others choose to order their lives usually, though not always, through a Calling.

"In any event, those earlier Sages were quite powerful, but as the magic was no longer required in the Anterianhi peace, the magic faded. As a rule, now, our powers are limited to an intuitive reading of emotions and body language, minor healing and sleep powers, emotional connectivity with others of like mind unto ourselves such as what Idamé and I often share when we are near to each other and is common amongst Healer pairs, and a few other useful tidbits. I know I have mentioned before about the sound 'blocking' magic by which I can communicate privately with a person even though others may be nearby, although some Healers and Moment-masters share that one, too. And some of our priestly functions have a sort of magical component, hmm, perhaps 'mystical' is the better word. We can offer forgiveness and absolution to those who harbor great internal struggles and guilt and will sometimes draw up individualized written Disciplines for those determined to begin anew—contracts of a sort that aid in binding them to a new way of life. But no more do we have the destructive powers, for they are not needed. And most of our healing powers are now dispersed amongst the Healers as a separate Order."

"But the Staff has destructive powers."

"It does. I think *most* of its powers are destructive. Yet the call of the War Wizard is quite different from that of a Sage. The War Wizard has within him, not what you might call a desire to kill, but rather an instinct to fight for what is right."

"Yet killing is involved."

"I understand that you worry for your brother." Curdoz spoke more quietly in order not to awaken the resting Idamé. "There is no reason in the world for any of us to worry for the morality and ethicality of Kodi's or of Nikal's methods, particularly if we as friends stick close and help to keep them grounded—admittedly an important part of our Calling. I feel very strongly now that that is *my* Calling. Should we gain the Staff, those two will perform a duty as proxies of the Taxiarch Meical whereby good has a fighting chance against evil. War involves killing, yes, but in the Imperfect Worlds where evil lurks, it is sometimes necessary, or evil will march over the lands in triumph. Meical, considering the fact He Himself is not attending to this current war in person has chosen two men He believes will best represent His role of Taxiarch. It is intriguing, as He has never chosen two men at the same time. It is unique. It says much for their innate character that you should have no fear for their minds and motives, and yet..."

"And yet what?"

"It is certain, in war, that though we may not worry for their minds and motives, we may worry for their persons. I wish I could say something definitively encouraging. They assuredly have the courage needed to face the enemy. Yet the danger of failure is there."

"We could lose," stated Rainwing flatly. She had been sitting on the floor listening closely to this whole conversation.

"We could. But the main point is that we do our best. We must presume that though our time is indeed dangerous it may be less so than at the time of Terianh the Great and the Eight Sages. Yet sacrifice will occur, perhaps very great sacrifice, and all of us friends will be at the forefront of it for that is our Calling, and we must prepare ourselves for it. We were *all* chosen, not just Kodi and Nikal."

"Yes, I know that now," said Lyndz, looking knowingly at Rainwing.

The rain continued to fall, the ship rolled, and Lyndz remained quiet and contemplative the rest of the evening.

The following morning dawned, and Idamé was much refreshed and cheered by this and even came above deck to take in the sun and the sea breeze. She liked the sea quite much at a certain level. She thought it beautiful and energetic and spiritually mysterious. She loved it when fish or dolphins jumped out of the waters and the calling of gulls. She admired the panorama of stars at night. Yet it also unnerved her, for it made her, as she would say, "feel like water." She did not like the movements of the ship upon the waves. She would tolerate it for about an hour, but then retreat again to her cabin. She could read only for short periods, but then she would simply lie there in her alcove with her eyes closed and her hand on her head as if she were nursing a headache. Which sometimes she was.

"Knitting!" Lyndz said suddenly later that day as she sat with Idamé to keep her company.

"What did you say, dear?" asked the Mother in a weak voice.

Lyndz scrambled through her belongings and retrieved her knitting needles and yarn that she used often to occupy her hands while she thought and when she didn't feel like reading. It was an activity too which reminded her of her mother. But with Rainwing's presence she was doing more of her thinking aloud with her new Etoppsi friend and didn't feel the need to occupy her hands so much.

"You can knit, Mother Idamé," she said, bringing the supplies over to her. "It'll help, I bet. You lie there and knit something. You don't have to knit anything special, of course."

"All right, dear, it's worth a try, isn't it?"

She did at least have to prop herself up on a few pillows. Lyndz swung open the little porthole for air and propped the cabin door open. Light streamed in.

"Oh, that's quite fine, dear," said the Matrimonial. "The window wouldn't open on Curdoz' ship." She began fingering the needles and yarn. After a minute she pulled it all apart. "You know I really must focus on something, though. I think I'll attempt a scarf. For Tiliruf, I think. Is there enough wool here, do you think?"

"Yes, Mother Idamé. Use it all. We can get more in Nant and have plenty when we sail in search of the Staff."

It did seem to help, and when Idamé was working away and the frown left her face, Lyndz called out the cabin door for Musca to come and ordered him to sit beside the Matrimonial, which he promptly did with good grace. Lyndz felt good about leaving the cabin and returned to Rainwing on deck.

She found her twin and Tiliruf sparring with practice swords. Nikal was at the helm giving the steersman a break, for he trusted Tiliruf when it came to training Kodi on his swordsmanship. Curdoz was standing as he often did at the railing looking out upon the churning sea, contemplating whatever it was Sages contemplate. Lyndz was unaware that at that moment he was pondering her recent encounter with Meical the Guardian, her questions of the day before, and her responses.

She sat down beside Rainwing who was watching the men spar, and the two picked up again on an earlier conversation.

"...so, were you involved in confronting it?" Lyndz asked, referring back to Rainwing describing a rare encounter, when as a Legionnaire in the Dragon Legion, she had to face a huge Winged Dragon.

"Yes! There were at least a hundred of us who took turns in groups rushing it and stabbing it with lances or pounding it with maces or casting javelins at it. It was terrifying yet exhilarating to say the least. Part of the strategy involves trying to damage one of its wings. For if you can hurt it badly enough it will fall to earth, and then it is easier to kill, though still dangerous in its agony. Of course, it is attempting to blast fire at you whether it is flying or on the ground, and it is easy to get scorched or maimed or killed despite the dragon armor we wear and our shields. We finally did bring it down and kill it. Sometimes we allow the Winged to escape, particularly if we are chasing it over the Infested Jungle, and usually they learn their lesson. Rarely does the same beast return. It can be years before another one ventures into the plain on our side of the Western River. This one was only the second Winged I ever saw the whole fifteen years I served in the Legion. It was a brute. One of our females had to have her right wing removed for it was so badly damaged. Sundasher is a hero to the people. She is a friend of mine, and like me a Follower of the Ancient Way, which is how we reference the old Monastic Disciplines. It's the few of us females who are not Bonded and spend time in study and contemplation. I go visit her when I can and even carry and fly with her on high so she can experience the exhilaration of being airborne. No one died in that incident, thankfully, but every once in a while, someone will be killed. A granite obelisk is placed, often in the hometown of the Legionnaire, as a memorial."

"What's the worst that ever happened to you?"

"Oh! Well as to that one time a group of ten of us were confronting a Wingless just as it was on the edge of the river getting ready to cross it near to an orchard on the southern border. It was spotted by one of our watchers from a platform in a tall tree about a mile away. Well, to make a long story short, I struck it with a mace, but as I swung forward with my arm, it turned its head and cast fire at my exposed right wing. My next blow stunned it, but so many of my feathers were scorched I couldn't fly for three months until new ones grew in."

"Was it painful?"

"Not especially. Yet it was an awful experience, I tell you, for not to be able to fly is really hard on us—a great handicap. It is so much a part of us. At least feathers can grow back, so I had little to complain about in comparison to Sundasher. Yet I have personally known three Legionnaires who have lost wings, Sundasher, and two males, and though they are honored and well cared for, it is tragic for them. If I should ever lose a wing, I think it would kill me inside."

"I can imagine," said Lyndz. "If I should lose my eyesight, or an arm, that would be horrid. I suppose I would have to adapt, but it would be very hard."

The two broke off their conversation when they realized the men had stopped sparring. They looked to see them standing with Curdoz who was pointing, looking outward upon the sea.

"Look!" cried Kodi, turning to his twin and Rainwing. A mile or more away at sea there was a great commotion. Dark shapes appeared sporadically above the surface only to retreat again below the waves. It went on for several minutes, and all the time the shapes kept getting closer.

Suddenly Nikal was there beside them having turned the helm over to another.

"None of you have ever seen them before, have you? They are the giants of the sea. Other than the rare serpent that escapes the rivers of the Infested Jungles, that is, but of course serpents are like dragons, cruel and vicious, and will attack ships. These creatures on the other hand are friendly to all. Curious and intelligent. They come close to learn about us."

"I've always heard about whales and have always wanted to see them!" said Lyndz.

"And I think I would like to see them from a different perspective!" said Rainwing, laughing. "Friend Lyndz, are you willing to fly with me?"

"Yes! Oh, yes!" Lyndz was beside herself with excitement. Kodi indicated envy. Tiliruf balked.

"I'll catch you another time, Kodi!" said Rainwing consolingly. "Tiliruf, you have no idea what you're missing!"

"There's a reason Humans don't have wings!" he said, displaying skepticism.

Then Rainwing walked to the bow as Hawking had done, and Lyndz went with her.

The Etoppsis grabbed Lyndz securely against her body, spread her wings and sprang skyward. Kodi and Curdoz applauded, and even Nikal smiled. He was the only one there who knew exactly what it felt like.

High they flew upon the winds of the sea. For Lyndz it was the most exhilarating experience of her life. "Oh! This is so incredible! Rainwing!" She had to shout over the wind.

Rainwing then swooped down in the direction of the great pod of whales.

"Are there different kinds?" Lyndz called out.

"Yes!" said Rainwing. She was a scholar, but she was also from Green Isle, a large island north of the Berugian mainland, and so she had by necessity flown above the sea countless times in her life on her way to and from her home in order to see her family. "There are many kinds. Some smaller, some even larger than these, and of various colors and even shapes. Those are Great Blacks, some of the larger types, and especially dark in color. They are rarely seen in this sea; they are much more common west of Nant. And to see such a large pod, surely this is an unusual occurrence. This is exciting for me as well!"

They swooped low, and low and behold one of the massive creatures jumped nearly clean out of the water in their direction, only to crash upon the waves in an enormous splash that got Lyndz and Rainwing wet.

They laughed. They circled and watched as the creatures rose and spouted wet airs high above their blowholes.

"That is how they breathe, you see!" called out Rainwing. "They are not like fish. They are much more like land animals in that way!"

The pod approached the ship and began to slow down. All on the ship could see them well, now. For fun, Rainwing decided to take Lyndz higher. She pumped her wings and rose rapidly.

Suddenly, Lyndz called out and pointed. "What is that? It's massive!"

In the distance, below the water could be seen an enormous shape. A vast cloud or darkness. It was so immense that it appeared as if an island had grown there from the deeps but did not yet reach the surface of the sea.

"I...I don't know!" said Rainwing, obviously startled. "It's as big as a mountain!"

"Is it moving?"

The waters above it appeared to be calmer, more like the waters of a lake, as if they were receding or being pushed aside. Considering its size, it appeared to be moving slowly, yet Rainwing supposed it may have been an illusion, possibly moving much faster than it seemed.

"When I first saw it, I thought it might be an enormous school of fish, for they can appear like dark clouds under the waters, but I have never imagined one so large. I would say it is more solid than that."

It was difficult to tell, and even as Rainwing dove in its direction to get a closer view, the great shape appeared to recede lower into the water until it disappeared altogether. The waves reappeared sharp above just as they were in the rest of the sea all around.

"We did not imagine that, did we?" asked Lyndz.

"Of course we didn't! There was something in that water! And I felt something. Like we were being watched!"

"I did, too, yes! Like a great presence!"

"Let us go back to the ship and tell them what we saw. I doubt they could see anything of it from their low perspective."

The men watched the pod of Great Blacks from the deck as they approached closer and closer. "I think I'll go and get Ida," said Curdoz. "She must see this!"

He turned, but then his smile left his face. Then quite suddenly he grasped hold of his head with both of his hands. He called out and then collapsed on the deck.

"Lord Curdoz!" yelled the prince.

Kodi ripped off his hauberk which he was still wearing from his sparring with Tiliruf and immediately went down onto the deck and raised Curdoz' head into his lap. "Curdoz! Curdoz!"

The man did not move.

Tiliruf stood shocked for a moment, yet finally broke out of it and said, "I'll go and get Idamé!" He ran to the women's cabin.

Nikal bent down beside the Sage. "He has a pulse. It is beating fast." He called for water from one of the sailors. "He's pale and sweating. I wish we had a Healer pair aboard!"

Tiliruf returned with Idamé running. "What's wrong! What's wrong! Oh Curdoz! Whatever has happened?" She bent down, and like Nikal had done, felt his pulse. When the sailor returned with a bucket of water, since there was no rag handy, she dipped a portion of her shawl in it and wiped his face with cool water. "Curdoz!"

"His heart is beating. I don't understand!" said Kodi.

"And he is breathing. It can't be the heat. It's not that hot, not with the winds."

On the bow Rainwing landed with Lyndz. There were other sailors and soldiers standing by watching what was going on with the Sage, but they drew aside and the two came quickly.

"What has happened!" said Rainwing in her loud voice.

"We don't know!" said Tiliruf. "Curdoz collapsed, but nothing seems wrong. His breathing and his heart are good, and he hasn't been hurt!"

"Step out of the way," said Nikal commandingly. With that he bent over and with strength lifted the Sage. Since there were only hammocks in the men's cabin, he carried him to the women's and laid him on Idamé's mattress in its alcove.

For several minutes Idamé nursed her friend, wiping his brow with cool water. Kodi removed the man's boots and stockings and loosened his shirt so that he would stay cool. The others stood by.

"It's as if he's fallen asleep," he said. "He was pale and his heart was racing as if he were agitated, but it has calmed down and he looks all right."

"Yes, his coloring is good now," agreed Idamé.

"Try calling him again, Mother Idamé," suggested Lyndz.

Idamé got close to his face and called, "Curdoz! Curdoz, dear! It's me, It's your Ida! Do you hear me, dear?"

Suddenly, and to everyone's astonishment and relief, the Sage open his eyes.

"Curdoz!"

"Where am I?"

"You're in my bed, dear."

Tiliruf snickered. Everyone looked around at him scathingly, but then Curdoz spoke again. "It is rather embarrassing, Tiliruf, is it not? A Sage in a Matrimonial Mother's bed! Whatever happened to your Vow, Ida?"

And then Kodi laughed too and Idamé went all pink. "Oh Curdoz! You had us so worried! I couldn't reach you with my mind, even though I tried! What happened, dear?"

"Vanaratu."

Lyndz caught her breath and looked at Rainwing who remained outside the cabin with her head in the door. The Etoppsis replied first. Her round voice filled the cabin, though she was attempting to be quiet and gentle. "Did he speak to you, Curdoz? We may have seen him from above, Lyndz and I! A vast dark presence under the water!"

"Yes. He spoke to me. It was overwhelming. I could not handle it."

"You fell, sir. You fainted."

"Yes, Kodi, I imagine you would too if a god entered into your mind and spoke to you. And it was more than words; he cast images at me. Like Visions from the Guardian. But they were like thoughts, or emotions. Finally, my mind settled when I realized what was happening and who it was, and I was able to manage. Next time he speaks to me I think...I think I will be prepared. There is a calming technique I can use. He will not speak to anyone else but me."

"Why not?"asked Kodi.

"He is not allowed to."

"You mean by the Guardian?"

"Precisely, Lyndz. He was given permission to speak only to me. And I am the only one Of the Mold with whom he has been allowed to speak in five hundred years."

"The whales!" stated Lyndz.

"You are ever the keen one."

Kodi and the others looked confused. Lyndz explained what she and Rainwing saw from the air. "...and those whales are his friends, don't you see? He's not been allowed to speak to people, and so he has instead made friends with the creatures of the sea!"

"And yet he is lonely, still," said Curdoz sadly. "Very lonely. So lonely, that I cried inside. The images I saw. Gods—his sisters and brothers on the Other Side of the World—even Qeteral faces of some he knew in Ulakel centuries ago. He misses them all terribly. All lost to him."

"So, he *has* been living in the oceans all these long years!" concluded Rainwing.

"Kodi, run and get my pipe and get it going for me. I need it."

Kodi returned promptly. In a minute the Sage was sitting up and smoking. He returned to complete calm and acted perfectly fine again.

"There are legends of a great shadow in the sea," said Prince Nikal. "Just as Rainwing and Lyndz describe. A vast black mountain that never lifts itself above the waves, and always the great whales come into those tales! But none as far as I know had ever speculated that it could be Vanaratu."

"But what did he actually say to you, Curdoz, dear?" asked Idamé.

"He will meet us here in this same place when we return from Sevarr. He knows where the Staff of Terianh is located."

"Did Meical tell him?"

"As a matter of fact, the Guardian took it from Terianh after the war and gave it to Vanaratu and told him where to take it."

"But Terianh didn't record that!" said Tiliruf, obviously doubtful.

"Because Terianh never knew what Meical did with it."

"Did he tell you where?"

"He did not tell me where, no."

"So, we're going to come back here and follow this thing, what? Across the ocean?"

"Well, Tiliruf, I do not know how big the ocean is, so I cannot say. He told us to prepare for a four-week journey altogether, there and back. And he is not a *thing*. He is..."

"...a World God, yeah, I gathered that. Sorry, my mistake."

"He understands the need for freshwater and assured me we would be able to renew our supplies when we reach our destination."

Nikal sighed deeply. "Some island, then, or land mass. Four weeks. That will still take a good deal of provender. Did he say in which direction we would be traveling?"

"West."

"Two weeks west! In past years Nantian vessels have sailed far in that direction and yet found nothing: no islands or other lands. They would be forced to turn back of course as their provisions had to hold out for their return. None travel that direction anymore except fishing fleets, and even they only as far as the Chain Islands."

"And no Etoppsis has flown so far, for there are no places to rest west of those islands," added Rainwing.

"An entire month on a ship!" said Idamé gloomily.

"Though with a docking midway, apparently. Yet, we can leave you in Sevarr if you wish, Mother Idamé," said Nikal compassionately. "There is a convent west of the city, and I can arrange an escort there for you. We will return for you before traveling east. My father will command me to return after the quest for the Staff in any regard."

"No!" she replied firmly. "I will not abandon all of you. I will manage it somehow. You will not leave me behind. I will face with you whatever it is. I am one of the Eight Friends from the Prophecy! We are in this together."

There was little to report over the next two days other than that they sighted and then followed along the coast of the island Kingdom of Nant.

Nant was an island kingdom situated between the southwestern coast of the Northern Continent and the Coast Islands, a chain that led to the north coast of the Southern Continent and the land of Berug. Geographically, Nant was the western terminus of the Coast Island chain. It was settled by Humans in ancient times and was a province of the Ralsheen Empire until the Anterianhi conquest. It was some time before the fledgling Anterianhi navy reached the island only to find that its slave population had risen up on its own to overthrow the Ralsheen yoke. It readily joined the new Empire, and the Eight Sages and Terianh appointed its first king, Luxindi, a former slave who had led the uprising. Nikal was directly descended from this first king, though through female as well as male lines.

It was small relative to the other constituent nations of the former empire, yet rich and prosperous. Fertile, the island produced many products, wines and brandies, linen and wool, various grains, iron ore and military armor.

Being an island, shipping and shipbuilding was an important industry, and when the Anterianhi Empire dissolved, the King of Nant greatly expanded the royal navy, and in time it took the imperial navy's place as the preeminent enforcement and protective force in the southern seas. They took on the responsibility of monitoring the coasts and keeping the Khestadone navy at bay. Aside from occasional piracy the latter was rarely seen outside the Khestadone Sea, the wide waters between the two enemy realms that led to the larger Sea of Siriné further south.

Like Eleni, which was occasionally at war with Barant in the far northeast or with the Ice Tribes, Nant, also being of a military bent was dominated by men. And yet in Eleni, women had nearly as many rights and options as they did in Solanto and were treated with a level of respect that adhered to the highest chivalric notions. Chivalry was not absent in Nant, for there were certainly a few, such as Nikal and Aron, who had the highest regard for all women. But since the time of Nikal's grandfather, upper class females had most of their rights taken from them in favor of an ancient dowry system.

Despite this unhappy situation, most in the old Anterianhi world still looked to Nant as an example. As stated, the army and navy were the biggest and most disciplined in the world, and most countries depended on them to keep the Khestadone threat in check. The realms prospered as long as Nant controlled the seas. Few in other countries really knew much about the unhappy limitations imposed upon its noblewomen, seeing rather the realm's great surface features: its power, prestige and wealth. Only a handful, such as Nikal and the Sages of Nant and close observers like Hawking, could see the poison that limiting the rights of women created in the ruling hierarchy.

As the ship neared the coast, a city could be seen at one point. It was obviously a busy stopping point for ships, though it did not have a deep harbor. Ships were anchored offshore. They passed it by.

Nikal stood and watched that place for some time, gulls crying overhead, a deep frown on his black-bearded face. Curdoz approached him privately.

"I sense you are in some pain, Prince. That place holds some unhappy memory for you?"

"That place does not. On the contrary, Lord Sage. That place holds my last happy memory." He attempted a smile, then turned away and walked back to the men's cabin and shut the door. No one else was privy to this exchange and Curdoz kept it to himself.

He did, however, make one comment to Kodi later in the day. "If anyone of us is to break through Nikal's gloom it will be you. Rainwing may know what ails him, but he does not open himself to her."

"I am trying, sir."

"Yes, I see you are. And doing a fair job of it. You have a real knack for getting to know people. All I can say is this. I think he has lost something or someone he values greatly. I think the latter."

In the evening a grayhawk landed on the prince's shoulder as he stood on the aftcastle. Around its neck was tied a small pouch within which was a folded piece of parchment. Nikal took the message, read it, and then stuffed it in a pocket.

Kodi was standing with the prince who allowed him to handle the little raptor. "Very useful, you see," said Nikal. "Aron and I exchange messages this way, though usually we do so back east before or during battle. I'll have to teach you the symbols we use for battle positions. Her name is Letti."

Kodi was intrigued. "I've often wanted a trained bird. They are used in Solanto, too, by a few. My cousin, Duke Amerro, has one. I have wished for a Bluetail. Do they live in Nant?"

"Ah! Majestic creatures, yes, and amazingly swift of wing. They are a large bird, though, Kodi. I've never heard of one being used as a messenger. The smaller hawks and falcons are easier to train and care for, I should think."

"Maybe so, but I still want one."

"Then they hold meaning for you?"

"When I see them in flight I think of the idea of *freedom*. And when they call out, it's as if they call for me to follow. Especially when I was stuck back in Felto, seeing one would make me daydream. So, yes, you're right, they do. Perhaps they're not so practical, as you say. Yet if it were independent, like Musca can be, it might work."

"Perhaps," Nikal smiled. "Are you sure there really is such an idea? As freedom? Sometimes I doubt."

Kodi looked at Nikal. "I am freer, for sure. I've told you my story. I can tell that you are not, though. For that I'm really sorry. Yet, how can I judge if you don't tell me your tale?"

Nikal eyed him. "You don't think that Prophecy traps us, you and I especially? Limits our freedoms?"

"I can't look at it that way, no. For me it gives me a new purpose."

Nikal reached up and held the top of Kodi's shoulder. Then he looked off over the sea.

"For me it adds to my responsibilities and is a burden on my heart when my heart is otherwise clouded." He sighed. "Don't get me wrong, Kodi. I am committed to the task ahead, and I care a great deal about doing what is right and following this path the Guardian wishes for us to follow. It is the Principles and the Disciplines that saved me from myself in my youth, through Sage Antonin's teachings and forgiveness. I am now lost again. Maybe it will be the Principles and the Disciplines that will save me from despair."

"But you say that last cynically like you don't really believe it."

"No, my faith is challenged. You are right. Yet I will tell you something. I look at you, who are in many ways untroubled and enthusiastic, with few errors or tragedies to darken your soul, and it gives me some limited joy, maybe even a dash of hope, to know there is a friend such as you near at hand. Your presence means much. Stick close. When we are in Sevarr, stay by my side. You may learn much. And like you have said before, this quest for the Staff binds us together. I deem you will know my story soon enough. There was more to that Prophecy than the portion in your great-grandmother's little book."

"Is there something I should be wary of?"

Nikal puckered his brows and thought for a minute.

"Yes. The crown prince. Considering your candidness, Kodi, I would advise you to steer widely of him. He will never be a friend of yours."

"His name is Lekktor, isn't it? You mean your brother?"

"Factually speaking."

Kodi pondered the word choice for a goodly while before replying. "He is dangerous?"

"Well, put it this way. He has recently become dangerous."

"What does he look like?"

"He is paler than I, tall, less hefty, clean-shaven, brown hair. You look more like a typical Nantian than he does. He takes after our Elenite mother, whereas I take strongly after my father. Eh, at least in looks. Though you are unlikely to see my mother. Oh," Nikal smirked. "Lekktor's nose was broken once. You will be able to tell it when you see him."

Kodi was learning to trust his instincts, and Nikal was giving him a good deal of information, even if it was in cryptic terms. "I'll break it for you next time, if you wish, and you won't have to get your hands bloody the second time."

Nikal laughed so loud and heartily that everyone on the deck of the ship looked in his direction. They could not hear the conversation, of course, over the winds. "Would that I had you for a brother instead!"

As Nikal had done to him, Kodi put his hand on Nikal's shoulder. "But don't you see, Nikal? I *am* your 'genuine brother.' The Prophecy says so. In which case Meical says so."

Nikal looked at Kodi and pondered this truth. Finally, he nodded. Together they stood and watched the sun set over Nant. Neither said any more to the other. And in the silence, the bond grew stronger.

From the other end of the ship where Curdoz stood, he watched the two and was cheered.

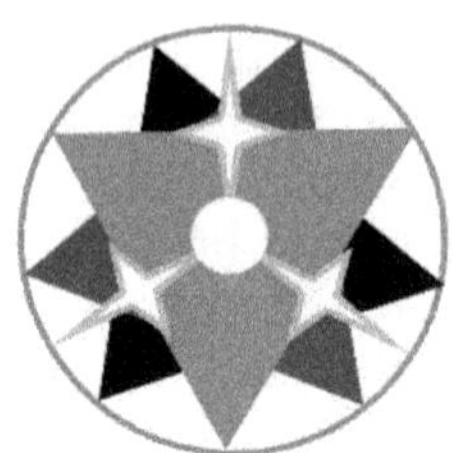

Chapter 16—The Truth Behind Nikal's Gloom

When they landed in the large port capital of Sevarr in late morning on the sixth day out from Tirilorin, General Aron was there to greet them along with Lord Ralle, High Sage of Nant. Both were gracious during the introductions, and Curdoz and Idamé were delighted to see Ralle, whom they both remembered from the Valley. He was close to their age, though unlike Curdoz he had remained as a scholar for many years in the Valley before being sent to replace the retiring Antonin.

Tiliruf stared at Aron a bit rudely until Kodi kicked him in the shin. Nikal had not made mention of the general's stammer, and Tiliruf too obviously thought his speech strange. Yet Musca took to the general instantly and was quite playful until Aron finally took a moment to bend over and scratch the dog's pointed ears. The latter licked him fiercely on the face.

Ralle's presence was not anticipated, for Nikal had kept silent, although it was Curdoz' intention to call upon him. Yet per Nikal's instructions, Ralle was approached by Aron soon after the prince had flown off to Tirilorin with Rainwing and Hawking. The prince and general had decided that Ralle was likely the only person in the capital who could be trusted with such delicate information. Someone of substance was needed who would know of Lekktor's recent scheming and who could be on the watch for more of it. And though the Sage had less authority in Nant in comparison to Curdoz in Solanto, he did at least have the weight of the Orders behind him and was a member of the High Council.

It turned out well that they did, for Nikal really did not wish to stay at his father's palace, for now it held one too many unpleasant memories, nor did he wish to subject his new friends to palace intrigue. Aron lived aboard ship much of the time, and his Sevarrian house was otherwise too small, and he had no servants. Therefore, Ralle led the little crowd to his manor which overlooked the harbor from a height. It was a beautiful place, but little time was taken for exploration of the city or of the gardens. Monastic servants assisted the travelers with baths and brought them good meals at midday, and during the afternoon several conversations took place with the Sage of Nant. Some of these were decidedly illuminating.

Aron had disappeared again, for he was working to ensure Nikal's warship was prepared and well-stocked for the journey ahead. As instructed, Kodi remained close to Nikal after those two had cleaned up. Kodi, as he always did after a bath, felt like a powerful new man, for though he had never explained it to Tiliruf, baths had become for him symbolic of his plunge into the Valley Lake in his Vision. Yet as he listened carefully to the current conversation between Nikal and Sage Ralle this bit of temporary euphoria was swiftly wiped away. Some harsh truths were finally revealed to him of his Nantian friend's struggles.

Ralle was saying to Nikal, "Of course the king will be gracious to your visitors and will wish to meet them all and hear of events. Mother Idamé's presence, however, might make a few people nervous. As your guest from another country, she will be welcomed by your father, but if she were one of my own here in Nant it would be illegal for her to even come to the city without invitation. Yet you need not even announce her name until you are with your father. No one in Nant will consider the symbolism of her shawl except for Order Members, and they will retain their silence."

"And of Lekktor? Aron says he has not returned to his station in Hildred. Why does he remain in Sevarr?"

"His Highness is taking advantage of his popularity due to his recent...nuptials. His prestige has grown a little now he is Bonded. He is playing it up."

Nikal sighed. "I had hoped not to have to run into him again. And...and Dira?"

"As secluded as your mother the queen. She hasn't been seen since their Bonding last week. To me it comes as no surprise. Why should Lekktor treat her any more favorably than your father treats your mother? Of course, considering her own trauma, she quite likely does not wish to be seen."

Nikal eyed Kodi and looked away from them and out a window. "And their Bonding last week?"

"Mother Superior Gilrian presided. She despises the contractual Bondings of the highborn, and I know you do, too. It is the only time she or any Matrimonial is allowed into the city, as you know, to squelch any likelihood that they would declare an Aura over one of the lords. The Lady Dira wore a veil, and her face could not be seen unless one was in close proximity, as I was. I could sense her emotion through my Gift as she walked by me. She was most distressed and unhappy. She...she was in tears."

Nikal swallowed hard and was silent for a while.

Though it was not admitted in so many words, the truth struck Kodi and struck him hard. His friend's pain was palpable—he could feel it across the room. It was all he could do to refrain from blurting out. There was a tremendous amount he didn't understand. How could such a horrible thing happen? Why were the laws so restrictive? Was there a law that had kept Nikal from declaring for her? Nant sounded to him a place as awful and restraining as the Principality of Hesk.

Yet now he understood fully why Nikal could not talk about it. It was assuredly the most treacherous and tragic thing that could happen to any man, that one's brother would deliberately steal the woman he loved and force her into Bonding him instead.

Ralle spoke again. "You are right even to keep this from your father. His prestige would be on the line if it were discovered that his elder son had used him in such a way as to hurt his younger son so deliberately. He would not be able to make things right without breaking the law, nor could he now change those laws without the Council, and they would not stand for it. Of course, you know all this already. For your own heartbreak, Your Highness, I am most deeply sorry. I suspected something was horribly afoot as I watched you during that Council meeting when the betrothal was announced. I saw you go pale and could sense your distress, and I...I saw the looks you and your brother exchanged."

After further pause Nikal finally turned around. "I see I have missed out on a friend, Lord Ralle. Thank you for all the information and for hosting me and my comrades."

"I know you were close to Antonin. I...I know I am not quite on his level. He fought harder than I do for the privileges of the Orders in Nant. For the Principles."

"I think it is only with these recent events, Lord Sage, that I have been able to see just how difficult such a task really is. So, no, I believe you underestimate your role. You have protected the Orders and stood for the Principles. Sevarr is a difficult place. It is why I do not like coming here often, and now I don't wish to be here at all. We will set sail as soon as reasonable the instant the king gives us leave. We shall certainly remain tonight." He paused. "And a Healer pair for our journey?"

"Oh, yes. The message you sent by the hawk to Aron. You requested a female pair, which I thought odd."

"I wished for Mother Idamé, Rainwing and the Lady Lyndz to have more of their own gender as friends for such a long journey."

"A pair is willing. According to Father Kienne, they are hearty travelers and are quite used to camping on their treks out to the provinces and doing without luxury. They are the Sisters Ulna and Maru. They await at Kienne's home."

Then Kodi made a request. "Lord Ralle, sir, Musca is very cramped on a ship. Would you consider watching after him until we return? A month is a long time for a large dog to be on a ship. I'll miss him, but he would be much happier here."

"Certainly, Master Kodi!" the Sage replied cheerfully. "The Monastics will happily watch after him!"

Another conversation to which Kodi was not privy took place between the three from the Valley. Kodi had gone with Musca, Tiliruf and Nikal to the harbor to check on Aron and to look over Nikal's ship. After Lyndz had bathed, Rainwing took her on a flight over the countryside. Ralle, Curdoz, and Idamé sat in the study. Unlike Enric who did not smoke, Ralle was quite the connoisseur, and the two Sages smoked their pipes together and with Idamé shared some wine.

"The Staff, should those two men come into its possession, will come with political ramifications here in Nant," said Ralle. "Nikal is favored by his father, and possessing the Staff will come with even greater authority. That is my suspicion, and I hope that is the case. Crown Prince Lekktor will resist it, for, at the moment, the two brothers, though most prefer Nikal, are considered equal generals under the king. The Staff will change that. The military Disciplines of the Taxiarch which that Staff will symbolize, will gain great traction in Nant, for they have a military nature in any regard. Not unlike the Berugians, if you ask me. He who bears that Staff will *command*."

"And you think it will affect Kodi as well?"

Ralle smiled. "He holds himself well for one so young. Confident."

"He has a charismatic personality and is becoming smarter and more subtle by the day, I swear it. He's catching up to his very astute sister, quite frankly."

"I can hardly keep up with him," added Idamé. "One day he is in my eyes a mere boy, and the next he is a great man, and yet the boy-like affability remains always the same."

"And he is a pillar for Prince Nikal, I see. Rather like General Aron. The prince is very private and will consult with few. But yes, back to your question. I think so. I don't think it will matter that much that Kodi is not from Nant. He looks like a young Nantian prince anyway, and to be a direct descendent of Bagarro himself will hold great weight in the hierarchy of the military and among the high lords. He will rise quickly, particularly at Prince Nikal's side."

Curdoz nodded. "Would you consider, upon our return, traveling with us to Tirilorin? Terianh, according to the Histories, was installed as War Wizard by three of the Sages in a rite in what is now Eleni. It will add to their legitimacy if we carry out a similar ceremony, you and I, along with Enric. And Tirilorin needs a reconnection with its founding history. I think such an event would do great good."

"I will plan on it! But you don't have the Staff yet, Brother Curdoz," he said with a wink.

"True."

Ralle turned his attention to Idamé, and a bit more soberly said, "Are you aware of the laws here regarding Matrimonials?"

Idamé put on her most disgusted look. "Rainwing has been informing me, and I learned somewhat during my stay in Tirilorin."

"You must not proclaim an Aura in this city, or you might be subject to questioning despite your status as a guest. The justices might try to impugn your reputation and integrity. The ability to detect Auras is doubted and ridiculed by the elite. I know it is unlikely, but if you see an Aura out and about while you are here in the city, you need to retain your silence and inform me personally, and I will do what I can to bring the pair together without anyone being the wiser."

"I think your laws here are hideous! I had no idea before that Nant had such restrictions. I don't remember it being discussed in the Valley."

"Matrimonials are to avoid places where high lords gather, and that includes the provincial estates of the lords and the capital city of Sevarr. It is an embarrassment, and I myself was uninformed until Antonin told me upon my arrival eight years ago. Antonin tried to fight the rules from their inception decades ago, always holding out hope for a reversal. King Monticu's father and his Council established these rules about forty years ago. The king's father was determined to Bond a young woman he had taken a liking to, but an Aura was proclaimed upon the young woman and his younger brother instead. It infuriated Monticu's father, so when he came to the throne, he pressured the Council to change the law. He didn't have to press them hard. The Council, all men, thought the idea a good one, for it increased their authority to establish these awful contractual Bondings. Huge dowries and local powers and prestige are on the line for these. And the highborn young women and their mothers have no control over their futures. At feasts they are mere decorations as they sit next to their husbands. Yet in the countryside and the villages, the Matrimonial Order operates as it would almost everywhere else. Though the elite pretend the Auras are superstition, the tradition is so entrenched amongst the common folk that, so far, the Council ignores it. It is quite typical for the Sevarrian city common folk, young lovers that is, to travel out to the convent west of the city to see if by chance an Aura will be proclaimed. Once every year or so I will hear of one such Aura. And virtually all Sevarrian Bondings take place at the convent. It is an inconvenience, but that is the way it works here. The only time Matrimonials are allowed in the city is if they are invited, such as crown prince Lekktor's Bonding last week when the Mother Superior presided."

Curdoz and Idamé both frowned and looked at one another. Idamé spoke first. "Nikal made no mention to us of his brother's Bonding!"

Ralle puckered his brow and considered before responding. "If he has not said anything to you, then I hesitate to say..."

“Your hesitation tells me much, anyway!” exclaimed Curdoz, sitting up straight and setting down his pipe. “Does this recent Bonding have something to do with the prince’s current melancholy? He obviously skipped the ceremony if it was last week and flew instead with the Etoppsi to Tirilorin! It does, doesn’t it?”

Idamé looked aghast at the portents.

Ralle puffed several times on his pipe. He stood and walked to the window. “So, he hasn’t been forthcoming with you. But why did he...” he paused. He raised his eyebrows and turned around. “I do know a little. General Aron told me what Nikal wanted me to know, and that was that yes, Prince Nikal was in love with the young woman. Her name is Dira, the daughter of Duke Rothee from Noess. The crown prince discovered his brother secretly loved this woman and in his jealousy of Nikal’s fame and father’s favoritism stole her from him. The law allows the crown prince to Bond first before a brother. That also came about through their grandfather’s changes, though it is Lekktor and Nikal to whom that law has first been applicable. Their father had no brothers. The situation is a great secret. His Majesty doesn’t know. Monticu isn’t the brightest to sit on the Nantian throne. Aron says no one in the court knows except for the two brothers. Oh. And their mother Queen Gatha. She apparently was the one who informed Lekktor, undoubtedly her favorite son, of the secret courtship. Aron refuses to tell me specifics as to how far the relationship progressed. We can readily presume she loved Nikal in return. I perceived her broken heart at the Bonding. Yet Lekktor schemed, and Duke Rothee perceived a better opportunity. To be the father-in-law and grandfather of future kings overshadowed possibilities with the second son.”

Tears fell from Idamé’s eyes. She dabbed at them with her shawl. “Oh, how wretched!”

Ralle continued. “I really suspect now Nikal must want you to know the truth, yet he himself is unwilling to talk of it, for it is obviously much too painful for him. That makes sense to me considering my earlier conversation today with him and Kodi.”

“So Kodi knows?”

“Well, he assuredly does now. Considering the fact you two did not, some of Kodi’s expressions during that conversation make more sense to me, so in retrospect I do not believe he knew beforehand. Yet it is perfectly clear Nikal wanted him to know, or he would not have questioned me about Dira and the Bonding in front of him.”

“They have become close this week. For which I am glad. Nikal could have had Rainwing inform us, though, even if he were unwilling himself to talk about it.”

Idamé replied. “Even if he wanted her to, Rainwing’s big voice carries all over that ship. Every sailor and soldier aboard would know the story. I suspect it is only today—just before we go to the king his father—

that he was willing for any of us to know. In the privacy of Brother Ralle's home."

"Of course. His own thinking is probably changing day to day. If it hadn't been for Kodi and Ralle, we still might not know."

When Nikal returned with the men, Ralle was determined to inform him he had felt compelled to discuss the situation with Curdoz and Idamé. Yet Nikal was in some way relieved.

"It is well, then, that they know." He turned to Kodi. "You may discuss this with Tiliruf and Lyndz, then all will know. In one hour, we will leave here and go meet my father."

"I will go along," said Ralle. "This meeting is about the Prophecy and the quest for the Staff. It is the business of the Orders. And obviously, only the middle portion of that Prophecy should be repeated and discussed."

Kodi then made it plain to Nikal what he now expected from him. "I want to know the whole of the Prophecy, Nikal. I want to know everything. It isn't right for you to keep the rest of us in the dark on it."

Aron agreed. "Thh...they must be made ah, aware, sir. If you wish it, I'll have Rainwing repeat it for them all."

"Go ahead, but for my part I never want to hear it again."

And so Nikal disappeared for a while. Rainwing had returned with Lyndz, and they all sat in Ralle's parlor, and the whole of the Prophecy was revealed to them, and the betrayal of the queen and Lekktor was explained.

All sat or stood about, shocked. Lyndz' and Curdoz' minds sifted silently the additional verses, attempting to determine hidden meanings. Yet if they had some new revelation, they kept it to themselves.

Tiliruf's jaw dropped after hearing it. "And I thought Nikal might be angry with me for some reason."

"You always think it's about you, even when I tell you it isn't," said Kodi.

"Sorry about that, mate. Just having a hard time trying to get to know the man."

"H...heee is difficult to get to know, Master Tiliruf," said Aron. "Yyy...yet you should not ever question his loyalty to thhhose who are loyal to him."

"He is warned by one with the shawl?" questioned Idamé. "But what am I supposed to warn him about? I don't have any insights into that Prophecy any more than anyone else does, other than what has already taken place and has become obvious."

"Which means quite simply it hasn't taken place, yet, Mother," said Lyndz, matter-of-factly. "But when it happens you will undoubtedly know it. You can't push it."

"Lyndz is correct," said Curdoz. He pondered for a moment and then looked at Ralle. "We can't force any of it. Yet it's ultimately about decisions that Nikal makes for hope in the end. And our roles in this are more critical than I imagined at first. Nikal cannot succeed without us. For the enemy's fate—it is almost certainly the Alkhan it refers to—to be sealed, correct decisions and sacrifices must be made. And we must retrieve the Staff of Terianh if we are to have a chance. If Nikal doesn't go after that..."

"But he's committed to it already," said Kodi.

"Unless he changes his mind."

"But what could change his mind?"

"I hope nothing happens that makes his choices even more difficult than they already are."

"Fff...for my part, I am ww...willing to make any sacrifice for Nikal to gain that Staff, for he must have it. He is the great hope for this war."

"I, too," said Rainwing. "I'd even give my wings for it."

"Me, too," said Kodi. "Er, I know I don't have wings. You know what I mean."

"What I want to know is why the queen would do such a thing to Nikal," stated Lyndz.

"It is a mystery," said Ralle. "Nikal is and has always been respectful of his mother. In fact, he is one of the only high lords in all the land that give women their due."

"What about this Prince Lekktor, eh?" said Tiliruf. "Maybe Kodi or I should take him outside for a bit of sword practice. You all say the secret must remain a secret because of the way the laws work, but that doesn't mean we can't rough him up a bit."

"Serrrrvants in the palace speculate Nikal already rrr...roughed him up, yet Lekktor denies it hotly."

"He broke his face," said Kodi, chuckling. Everyone looked at him. "Well, he didn't admit it straight up, but I know it's true."

"He dd...didn't tell me!" Aron laughed gleefully. "Lekktor told everyone hhh...he fell hard and crashed into a bedpost!"

"He must be trying to hide that little affair from the king," said Ralle. "The Healer pair who mended him were convinced there was more to it than an accident. The last thing Lekktor wants is for his father to start asking questions. Lekktor knows he has hurt Nikal deeply, and he knows Nikal cannot reveal it without their father losing face and causing scandal. Yet now he fears Nikal."

"Well, he's about to fear me, eh? Maybe a situation will present itself for me to challenge him to some friendly swordplay."

"He learned from Jaden, like Nikal did," said Kodi.

"That's right!" exclaimed Tiliruf, chomping at the bit.

"No!" said Curdoz, emphatically, though he had a smirk on his face. "You will do nothing of the sort. Nikal wishes us to depart Nant as soon as the king gives leave. We don't have time for that sort of nonsense."

"Unfortunate," said Tiliruf pouting.

Aron was laughing. “I also look fff...forward to the opportunity to present itself, Master Tiliruf. I...I...I have known His Highness as long as I have known Nikal, and I can tell you plainly Lekktor is a great horse’s ass.”

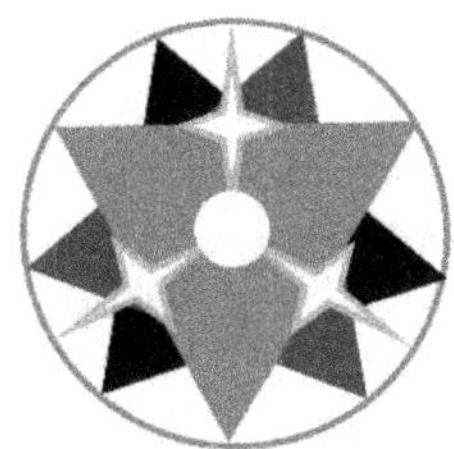

Chapter 17—One With the Shawl

There were a few carriages in the city of Sevarr, nothing on the order of Tirilorin. It was a gorgeous city with its white stone buildings on hills overlooking its large harbor. Across the harbor a large river plunged over cliffs in a great waterfall and added to the city's stunning views. Yet the streets were narrow, and there were many switchback curves and inclines. Many were on horseback on the cobbled streets. Yet walking was the norm, and so some two hours before the sun set, the party of nine set out from Sage Ralle's manor and made their way to the palace of King Monticu.

The prince walked resolutely, and beside him, each with his sword at his side, were Tiliruf, Kodi and General Aron. They were a formidable force, truth be told, and drew many looks. The others walked behind, and though Etoppsi were seen more commonly in Nant than in any other Human country in the world, Rainwing nevertheless drew stares. Most had heard that Hawking's delegation had departed already, so they were surprised to see another Berugian so soon and wondered what it could mean.

Prince Nikal was hailed often, and commoners bowed to him as he passed, and though he would always acknowledge the people, particularly soldiers and officers, it was clear to Kodi that his cheerful greetings did not reflect his true mood.

"How long will this take, Nikal? Will you have to speak at length regarding Tirilorin and its position?" asked Kodi.

"No. As a matter of fact, Hawking has delivered the messages already. My father will know already of Tirilorin's declaration of war and most of Jaden's immediate plans. Our meeting will focus on our quest. Rainwing will tell him of the nature of the Prophecy, and Lord Curdoz will display its importance through its duplication in the Seeress's little book. I will have to explain little of that myself."

"You seem nervous about the meeting. Is there really a reason to be?"

"I do not fear my father, no. Securing his blessing for the Staff quest should not be difficult, although it does delay my return to the east by at least a month, which is unfortunate. I think he will be intrigued, altogether. I am mostly anxious about the possibility of seeing Lekktor, for he assuredly knows I have returned."

"You fear he may cause some sort of trouble?"

"His behavior is no longer predictable, so I don't know what to expect. I think mostly I am afraid that I will lack patience should he interfere."

"Yyy...you must not, ah...allow yourself to veer from your goal, sir, which is to secure your father's ah...good graces and blessings for our journey. Ignore yyy...your brother."

"You think he'll even show himself, eh?" asked Tiliruf. "After all he has done. I know I wouldn't."

"Well, if he does," said Kodi, cracking his knuckles, "you're not alone, Nikal. Don't forget it. We all stand with you."

"Egggg...exactly, Kodi," said Aron. "C...c...couldn't agree more."

And Aron cracked his knuckles, too.

When they arrived at the palace, the prince was greeted enthusiastically by guards and servants, and Nikal was required to put on a gracious show. Kodi had seen how Nikal could perk up when there was business to attend to. Even on the ship when soldiers, sailors, or the captain would speak with Nikal, he had always squelched his gloom so as to act with proficiency and confidence. It intrigued Kodi greatly, for it had never occurred to him before he met the Nantian that a man could act as two different people. He remembered Jaden saying something about it—that Nikal was a private man, yet when required to lead, he led. He understood better what he meant. Kodi, who was in general outgoing and cheerful, wasn't sure this was a strategy he could use, yet he nevertheless paid attention. He supposed it was like role-playing. Yet in Kodi's case the roles he himself played all interrelated and did not require such different personae to achieve. He was extroverted by nature. With Nikal, on the other hand, Kodi often believed he was witnessing an actor on a stage. Behind the curtain the man was reserved, yet with deep emotions and serious demeanor, and even a caring and warm nature to those who could break through the gloom. Yet once the curtain was withdrawn and he found himself in front of the crowd, he was another: the great prince of Nant, captain and hero of the eastern war, a favorite of the Nantian people.

Messages had been sent already, and so the king was expecting his son and his guests. When the group was admitted into Monticu's private audience chamber, the king stood from his chair and walked forward. He was a handsome man who greatly resembled his second son, yet close perhaps to Curdoz' age. He indeed looked kingly. However, his eyes, though bright, did not hold the depth of perceptiveness that Nikal's so definitely did.

He greeted his son amiably, and as Nikal introduced the others, he was clearly impressed. Yet the presence of Curdoz perhaps more than all the others was a real indication to the king that there was some great purpose. That a Sage would travel so far from his assigned country meant something.

"...yet you are not mere travelers," he said, as he eyed him. He then looked at his son. "What is the meaning behind this gathering of such illustrious persons, Nikal? You brought them from Tirilorin. Hawking said you would make everything clear."

The king invited everyone to sit. There was even a stone bench for Rainwing. Nikal began to explain about the Meicalian Prophecy, but then turned this part of the discussion over to the Etoppsi female. She, with the help of the Solantine Sage, explained everything thoroughly. Only the middle portion of the Prophecy, as agreed beforehand, and duplicated in Deroges book, was revealed to the king. Curdoz had the book and Lyndz' deciphered interpretation with him, and though he did not choose to discuss Deroge's relationship to the twins, he did explain her reputation as a Seeress.

"The Eagle Staff of Terianh! In our time!" Monticu then turned to Sage Ralle. "And what do you make of all this, Lord Sage?"

"You can be assured, Your Majesty, that it is all true and these are great portents. There is great reason through my discussions with our guests to believe that our revered Meical the Guardian is taking a guiding role in our conflict with the Khestadone. He is making use of these persons based on their specialties and Gifts, including those of your own son. It is a great defining moment in our country's history! Should your son gain the Staff of Terianh, it will improve our chances in defeating the Alkhan and Alkaness once and for all and returning peace to the northern world."

"But this about Vanaratu the World God. Lord Curdoz, explain what you know of this."

Curdoz then explained his communication with the elusive Vanaratu, and Rainwing described what she and Lyndz saw from their flight. King Monticu was utterly astonished.

And thoroughly convinced, apparently. "It is a long journey and potentially dangerous, my son," he said to Nikal. "Yet I shall not be the one to deny your destiny. You must go, and go with my blessings! The war will manage without you for a while longer."

Nikal nodded appreciatively to his father, though everyone else had turned in the direction of a side door being opened.

The man was brown-haired and clean-shaven. He was lighter in complexion than the king and Nikal, not anywhere near as muscular or handsome, and with a nose sporting a large hump in the middle. Yet otherwise, his face was clean, and no bruises or scars shown. The Healers had done their job well, yet the broken nose was something they could not fix.

Though he looked nothing like Monticu, he wore princely clothes with a sword at his side. Beside him walked a woman.

This woman was obviously Nantian with her darker complexion, and she was indeed so beautiful and shapely in a silken blue dress that Tiliruf shuffled, and even the disciplined Kodi was forced to stifle that surge in his groin that always seemed to plague him in the presence of perfectly shaped or stunningly beautiful women. However, upon the woman's striking oval face was a look stoic and unseeing. She did not look in the face of the king or of those of any of the visitors.

"And just where is my illustrious brother going, Father, may I ask? This sounds to me quite intriguing. I should like to know the details!"

All had properly stood at their entrance, including the king, but Kodi could sense the strain in the man standing next to him. Nikal stared with wide eyes at the beautiful woman, ignoring utterly the man.

"Ah, Lekktor!" said King Monticu. "You have brought with you the new princess! Dira, it is lovely to see you again. You have been too much secluded since the ceremony last week."

Being thus directly addressed, she still refused to look into his face and only nodded.

This did not seem to bother the king who turned to Nikal. "It was most regretful you missed your brother's Bonding Ceremony, yet General Aron informed me of course that an opportunity had presented itself and you felt the need to take advantage of it. Tirilorin's declaration to fight with us in the war was indeed a great coup, and you and Royal Hawking should be proud of your influence on that. But it was a grand affair, and the Lady Dira was lovely. Unfortunately, your brother a few days beforehand had a most unfortunate accident with a bedpost, in *your* bedroom oddly, and though the Healers worked on him, they could only do so much. It is only in the last few days the remnants of his bruises have faded."

Kodi stifled himself and hoped desperately that Tiliruf would not snicker at this, yet even the Tirilorine was not unaware of the delicacy of the moment.

"Yes, Father, that story is quickly growing old," said Lekktor in an aggravated tone. "But yes, indeed I wanted very much for my dear brother to meet his new sister-in-law!"

Kodi shifted, as did Aron. It was clear now exactly why Lekktor had deigned to allow Dira to leave her imposed seclusion in their rooms. He had ordered her to come with him.

Nikal remained silent, and Lekktor pressed his advantage. "The law allows you now to find your own Bondmate, Nikal! I wish you well! Though I doubt you shall ever find a lady so lovely as *my* Dira."

Aron's hand went to the hilt of his sword, though perhaps no one other than Kodi saw this. The general was assuredly angered by this subtle provocation and gave Lekktor a deadly look. Kodi feared he might attack the crown prince then and there.

The king obviously expected a reply, and so Nikal swallowed and finally spoke in a quiet tone, all the while his eyes on the woman. With slow and careful words, he said, “Assuredly there are none, none in all the world, who could compete with the beauty and perfection of the Lady Dira, and I can assure all that there will never be such a one as she to grace my side.”

The naive Monticu replied. “Ah, Nikal! You speak as though you shall not pursue a Bondmate and a family! I think I know you better than that! You are capable of great love, I know.”

“No,” Nikal said, and then turned his eyes from the lady to his father. “This quest and the war preclude it.”

“Ah, well, perhaps after you acquire the Staff of Terianh and the Khestadone are defeated, you shall have a change of heart!”

Lekktor laughed with much exaggeration. “The Staff of Terianh! What nonsense is this, Father? And who are all these folk?”

It was then that Curdoz took charge, responding before the king could take a breath. He bowed to the crown prince. “Greetings, Your Highness!” he began with exaggerated cheerfulness. “I am Curdoz. I am the Meicalian Sage of the Kingdom of Solanto. I was so hoping to meet you, and to place a face on one I have heard so much about! I am sure you know Rainwing of Berug and General Aron, and my Brother in the Orders, Sage Ralle. These others with me are Master Kodi, the Viscount Fothemry and his twin the Lady Lyndz. They are descendants of the great Anterianhi General Bagarro, and with them is the Mother Matrimonial Idamé. These traveled with me from the Kingdom of Solanto. And also Swordmaster Tiliruf, son of Genehbro of the House of Terianh. We are gathered as your brother’s very good friends, of course, as directed by Meical the Guardian through a Prophecy and by way of Meicalian Visions. We have been ordered by the Guardian to seek the Eagle Staff of Terianh the Great, which your brother His Highness Nikal has been chosen *personally* by the Guardian Himself to possess and with it to command all the nations in the war against the Khestadone. Your brother is indeed a great man, one of the greatest of all men in our time. I know you must be most proud of him! Your father has just given us his formal Blessings upon our journey to seek the Staff, and we shall take our leave upon the morrow. So, as you see, Your Highness, you can be reassured this is not nonsense at all. When your brother gains the Staff of Terianh, great benefit may result in our conflict with the Alkhan and the Alkhaness.”

During this little address on Curdoz’ part, the face of the crown prince grew pale. He did not like hearing words that lifted his brother to further greatness, nor did he like the deadly stares given him as he looked around at each of his brother’s ‘very good friends.’ Even Lyndz and Rainwing looked as though they were capable of stabbing him. Tiliruf fingered the hilt of his sword and oddly winked at him, adding to his anxiety.

The whole time Curdoz spoke, behind Lekktor, Nikal continued to look at Dira, whose face was turned downward. All the rest in the room were focused upon Lekktor and Curdoz.

Except for Idamé. She kept looking back and forth between Dira and Nikal. The poor Matrimonial was beside herself with deepest sorrow for the two and immense anger that the laws of Nant resulted in such horrible circumstances. That Lekktor had come deliberately to taunt his brother in front of their father and friends made her believe the crown prince the wickedest man she had ever in her life come across. She wanted desperately to be able to intervene and turn the whole horrid situation around. As a Matrimonial it was her Calling to bring together those who were in love, offer counseling, and perform the Bonding rites. Love between two people was to her a central theme of Creation, for it brought joy in the world. Everything else happening in that audience chamber was to her irrelevant in comparison, even the Staff quest, and the sham conversations and pretense in front of the king were almost unbearable for her. Her heart wept for Nikal and Dira. Her face turned red, and her heart began to pound as her frustration and anger built.

And then it happened.

Dira, who had thus far kept her head lowered in order not to meet the eyes of the others in the room, especially Nikal, knowing how it would affect her, made the error of looking up just once. And when she beheld her lover and read the pain there as he looked at her, she wept.

The king did not notice this, and of course Lekktor was paying no attention to her whatsoever. He was processing all this information Curdoz had cast at him, anxious as to how it might affect his future. He was not liking in the least what he was hearing, for anything that might bring glory to his brother would surely bring nothing good to him. So, when Dira fell to the floor in tears, it was Nikal who brushed behind Lekktor and was suddenly and naturally at her side.

When the green light visible only to her appeared strong above them, the tragedy of it all was too much. Idamé gasped...and fainted.

When she awoke Curdoz and Lyndz were at her side. Lyndz was fanning her face. Rainwing stood by as well.

She looked around, "Where am I? What happened?"

"You're in a waiting side chamber, Mother Idamé, on a divan. Are you all right?"

"You fainted, dear friend! In the audience chamber," said Curdoz.

Then it all came back to Idamé in an instant. "Where's Nikal! Where's Nikal! I must see him! I must see him, *now!*" She sat up and grabbed Curdoz' arm, panic in her eyes.

Curdoz looked at her and puckered his eyebrows, worried. And then his eyebrows shot wide.

Lyndz gasped, "No! Oh, no! Mother Idamé, it can't be!" She realized exactly what Curdoz had. There was only one reason why the Matrimonial would be that desperate to see Nikal.

"I'll go!" said the Sage.

Back in Monticu's audience chamber Nikal was pacing, attempting desperately to retain his self-control. His mind was tortured. Lekktor, greatly annoyed by the whole situation, was forced to withdraw with the distraught Dira. The king, stupid in his ignorance, was utterly oblivious to the meaning behind any of it, making idiotic excuses.

"So sorry that that happened! Lekktor tells me the poor girl has been rather emotional. I was quite surprised she was willing to come out this evening. I do hope she doesn't prove to be too frail a companion for Lekktor."

"If you were to ask my opinion," said Sage Ralle, who was moved by the situation, "I would say she is most unhappy. I perceived her sadness during the ceremony. Perhaps this contractual Bonding was not a good idea, Your Majesty. Much more thought should have been given to it, and her own opinions taken into account. Perhaps the two are not compatible."

"It is immaterial," said the king, coolly. He might be dense, but he was still a king. "It is the law, as you know, Your Grace. I'm sure in time she will grow used to her new situation. She should be happy. She will be queen someday."

"Her Majesty is happy?"

Monticu frowned at Ralle's presumption, but then he smiled. "It is your wont as a Sage, I grant, to give the women such equality on a par with the men."

"Because all of us Of the Mold, male and female, are indeed equal, Your Majesty."

"Old Antonin always fought me on it, even more so than you. I cannot agree, of course, but it matters not, Your Grace. You have your views you feel required to espouse, and I respect that. And I have Nantian law to uphold. Women do not have the will and fortitude of men. Their purpose is to serve the needs of their husbands."

Aron held his tongue, as did Kodi and Tiliruf. All the men were decidedly uncomfortable at this exchange, yet they were determined not to exacerbate the situation. Even Tiliruf who had few relationships with any women, and the few he did have were not especially healthy ones, found the king's misogynistic views troubling.

Curdoz appeared again in the audience chamber.

"How is your Matrimonial friend, Lord Curdoz?" asked the king. "How odd it was that she collapsed at the very time as the young princess broke down!"

"Yes, it is odd, I admit, though I should think nothing of it! She is perfectly well, thank you, Your Majesty!" The Sage spoke with exaggerated cheer, like he had a few minutes ago with Lekktor. Kodi had grown used to the Sage putting on such sham exaggeration. It was not dissimilar to the first half of his conversation with poor Onri on the Ramp. "I think the sea journey has worn her out, you see, and we must return soon to my Brother Ralle's home so she may rest well before our departure tomorrow. But while we wait for her to recuperate a little, I'd like to speak to His Highness. I have had a bit of an idea I wish to share with him! Your Highness, Prince Nikal, if you will come with me. I'm sure we shall return shortly, Your Majesty. Swordmaster Tiliruf. Master Kodi. You should show your swords to His Majesty! I'm sure the king would be most inspired by their histories!"

Nikal followed the Sage out into the hallway. Servants were bustling about, and the prince had to whisper. "What is the matter, Lord Curdoz?"

Curdoz scoffed. "Everything is the matter! What horrors that you have a brother such as that and a father as shallow and unaware as Monticu! There is a matter for Idamé to discuss with you. She needs to see you at once."

They entered the waiting room where Rainwing had carried Idamé, and the instant Nikal went inside, Rainwing, Lyndz and Curdoz took their leave in order to wait in the hall.

"...but don't you see, Nikal! The two of you are meant to be together! It was intended for you to be a Bonded pair!"

Nikal's eyes were bloodshot as he squelched hot tears. The news had nearly broken him. He paced the room in great strides. Finally, he stood still and faced her. "Just what do you expect me to do about it, Mother Idamé!"

"Explain it to your father! He is the king! Surely, he can decree your brother's Bonding to be null! Or the Mother Superior!"

"It is a legal contract! They can't do that! The law would have to be altered, and they are not granted that authority in Nant. Do you want the whole of the High Council to learn of this? I don't think you understand the danger, Mother Idamé. They don't want to believe in Auras! Auras represent to them a lack of control over their choice of Bondmates. Auras are rare, perhaps, but the very notion of Auras allows women in general to have equal say as to whom they Bond. The men don't want women to gain back the old privilege! They would ridicule you and they would pressure my father into removing my authority in the war in the east. Is that what you want? They would accuse me of trying to do anything to steal Lekktor's wife rather than the other way around. They would not stand for it! Don't you think I would do it if I could? I would give it all up. Dira is all the world to me!"

Idamé was the one doing the pacing now. "Run away with her!"

Nikal looked at her, amazed.

"The Guardian would understand if you did," she continued. "This is your chance! You could flee with her on a ship, or better yet Rainwing could fly you both to Tirilorin, or even to the Valley of the Gifted. They would understand. And you would be safe from the repercussions. You and Dira could live there in peace the rest of your lives."

"Peace!" he said, mockingly. "Much of the world is in a state of war that is about to explode in an inferno involving nearly all the countries once the Alkhaness gets involved, and you think Dira and I should abandon all and go and live in the Valley in peace! Think what you are saying, Mother Idamé! Don't think though the idea isn't tempting! All this time I have wanted to run away with her, plotting little plots in my mind as to how to remove her from my brother's clutches, and every day I am torn to shreds as I see my duty in conflict with that notion."

"But there are other generals, Nikal!"

He looked at her hard. "It is the Staff, Mother Idamé! The Staff! Think of the words of that Prophecy and pretend to take me out of it. I have already pretended it. What awful choices the Guardian has set before me! So, this is your warning in the Prophecy, is it?"

Idamé was constantly dabbing tears with her shawl, even as she paced. "I know it, Nikal! I am so very sorry!"

"And I think of Kodi, too. Would you want him to be alone in the use of that Staff less than twenty years old? The Alkhan and the Alkhaness focused on his destruction? He is no commander, yet. He is most courageous and capable, yet he knows little of war except what he learns in books."

At that, Idamé steeled herself and squelched the tears.

"No, of course not. You're right, of course."

Nikal reached out and took her hands into his.

"How often have all of you said to me the last week that I am not alone! And how much I appreciate the words, hanging on them, actually, though I may not display my thankfulness as I should. But I don't want you all to be alone, either. We have great strength as friends, I see that now. The Guardian has chosen me for this task because He thinks I am capable. Rainwing and Hawking are right. I am capable. Though I have not the foresight to know all outcomes, I know where my talents lie. It is why I continue to lead in this war even though my heart has been elsewhere for some time, or I might have bucked the law and disappeared with Dira long ago. I cannot destabilize the family and the country with such scandal, and even Dira would not want that."

"Of course, you are right, Nikal. I see that, now. Your decision is surely the best one. But there is something you are overlooking! A time of instability may still come, for your family may now have its end, for the

Aura prevents Dira bearing heirs to Lekktor. Nor can you, Nikal, sire heirs without her. The magic connects you."

Nikal paused for a long moment as he grasped this truth. An end to his father's House was unfortunate and would surely have ramifications. His House had ruled Nant for centuries. There would be conflict as the Houses of distant cousins maneuvered for advantage. Yet at a personal level it was a consolation to know the truth. It had been his ongoing nightmare to imagine Dira lying there as she allowed Lekktor to expend his uncaring carnal urges. She would hate Lekktor, and so knowing she would never have to bear his children might bring her some solace, however limited. He wished there were some way to get the information to her.

Idamé, however, apparently read his mind in his silence. A scope of her professionalism now exerted itself. "You've made your decision. If she knew of the Aura? Consider her lack of independence with a hateful husband, and guards outside her doors. How would you get the information to her without Lekktor knowing? Would it even be helpful?"

"If Lekktor knew, he would be infuriated, I know. He would treat her more horribly than ever."

"And mightn't she divulge the knowledge to try to hurt him in a moment of anger? Perhaps it is best she does not know. Her only value to your brother is her ability to produce for him an heir."

"And if he knew the truth, she would become no more to him than a slave. No. It must remain a secret, Mother Idamé."

She nodded. "The three waiting in the hallway know, for they read through my distress."

Nikal considered. "I suppose I don't see much point anymore of keeping such secrets from the friends in the Prophecy. I will tell the other men, and Ralle, too. Kodi would glean it from me in any event. I don't seem to be able to keep any secrets from him for long anyway. He is persistent in such a friendly way. How can anyone not respond? Like a Meicalian Healer might, he places his hand on my shoulder and I feel at ease."

Idamé smiled for the first time that evening. "The brother you should have had."

Nikal sighed deeply. "And thinking of our bond is of some minor cheer even in this misfortune. It has become clear to me that Kodi needs me, and I need him. It is another reason for us all to plow ahead."

"Is there any hope by which the Lady Dira can be relieved of the torture of your brother's presence? Is there a way to separate them on occasion?"

"I don't know, but I will think on it. Maybe Lord Ralle can somehow provide her companions or kind servants. But for now, you and I need to put on the pretense of pleasant faces like the Lord Curdoz and do what we can to take leave of my father and get back to Lord Ralle's home for the night. This palace sickens me."

"And me. I am so sorry I ever came tonight."

Nikal held and patted her hand. "But then the truth of the Aura would not be known."

"Nor its magic imposed had it never been seen! And the tragedy made that much worse."

"The tragedy is none the worse for me or for Dira than it was before. That Dira will not have to bear a child by a man she hates, that it prevents Lekktor from siring an heir through his future queen...it was worth your distress. And mine. That is what I think." Nikal turned around and looked at a painting on the wall of one of his ancestors. "The High Council will suffer the effects of a law they should never have made. Lekktor will have no heir, and he will rue the day he stole Dira from me."

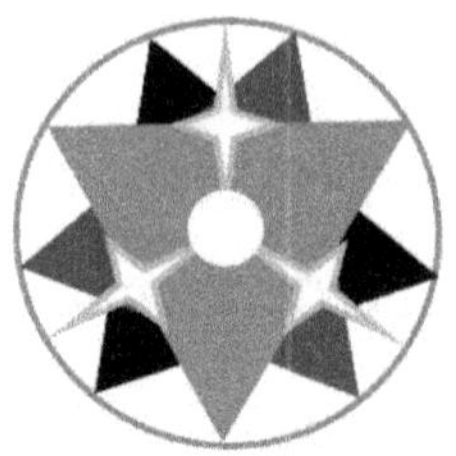

Chapter 18—Sea Voyage

Nikal's ship was the largest in the fleet, a warship, and not a mere transport vessel like the one that took them to Sevarr. It sported three masts with several sails. Its weaponry was formidable with ten fireball launchers mounted on its decks which operated like catapults, and below decks were fourteen massive crossbows which could shoot bolts or grappling hooks larger than Berugian spears. These could be aimed in multiple directions through hinged windows during a sea battle. With no exceptions, the sailors were also soldiers and weaponry specialists, the handpicked elite of the Nantian Navy, every man a multi-talented warrior.

It was a strapping, boisterous crew which appealed to Kodi and Tiliruf who were able to fit right in, but they were also self-disciplined and gentlemanly as required. The prince and General Aron could be tyrants to any under their command who mistreated a woman or did not display proper decorum when on duty. Rum drinking was allowed, though still strictly rationed, and any man who made a fool of himself was punished.

Cleanliness was a constant objective both for the ship and also for the men on board: every man was required to wash himself thoroughly every third day with soap, a scrubrag or sponge, and a bucket that he had to share with several others in order not to over-use the freshwater supplies. Nor was there spare water for shaving. It was not ideal, and Kodi missed his recently acquired daily bath habit while in Tirilorin. Yet he and Tiliruf, essentially under Nikal's command now, adapted to the discipline. These bathing routines typically took place in the early mornings, and the women held forth in their cabin as the laughing, joshing men were necessarily bared as they accomplished this task on the main deck so the soapy water could be doubly used for scrubbing the deck.

"So that is what Human male bodies really look like," said Rainwing, as she peered out the cabin door on the third morning, the day they were expecting to meet up again with Vanaratu. "Fascinating. Some have much more hair on their bodies than others. And no pouch of course, solely an Etoppsi trait. The penis is..."

"Rainwing!" exclaimed Mother Idamé. There was laughter from some of the men, including Kodi, who were close to the cabin door and heard Rainwing's loud voice. Idamé tried to close her eyes as she shut the door. "It isn't proper to watch them!"

Muffled male laughter continued to be heard through the door.

The Etoppsis had seen her female Human counterparts already, for they were more attuned than the men, even, on the idea of staying clean. They would remain privately in their cabin, carefully mopping and drying spilt water on the cabin floor after their own sponge baths. "That is what I have read in books on Human culture, but I don't understand it. And why do they laugh and carry on so?"

"For small children to be naked is not improper, but as adults, men and women are usually only naked *together* when making love and as Bondmates," said Lyndz, trying to explain. She knew Idamé wasn't likely to be forthcoming about such a topic, even though Rainwing was only being naturally curious. "It is part of the intimacy and attraction between a man and a woman when they decide to become bondmates. And the reason the men are laughing is because nakedness in all-male or all-female groups can have a funny and fun element to it. It's difficult to explain, but there's a playful kind of friendly bonding that goes on."

Rainwing shook her head. Etoppsi were never so silly about their bodies. "I think it is peculiar to cover your bodies anyhow; I think your race very handsome."

Sister Ulna, a native Nantian, was snoozing, in and out of wakefulness, and wasn't alert enough to engage in the conversation, but Sister Maru, a tall woman with cropped blond hair and fair complexion was sitting on the edge of her bunk, putting on her boots. Nearly as much as Lyndz, she enjoyed the give and take teaching and learning with Rainwing, the consequence of the two races being so different and living apart. "But we do not have that tight protective fur, Rainwing," she said rather scientifically. "The circumstances of the environment must be almost perfect for bared Human bodies to be comfortable, you see. It is usually too cool, or too windy, or too wet or too dusty. We white-skinned northerners—I'm from Eleni myself—have to be alert to the hot sun burning our uncovered skin. The olive and brown Nantians and the dark Essemarians and Hralindis don't have to worry about it, because their skin is better adapted to the sun. So, I wear a bonnet to protect my face on deck. I can allow the sun to darken my skin temporarily, but it takes many days of not getting too much exposure at one time. But clothing keeps our bodies cleaner and generally more comfortable, and it protects our skin from scratches and bruising, which can happen quite easily for us. As far as shoes are concerned, they help us walk or run much faster on rough surfaces. Otherwise, our feet would hurt quite dreadfully. You Etoppsi don't need shoes."

The Etoppsis considered. "I've noticed the males on board remove their shirts when they work in the heat. And it seems perfectly natural, yet I have never seen you females do so. Why not?"

Maru chuckled. "It is because most Humans believe it is not as appropriate for women to bare their breasts in front of men who are not their husbands, or at least close family, yet the reverse is not true."

Rainwing stood there staring. "That does not make sense at all!"

"It's a cultural thing, but I agree, Rainwing," said Lyndz. "It really is stupid."

"Lyndz!" exclaimed Idamé.

"Oh, Mother. You know it to be true. It's hardly fair for men to feel free to go bare-chested when they labor and for women to have to keep themselves covered all the time. I'd love, just like Kodi, to take off my shirt on a hot day!"

"But it isn't proper, dear! Young women baring their breasts would arouse the passions of the men."

"Maybe not so much if they grew used to it!"

Maru laughed. She and the snoozing Ulna were closer in age to Lyndz than they were to Idamé, so she perhaps better understood Lyndz' point of view. "Lyndz brings up a fair point, Rainwing, that women are expected to conform to stricter rules of modesty around men. But like Mother Idamé implies, these rules have come about because of the more flawed Human sexual nature and the fact that, compared to Etoppsi and Qeteral, many Human men—certainly not all—are less controlled in their impulses, and so their lust can cause them to act wrongly, against the Discipline of monogamy. So, it's considered wise for women not to bare themselves in front of strangers."

Idamé put in. "Same-gender groups don't have to be concerned. But group nudity is nearly always associated with swimming or bathing or sunning. Lyndz is right about the playful bonding. I remember the times in the Valley when all us girls would swim without our clothing in the Lake and lie there in the sun during high summer. What enjoyment we had! The men had to remain elsewhere, although they had their days at the lake, too."

"They have something similar in Tirilorin," said Lyndz. "They have different days on the beach for men and for women. Kodi went a couple times with Tiliruf and his friends to swim and play in the waves. I would sometimes go with my girlfriends to the river near our home, but we'd have to warn Kodi, and he'd make sure he and his friends stayed away until we came back, because they would go almost every day. It was the typical manner the boys and men of Felto took baths in the summertime, by taking soap to the river."

"So, what you are telling me is that Humans, even though you wear clothes all the time, enjoy being naked, at least when it's warm," said Rainwing.

"Particularly when Humans are fit and healthy," said Maru, "they like the appearance of their bodies and others. Human shapes *are* attractive, Rainwing, just as you say, and that is why Humans are often depicted naked in art and sculpture. Men and women like to show off how beautiful and fit they are. Men tend to be more animal-like and spirited about it and enjoy the look of their own musculature. Which is probably another reason they so often remove their shirts, in addition to the fact it helps them cool down in the breezes. They actually want others to see how muscular and powerful they are. And with Lyndz being on board, some of the unbonded ones wish to appear physically attractive to her."

Lyndz giggled, "And I do like looking!"

Idamé couldn't help laughing too, though she seemed to embarrass herself by doing so. "Oh, Lyndz, you're so silly!"

"And really, Rainwing, that crowd of rowdies out there doesn't care a whit if we see them fully naked. Remember, men tend to be less modest. Mother Idamé's just trying to preserve some decorum. Human decorum."

"Well, some of that makes more sense," said Rainwing nodding. "What you described then is like Etoppsi culture. We take tremendous pride in our bodies, obviously, and like you say the males are more the trumpeters. Though we females in the Dragon Legion are keen on our muscularity, too. Yet all have great reverence for our bodies and for one another's, for they are the Creator's art as expressed through the Mold."

"Your people are still beautiful even when you are old. Royal Hawking is quite striking, for instance," observed Idamé. "As Humans grow older, our bodies no longer match the youthful Human ideal. We age quite differently than you it seems. We can sometimes be a bit self-conscious about it, and that is yet another reason we clothe ourselves."

"Clothes are important socially, too," said Maru. "It isn't only about covering and protecting the body."

"Yes," agreed Lyndz. "Making and wearing beautiful clothes is important, especially to women. There are different sorts of clothes meant for different activities and events, Rainwing. You saw the women's dresses, and fine attire on the men, at the Grand Dance in Tirilorin. And like women, men want to look dashing in fancy clothes, or at least some of them do, like Tiliruf. I always like to look at Tiliruf. I think everyday in Tirilorin he wore something different. Kodi thought he was nuts and teased him for it. Kodi doesn't care about fancy silks, satins, and flamboyant colors. He's more practical. He likes good-woven linens, and woolens and leather.

"Let me tell you more about my brother's attitude about being a man and having a man's body, Rainwing, because in some ways he's a good example for you of both the comparative freedom men have, but also societal expectations they do have to consider. I admit in a way our focus at home centers in large part on Kodi as the epitome of self-confidence and man of the house, especially when Father isn't home. Mother listens to his tales with a smile on her face and lets him get away with his little lies trying to cover his ale-drinking fun with his mates, which he's been doing pretty regularly since about thirteen. She knows more about his ocassional heavy drinking than he thinks she does. No way she'd dare let me drink like that!"

"An occasional wine is the only proper option for ladies," said Idamé.

"That's ridiculous, Idamé," said Rainwing. "Female Etoppsi drink everything, just like males!"

"Oh, listen to you two! Anyway, Kodi gets away with everything, and I don't. And you know? In Mother's case it's partly because of Kodi's very voice, because he has that confident soothing low pitch which reminds her of Father. So, when he lies, he's pretty suave about it. Not that he's dishonest, but rather he's just determined to do what he wants when he knows there's no harm in it, and at the same time doesn't think we women need to always know what he's up to when he disappears with his mates."

"Women are secretive, too," admitted Idamé.

"Quite right we are!" said Maru to everyone's laughter.

Lyndz continued. "Grandpa dotes on him, the son he never had, though there's nothing Kodi wouldn't do for him, of course, he worships his grandfather. Ansy the house servant..."

"She's your grandmother now, dear," said Idamé winking.

Lyndz' eyes got big. "She *is* my grandmother! Idamé, I've never thought of it that way! You're right. She Bonded Grandpa just before we left home, Rainwing. Maru. Idamé saw their Aura, and it was a great surprise! She's been our servant since I was a girl, and of course I'm talking about the past, not the present."

"Oh, that's charming!" said Maru. "But that's another little tale of its own, isn't it? Go on with telling us about Kodi, dear. But I'm always up for love tales. Save it for when Ulna wakes!"

Lyndz smiled. "Yes, of course. Well, Ansy's always spoiled Kodi and spends hours meticulously laundering and mending his clothes and pampering him. She cooks dinners based on what Kodi likes best to eat and dishes second helpings onto his plate, and he definitely eats like a horse. Biscuits! He can eat ten big biscuits at one sitting. She even brings him his dessert first! Every time!"

"Now that is a bit spoiling," said Idamé. "We older ladies do tend to have a sweet spot for the young men, don't we?"

"For sure! See, Rainwing? Half of a man's sense of privilege is because we women let them get away with it and even encourage it!"

They all laughed, and then Rainwing admitted, "Etoppsi females do similarly, I'd say. There can be a bit of confident charm on the male's part that warms us to them. It isn't only the young male. Hawking has a bit of that at 102. Some males can be demanding, but I know that isn't the case with most, including your brother. The other half of their sense of privilege is as they learn its benefits from watching how other *males* make use of it and encourage their male counterparts to do the same. It has the hint of manipulation in it, but again, exactly like you say, we let them get away with it."

"Yes, I think you must be right! I haven't considered the psychological underpinnings. That's such an interesting observation."

"You should read Seabreeze Stargazer. She's a brilliant Berugian philosopher. I'm sure there are copies at the Library in Tirilorin. But we're getting sidetracked. This is all so interesting. I like this you using Kodi as an example."

"So, Kodi runs around and works without a shirt all summer whenever he can get away with it. He works hard like a dog all day. He's oblivious to pain and cuts and bruises and never complains about anything, works his muscles to their maximum, and doesn't mind doing the nastiest tasks and getting filthy dirty. But then he really likes getting clean for the evening. He's almost obsessive about it. When he can't swim and bathe at the river, he does bucket baths in a room behind the kitchen. After a bucket bath, he saunters lazily buck naked from the washroom, through the house, still drying himself off with a towel, upstairs to his bedroom, won't even close the door while he's dressing, not caring a fig whether any of us sees him. Sometimes he'll even pause in the parlor doorway, drying his hair with the towel, and ask what's for dinner! Just so we'll get a good look at him, of course. He's an impressive pretty thing to look at, and he knows it. He's wishing we'll say something, fishing for compliments and good-natured teasing. And makes Grandpa laugh! And Ansy pretends to be embarrassed, squealing to him to get his clothes on!"

"That's so funny!" said Maru. "My brothers were all exactly like that growing up!"

"He gets that body self-confidence from our father. Father's not so different himself when he's home, maybe a tad more modest in front of Ansy. Father's still quite young and handsome, only thirty-five years old now, and still has a muscular, youthful body which he's also very proud of. He and Kodi look more like brothers than father and son. Father is hugely complimentary of Kodi's physical fitness, work ethic, and cheers loudly for Kodi at competitions at the local fairs."

"He compliments you, too, dear, I'm sure."

"Oh, he does, Idamé. He can dote on me, too. I'm not saying he doesn't. Father definitely has a jovial side with us all at home and treats Mother like a queen. Now it's true as I've explained before to Idamé that he can be stern with Kodi, but it's always in private, never willing to goad or embarrass."

"That's a good manly Discipline for a father to maintain," said Maru. "He should never chastise his children in front of others. Sons especially can take on powerful resentment when that happens."

"I agree, though I won't say Father hasn't caused Kodi to ever be resentful, because he definitely has. Idamé knows some of that story. He has strong views and doesn't like anyone bucking his authority. He and Kodi have had some major struggles the last couple years as Kodi has become his own man to Father's resistance. But in general, they like doing things together, especially hunting and fishing. Now that's the informal setting of close family. But back to what I was saying about body exposure, too, Kodi is perfectly at ease in the all-male crowd.

"Yet then, here, Rainwing, is where Human decorum exerts itself. Kodi's fully clothed at family meals, around house guests, dresses cleanly and acts with appropriate demeanor doing business in town for Mother or Grandpa, and takes especial care when he's required to engage in settings where girls and unbonded young women might be present. Though they've all noticed him from time to time working shirtless and wrestling and running at the fairs and comment privately to each other on his muscularity. He's got that smooth brown skin which stands out exotically in Felto. Maru talked about men's lust, but women can be guilty too of tempting men with strong flirtation, and the proper man has to be careful about exposing his body in such a way that it might inflame sexual thoughts. A few women are so bad they attempt entrapment. That's when they seduce a man they really desire so as to become impregnated by him."

"That's terrible!" said Rainwing, her eyes huge. "Etoppsi females would never allow conception without the male's consent and loving committment!"

"It *is* terrible! When that happens, the man who has any scruples will Bond the woman, even if he doesn't really love her, in order to be there as a father for the child and to preserve their social reputation. It's rarely a happy Bonding despite how the woman might have convinced herself it was going to be. Very selfish. So, there are some who really come on strong to Kodi since he's handsome and because our family has wealth, you see. He'll smile and laugh with them, but that's all. He's determined not to be tempted by those he knows he will never love that way. I'm proud of Kodi. He's self-disciplined. Self-assured and occasionally cocky, but definitely self-disciplined where it really counts."

"One of the finest of young men," agreed Idamé. "And one doesn't have to be young to admire a physique like that. He's kind of like what I've read about the Qeteral—very attuned to the gift of the beautiful body and nature. Qeteral men go about without covering the upper body most of the time, and of course their race is devotedly monogamous."

"You're right, Mother. Kodi'd fit in great, wouldn't he? Though of course he's got some black body and face hair, and Qeteral, both men and women, only have long, dark head hair. Entirely smooth-skinned."

"And did you read," put in Maru, "that the Qeteral can adjust to extremes of cold weather without having to wear winter clothes? One layer of loose-fitting linen is almost all they ever wear. And sandals. No boots. They resist fiery heat, also, and barely sweat."

"I read that before, too," put in Rainwing. "Maybe I was expecting Humans to be more like Qeteral that way. When I flew to Nant that first time, I was surprised at the amount of clothing Humans wore. You're enlightening me. And all that about sexual nature in Humans I have read, as it's so different. Etoppsi and Qeteral females have full control over pregnancy, but that's not the case with you Humans, and so I can see how that impacts your culture. It sounds like it can prove quite tricky. You have a natural desire for others to perceive you as beautiful and attractive, but at the same time you have to have a certain amount of care and that Human decorum you talk about."

"There are definitely similarities between Qeteral and Humans," said Idamé. "And there have been a handful of Bondings between the two in the ancient past. But Qeteral have an innate magic and the pure monogamy instinct that determines their differences. Humans have no magic of that kind, and though monogamy is an understood Discipline of Human culture, it has a lot of cracks in it. It's more a matter of character than it is instinct..."

The 'females' continued this interesting conversation, talking about body perception and more about physical variances and sexual differences among the three races and how those differences impact the culture in each society. Idamé buried some of her embarrassment about such topics and put on a bit of the intellectual like the others.

Rainwing's description of Etoppsi Star Revel was particularly enlightening, and very amusing. There appeared to be two levels of Etoppsi sexuality. The first stage, during the puberty years into the mid-twenties, involved multiple mating experiences with many others, all geared, however, to the hunt for one's eventual monogamous mate. Once that mate was discovered, typically by the late twenties, the second stage began. Etoppsi sexuality settled down permanently into devotion to one's Bondmate and family, and like with the Qeteral, there was no such thing as adultery. Lyndz noted that Human sexual experience seemed closer to Etoppsi than it did to the Qeteral, who, ever and only, had one mate, except for the possibility of another following widowhood. She had read that Humans in the eastern countries were particularly open with youthful sexual encounters, whereas such were more secretive and guarded in western countries.

Idamé was not unaware of some of the different mores in the eastern countries, but she was too conservative and western in her views to believe this to be a good thing for Humans at all, considering the risks. She believed all Humans ought to be exactly like Qeteral. She was a bit shocked when Lyndz admitted that her own views on the subject were mixed. In some ways, Lyndz wasn't sure that experimentation couldn't be a useful growing experience for some. Idamé tut-tutted this, but Maru seemed to agree and asked Lyndz to explain her point, which she did. Human women on Dumhoni had very clock-like fertile cycles, and she was not unaware of girlfriends back home who had taken advantage of their infertile times and had had an encounter or two. They implied they had learned important lessons about men's bodies and the responses of their own during those enounters. That use of timing was of course the main method followed too by most Bonded Human couples to limit the number of children in the family. It was only the ones who deliberately seduced men during their fertile times that Lyndz had such genuine distaste for—the ones who attempted to entrap unwary men. Another point Lyndz brought up related to prostitution. It was said that prostitution was rarer in the eastern countries, and it was speculated that maybe it was the more open experimentation there that made prostitution less tempting. Nevertheless, she had to acknowledge Idamé's view of risk was valid. How, for example, could a young man wishing to experiment be certain that the young woman was not actually attempting entrapment rather than limiting encounters to her infertile times? Maru thought Lyndz' views had merit, and in support brought up the point that eastern women in comparison to western women were more socially equal to men, and that in acknowledgement of that, she wondered if the very idea of entrapment among eastern women was taboo. Entrapment was perhaps in a way a symptom of inequality whereby insecure women felt compelled to force a relationship of their own choosing.

Some of these subtleties went beyond Idamé's area of comfort. Most of this latter part of the conversation was between Maru and Lyndz. Lyndz did reassure Idamé that in her own case she didn't think the idea of experimentation need apply to her. She was perfectly willing to wait until she found her life-mate, and that was certainly the expectation of all properly raised ladies of class in western countries. Idamé's eyebrow settled a little. Everyone was of course in total agreement that it was the Design of Life and a high Principle that children were meant to grow up with parents who loved one another, and that prostitution and the need for the Orders to maintain orphanages due to unwanted children indicated significant failings in Human sexual expression.

When late-sleeping Ulna finally roused herself, they all prepared themselves for what was expected to be an eventful day.

It would be wrong to say that Nikal had cast aside his gloom, for painful memories of Sevarr would continually creep into his mind and depress him. At the same time, however, his conversation with Idamé regarding the Aura had recommitted him to the fulfilling of the Prophecy, and also established within him a determination to do his best by Kodi who was to share with him the Staff of Terianh, and the others who were equally determined to claim his friendship. The commitment and the determination therefore had galvanized him, renewing his energy and focus. His gloomy frowns were less common. He talked more often and regularly not only to the persistent Kodi but to the others as well. This new openness on his part was just what the other friends wished for, and they renewed their efforts to strengthen their connection to him. He rarely walked away anymore during lighthearted conversation which before had annoyed him. On occasion he would display his appreciation for the friendships with a smile and a kind word or even a touch on a shoulder. Even with Tiliruf whom he considered spoiled he would be more likely now to smile at jests. Tiliruf was slowly changing, and Nikal apparently noticed the improvement and change in attitude. Quite possibly he noticed it sooner than the others, and thus the prince's patience with the Tirilorine, whose potential was so great, increased.

Yet alongside Aron, it was with Kodi that Nikal felt most at ease, and it was rare that Nikal did not keep one or the other, or even both, close by him at all times. Those two read him best, Aron by way of long association, and Kodi by almost Gifted instinct, and both by fraternal affection which Nikal reciprocated.

Tiliruf might have felt left out by this threesome if Kodi did not make additional effort to ensure their own friendship remained solid. They two were more likely to spar during swordsmanship practice than either was with Nikal or with Aron, and Kodi enjoyed going below decks to exercise with Tiliruf with the weighted equipment. Both joked with each other often and played games with the sailors, activities that Nikal rarely engaged in even before Dira was lost to him. Therefore Tiliruf, though he noticed the growing bond between the prince and his best friend, so far did not seem to mind it. Kodi had sufficient charisma and friendly energy to spare for everyone, and Tiliruf did not feel neglected.

Aron was a delight to be around. Like Tiliruf he had curly hair which gave him that same handsome, sort of rascally look, yet of course he was black-haired like most Nantians with a trim black beard, and darker skinned even than Nikal, with some recent Eastern ancestry as they found out. He bore a black, star-shaped tattoo on his right lower arm to cover an old battle scar. He was the epitome of gentlemanliness, soft-spoken and yet very, very funny. His stammer they all grew used to quickly, and even that seemed to highlight his soft-spokenness. He seemed to read right through people and understand them. And his drollness would surface in the most amusing ways.

"Ah, Lady Lyndz, you shouldn't walk, ah, so sprightly across the decks, the ah...saaaailers tend to drr...rain their rum rr...rations to calm themselves."

Lyndz laughed. "I didn't know I walked 'sprightly!' Exactly how then should I walk, General?"

"Ah, well I believe it ah, would be helpful if yy...you'd acquire a limp rrr...rather like this." At which point he demonstrated a most absurd stumbling movement as though his whole left foot had been removed. Everyone guffawed. "See, if yy...you do it like that, they might stop getting muscle cramps from flexing so hard ah, around you."

To Tiliruf he was brutally funny, though it was clear he liked him quite well. "Yyy...you are the spoiled emperor's kid, aren't you? Ah, do serrrvants wash yyy...your hair back at that big palace in a big marble tub? And massage your back and feet? That must feel rr...right nice, 'specially if it's by the hands of a ww...woman."

Tiliruf snickered. "I ain't the emperor's kid, General."

"Maaayyybe so. But yy...you're the kid of the kid of the kid, and yy...you live in the emperor's palace, don't you?"

"Eh, I suppose I do."

"And yy...you have servants by the hundreds runnin' 'round the place."

Tiliruf didn't even nod, afraid to give the man more bait.

"Ssoo, does she wash yy...your back and yy...your feet? Ah...tell the truth now, Swordmaster."

Tiliruf turned slightly pink. He refused to answer.

"That's, ah, what I thought," stated Aron with a wink. "That's proh...bably not the only body parts yy...you let her massage and wash for you now, is it? What a treat *that* must be!"

The sailors and Kodi nearly rolled off the deck and into the sea.

Even with Idamé he was hilarious. Aron had never really known any Matrimonials personally, and because one was required to detect the Aura promised in his long-ago Vision, her presence on this journey intrigued him immensely, and he thought it auspicious. She became to him a sort of motherly confessor, and he had chosen to share with her the Vision he had as a youth. "So, I ah, rr...reckon yy...you're going to see an Aura over me and some ll...lovely lady one of these days, and it won't be yy...your typical green light. Yy...you had better be careful and stand way back."

"What do you mean, Aron, dear?" To Idamé, the virginal, self-disciplined Aron was to her the exemplar of virtuous masculinity. In her mind every man should live his life as pure as he before he settled with his Bondmate.

"Well, yy...you know it's going to be fiery explosions, crashing moons, shooting stars and lightning, or it'd better be, con...considering how long I've been puttin' off love-making. And yy...you'd better Bond us right away, so I can catch up quick on wwh...hat I've been missin'."

This candidness did not in the least alter the Matrimonial's high opinion of the general in any way. "Certainly, dear!" She patted him fondly on his bearded cheek.

Most of the general's witticisms were expressed with the most settled expression, nary a hint of excitement or chuckle in his voice, and then he'd walk away as though all he'd said was a simple 'good morning,' leaving everyone behind clutching stitches. To a man, every sailor on board, many who had known him long years, had the highest respect and admiration for the gentle general.

Yet underneath the usual gentleness and humor was a man iron hard, and his swordplay with Nikal and Tiliruf—he himself was a skilled master—could be ferocious and heated even if it was controlled, and with the still learning Kodi he gave no quarter, unlike the other two who typically eased up in order to teach him and improve his stamina. Aron would have none of it and crushed Kodi over and over.

"You're not much of a trainer, are you, General Aron?" quipped Tiliruf, nursing his best friend after one of these more brutal bouts.

"Losing is the best training," said Aron, coldly. He never stammered at such times.

And there was a rare instance in which one of the newer sailors had the nerve to eye Lyndz provocatively down her shirt as she climbed backwards down the steep stair from the aftcastle to the main deck. Aron noticed, gave the man a deadly look and knocked him cold with a vicious fist. He refused to allow the Healers to work their magic. Lyndz felt terribly sorry for the poor man, but she understood that discipline had to be maintained, and Kodi warned her not to intervene.

To prepare for all contingencies, it had been agreed beforehand that Curdoz would remain on a mattress in the women's cabin that day with Maru and Ulna close by. He believed he could handle his next communication with the World God, yet it was prudent to take precautions. If he fainted again, he would be on a bed, and Ulna, who had some mind powers in addition to her Healing magic, would be present to lend Mind Support to the Sage.

Rainwing had promised Kodi a flight, and Nikal had given him a break from assisting with the sails. Therefore, Rainwing, as she had before with Lyndz, wrapped him tightly in her grasp and leaped from the bow.

It was an exciting moment and Kodi thrilled in the pleasure. He knew he was perfectly safe against Rainwing's body, and whooped and hollered as she dived, circled around, and lifted him on high. The cooling air created for Kodi a new dimension of exhilaration.

"I'm going to try something I've never done before carrying a Human," Rainwing called out. She sensed Kodi's desire for fun and adventure. "You willing?"

"'Course I am! Do what you want! This is tremendous!"

With that the Etoppsi female went into a nosedive which promptly took Kodi's breath away as he realized what she was probably going to do. He grinned hugely, his heart pounding. Right before she hit the surface of the water she angled up, yet still with tremendous momentum she plunged into the crest of a wave, under water for two seconds, and then pulled up again with powerful pumping of her massive wings. She lifted high and did it all a second time and then a third. Kodi was soaked to the skin through his clothes, but he didn't care in the least. To him this was the most thrilling thing he'd ever experienced in his life. He laughed and hollered, and Rainwing was equally pleased to offer him such extreme excitement.

"That is how *we* take baths!" she boomed.

He laughed more as they flew high.

"Look!" he called suddenly.

Below them in the distance some two miles away was again a large pod of Great Black whales, steaming and swooping in and out of the waves in the direction of Nikal's ship. Rainwing rose high again looking to see if the enormous black, underwater mountain would reappear.

It did not this time, and yet suddenly both she and Kodi sensed a powerful presence nearby. It was as though sounds lessened and the winds stilled.

"Whether Vanaratu appears near the surface is probably not important, Curdoz said to me the other day," offered Kodi when they continued to see nothing unusual. "Though I really wish I could see what you and Lyndz saw!"

Soon the pod of whales had surrounded the ship, and Kodi and Rainwing could see that everyone on board was standing at the rails looking and pointing. Finally, giving up on searching any further for the elusive black mass, Rainwing and Kodi flew back to the ship. Despite not siting Vanaratu, they were still in for a surprise.

Just as they landed on the bow an enormous creature, four or five times the size of the largest of the Great Blacks, broke the surface. It was larger than the ship itself, a massive giant of pinkish-white flesh, though coated in many places with black barnacles.

"A Pearl Colossal!" boomed Rainwing. "Hardly anyone ever sees them! It is believed they are the largest of all the great whales!"

The calls and whoops on the ship at the sight of the Colossal were telling. None aboard had ever seen one before.

Nikal emerged from the women's cabin where Curdoz was. "Drop sails!" he called out.

The crew completed this task rapidly, and the ship just bobbed up and down the waves in place.

"What is that?" called one of the sailors pointing off port in the direction of the Pearl Colossal. It appeared to be carrying something, something made of rope, net-like and with long trailers.

Curdoz himself appeared. He was fine, although Sister Ulna, a dark-haired Nantian, short and sturdy, followed him closely as he moved around the deck.

"It's a harness," he said. "We are to attach it to the ship."

"It's going to pull us?" asked a shocked Rainwing. She looked from the rope contraption to the Colossal as it settled itself with a quarter of its huge body still above the surface.

"It is indeed."

This task took well over an hour. The most powerful divers and swimmers were employed into the waters to grasp hold of the trailers and bring them to the ship. These then had to be lifted up the rope ladders to the hinged windows where they were woven through and attached to the ship's beams. There were iron eyehooks in the keel and in other locations on the side of the ship that had been used in the activity of launching it from the shipyard two years before, and divers were employed to string the strange ropes through these as well. All the time the Great Blacks were circling the ship as Curdoz and Nikal called out orders, and the Pearl Colossal floated as if sunbathing. Apparently Vanaratu himself was issuing directions directly into Curdoz' mind on how best and in which location the various ropes were to be attached. It was admittedly a strange and unique operation.

The swimmers, and Kodi was one of these, on occasion were able to reach out and touch the Great Blacks, for they were friendly and curious. The Pearl, however, was slightly far away for this to be deemed safe, for the swimmers remained necessarily close to the ship.

Finally, the task was completed and Curdoz had Nikal order the men back on board.

The Pearl disappeared again below the water and when it reappeared the vast harness was over its massive beak. The ship jerked as the ropes went taut and, in a moment, they had gained rapid westward momentum.

Even so, the sails were unfurled to achieve maximum velocity and to ease the Pearl's load, and Aron believed that they were traveling faster on the sea than Humans had ever before traveled. "Two www...weeks at this speed will take us far beyond the nnn...known world of Humans."

"Or Etoppsi," added Rainwing.

"There is something *pleasant* at the other end, eh?" Tiliruf finally asked the unspoken question, looking directly at Curdoz. The friends were standing near to one another close to the bow.

The Sage sighed. He appeared to be all right after this most recent communication with the unseen Vanaratu, though marginally pale and sweaty. Idamé had procured something for him to eat, and he sat watching the Pearl Colossal.

"His information is limited."

"Surely he has told you something, Curdoz," chimed in Lyndz, "regarding our destination."

"He has, yes, told me something."

They all waited.

He sighed again. "These were his words: *Great sacrifice is to come to the Eight. She takes yet she gives. To lose is to gain. Hold firm. Meical watches from afar. The Guardian is aware.*"

When they looked at him oddly, he repeated it.

"Eh, what sort of *great sacrifice?*" asked Tiliruf with trepidation. "And who is this 'she?'"

"I am afraid I do not know. The Prophecy alluded to 'giving' and 'gifts', perhaps on the part of each of the Eight Friends in order for us to get the Staff, and I took it to mean the Gift of friendship and camaraderie. Yet these words of Vanaratu's imply sacrifice and a test of resolve. Who 'she' is I haven't the faintest notion. Yet, I think it is now safe to assume 'she' has the Staff, whoever 'she' is."

"You know, you really need to start asking more questions, Curdoz," said Tiliruf. "This Vanaratu chap needs to be more candid."

"He's a god and he can do what he likes," said the Sage, aggravated. Yet he sighed again and eased up. "I understand the fear of not knowing, Tiliruf, and I'm sure you speak well for all of us on this, so don't think I'm annoyed with you, but I feel confident Vanaratu will tell us little more than what he has done already. He isn't very chatty. Yet know this. The statement 'to lose is to gain' is an axiom as old as the world itself and applies to all of life. Always must we give up one thing so to gain another, and often the new thing is better than the old."

Nikal looked away. "Not always."

"No. Not always, no, and perhaps that is why I was hesitant to answer at first. The idea of sacrifice is never especially pleasant."

"It pains me to think of any of you sacrificing for me to have that Staff. I have half a mind to end this whole affair."

"Then, ah, the wwwar wwwould surely be lost," said Aron.

"That Staff is not a possession of yours or Kodi's," said Curdoz with emphasis.

"It's for all of us," agreed Lyndz. "That Staff is a *key*, and the Guardian wants us to have it. Nikal and Kodi are to wield it."

Kodi spoke. "I think knowing that Meical is Himself watching and is aware says a lot. At least it does for me. Maybe there is some test of resolve involved, but I don't think He's deliberately trying to cause us suffering. It isn't how He works. Curdoz has at least taught me that. The Eight Friends has meaning in that we are exactly that—friends. We are meant to help each other get through this, and we are the ones chosen to achieve certain tasks and to lead in the fight. He didn't pick us to lead us to a butcher's shop."

"Exactly, Ko." Lyndz nodded. "I think when Vanaratu says to 'hold firm' he means to have faith."

Tiliruf turned his head and rolled his eyes so no one could see. He wanted to believe Kodi's words, but the idea of having faith was in his mind the same as not having the ability to direct one's own future. He didn't like it, and here he was being pulled by some great monster into the vast unknown blue. But he had promised his father he would not argue with the others on such topics.

"Do you think 'she' is a World Goddess?" asked Idamé.

"No. The only two World Gods still in Our Side of the World are Vanaratu and Siriné, and Siriné is trapped in the Serpent Sea. All the others—the Favored of Meical are on the Other Side of the World, and the Condemned entrapped behind the Teeth of Meical. The Barriers solidified long ago, and only with Meical's direct intervention can they now be breached."

"If she's not a goddess she must be very old if she was the one who took the Staff from Vanaratu centuries ago," offered Lyndz.

"You know, what's even the point of speculating, eh? If Curdoz isn't going to ask the questions, then we're only going to be guessing."

"I will attempt to ask when I deem the timing right," said the Sage. "I'm still trying to get to know Vanaratu. So be patient, Tiliruf. We are on a quest, you know. Those who seek do not always know in advance the outcome of their search."

"Yyyet, ah, we must pre...pare our minds," said Aron. Quite humorously the general took his rum flask out of his pocket and with deliberation he opened the lid, held it up, winked at everyone, put it to his lips and swallowed two large mouthfuls. "Ahhh."

"A good smoke does sound like an excellent idea," said Curdoz. He then looked at Nikal. "Perhaps the Eight Friends do deserve a bit of a respite, Prince."

"Not the men. When the sun sets, perhaps. At sundown Tiliruf can share a couple of the bottles buried in that trunk of his."

"How'd you know they were there, eh?"

"I, ah, nnn..know the smell of Nantian brandy. None better," said Aron. "Yy...you're not as ah, sneaky as yy...you think you are, Son of Emperors."

"And what Aron knows, I know," said the prince. He actually winked at the Tirilorine.

Tiliruf grinned. "'Course, I'm happy to share, eh?"

Mother Idamé tssked. "I really don't think you should drink so much."

"Why not?" asked four or five male voices at the same time.

The consensus obviously against her, the Matrimonial made a little face of disapproval and said no more.

The men went about working with the rest of the crew and took turns with one another at swordsmanship practice and exercising with the equipment below decks. It was also important to check regularly all the ropes and knots that attached the ship to the harness and the Pearl Colossal and to ensure that nothing was being damaged or stressed. Yet the ship appeared to be holding up well.

Watching the Colossal and the Great Blacks, too, who swam alongside, was in itself a sight to behold, and the women and all the crewmen on deck were often in awe. It was as though they had become participants in a fantasy or wrapped in a legend of epic proportions. Yet, too, there was a brooding sense if not of fear at least of angst as to what lay at the other end of the journey. Not all had the faith that Lyndz spoke of. However, duty to the prince held the crew in check, and the Eight Friends and the Healer pair did their best to comfort each other and to keep the crewmen happy. The women aided the crewmen in the constant need for cleanliness and orderliness, doing their best with limited water supplies to launder and scrub the worst of the filth—though thankfully sea water could be used for some of this—in order for all to manage as comfortably as possible. It was a struggle, and life aboard a sailing ship was by necessity a difficult undertaking. For some, such as Kodi and Rainwing, learning and adapting to struggles was second nature, and they thrived on this long journey. Yet even those like Idamé and Tiliruf, for whom doing without comforts was met with some grumbling, adjusted. All of them learned, and all of them grew. And the labor and the struggles brought them all closer together.

And there were other tasks. Lyndz would practice a little with her Moment Mastering, all the while trying to quicken her ability to enter the Mode, thinking speed could be useful. Curdoz spent much time writing in his journal. Tiliruf had at first taken to gambling at Fifty-twos with the sailors until he kept winning and Aron forced him to give it up and to spend his rest times more fruitfully. Now, he had to settle to reading the book about Terianh that Theneri had given to Kodi. He knew a great deal already about his ancestor, of course, yet most of his focus had been on the founding and administration of Terianh's new empire after the Conquest. This was an historical interpretation that he had not come across. As he read, however, particularly now that the Eagle Sword had come to him, he began to find renewed interest, even a connection to his ancestor that grew in his mind day by day as they traveled west.

Idamé was now knitting almost non-stop, and over time churned out several scarves and caps that she had given away to some of the eight friends, the Healers, and even to the sailors. Lyndz had, with money Curdoz had given her for the purpose, bought oodles and oodles of yarn before they left Sevarr, enough to keep the Matrimonial busy for weeks, as it helped her deal with being on the ship and the rolling waves. The sailors were appreciative of the Matrimonial's motherly ways, and she would always chat with them and pat their cheeks. And when they would wear her caps or scarves, which they often did in the brisk winds on deck, she would pour out even more affections.

Occasionally, Rainwing would take flight, and Letti the grayhawk would take off with her. At other times, she engaged in storytelling when groups of sailors were given breaks, for they were fascinated by her tales of life as an Etoppsis. They especially liked hearing about her time in the Dragon Legion.

Curdoz gave up on trying to make Kodi learn the Discipline of Emptying of the Mind. He simply wasn't getting it, and Curdoz had now decided that if Kodi's and Nikal's Meicalian Gifts were to be through the wielding of the Staff, then it was altogether a different sort of magic. Meical, in proclaiming their role in that Prophecy, Curdoz told them, the sorts of mind Disciplines used by the Gifted when they trained in the Valley were not likely to apply to them or make a difference.

"You mean...are you saying Nikal and I already have mastered the Gift?"

"I'm saying that you will not be able to master it until you gain the Staff. You and the Staff will be connected, I'm quite sure, by magic. I could be wrong, but I do not think you will have any other sort of Gift besides the ability to make use of the Staff. There could be more than meets the eye, for you will be entering into a magical realm that hasn't been experienced since the days of Tiliruf's ancestor and the first Sages. The Guardian was Himself present for much of the time and communicated with them."

Nikal wondered. "But..."

"Don't ask me," Curdoz shook his head. "I do not know how He will communicate with you or if there will be some revelation once you begin using that Staff."

There were times when the Pearl Colossal would disengage and hunt for its sustenance sometimes for hours at a time, and the Blacks would disappear too for the same reason. At these times the harness was pulled in and balanced on the bowsprit as the sails would keep the ship moving in its westward direction. Vanaratu would disappear it seemed for days at a time before he would reappear as a powerful occupant inside Curdoz' mind. And some of the others, particularly any who were Gifted or who had ever experienced a Vision appeared also to sense his presence.

Three days after the appearance of the Pearl Colossal, the World God returned, and Curdoz did communicate with him throughout the day. Generally, Curdoz would lie back in his cot in Nikal and Aron's cabin, or on Lyndz' mattress in the women's in order to be close to the knitting Idamé, close his eyes, and enter Vanaratu's world. There were images of unparalleled beauty as the world was fashioned by gods out of fires and muds and rock and water. There were faces of gods so beautiful that Curdoz was moved. There were mountains and forests and rivers and seas, and below the seas were creatures uncounted, strange lights and darkness mixing in a world of utter strangeness. Too there were visions of stars and of Solvermoon and Orohmoon. There were faces of Qeteral and Etoppsi and Humans from an era long ago, more Qeteral than all others. There were also images of destruction and war and a face of a female being, completely deranged and yet full of fearless pride.

Finally, Curdoz attempted to reach out with a direct question.

"Is that Siriné?"

It is.

"She is on your mind often, Vanaratu."

There was silence for a long moment. *She is the object of many errors on my part.*

Curdoz then sensed through the connection a surge of remorse and painful sadness, and even as he lay back, tears came unwittingly as the god's emotions transferred into his mind.

"You must share with me, Vanaratu. The Guardian wishes me to be your friend."

And so, a god opened his heart to a mortal. After nearly five centuries the true story was known, and Curdoz later shared it with the others. Not all of Vanaratu's communication was words. There were many scenes which flashed across the Sage's mind, and surges of emotion which he had to make sense of. This is how he rendered it in his journal:

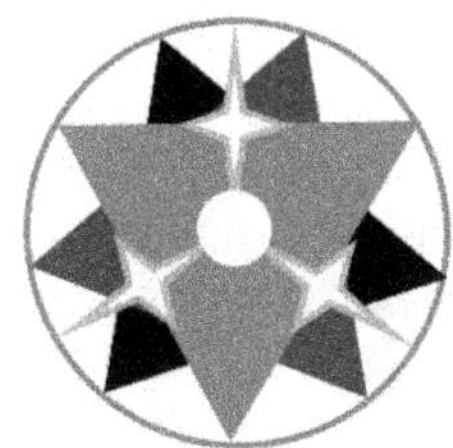

Chapter 19—The Tale of Vanaratu and Siriné

After the Great War in the Deeps of Time, the rebel gods were Imprisoned behind the Guardian's Teeth, and those world gods that had been favored by Meical were entrusted with the Other Side of the World to be their domain of peace until the End of the World, leaving the Three Peoples of the Mold with the Northern and Southern Continents and all the great and small islands of This Side of the World. All were at peace for long years. Eventually, however, Siriné's heart grew selfish, for she had hidden from the Guardian her lust for the male Humans that she had watched during the Time of the Fashioning of the Three Peoples. Meical was not aware of this, or He would have attempted a Cleansing. As it was He had shown her much favor, for she was the most beautiful of all the gods, and she had aided Him in the Great War. But as the years passed and Meical did not return, the lust in her mind grew, and she chafed at His command to remain on the Other Side of the World.

She tempted therefore her brother Vanaratu to join her, and because he remembered well the beauty of the Three Peoples and their tuneful voices and laughter, he desired to see them again and to learn what secrets they held from the Creator, and together the two gods left the Confines and returned to This Side of the World. They were greeted as the gods they were by the Three Peoples, for time was not reckoned the same for them, and uncounted generations had passed among them since the Great War, and nearly all of the events of that earlier age had been forgotten. Though Siriné lived with the Humans, Vanaratu found that he loved to wander the skies with the proud Etoppsi, the First People, and to walk in forests and meadows with the Qeteral as they sang with their beautiful voices and spoke to the birds and other creatures of the world. In time his heart was captured by the beauty of the Qeteral People, and though he would still visit the Etoppsi, he chose to make a home among the Second People.

For many years Vanaratu was content. But upon a time, he stumbled upon a Qeteral princess as she bathed in the Diamond Pool, a beautiful water garden the god himself had crafted as a gift to his Qeteral friends, and his wisdom abandoned him for a time as he watched her. He grew suddenly lustful, for her naked beauty captured his imagination, and he approached her with dishonorable intent. When she resisted his advances, Vanaratu's wisdom returned to him. He expressed his sorrow to her and begged her forgiveness, which she granted, but in fear of himself he fled from the land of the Qeteral. The world god repented of breaking Meical's Command.

He found his sister living in proud luxury among the Humans, the Third People. He said to her, "It was wrong of us to come here. I find that my body craves that of the Qeteral females, and I recognize now in your eyes your own lust for the Human males. The Creator forbade us from bonding with the Three Peoples of the Mold, and Meical Commanded we live apart after the Great War. I repent for the failure I could not foresee, and I will return to the Other Side of the World. I urge you, my sister, to return with me, so we do not cause harm to the Peoples."

But Siriné had allowed her lust to build over the years, in addition to a desire for power, and she refused. "You may go, my brother, but I will not. I will find the perfect Human male who deserves me, and when I do I will not give him up. Go. But do not be surprised if the Barrier to the Other Side of the World has become impenetrable to you."

Vanaratu realized that there may be truth in Siriné's words, and he sped across the Divide until he came to the Barrier and found that he could not pass through. He called the names of the other gods, his brothers and sisters, but they could not hear him. In his despair he returned to Siriné and warned her. "The Other Side of the World is closed to you and me! It is a sign that we have failed, my sister. Take heed and before further doom falls upon us, let us you and I retreat to some solitary island in the sea and bide our time until Meical should come again, and we will plead to him our repentance for breaking His Command. If we do this now, no great harm will have come to the Three Peoples, and Meical is good, and He will forgive us."

Siriné, however, laughed and replied, "No. I will plead nothing. Meical has too many worlds to watch and will not come here again."

Vanaratu's words having had no effect, in sadness he left her and stood upon the edge of the sea and called out, "Where can I go so that I never bring harm to the Three Peoples?"

Suddenly he saw in the sea before him a team of dolphins splashing in the waves and cheering the sunshine with their laughing voices. Vanaratu was struck with inspiration and plunged into the sea. As he swam in and out of the depths, he discovered many beautiful and intelligent creatures and made friends with them. He had learned their languages during the time of Creation and knew too from the Qeteral the languages of the gulls and other birds that traversed the oceans. He was happy here and remained, swimming tirelessly through the seas as only a god can, and for many years he forgot his troubles.

However, in time he learned of the travails of the Three Peoples, the enslavement of the Humans, the Hiding of the Qeteral, and the wars of the Etoppsi in their attempts to guard their lands against the Ralsheen Imperial armies. Vanaratu rightly suspected his sister Siriné was at the root of these events. One final time he spoke to her, calling to her from the shores of an island so as not to let the Peoples of the Mold see him again. And she came. When he saw his sister, he barely recognized her, and no longer thought her beautiful. "Sister, what have you done in your lust and desire for power? I hear from the birds of the air that you demand sacrifices and require that the Humans worship you. The Qeteral have hidden in fear, and the Etoppsi have taken up arms to protect themselves!"

She smiled cruelly. "What have I done? I have brought order to the Empire of the Humans. I will find soon the Qeteral, and they will serve me with their magic. I found the Man I have sought after for so long, the Emperor of the Ralsheen, and because he satisfies my desires, I will aid him in his triumph over the Etoppsi. If they will not serve him as their master, they will be destroyed. I have done as I will, for it is only my will that matters. Go, Vanaratu. You have your friends in the sea and they do not interest me. I have what I want, and in time I will rule This Side of the World. Go, and trouble me never again." In a demonstration of her Power, she then struck out at him, burning him with fire and lightning.

Vanaratu screamed in pain that he had never experienced before, and in terror of his sister, fled. He fell into despair and retreated into the depths of the sea and ignored the plight of the Three Peoples. He had made a vow long ago to avoid the Three Peoples so as not to be the cause of any harm that should come to them. But now he used his vow as an excuse to do nothing in his fear of his sister Siriné, and the only comfort he took was the knowledge brought to him by the seagulls that the Etoppsi still fought, and the Qeteral whom he loved most of all remained hidden by way of their magic.

In time, the Guardian did indeed return to this world and initiated the rebellion against the Ralsheen. He freed the slaves and placed Terianh the Great at their head. The Conquest took many years, for the Emperor and Siriné held up long in the land of Tolos, their navies supplied their needs from the islands, and the armies of the Anterianhi could not reach them, as they had few ships and no expertise to build them. Finally, Terianh defeated the emperor in the last battle, Meical released the Dragon Scourge upon the land of Tolos, and the hegemony of the Ralsheen ended. Meical then found Vanaratu in the deeps and spoke to him.

You disobeyed me in your foolishness and pride. You attempted to appease my command by hiding in the sea. A time presented itself in which you might have redeemed yourself, for if you had fought Siriné with all your might you would have distracted her from her obsession until my return, for you knew I would return. You had it within you to do this, but instead you chose to avoid the Peoples of the Mold pretending you would have caused more damage, but how many thousands perished before their time because you chose ultimately to do nothing? I am ashamed of you, Vanaratu!

And Vanaratu's tears of shame were a flood that ran through all the oceans. His anguished cries reached throughout the waters, and all the great whales and the dolphins his friends rushed to him to console him. But when Meical saw this, his heart was softened. And he spoke again to Vanaratu.

The love these innocents have for you is an indication of the deep sincerity and goodness of your heart. Their friendship for you moves me, and it is true there was never any command not to commune with them. However, they exist on the Other Side of the World as well, and if you had remained there as you were commanded you would have had them all as your friends and more besides. Nevertheless, you deserve a new opportunity. I am in need of you, Vanaratu, and you can still aid me.

Vanaratu's tears abated, and he bowed with deepest humility to the Guardian. "Yes, My Lord Meical. I am prepared to be obedient."

You are to find your sister Siriné and take her to the Serpent Sea in the South of the World. You will ignore all her pleadings and do your duty to me and the Three Peoples. When you capture her, call out My name, and I will come to the Serpent Sea. Siriné will be Transformed, and in her Transformation, she will be required to devour as many as she can of the vicious serpents that spawn in the Jungle rivers and make their way to that sea. Since she demands lives to satiate her appetite, she will have them, and fewer serpents will then escape into the oceans to trouble the Peoples and their ships. But Siriné will not be the only one who is Transformed.

Then, Vanaratu went willingly, and after much searching, he found Siriné hiding in the mountains. She fought him long with fire and lightning, but Vanaratu fought back now with tempest and water and proved the stronger, and though she pleaded with him, his ears had now closed to her. Though she tried to flee, Vanaratu was successful in chasing his sister to the shores of the Serpent Sea. There he held her until Meical was able to free himself from the burdens of the end of the war and the installation of Terianh as Emperor, and when He came to them, He spoke harshly to Siriné.

Your lust and cravings have been the cause of suffering not experienced since the time of the Great War. If you had come to me then and told me of your weakness, I could have helped you, but in your pride, you hid your heart from me. Your choices have doomed you, and there is no healing for you. The Teeth are unbreakable, or I would put you there. Since you cannot leave the confines of this world, I condemn you to remain here in the Serpent Sea. You will be transformed such that your wrath and appetite will be better demonstrated to the world, and all will fear you and avoid you.

Then Meical the Guardian reached into the heavens and gathered his Power, and he struck Siriné with great might. Her once beautiful body melted into the Sea, and Meical caused the water to spin until a vast whirlpool was formed so great as to dwarf an island. Her new form was of such immensity that she could not pass through the crooked straights, and she was trapped, with the shores of the Serpent Sea her prison. Storms and lightning announced her approach and the Peoples never again sailed that sea willingly. Despite his sister's treachery, Vanaratu cried. "Great Meical I am ashamed it came to this. My own choices and actions in part brought the downfall of my sister."

She would have fallen I think without you, Vanaratu. Yes, you should have fought her, for that is the Great Requirement in the ongoing Cosmic Battle against Evil. Failure is never defeat when it comes to fighting evil, though one perish in the fight. Yet in the end you did your part, Vanaratu. But I cannot leave you as you are, for you are still strong and beautiful in the eyes of the Three Peoples, and they would worship you in time if you should follow through with the lusts and desires in your heart which you have admitted and yet have thus far resisted. But I am telling you that coming to This Side of the World was your first great error, for despite your will, you will always be tempted as was your sister. A Cleansing I withhold at this time. Therefore, you too must be Transformed, so that you are no longer tempted. The Other Side of the World remains closed to you. But if you remain a friend and do your duty to Me, then there is hope.

Again, Meical reached up to the heavens to gather His Power, but He did not strike Vanaratu, but placed His hands with gentle firmness upon Vanaratu's shoulders. Then, Vanaratu's body was Transformed into the likeness of his friends of the deep oceans, the great whales, but of such vastness and size so as to rival the whirlpool of Siriné. And many godly powers remained to him. When the sea creatures saw that their friend had been remade in their own image, they rejoiced, and even Vanaratu was grateful to Meical for his mercy. And Meical spoke to Vanaratu again.

There may come a time when I need you. Siriné remains ever a danger to the world of the Three Peoples. But I give you your freedom to travel the seas and oceans with your friends. But have a care, Vanaratu, for your vastness is such that your very movements could topple ships and destroy the harbors and coastal lands! You should remain below the waves until you are far, far out to sea!

He spoke the words in friendly tones, but then he struck a note more serious, and Vanaratu's joy was tempered.

Vanaratu, a time will come when you will grow weary of the seas, and the seemingly boundless oceans will appear small and become a prison for you little different than the Serpent Sea to Siriné. You will miss the beauty of the forests, and the ability to run swiftly across the plains. You will miss skipping across mountains in the sun, and the skies are closed to your flights to Solvermoon and Orohmoon in the night.

Vanaratu knew Meical's words were true. "My Lord and Master, Meical! Is there hope for me?"

Indeed, I said so. There is always hope. But be mindful. The Creator expects more from the gods than from the Peoples of the Mold. Your powers are greater, your tasks are greater, your failures are greater, and your punishments are greater. This is why you were meant to live apart from the Three Peoples. Yet you chose to come to the world of the Three Peoples, and now you dwell here.

Vanaratu thought long on these words. Finally, he replied. "You are saying that I must never again make an error in judgment. I do not know if there is hope there. Perhaps I truly am doomed."

No, Vanaratu. There is another way.

"But what is it, My Lord?"

I cannot give you the answer. You must discover it on your own.

Vanaratu was troubled in spirit, but Meical placed his hands again upon Vanaratu and smiled warmly, for Meical had come to have great love for him in his sincerity.

I claim you as mine, Vanaratu.

Then Vanaratu felt within himself that sense of hope which he had not felt since before he had left the Other Side of the World.

Do me this favor, for I must now go to another world that needs me. Take this the Staff of Terianh to Vanayema across the western sea. I foresee a future when it will be needed again, and in that time, you will have many chances to serve me.

Then, like a bolt of lightning, the Great Guardian Meical, Messenger of the Creator, shot skyward into the Sun, leaving this world once more.

Afterward, Vanaratu looked upon the turmoil of Siriné. Then he turned and made his way carefully through the straights and into the deep oceans. He went far out to sea so as not to trouble the coastlines. First, he took the Staff and delivered it, and then he frolicked with his friends in the deeps and in the foam. After long centuries his heart did find the oceans confining, but he bided his time, and though he was lonely in his heart, he took comfort in Meical's claim upon him and did not despair.

It was with some storytelling skill that Curdoz repeated it now a second time. He had already told it that afternoon to the women in their cabin shortly after his long communication with the World God, and they had listened in rapt attention, Idamé and Ulna dabbing tears from their eyes, Rainwing and Lyndz and Maru committing it to memory. Even now with the four other men in Nikal's cabin, passing around Tiliruf's brandy as they were, the men were moved by the Sage's telling, but none less so than the prince.

When Curdoz was finished, Nikal was the first to speak. Maybe it was in part the influence of the drink, for all of them had had quite their fair share, and it was well past the time when most of the off-duty sailors had gone to their hammocks below decks. But perhaps more than the drink, as he looked around and weighed the characters of the men present, he grew emotional and felt strongly and deeply connected to all of them, even Tiliruf, as though they were now a part of him. They could not replace his love for Dira, yet they had certainly captured a different place in his heart, arresting a troubled mind that otherwise might have descended into despair.

"I really do feel for Vanaratu, and his pain is something that I understand. His story moves me deeply. He has suffered in his soul for centuries for his choices, desperate for opportunities for redemption, and only sea creatures to give him the love and friendship he needs. What a fool I am.

"Here I am drowning from conflict that has affected me at most three weeks, the Guardian reaches out and offers me instantly opportunities for redemption and even fulfillment, superior colleagues to aid me, and the truest possible friends to stand at my side." A few rare tears fell from his eyes as he sat on the edge of his bunk. He tried to cover them by swallowing another mouthful from the bottle and wiping his arm across his eyes as he passed it on to Kodi sitting across from him on Aron's bunk. "Why do I still feel lost?" he inquired.

"Your loss is the result of the wrong-headed laws passed by others long before your time," said the Sage. "You could not have foreseen such an event."

A few more tears flowed. "But I knew of the law when I met her."

"Sounds to me you were acting on the truest and best sort of instinct," said Kodi. "I'd say you were living your life in the right way in spite of the stupid laws. I know I'd have done the same. What is love if we deny it when we finally find it?"

"Ah, Kodi is rr...right, Nn..nikal." Though Kodi might have guessed it, Aron was the one present who really knew of the level of intimacy shared between Nikal and Dira. "Yy...you must not ah, second guess yy...your relationship with Dira. She ll...loved you, and she still does."

Nikal rubbed his face. "I'm regarded by many a great captain and general—a hero even. I've defeated armies, vanquished some of the Alkhan's champions in single combat. The people believe I am strong. Somehow, I've got to get control of myself again if I am to wield that Staff, and, like Vanaratu, do my duty, maintain hope, and let the rest fall where it may."

He breathed deeply to let some of the intensity dissipate and brightened up a little under the influence of his friends, even challenging Kodi to a game of Kings and Castles. Aron and Tiliruf played likewise with a second set. Kodi and Tiliruf and Curdoz smoked pipes, and the brandy bottle went round slowly.

Curdoz, nursing a decanter of wine, watched the men at their games for a little. Then he went and sat at Nikal's tiny desk, and in the light of a hanging lantern began his written interpretation of Vanaratu's tale.

The next day a few of the Eight were together on deck when Lyndz asked Curdoz what he knew of Vanayema.

"The name is curious, isn't it?" he replied. "It is similar to Vanaratu; his name is from an archaic pre-Ralsheen language meaning *ancient artist*. He is often cited in the Ancient Book as the god who would take the creations of the other gods, such as the mountains, and give to them specific shapes, detail and color, or shifted rivers and fields and hills and trees so to create beautiful panoramas and fertile lands for the eventual coming of the Three Peoples. He worked closely with Noromoray in the designs of rivers and lakes. The name Vanayema is also of the ancient form and thus makes sense to me that Vanaratu used it when he told me his tale. It contains the root *vana* which is the part that means *ancient* or even *first*. The other part of the name, *yema*, is..."

"*Mother*," said Rainwing.

"Correct."

"'Ancient Mother!'" said Tiliruf. "Well, what does that mean, eh? Is she some sort of gray-haired old magical woman?"

"Or 'First Mother,'" suggested Lyndz. "Have I heard that name before?"

"Possibly not, Lyndz," continued Curdoz. "Unlike the names of the World Gods which retained their ancient form, Vanayema was not a goddess, and her name was rendered into Anterianhi interpretations of the Ancient Book as 'Modela.' If we presume she is the same individual."

"Modela!" exclaimed Rainwing. She looked at Curdoz with extreme wonder on her furred face. "Do you really think it, Curdoz! That's extraordinary!"

"It is. Yet, I know not what else to think. Considering that Vanaratu used the more ancient name, I'm inclined to think it is."

"Remarkable!" said Idamé.

"Amazing!" said Lyndz.

"Who is Modela, eh?"

They all looked at him.

"Oh, Tiliruf!" said Lyndz. "You didn't read any of the stories derived from the Ancient Book? The old Sages created all those tales out of the Ancient Book, putting them in collections. My grandfather has a collection which he would read from to Kodi and me as children, and there are at least thirty different collections in the library in Tirilorin! I saw them there."

"Ask me anything about Anterianhi and Tirilorine history, and I can tell you about it, eh? All that ancient stuff is..." He looked at her and caught himself, remembering his promise to his father. "Oh, never mind. The simple answer to your question is no. I'll leave it at that, eh?"

In his mind the Ancient Book was attached to Meicalian 'religion.' He had avoided it his whole life because of that, and his father certainly never read him stories from it, nor did his nannies or tutors.

"You might," said Rainwing, "consider her to be the grandmother of all the Three Peoples."

"The legend says she was the first female rendering of the Mold itself, on our world: the embodiment of the Creator's feminine nature. She had a counterpart, of course, Vanayisu, or 'Modelo,' the masculine embodiment of the Creator. They are the female and male 'model' from which the Three races descend. Their firstborn children were born in the Valley and shaped by the Mind of the Creator and Meical into the Etoppsi, the Qeteral, and lastly the Humans. We call that shaping into the three forms 'the Molding,' hence the Three Peoples of the Mold."

"If she's still around, what happened to *him*, eh? This 'Modelo' bloke."

"You know, for someone who pretends he doesn't believe in this sort of thing, you sure ask a lot of questions!" said Lyndz, harassing him.

"Just making conversation, eh? Nobody else seems to be asking, or at least asking the *right* questions. I don't like going into things without knowing what I'm going into. The rest of you mates seem like you're willing to march down a dragon's throat as long as somebody's pulling you along, or in this case floating along being dragged by a giant sea monster. On top of that you put up the sails when the winds are good to make us get down the dragon's throat even faster!"

"You chose to come, didn't you? That's what I remember anyway," Lyndz replied.

"I reckon I did. I reckon it's 'cause I think all of you are kind of good for me, in a way. It's just that every day it seems like we're getting closer to the end of a limb, and I'm afraid it's going to break off and there won't be any way to get back to my safe, sturdy tree trunk."

Curdoz chuckled. "I like your analogies, Tiliruf. You're not so far off, I must say. I know you don't feel the confidence that Kodi often speaks of, and I believe your angst is perfectly natural. But the choice to go forward has been made. You're stuck with us."

"Good thing I like you so much. So you still haven't answered my question, though."

"He fought in the Great War with the gods and died in that ancient time. That is the legend, anyway. Berug the Magnificent, the great Etoppsi king, was then Chosen by Meical to take his place as War Wizard, as the

War went on for long years. Perhaps we shall find out more of the truth. No legend took up, however, with what happened to Modela, his Bondmate."

"How do you act so calm about Vanaratu's warning about the giving and the taking and the sacrifice and all?"

Curdoz' smile faltered. "I do worry about it. I suppose I just don't show it. Nikal and I have talked privately about it, and we are both quite anxious. We are at the end of a limb, just as you say, Tiliruf. I wish I could offer words of wisdom to ease your mind, but I cannot. The only thought I can offer is this, though it isn't likely to ease your mind. Nikal has suffered greatly and has already made tremendous sacrifice to fulfill the Prophecy and gain the Staff. Without the Staff, it seems that by the Prophecy we would have little hope in the conflict with the Alkhan and Alkhaness."

Tiliruf looked at him and replied with a nod. "Well, at least you're being honest about it, eh? I, er, suppose I'll do my part, then, whatever it is."

Idamé patted and kissed him on the cheek. "You're such a dear, Tiliruf."

He turned a bit pink.

Lyndz noticed that these moments of embarrassment were coming more often of late. She thought it sweet, for it appeared to make the typically self-involved Tiliruf a little more human to her. She smiled but kept her observation to herself.

On day nine from the time they met up again with Vanaratu, and the Pearl Colossal began its long labor of pulling the great ship, a storm rose in the west and barreled down upon them.

Storms at sea can be terrifying, and this one absolutely was. The Pearl Colossal had disengaged for the safety of the ship, and Vanaratu had disappeared the day before the storm came. The ship was on its own. Nikal and Aron worked the crew hard as they were required to tie everything down and to remove the ropes connecting to the harness from the inside of the ship. The hinged windows had to be closed and sealed, and so the interweaving ropes had to be withdrawn. This task was barely achieved before the waves began to grow to storm proportions, and the rains began to fall in torrents. In addition to the safety precautions, there was the need to try to use the drainage systems built into the deck in order to replenish some of their freshwater supplies used for washing. They had some success at this before the waves themselves began to splash ferociously. They sealed the water barrels and rerouted the drains off the sides of the ship, but eventually there was so much water from rain and wave that the pumps had to be worked down below to remove excess water. Rainwing was a powerful help at the working of the pumps, and did not tire. She was undaunted by the storm. In fact, there was little in the world that caused her real fear.

But the ship was perhaps the best-built on the sea, and it withstood the onslaught even as it went on for two days and two nights.

During this time, of course, Idamé was rather wretched, and Ulna and Maru had to keep her sedated much of the time. She would awaken and eat a little, and during these times she attempted to be controlled and brave, but eventually the pronounced bobbing of the ship upon the large waves, the thunder and winds, would work upon her fears. Even knitting didn't help, and she would have to close her eyes to the ever-churning world.

When the rains finally ended, and the winds calmed again, still the waves continued high and dangerous. They could not risk the long process of reattaching the harness, and it rested still, hooked over the bowsprit useless. It would have been much too perilous to engage the swimmers and divers in the waters.

The whales had for the time being disappeared, and as Vanaratu had still not returned, the crew was left upon its own devices.

The end of the storm had nevertheless brought them hope again, and the clouds were beginning to dissipate with bits of a morning sun shining through from time to time. The waves were now manageable and Nikal had just raised sails when suddenly Curdoz received in his mind an urgent message from Vanaratu.

My friends warn me! You are in greatest danger, Curdoz! You must fight them until I arrive! I will be there soon!

"Fight whom! Fight whom, Vanaratu?"

They escaped the diligence of the Dragon Legion or the hunger of Siriné. They are inflamed by the angry tears of the gods behind the Teeth. And the image of a great and hideous monster was cast into Curdoz' mind.

Curdoz sat up from his bunk and raced out of the cabin to find Nikal.

He found him issuing orders.

"Serpents, Nikal! Serpents! Sea Serpents are about to attack!"

Nikal and the rest looked at Curdoz, momentarily dumbstruck. Yet when suddenly there was a huge crash against the starboard side, Nikal yelled at the top of his lungs in a huge voice.

"Arm yourselves! All hands! All hands!"

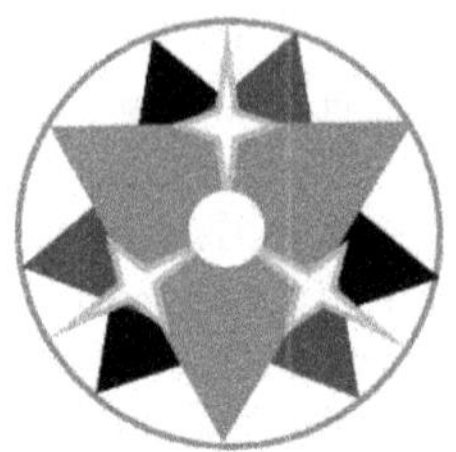

Chapter 20—Fight at Sea

"To arms! To arms!" yelled Aron, taking up the prince's order from his position on the aftcastle. Gone was his stammer as it always was when he was in a fight. He rang a bronze bell, urgent and loud. "Lower sails! Lower sails! Serpents! Sea serpents!"

Men were running, descending and ascending from below decks where they retrieved their swords. In a moment they changed from sailors to warriors. As the sails were being lowered but before the task was fully complete, Nikal yelled again and pointed off the port side as a great and savage head rose high out of the waters. Crowned in thorny plates and with glowing yellow eyes like their dragon cousins, it opened wide its enormous maw displaying dozens of sharp, huge, vicious teeth. The sound that issued from it was as a roar followed by a high-pitched scream. Perhaps such water creatures did not breathe fire, yet this did little to limit the deadly danger.

Spawned in the distant headwaters of the great rivers of the Infested Jungle, these creatures, small at first though still dangerous, would make their way either to the Serpent River in the east or the Western River on the southern border of the Kingdom of Berug. The former emptied into the Serpent Sea usually to end their brief lives in the Whirlpool of Siriné, for she was all the time hungry and required sustenance to sustain her wrath. The latter rarely escaped the vigilance of the Dragon Legion, for great iron sieves were positioned across the Western River, trapping them, and there the juveniles would be skewered by the Legionnaires. Yet some few in either direction would inevitably escape, those from the Serpent River through the Crooked Straights past the Khestadone Sea and out into the oceans of the world, and those from the Western River directly into the Great Western Ocean by way of the river's mouth. In time they would grow huge upon the abundance of the oceans. They did not deliberately go about hunting ships, but on occasion they would find themselves in the Human shipping lanes between the Northern and Southern continents or on the Outer Route north to Solanto, and then they would attack. Often the ship would flounder and those aboard would meet brutal death, and at other times the creature would be defeated at the hands of brave sailors armed and intent upon saving themselves and their ship. These survivors would tell fearsome tales. But again, these were rare, and there were none on Nikal's ship who had ever seen such creatures before.

The great monster leaned forward in a swift motion and snapped viciously at Nikal, but the stout prince stepped aside and pricked its fierce jaw with his sword, causing the creature to snap back, quantities of blood dribbling from the wound. In anger it then lifted itself higher to a level even with the middle of the center mast and launched its huge body over the whole of the ship, breaking one of the lower sail yards in the process. One of the catapult launchers was smashed, although these were useless for such a fight anyway. The beast then began to slide its unimaginable length across the rails of the ship damaging those on the starboard side where it had crashed downward. It was trying to wrap itself around the ship to crush it or to draw it below the waves.

Along with Nikal the sailor-soldiers were hacking at its body as rapidly and savagely as they could. Yet even as they stabbed and slashed, its long body moved across the decking before they could do enough damage to any one section of it. Its hide, though nothing like the hard scales of a dragon, was nevertheless leather tough, and only the most powerful men with the sharpest of swords had any real effect. Blood, nearly black, began to build on the main deck making it slippery and treacherous. It was difficult for the defenders to maintain their footing.

All of this action took place in a matter of moments when Rainwing burst in wrath from the women's cabin. She grabbed an enormous piece of broken wood from the downed sail yard and launched herself off the ship. Just as a second beast's enormous head rose out of the waters on the starboard side, she slammed into it like a battering ram and beat furiously on its head before it could assist its fellow creature's attack. This obviously hurt the monster, and for a little while it disappeared again below the waves. Yet Rainwing could see it below the surface as it charged at and knocked hard against the ship causing it to rock violently.

Many men on board lost their footing just as the head of the first beast rose again from the port side in preparation of winding its unfathomably long body a second time over the deck. Once it did, it would crack the ship like an egg.

Tiliruf and Kodi were now earning the keep of their famous blades as they stood with the prince and other swordsmen slashing away at the body of the beast. Men were yelling in their fierceness, intent upon the fight.

"Man overboard!" called Aron, as he swung a wooden saver over the side.

Rainwing heard him, however, and in a moment had swooped downward, scooping the grateful man out of the water and restoring him topside.

Tiliruf was watching this out of the corner of his eye, but when he turned back to Kodi, he was gone.

"Kodi!" cried Tiliruf. "Kodi!"

There were probably thirty yelling men on deck at this point all stabbing and slicing into the slithery thick hide of the sea serpent. Yet Kodi was nowhere among them.

Tiliruf needn't fear however, for his friend returned promptly with his bow of ambernut and the quiver of arrows from King Carlomen slung over his shoulder. He found a prime spot and in a split second he had an arrow fitted to the beautiful weapon. Just as the monster launched itself across the deck for its second pass, Kodi released an arrow striking it through its savage left eye. The beast roared and screamed, wavered, and crashed backward into the water.

"Great shot, Kodi!" yelled Nikal. "I'll give you your knighthood for that!"

Men cheered and Kodi grinned.

However, in its agony the part of the monster's slippery gray body that was over the surface of the deck began to buck dangerously upward, then back and forth trying to loosen its grip, and the ship rocked again. It smashed into the lower, thicker part of the center mast, yet it did not break, however the movement destroyed another fireball launcher and damaged more of the railings. Defenders were knocked over and sent plunging into the sea where the railings were now gone. Many of the others had to stop their attack to try to help those in the water.

The great body of the beast suddenly started sliding backwards, and in another moment or two it had removed itself entirely from the ship, and for a brief time the crew had a respite. Rainwing was kept busy scooping men out of the water and others were being pulled up by ropes.

If there had only been one monster the attack might have ended at this point, but unfortunately the second beast that Rainwing had first fought, having now recovered its senses from the Etoppsi female's powerful head blows, raised itself again out of the water and plunged down directly upon the men that they had not yet rescued, lifting high two of them screaming frantically in its maw. In a scene horrible to behold it bit down upon them and swallowed.

"Fight on!" yelled Nikal. "Fight on!"

Enraged, Rainwing attacked savagely again with the broken yard piece, cast it into the maw of the beast as it roared in delight at the taste of its victims. The wood stuck there like a tossed spear and buckets of black blood poured forth, the monster's screams silenced as it fell with an enormous splash downwards. Thus so damaged, it did not attack again.

They all hoped the fight was over, yet the horror of losing two of the sailors in such a terrible way was now washing over them in grief.

However, Aron called out, and Tiliruf, Nikal and Kodi raced up to the aftcastle. Coming towards them were three more unchallenged monsters who had risen up in the water some two hundred yards aft, racing at them like gargantuan snakes.

"We can't fight them all!" yelled a dismayed Tiliruf. He had been very brave and fought as hard as any of them, but for one who had lived a life of luxury and indulgence, what was happening now was forcing him into a shocking realization; he had entered into a dangerous sort of world of which he now doubted he was truly prepared. Fighting Khestadone men in a land battle with his ancestor's famous sword when he knew in advance he was one of the best swordsmen in the world was what he had pictured in his mind, not savage, slavering monsters in a watery sea attacking his transportation and swallowing men whole.

"Yet fight we will!" called out Aron, winking at him.

Aron's oddly placed smile seemed to give the young man more courage. He held his sword steady.

The general, Nikal, and Kodi seemed undaunted and ready. As the beasts raced forward, Kodi raised his bow yet again, and with another mighty release, pierced once more the eye of the closest, causing the maddened monster to roar in agony. It swerved aside and vanished into the deep.

All were astonished by Kodi's cool precision, his relative youth and inexperience seeming not to handicap him in any way. Unlike the self-doubting Tiliruf, he fought with the same dutiful courage as Nikal and the others of longer experience. Hot and fierce in his resolve, he was a true warrior now. Yet there was not a spare moment for the rest to offer him further congratulation as the two remaining beasts were now upon them.

It was as this new attack began that Vanaratu arrived. No one saw him, and yet the water around the bobbing ship went suddenly still, the winds stopped altogether, and the light of the morning appeared to go dim.

Lightning from the deep erupted nearby striking the two monsters in a display of unimaginable power. The thunderous sound emanating from this massive release of energy was deafening, causing the ship to shudder as if in an earthquake. Men knelt on deck and covered their ears, yet they could not close their eyes, mesmerized as they were by the vast and terrifying magic employed by the invisible world god. The huge bodies of the two beasts were lifted into the sky—they were surely each three hundred feet in length—then more lightning like jagged, glowing white swords slashed their bodies into pieces, dropping these in shocking chunks of bloody monster flesh into the sea some two hundred yards away.

The lightning ceased and the thunders ended, and all seemed deadly calm for a moment as ears adjusted to normal. The men then raced to the sides to assist those dozen or so still in the water, only to discover another though different sort of magic being employed, if magic it could be called. Circling the ship was a school of dolphins jumping in and out of the now calm water, and each of the men in the water was being assisted by one of these playful creatures, allowing them to hold on and keeping their torsos up and out of the water. None were in danger anymore. Eventually Rainwing retrieved them all, two or three at a time.

The women emerged from the relative safety of their cabin. Lyndz was anxious, having wanted to fight, vowing silently to herself she would learn the use of some weapon if only she could find someone willing to train her. She squelched her desire for the time being, as there was too much else to do. But a fire was kindled in her soul that from that point on never went away. It was a turning point, for she was beginning now to set aside her more sedate past in favor of living by way of action.

All those men who were hurt were brought to the aftcastle deck where there was remarkably no damage and little blood. All on board were then accounted for except for the two who had been killed and swallowed by the second monster, yet these two were grieved by many. There were several with broken limbs, and one man had a leg crushed so badly by a falling yard and sail that a makeshift surgery had to be undertaken to remove it. Ulna and Maru along with many others were kept busy treating the wounded.

In the meantime, the rest on board were busy working hard to clean up and assess the damage. Kodi was at work with several men trying to restore and rebuild the broken railings, for this was a serious safety concern, and there were replacement yards that could be employed to repair the ones on the central mast that had been broken. The men worked like ants the remainder of that day and into the next, Vanaratu's magic keeping the water around the ship calm as a late summer pond in evening, and Lyndz and Idamé working to bring food and water to all of them as they labored.

Curdoz assisted the Healers, and he was able to use his magic to sedate the men as bones were set so as to ease their pain from the procedure. He had grown now so used to the powerful mind of Vanaratu that he was able to carry on a mind conversation with the god even as he worked.

"Your people are great fighters. I could feel their resoluteness and bravery many miles away. A few of them have powerful minds, like yours. I wish I could touch them and speak to them! I want very much to know them and to see you all face to face. I am sorry I was not near enough to stop the attack before it happened. I was scouting many miles ahead. Yet it was because of it that I discovered the serpents through my communications with the creatures of the sea. When I turned back to hunt for them, I could see them then in my mind and that is when I warned you."

"You saved us in the end, Vanaratu. Thank you. We could not have fought all of them."

"I am not so sure! You were the cause of the demise of three of the five! What heroes you must have on that ship!"

"There are assuredly heroes here, as the Guardian Himself has Called them to the tasks at hand. I am surprised there were five serpents. Never have I read a tale of a ship attack involving more than one sea serpent! Even one is enough horror."

"I am amazed, as well. Yet these were together. I suspect something."

"What is that?"

"These were given orders by some powerful mind through powerful magic. They almost assuredly escaped long ago from Siriné's hunger from the distant Serpent Sea rather than from the Western River and the diligence of the Etoppsi Dragon Legion. They had a magical link between them which I sensed as I approached them, or otherwise they would not have worked in tandem, and I now detect others in the vicinity. They shall soon be dealt with, and the ones you have damaged, one has now died from its wounds and two more are now being savaged. There are sea creatures that are not as gentle as the ones you have encountered. You would wish no more to encounter them swimming alone in the waters than you would the serpents. Yet they cannot attack ships. They do my bidding, but I would not call them friends."

"You mean sharks, yes. The Alkhan of Eastrealm Khestadon can control the minds of many savage land beasts according to the Etoppsi and the Nantians, particularly the bears and desert wolves. Could it have been he?"

"It is possible still to speak to Siriné, even though she is crazed and mad, and the Alkhan's lands border the Serpent Sea. He could have gained access to her mind. As I recalled my tale to you the other day, I realized suddenly that Siriné was still near when the Guardian told me where to take the Staff of Terianh. She might know that Vanayema has the Staff and that some might seek it out someday."

"Even Meical makes errors. You suspect the Alkhan discovered this information from her..."

"And ordered these beasts to guard the way to Vanayema's home, yes. Yet only with your help have I now been able to realize it. Yes, that is what I suspect—to prevent the return of the Staff of Terianh to the world of the Three Peoples. It is, in itself, more dangerous to the Alkhan than an entire army of your brave Nantians. I have not been in these far-western waters in many a year or I might have known about the beasts. Yet you need have no fear of them again. However, the idea that Siriné could be communicating with the Alkhan is a dangerous proposition."

"Yes, it is, and I shall ponder it more. Do you think the Alkhan could still be in communication with these creatures?"

"The magic was implanted and finite. It connected the beasts ordering them to work together, probably to attack any ships that ventured this way. No. I do not think the Alkhan will know that we have encountered these remote watchdogs of his. Yet he may have sensed a surge in his mind when I employed my own magic, though he will not know what it means."

There was excitement coming from the mind of the god. He seemed as eager as Kodi often did. Youthful. Vigorous. The eternal loneliness had been temporarily thrust away into a far corner of his mind.

"You seem oddly different, Vanaratu. There is emotion I have not experienced from you before."

"I have not employed such power in many centuries. It was exhilarating. I think the fight helped me connect to you and your brave people on your ship. I feel...less sad. Yet my ability to fight with you or for you is limited. I am not allowed to fight against any of the Three Peoples. You must fight your Khestadone enemies. The Staff will help you once you acquire it."

"If you keep our path free of sea serpents, we will be grateful."

"I am most sorry for the two men you lost today."

"They had many close friends aboard. Yet the two shall now dance among the stars. The danger of our task is perhaps better understood now by the others. They will be wiser."

"I cannot talk to any of them, yet would you tell me about them? And along with you I shall celebrate and honor them. Maybe in this way I can know them, and they will in a sense be my friends, too."

"I am most happy to tell you about them, Vanaratu." Curdoz said this, smiling to himself, and then considered whom he thought Vanaratu would most enjoy learning about. "I shall start first with the one I have come to love as though he were my own son. His name is Kodi..."

His remark during the battle was no mere jest, and after death rites were offered for the two lost sailors and the ship was repaired and again on its way, being pulled by the Pearl Colossal as before the storm, His Highness, Prince Nikal of Nant, knighted Kodi of the House of Fothemry. It was a brief but stirring ceremony with all aboard present, Lyndz and Tiliruf beaming while Idamé dabbed at her tears. And since it had not been done before, Curdoz took the opportunity to offer a blessing upon the ambernut bow and upon the sword of Bagarro. The bow especially, along with its master, was now a part of legend, for the sailor-soldiers upon Nikal's ship would surely tell the harrowing tale upon their return to Human lands.

Though there was no precedent of such for a female in Nantian history, Nikal was determined to offer the honor to Rainwing, but she explained to the prince that in Berug she had already achieved such status and honor from King Eagleron and Queen Silverwing through her service in the Dragon Legion. Nikal's proposal was a redundancy. Nevertheless, the prince expressed public gratitude to her for her heroic actions, and all those on the ship saluted her. She may not before have had many male friends among her own people due to her position on celibacy, but she could count many Human men now as both friends and devotees. In her future traumas and struggles, she would find them loyal.

"Am I supposed to call you 'Sir Kodi,' now, mate?" asked Tiliruf, offering his friend another swig of the brandy bottle.

It was late the third night after the serpent attack. The death of the two Nantian sailors had dampened any call for a ship-wide celebration of Kodi's or Rainwing's achievements, yet the Eight Friends gathered in Nikal and Aron's larger cabin where the other men had also been staying. They might have invited the Healer pair, except that Ulna and Maru were wiped out from all their Healing work of the past few days and had retired to their bunks an hour ago. Nikal sat at his desk writing letters to be delivered eventually to the families of the two men who were lost, yet he often looked up and would on occasion make a comment or two and take a swallow if Tiliruf brought the bottle over to him. Otherwise, he remained relatively quiet. Letti was perched near him in a wicker cage.

Even Idamé had deigned to come despite being warned that liquor was to be consumed, yet she need have no fear with such a mixed crowd. None of these men were ever likely to drink to excess or get seriously out-of-control around women whom they respected. Besides, the Matrimonial could never deny Kodi her presence when it was requested. So, she too sat by watching Aron play a round of Kings and Castles with Lyndz and drank from a goblet of wine that Curdoz had poured for her. She was knitting another scarf, a green one she had decided was to be for Kodi.

Lyndz was in a spirited mood, however, and took a taste or too of the brandy when Idamé's attention was elsewhere. Tiliruf chuckled at each of these daring feats, and Lyndz would wink. He would then try to embarrass her by offering her more when Idamé was actually paying closer attention, which would earn him a scowl from the Matrimonial and to which Lyndz would be required to pretend he was 'being silly,' and would remind him she already had a goblet of wine at hand.

Kodi swallowed a smallish mouthful and responded to his friend's query. "Just you. The others shouldn't have to. I'd be right embarrassed if Curdoz started calling me 'Sir.'" He handed the bottle on to Aron and then reached up and scratched his own scruffy face.

Tiliruf reached up and rubbed his own face, likewise. None of the men had shaved since they had left Nant. Tiliruf had never allowed himself to grow a beard, and he was finding his own scruffiness to be both itchy and interesting. He and Kodi would, out of a sense of fun, reach out and rub the cheeks of the other to feel the hair growing there, and whenever they walked by it they would each have a look in the tiny framed mirror attached by nails on the wall in Nikal's cabin.

"You're always going to be 'Ko' to me," said Lyndz. "And you don't look a bit different than you did before."

"He lll...looks bigger and ah, tah...taller if you ask me," teased Aron. "There are at lll...least two mm...more hairs on his chin." The comment caused Kodi to automatically rub his face again.

Rainwing had been given by Tiliruf her very own bottle of Nantian brandy, which she was treating as tenderly as Curdoz was his wine. "I think the beards make you Human males more handsome. They make you earthier and more rugged. Appropriately masculine, I should say."

"I think not," disagreed Idamé. "I think Tiliruf and Kodi and all the rest should shave the first instance they can. You look cleaner and healthier without them."

"Ah, you just want us to always look barely out of boyhood, Mother Idamé," quipped Tiliruf.

"It is easier, I admit, to pat you on your cheeks that way," she replied, teasing him back and reaching over to offer this motherly affection to the Tirilorine. "Too scruffy. You look a bit like a scoundrel. A shaven face is a more innocent face."

Tiliruf had by now come to have strong affection for the Matrimonial, even if she did sometimes make him feel nervous and guilty, and so had grown used to her patting his cheeks as though he really were a boy. She did it to most everybody anyway, whether they were nineteen or fifty-nine, yet it would always cause Tiliruf to turn red when she did it to him. He never stopped her, though.

"But he *is* a scoundrel, Mother Idamé!" said Kodi, laughing at the Matrimonial's naïve observation. "You don't know him like I do."

Actually, he had a good notion that most, even Idamé, knew that Tiliruf had a questionable lifestyle back in Tirilorin. He did, however, hope that the Matrimonial wasn't too keen on the details.

"Well, he's a sweet scoundrel, then. And he's your friend; you shouldn't talk about him that way."

Tiliruf thought this observation delightful and laughed. "See, mate. The honorable Matrimonial says I'm a 'sweet scoundrel.' Lyndz, you don't mind that I'm a sweet scoundrel, do you?"

"Hmm?" The question caught her off guard for a moment. Pretending to be intent on her game with Aron, she then took a move on the game board—one she quickly regretted. "What did you say?"

"Eh, never mind."

When Aron countered, Lyndz looked at him. "Oh, General! Don't you dare let me get away with that mistake! You take that back!"

"Exactly," said Rainwing who had been watching the game closely. "We females don't need you males coddling us."

Aron chuckled. "All right, ah, all right! I ju...just thought I'd be nn...nice."

The Etoppsis tssked.

In two more moves it was clear that Lyndz' error was costly. She conceded.

"Sorry I messed you up, Lyndz, eh?" offered Tiliruf.

"You didn't mess me up!" she said, self-conscious of the fact that his attention and question might very well have caused her to do so. "But to answer your question, I think you and Kodi good looking enough with or without a beard. Some men look especially nice with them like General Aron and Prince Nikal. I suppose when they are thick and full and kept short and trim like theirs, they look quite nice. I don't like the long, straggly beards like on some of the Solantine sailors on Curdoz' boat. When you're still so young, though, I suppose I agree a little bit more with Mother Idamé. Makes you more...fresh, I suppose."

"So, ah, yy...you're saying I'm ll...looking rr...rather old?" asked Aron with a pretend pout.

"No, you're twisting my words, General," she replied sweetly as she reset her pieces for the next player. "I said *you* are very handsome with a thick, trimmed beard. But why are all you men asking me such silly questions?"

"Because you're the eligible one, dear," said Idamé, knowingly.

They all laughed jovially.

Kodi then sat in Lyndz' place to challenge Aron, the winner.

"Lord Sage, you have been rr...right quiet," said the general looking in Curdoz' direction. The Sage was sitting back in a chair by the desk close to Nikal. He had been writing in his journal, but he had set his quill down some time ago and was now stone still, looking past them as if deep in thought. "Are yy...you talking to Vaa...anaratu?"

"Ah! No," he said, stretching and coming back around. "I suppose my mind is wandering."

In fact, there was much on the Sage's mind. The possibility that Modela would require some sacrifices from them to gain the Staff was a continual source of discomfort for him. Also, he had begun wondering about events in Solanto. The King's Council meeting that Prince Filidor had called would now be long over. He desired very much to know what that had been about and if Mannago's suspicions were born out. Based on Deroge's Prophecies, in addition to his own Vision, Curdoz had begun wondering lately if there was some connection between events in the north and those in the south and east. That the Alkhan had implanted an order in the wild minds of vicious sea monsters and then sent them on a sort of 'mission' hundreds of miles away across the seas made him wonder whether the Ice Tribes, who it was believed still revered Siriné, were being influenced in some way by the Khestadone rulers. Perhaps the timing of all these events was not mere chance. In addition, he felt the mission to the Qeteral was also tied to the situation. He could not forget that his and Idamé's Visions had shown Qeteral in the far south of the world on the shores of the Sea of Sirinė. It was difficult to make sense of it all. And time was passing with little to show on their own part in countering the evils in the world aside from assisting in convincing the Tirilorines to go to war. That was something, he knew. Yet he still knew more needed to be done and done quickly. Despite the speed of the Colossal pulling them, he believed they were moving slow as turtles.

With Kodi and Lyndz both taking up on Aron's observation, they pressed him, and so he opened his tongue and shared with them his thoughts.

When he was done, they entered into a conversation. None of them could disagree, nor were any particularly skeptical of his observations, and some of them shared the same sorts of anxieties. Nikal expressed his own disquiet about the war in the far east, the fact he had been gone long already, and that his return to command the war would still be a long day away. He wondered what advances or new events would take place upon the part of the Alkhan and Alkhaness while they were gone.

Aron expressed concerns about Lekktor's growing influence at court and the damage he could do.

Tiliruf said little, for all these complexities had not really occurred to him before, and he learned a few facts that he had heretofore, because they were associated with Visions or Prophecies, not been privy to. He had resisted allowing Kodi give him details. It opened his mind a little more, yet he continued to harbor skepticism regarding the role of 'powers' in the world influencing events. His own role appeared to be, at least for now, a follower. He was not in a position of influence and doubted he ever would be. Yet this last thought did make him wonder if perhaps his doubts were a copout of a sort, and he didn't like that. But like many things, he kept it to himself.

Lyndz and Idamé were fairly reserved in their remarks, for along with Rainwing they harbored the secret of their future mission to Westrealm, and they didn't want to give too many of their internal thoughts away that might give the men cause to interfere in their plans.

Kodi understood Curdoz' concerns, and yet he was of the mind that what they were embarking on right now was, in itself, important. He expressed the idea that all they could do was do their best day by day to fulfill the wishes of the Guardian. To him it was all a struggle to overcome obstacles one at a time along the way. "I feel we're doing all we can do at the moment," he concluded.

Rainwing agreed. "The Eight Friends has meaning beyond the Prophecy, and our travels together, this very journey across the sea to find Modela is what we are at this time meant to focus our energies upon."

"I think we're meant to learn as we go," added Kodi. "It was Mother Idamé back in Tirilorin who said we're all growing and changing."

"You're saying it's the effort and the growing that matter," said the prince. "That is about the only thought lately that has kept me from going mad on the inside. You and Rainwing seem the best to show your faith. Lord Curdoz, there is no doubt that all of these are valid concerns and that at some point we will have to face all of them. I think we all agree that we are caught up in great events. That a very World God is nearby talking to you and monitoring our journey in the sea is sufficient evidence for that. Yet, regarding events in Solanto, the fact you are not there must be agonizing. It is the same with me, at the moment, not being with my armies in the east. It is as if we are momentarily out of our proper places and helpless."

"And yet we grow," said Rainwing. "It never occurred to me of course when I flew with the delegation to Nant that I would find myself caught up in all this. Like Kodi I get excited about it and feel like the Guardian is using me for a positive end. Yet I can understand the mind struggles you all are facing, and chances are there will be many more and greater struggles to come. All we can do is take it step by step."

"I'm sure it is the recent dangers and the loss of our sailing comrades that brings it all home to me," said Curdoz. "And sharing thoughts with Vanaratu, for it forces my mind to work. Yet even he is growing along with us."

"Then, ah...we must, as I ah, have said beeee...before, we must prepare our minds." Aron winked and took a sip from Tiliruf's bottle. "But it is nn...not with brr...randy that I mean, for I am only being funny."

"Not you, surely," said Tiliruf.

Aron laughed. "It is as Rr...rainwing has said alll...already. The...ah...Eight Friends has meaning."

"We gain strength and faith through each other," said Lyndz. "We just have to keep ourselves moving forward and helping each other move forward. We can only do what we can do where we are. I worry like Curdoz; in fact, I often feel I have a thousand things running around my head all at the same time, and like Nikal says I could go mad if I let myself."

"I am grateful in the moment," said Idamé. "This peaceful moment, even if it is over tomorrow. All of you are family to me, and though I wish I was safe at home in Solanto or even Tirilorin, I would not give up what I have gained from coming to know all of you." She dabbed a tear. "And Enric and Hollina and Maru and Ulna and the rest. And who is to know how safe Solanto is at present. So, Curdoz, dear, we must just take it one day at a time."

Nor did the wise Sage ever really think otherwise. Yet it was good to express his thoughts, and it was good to hear the others express support for one another.

This gathering and this conversation, along with many previous ones and those to follow would have a great impact upon the friends and their ability to help each other in the times ahead. As Rainwing said, there would be greater struggles to come.

Chapter 21—Modela's Island

The Pearl Colossal had disengaged from its harness sometime in the night. White gulls flew by the hundreds to and fro, and the bright morning sun shone gold upon a green land. In the distance dominating the striking scenery was a tall, broad conical mountain. Snow embraced its tip like a starred tiara. At the base of the cone was a series of rocky hills. Waterfalls and plumed cataracts could be seen flowing outward from them in many places, swift and white. Covering most of the landscape were trees, from this point appearing taller than anyone on the ship had ever seen. Directly in front of them issuing forth from the edge of the forest, a clean river emptied across white sands into the sea.

Your ship will be safe, Curdoz. Vanayema will find you. She knows you are coming.

After anchoring the ship in place, it took three trips for the three rowboats to complete the ferrying of the adventurers and the ship's crew to the sandy shore. They followed the river upstream a little way where it was all freshwater and sparkling, and it was here that the men took with them into the stream soap and razors, and like boys in a mountain river, swam and bathed.

Rainwing led the women on a longer hike upstream to a point where a little creek added to the river its own waters. They followed this smaller watercourse a short distance where they discovered an inviting deep pool surrounded by flowering shrubs, and with a low plume of water pouring into it. There they themselves engaged in long and grateful baths. Even Rainwing plunged her huge body, wings and all, into the clean waters. Etoppsi lathered their short fur sometimes, and Rainwing did so today, but she used no soap on her wings, for this would have destroyed the natural oils that kept her feathers whole and glossy. Emerging from this she shook herself and sat upon the banks of the pool. She worked her natural oils into her feathers with her large hands, spread her wings wide and dried herself in the sun.

Many birds, each with unique song, trumpeted harmoniously among the shrubs and high in the tall trees. Occasionally one would take flight, displaying multi-colored plumage with long trailing double tails, bright and cheerful. Though the kinds of trees and other plants and the sorts of birds were ones for which they knew no names, to Idamé, Ulna and Maru the place reminded them a little of the peaceful contentedness of the Valley of the Gifted. It was a magical sort of place, certainly.

Assuring her they felt safe, Rainwing left them and took flight from the stream bank in order to explore. She flew high, and they watched her until she disappeared towards the center of the island and was blocked from view by the surrounding trees.

The women washed their clothes and laid them on warm rocks or over the tops of the shrubs in the sun to dry. They then put on dry undergarments, and afterwards ate some of the provisions they had brought with them from the ship.

It was hot, and yet the beams of sunshine fed them through their skin with strength and health, and Ulna and Maru placed their hands on each other and upon the two other women like Xeno and Danly had done with Kodi in Thorune. Idamé then fell asleep in a shady spot on the soft ground near to the pool, grateful finally to be able to lie perfectly still upon motionless, solid earth.

Maru also sat down in the shade to protect her white, Elenite skin—she had even washed her bonnet, for it smelled to her, she said, 'of sea spray and fishiness.' Ulna and Lyndz sat on a rock beside the pool and absorbed into their olive skin more of the rays of the sun.

"Lyndz, you're a goddess, truly. Youthful. Serene. Every woman dreams of being beautiful as you are so naturally."

"Sister Ulna, you're so sweet!"

"Ulna's so very right, dear," said Maru. "Don't you *dare* take the Vow! Find you a good man to love on that gorgeous figure and make your babies!"

They all cracked up in laughter.

"I'm not taking the Vow, don't worry. But I've got work to do, Sisters. It will be a while before I settle down. Tell me, is having taken the Vow been a difficulty?"

"Yes and no. Mostly no," said Ulna. "It's hard to explain, dear, but I'm happy with my choice. The Guardian is close to me, I feel."

"There is," said Maru, "an erotic element in the connection to Him. Although I doubt I've ever really admitted that to anyone except Ulna. I do not feel *lonely*. But you cannot possibly understand..."

"Oh, but I think I might, Maru," said Lyndz, interrupting. "Really. You know I've had a Vision, and honestly, I didn't tell the whole truth to anyone, even Kodi, when I described the emotion. I told Kodi that Meical reminded me very much of him and my father. And there were strong pieces of them in what I was feeling. But there was a greater *erotic* quality to the figure I beheld. He was young and beautiful, and it really moved me, just in the way that perhaps you're describing."

"Oh, dear! Yes, Lyndz, I don't know I could describe my Calling Vision better than what you are doing," said Ulna.

"I'm convinced," said Maru philosophically, "that it is more common for women to see Him in Visions than it is for men. I believe it is connected strongly to the need for what I call a 'masculine balance.' Men need that less than women do, of course. And the men who do see the Guardian in their Visions have perhaps not had the best male role models in their lives to draw upon. Most particularly the fatherly. And so, they have a greater need to actually see Him, and be encouraged from the memory of His face in their Vision."

"You know, that does make a good deal of sense to me," said Lyndz. "But what you mean, really, is *all aspects* of the masculine balance. At least for women. Including the erotic element, but also the fatherly and brotherly. And that is precisely what I experienced when the Guardian presented Himself to me. I often review the encounter in my mind, and what it does for me is confirm the goodness of Kodi and of my father as excellent men in my life. But in my case has left me open to a bondmate someday. Really opened my mind to it, as I hadn't imagined much that kind of intimacy before the Vision. But I'm guessing that in *your* case..."

"Yes, in our case, the Guardian has in part *fulfilled* the role of bondmate and made it easier for us to adhere to our Vow."

"That is so incredibly interesting," said Lyndz. "But what about the other way around? What gives *men* in the Orders the *feminine balance* in order to subdue erotic needs?"

"I believe it's quite different altogether," offered Ulna. "From my conversations with male Healers, it seems that rather than a feminine balance they are instead adhering to the dictates of the Guardian as one would a king. A good king, one deserving of great loyalty."

"Oh! So as their overlord, in a sense, He directs them or even orders them to refrain from sensual passion. They draw strength directly from Him by way of the memory of their Vision and meditation. They follow the dictates of the Vow out of sheer loyalty, not wishing to disappoint Him."

"Brilliant, Lyndz, really! I have absolutely got to write all this down as soon as I get a chance," said Maru. "What a superb theory we've come up with! On our journey home we'll have to discuss it sometime with Mother Idamé and Lord Curdoz and see what they think. All that said, however, I suspect the theory doesn't work for every Order member. There are those few who in time fall in love with another. Many of those end up subject to an Aura, but there are those who don't. In both cases, they seek out a Dispensation."

"The Aura couples receive them without question by the High Priest," said Ulna. "The others endure a lot of scrutiny; some few receive the Dispensation, but most don't."

"What happens to those who don't?"

"A few will actually leave the Orders and begin a family."

"I'm not sure how I feel about that—the idea that individuality and personal choices based on love can't somehow have an outlet and the person remain in the Orders. War Wizards are understood as being an Order, and they are not prevented from Bonding. Trust me, Kodi's not going to deny himself once he falls in love. And me, too. I'm going to do what I want, and my Vision seems to have left me with that choice."

"I have to agree with you. There are those few in the Orders for whom the Vow doesn't work. Events present themselves. People change. There is no reason for anyone to experience a sense of loneliness or imbalance of that kind. There has been chatter from time to time on reforming that piece of the system. I think the High Synod is fearful too many will seek Dispensation if they loosen the rule. I think, yes, it will make it easier, but I don't foresee a flood. Most Order Members are quite happy with their choice of having taken the Vow."

The three chatted for a little more but soon grew quiet, as each fell into her own silent thoughts. They were lazy and relaxed. Lyndz dipped her legs into the water, the sun was quickly drying their clothes, and Idamé continued to snooze contentedly. This was the morning plan; the men were doing similarly downstream. None had forgotten the recent death of the two sailors, the fight with the serpents and the storm, but the charms upon that land were those of healing and contentment. Always there was the beautiful call of a bird or the tuneful play of the low waterfall, or the tender touch of the breeze.

When Rainwing returned, she had much to say.

"I have rarely seen such fanciful places as I have here. It is a large island with the volcano in the middle of it. Everywhere I look there is water flowing or in shaded pools, and beautiful trees and colorful birds. It is enchanting. Most importantly I saw a Human-like house of wood and stone set next to a crystalline stream, but I did not descend to it. If that is where Modela lives, Curdoz did not want us approaching her alone. Yet if she was looking up, she likely saw me. I did not see anyone; perhaps no one is home, at the moment. It is set in a clearing, and there are many fruit trees around it, and small pastures, and a large vegetable patch. There were goats. It looks like a small farmstead. Perhaps she lives alone—it is difficult to say. It would be hard for one person to manage such a place, in my opinion, yet perhaps if it is Modela she has magical Gifts she employs to aid her in taking care of it. I flew towards the volcano. It is massive, of course. There are volcanoes in the land of Berug, but none I think as large and tall. I doubt it has erupted in thousands of years. All the land about is heavily forested with old trees. The beaches are all low and sandy on this side, with high cliffs on the other, and there are numerous little rivers that begin high in the mountain and hills and make their way to the sea. Enchanting. Enchanting. I, myself, tend to prefer open lands and fields, and yet this place draws me somehow."

"It is both wild and tame, like a garden," observed Ulna. "There is no stain anywhere. There is not a browned leaf or a deadened flower."

"It does seem like a paradise and yet familiar at the same time," said Lyndz. "I feel, well, I feel a bit like a little girl again, playing outside in the spring sunshine with my mother watching me and laughing."

"That's interesting, because I feel similarly," said Maru. "Nothing about this place is remotely like Eleni, and yet I feel at home, and I too am reminded keenly of my mother. She and I are very close, though I have not seen her in many years. We write letters, of course, but they can take many months to arrive."

In fact, all of them had like thoughts. Even Idamé when she woke from her nap told them she had just experienced a dream in which her mother appeared, a woman who had died many years before. "I do not dream of her all the time, of course, and yet this one dream was vivid: she was alive and holding my hand as we walked in a green wood. And then we were sitting at the kitchen table drinking tea together. She was smiling and happy to see me."

Their clothes mostly dry now, they put these back on themselves and began their march downstream.

None of the men except Curdoz, sitting under a tree smoking his pipe as he was now doing, were inclined to put their newly laundered shirts back on their torsos in the inviting sunshine, yet all had returned to their clean, though still damp breeches in anticipation of the return of the women. Kodi and Tiliruf among others had shaved and looked fresh. All were relaxed and sleepy, lying about upon rocks or under trees. Some were napping. They were as much enchanted by the clean waters, healing sunshine, and island airs as were the women.

When questioned by Lyndz and Idamé they admitted also to images of childhood homes and indeed of their mothers, though as men often do, they had until then kept such thoughts to themselves. At least those who remembered their mothers, anyway. Tiliruf was one among two or three others who had little or no memory of their mothers, and yet even these few felt nostalgic. Tiliruf, however, refused to express himself, and just shook his head and smiled when Lyndz questioned him. Yet she didn't press him. It was all very personal.

Curdoz was most amazed by the women's observation. He too was thinking about his mother, before she died, how beautiful she was, and how important she had been to him, keeping his father's sternness under control. He had not thought about her since perhaps his uncle had died, and yet now he found himself missing her.

General Aron was quiet, rather like Tiliruf, though no one noticed this, and no one questioned him. For which he was glad. As he listened to all these observations, he was wondering much to himself.

Unlike the rest, he had not been thinking of his mother at all.

Aron had other images running around in his usually calm mind, wild and splendid images set off by the paradise-like setting with its cool waters and warm, healthy sunshine. The island had captured his soul in a way that no other place he had ever traveled to had ever done. He realized it even as he stepped foot upon the sands. He was convinced he had been here in his dreams particularly at times when he felt especially lonely, longing for companionship of a certain physical and emotional kind. The place brought upon him dichotomous emotions of longing, both exotic and familiar.

He believed it to be a place he would find rest and contentment...among other more interesting activities: there was a woman in those dreams, exotic and voluptuous. He had no intention of relating these activities aloud to anyone there, definitely not so sober. He suddenly remembered the game of Fifty-twos years before when, drunk on quantities of undiluted rum, he had told of his boyhood Vision to the prince his friend, among others—the time about which Nikal had teased him in front of Dira. He laughed to himself realizing he would have to be at least that drunk now and with a chosen few like Nikal and Tiliruf and Kodi before he would share the imagery occupying his thoughts. To him it was strange when the old Vision came suddenly and vividly to his mind.

He looked over at Mother Idamé as she was talking with Curdoz and raised an eyebrow.

Around the second hour after noon, they all returned to the shore. They were getting ready to divide into various parties, some under instruction to return to the ship to retrieve the water barrels and others to go about on land, some to hunt for food sources and others to set out in search of the house that Rainwing had spotted.

It was just as they were all about to go forth and explore when she appeared.

Upon a horse bright white, a woman in flowing white rode towards them along the beachfront from the direction of the sun. As she dismounted and approached, all came together as a group. They stood and waited. Yet as she drew closer and her form and features became more distinct, none were prepared for what was then revealed to them.

Kodi was the first to speak. His jaw dropped and he exclaimed, "It's my mother! Lyndz! It's Mother!"

There was Elisa, the Countess Fothemry, with her light brown locks and blue eyes, her skin white smooth. Lyndz could not speak.

The sailor standing next to Kodi looked at him oddly. "No, Sir Kodi! I beg your humble pardon, but it be me own mum! And yet, yet she be as I remember her when I was but a wee lad! She be quite young again, I say!"

The sailor began to walk towards her when Curdoz reached out and held his shoulder.

"Wait!" said the Sage loudly and firmly.

For Curdoz, too, saw walking towards them his long-deceased mother, and though her image reached in and touched his inmost soul most profoundly, he knew that what he saw could not be reality. In some way reality had been altered.

Nikal also saw his mother, the Queen of Nant. As with the others, she appeared to him to be much younger than she was now. And unlike the stern sad face of which he was most familiar, the woman before him nodded at him and smiled kindly.

Rainwing's vision was decidedly different. She saw not a Human woman riding a white horse but rather an Etoppsi female, powerful and beautiful, which had winged its way low along the coast and settled on the sands before them. She had light gray fur and bright silver wings, just like the female topling who had inherited them. "But...but! But she is *my* mother!" she said in her loud voice. "You mean each of you sees your own *Human* mother?"

When the realization hit them that in fact all were seeing in the approaching woman their own mother, and in fact, like the sailor beside Kodi, they saw the much younger woman they each remembered as a child, many of the sailors began to back away and grumble, wondering what witchery had caused such an illusion. Yet most of the rest stood resolute and waited. In another minute she had come within twenty feet of them and stood.

"You need have no fear," said a voice. And not only did each look upon their mother, indeed each believed they were hearing her speak.

Nikal called out. "Why do we each see in you our mother? Are you the one they call Modela? The one Vanaratu the World God knows as Vanayema?"

Tiliruf and the two or three sailors who had no memory of their mothers also saw before them a woman kind and loving, one who appeared to reach into each man's heart and hold him close. Whereas the sailors had not the luxury of a painting or image of their mothers, there was a painting upon the wall in Genehbro's bedroom with which Tiliruf was quite familiar, one he had looked upon many times over the years. Before him stood the living manifestation of that painting, Róssela, who had died soon after giving birth to him. She was stunningly beautiful, her long blond hair flowing in lovely curls, a trait he inherited from her.

Moved by repressed longing and despite Curdoz' order, he walked up to the woman. He looked into her face and said to her, "I...I am so sorry!"

She looked at him with a compassionate expression and said to him, "Oh, my Tiliruf a'Terianh! You need not be sorry! The fact that *you* lived is a joy to me!"

She then looked at Nikal and answered his question. "But I *am* Gatha your mother, Nikal, Prince of Nant! And I am Elisa, Lyndz and Kodi of the House of Fothemry. And your mother, Curdoz, my dear, sweet Luvin. Your new name from the Guardian is a strange one to me! Yet I am proud of the great man you have become, friend of Meical!"

Curdoz smiled at her. He could not feel threatened by the person in front of him, even if he was wary. "You know all our names?"

"I know the names of all my children since the creation of the Mold. For I *am* the Mold. You are correct, Nikal. Those names apply to the one whom you see before you. From my loins long ago sprang the forms of the Three Peoples." She looked at Rainwing and spread wide her vast wings, though only Rainwing could see these. "First born were Rainwing's people, the powerful winged Etoppsi of the sky. Second were the magical Qeteral of the forests and gardens. Third were the passionate Humans. All shaped from the Mind of the Creator, enhanced by clays from the Valley, watered and nurtured. I know all of you and all your names, for all of you descend from me. I know the names of all your parents and grandparents and the names of all your forebears to the Beginning. Some of you have children and I know their names. As all of your children are born to you, and their children, too, I shall know them as well. I am the mother of all, and it is in the form of your mother that you know me."

It was at this point that Aron stepped out in front of them all. Upon his face, with its curly dark hair and dark, trimmed beard was a look so clever that they all looked at him with wonder. Upon his lips was a smirk, and those who knew him were reminded of the look he often used before he would offer up one of his hilarious observations.

Tiliruf, though he stood close to the woman did not touch her. Aron, on the other hand, reached out to her with a slow and deliberate hand, and as it neared Modela's face, Mother Idamé shrieked. "Oh, my! Oh, my! Oh, my! Oh, Aron! Oh, my!"

Aron paused just before his fingers reached her cheek, and the woman looked at Idamé, and then at him, sudden amazement on her face.

He called her by her name. "Vanayema, I...I see nn...not the face of mm...my mum. Sheee....she was an ugly old wench, she was. I took after my ole dad, thannn....thank the Guardian. He was a right handsome fellow, I mmust say. Yyy...you do not fool me with your magic, deary. You are a woman, beauuutiful and fair, the most beautiful and fair I ever saw. I...I have dreamed of you. The others mm...might see the face of their mums. Not I."

When he then touched her face with his brown hand, she was astonished. "I thought I knew you! Even as you walked towards me I knew you! Why do I no longer remember? Who are you that Meical now hides you from me? He has never done that before!"

Tiliruf backed away. What was taking place between the general and the woman who looked like the painting of his mother was far too strange. A little distance he thought was called for. He went and stood with Kodi and Lyndz.

Idamé kept pointing. "But! But it's the Aura! The Aura is there!"

"I nnn...knew it," said Aron with dry emotion. "Had to be. Is there ah, lightning and ah, crashing moons? Ah...after allll these years, it's about time, d...don't you think, Vanayema? I will call you that. It is a mm...more beautiful name than Modela."

The woman stood uncertain at first, but finally she spoke again in a softer voice. "It has been long. So very long. Vanayisu fought with his many sons in the Great War and now dances among the stars. Does Meical send me again a companion after long millennia?"

And when she reached out herself and touched the face of the general, the magic changed.

"Oh, my! Oh, my!" repeated the flustered Idamé. "I...I don't believe it!"

No longer did everyone see the image of their mother. Before them stood a ravishing young woman, in looks perhaps five or ten years younger than the general. She had luxuriant flowing brown locks and mesmerizing green eyes. She was buxom, very, altogether with a most inviting figure in the eyes of all the men there, and upon her face was a look both knowing and 'lusty' as Tiliruf later described it. Not even to Rainwing did she appear as her Etoppsi mother, but rather a Human female in white garments, and she could now see the white horse standing beyond, waiting patiently.

"Is that how General Aron sees you?" asked the Etoppsis.

Modela looked at her and then again at Aron. She touched his face yet again, and he hers. The look between the two was not dissimilar to that of Manwul and Steffia back at the Grand Dance in Tirilorin, the one for which all around them laughed and to which some of the Sisters blushed.

"Aron is your name?" She said laughing. "'Arrono' was what I called Vanayisu! 'My beloved mate!'"

"Wh...wh...whyyy does that surpriiise you? Nnnothing surprises mm...me anymore."

"Your face shines as the sun. Your form is as those of my first Human sons, handsome and strong."

"Ah, ww...well, you should have seen me in the river swimming a while back if yy...you think I am handsome with *this* stuff on me. I'm mmm...much more fetching without." He fingered his shirt and rakishly winked.

Even Tiliruf, dealing with the aftereffects of having seen a living vision of his deceased mother, laughed. "Eh, you're cracking, General

Aron, mate! You're telling me you're in love with a woman you haven't known five minutes?"

Back at the river Aron had determined to keep his mouth shut, but in the presence of Vanayema his vision had come true, and he was so punch-drunk it didn't seem to matter any longer whether he'd really been drinking or who else was listening. There was nothing that could embarrass him anymore. "Nnn...no. I have ah, said already. I have dreamed of her since I was a teenaged boy. I nnn...know this woman. Mmm...every square inch, if yyyou know what I mean. I'm surprised she isn't pregnant with my kid already."

Virtually every man there burst asunder, as did Lyndz and Rainwing. Curdoz and even Nikal smiled. Idamé and the two Healers flushed.

"Bit randy aren't we, eh? Well maybe we ought to leave you two alone for a while?" quipped Tiliruf. "Unless you're of the mind we should all stand by and watch! Maybe I could learn a trick or two, eh?" He folded his arms and stood back. "Go ahead, mate."

This garnered much additional laughter.

"But...but this is all so illogical!" said Idamé, finally giving voice to her inner thoughts.

"What's logical about Auras anyways, I'd like to know, eh?"

Modela spoke. "The Aura is some of the oldest of magic, my son Tiliruf a'Terianh, and though your skeptical father may never have told you of it, indeed one was there when he met Róssela."

Tiliruf looked amazed. He did not reply to this information, uncertain whether he believed it. It was even weirder to him that this magical woman who only a minute ago looked exactly like his mother—now appearing to all as an exotic buxom beauty—still referred to him as her 'son.' She looked no older than he. The world was surely turned on its head.

"The Aura has defined the origins of some others standing before me today," added Modela. She then turned to Idamé. "You, my dear, have a great Gift."

Idamé nodded. "I...I am prepared to administer the Bonding rite if this is indeed what the Guardian desires, and if you and the general so wish it."

"I ah, suppose I can ah, wait a wee. Beee...besides, I...I have allll...ways expected a grand affair."

Aron then stood back and bowed low to Modela. "Ah, www...will you become my Bondmate, Vanayema? Though my life be short, for unlike you I am mortal, I wish to be yy...your companion for a time, if yyy...you will have me."

His demeanor in his proposal was so charming and humble that the women were oohing and aahing at the sweetness.

"I will certainly have you, Aron, for it is clear now to me that the Guardian has anticipated this for some time, though for what end or purpose I know not! Perhaps He grants me a blessing after long millenia." She then turned to the crowd. "Tonight, then, our union will take place, and dear Idamé can perform her duty by the Guardian. And if my handsome Aron wishes a grand affair, he shall surely have it!"

"But he's wanted this all his life," said Kodi to Tiliruf when they were back on board, rummaging through their trunks for their best attire to wear for the Bonding ceremony which was to take place at Modela's home. "Why does it bother you? You were the same when it was Manwul and Steffia."

"But it's mad, I tell you! She's...well, she's his *grandmother!*"

"She's *everybody's* grandmother. She's hundreds of generations removed anyway, so it's not like it's his sister or something!"

"It's still mad. Some magical female...what would you call her? A 'creature?' I mean she's not really fully Human, or at least not 'only' Human. I mean she's got Qeteral and Etoppsi blood, too, eh? But she makes herself *look* Human. Except to Rainwing of course. In fact, she makes herself look like everybody's mum! I was convinced she *was* my mother come back to life! It was mortifying!"

"You're only mortified because you talked to her like she really was your mom, and it turned out she wasn't. And what she said to you was beautiful."

Tiliruf ignored this. "And then she transforms into some busty, lusty damsel! Which is what Aron apparently saw all along! And he falls for her! He would have dropped his trousers and mounted her then and there if we weren't all standing around. Poor deprived bastard. What do you think about it, sir? Am I right or not?" He looked over at Nikal who was gathering by request some of Aron's best clothes and also putting on his own best from his trunk.

"I...I think many things. It is a confusing situation assuredly, so I understand your perspective. It has all happened so rapidly and unexpectedly. Though I cannot contradict the magic of Idamé's Aura. Or Aron's attraction. The Guardian Himself was wanting this. In that regard it is inspiring. It is a good thing, I suppose. Yet, despite it all, I admit my heart is much pained."

Curdoz paused in his dressing and looked at the prince. "In what way, Nikal?"

Nikal sat on his bunk and was silent for a moment. "I think I understand now what it is in the Prophecy I am required to give away in exchange for the Staff."

Even the cheerful Kodi stopped at this and dropped his jaw. "You mean you think you're being asked to give up...give up *Aron?* Because he is your friend? I didn't think of it like that."

"He is my best and oldest friend. We have known each other twelve years, since we were both seventeen and eighteen years old, I think. It is an unhappy thought to think of leaving him forever, here on this island, for who's to say we shall ever return? In fact, I know we shall not. I fear in my heart I will never see him again once we leave here. It's almost as hurtful as giving up Dira. Yet I cannot deny what I saw today with my own eyes. I have always wished for my friend this greatest happiness, a female companion who fulfills him and makes him whole. For a short time, I had that with Dira..." He paused, then shook his head to retain his composure. "Like Kodi says, Aron has wanted this all his life, since the Vision he had as a youth. Such a good man, and disciplined. And such a passionate man with much to offer a woman. This is what the Guardian wanted him to wait for, and the blessing of the Guardian should not be denied."

"Indeed," said Curdoz, "it should not. You speak wisely, Nikal. The Prophecy is being fulfilled, at least in part. I fear you are correct. You are giving your friend away. And you will stand beside him tonight in the place of honor. And so, Aron is giving up much as well, though it may not be apparent to him just now. His thoughts are on Modela."

Kodi looked at the prince sitting there. "I'm really sorry, Nikal."

"So Nikal is sacrificing Aron, and Aron is sacrificing Nikal. What else are we going to have to give up, eh? Eight Friends and eight sacrifices, or 'gifts' as this Prophecy thing calls them."

"But Vanaratu said 'to lose is to gain,'" said Kodi, trying desperately to find something reassuring to say.

"Well, we know what Aron is 'gaining', eh?" quipped Tiliruf. "I mean, by the Guardian's Nuts, eh? He gets to lie back in sweet contentment on this perfect little island and have his big happy stiffrod satisfied every day and night for decades if he wants it, by that...that handy amorous pretty piece of curvy female flesh! Not a responsibility in all the world, and nobody to interrupt! What more could any man want than that, might I ask, eh?"

Nikal chuckled. "Not one to mince words, are you, Tiliruf? There's a Sage of the Guardian standing right there, you know?"

"Yeah, well, sorry about that. You only made me promise not to talk like that around the women. I've done that. Better than Aron today, anyway, eh? With his 'I'm surprised she isn't pregnant with my kid already' remark! Right ruttish that was, eh? Ha! So, does 'the Sage of the Guardian' disagree?" Tiliruf asked with a hint of mocking sarcasm.

Curdoz chuckled. "No. I suppose I do not. I am sure you speak the truth, Tiliruf, as you see it. But I should look at it from a more wholesome angle which I hope someday you will, too. The man is in love, and Modela is smitten by him. They are committing to each other. There is much more to it than..." He paused and cleared his throat.

"Happy stiffrods getting satisfied," concluded Kodi, chuckling hugely.

"Nope. I don't believe it," said Tiliruf.

"Of course, you don't," agreed Nikal. "You're a scoundrel!"

"Thank you, sir! Best compliment you've ever given me, eh?" He bowed.

"A 'sweet scoundrel,' don't forget!" added Kodi, shoving his friend on the shoulder.

It must be said that despite the underlying grief on Nikal's part, and surely none of them liked the idea of never seeing their fun and funny friend Aron again, Tiliruf's crudeness achieved a useful effect, better at the moment even than Kodi's usual empathy. They, Nikal too, had to admit that in the long run some things were more important than others. The good Aron, whom they all admired, was to be happily Bonded to the woman, literally of his very dreams. After having fought hard in the east as a general in the army, he now was to dwell in a land of peace and unimaginable beauty. He was still quite young with the promise of a long life ahead, and he was as happy and playful about the prospects as a puppy. They could not refute such joy, though they themselves were to lose his companionship apparently forever. They could see no alternative. The chances of them returning to this place were non-existent, and Modela could not come to mortal lands and survive, certainly not in peace. Apparently, the Guardian designated this place as her protected home eons ago, and the only ones who could come here were the ones given permission by the Guardian Himself. Aron was being given an extraordinary gift. Whether it was a reward for his long self-discipline under Meical's orders, depriving himself of feminine affection and concupiscent desires—like Kodi he was no Vow-taking Monastic—or for some unknown purposes they could not know. For Nikal the loss was great, but he was very lucky that Kodi and the others were there, for it helped.

In fact, it helped a great deal. Eventually, Nikal would rely on them more and more. The loss of Aron would draw all the travelers, particularly the four remaining men, closer together. That, in itself, was important, and yet it was just a part of a bigger whole. In time it would become clear that Meical did indeed have a purpose in mind for Aron, and eventually they would all benefit. If all went well, the Bonding of ancient Modela to the young Aron would have far-reaching implications. But the travelers could not see this, now. Neither could Aron or even Modela at this stage. But the Vision of Meical the Guardian is a grand one, and on the whole a good one, and this was one of the worlds assigned Him long ago and one He loved quite passionately. He knew well the Mind of the Creator and the Creator's zest for the beautiful, the extraordinary, and the loving. He knew, for He and his many brothers and sisters scattered throughout the Cosmos sprang from that Mind in the Time Before All

Times. Perhaps Tiliruf thought it was madness, but there was method behind it all. The Guardian could not be plain with them for two reasons. One, He could truly only see a little into the future, and there was much He did not know, particularly as it had to do with the Alkhan and Alkhaness. The Khestadone realms were mostly dark to Him. Wrong choices upon the part of key players could still wreak havoc with His hopes, and the evil powers could do much damage in such an event. The situation was precarious. He had been thwarted before. There were worlds He had lost altogether. But the second reason was that, should all go well, being plain would quite spoil the surprise. And in His wisdom, He knew mortal life is best lived when there are many surprises. To know all in advance was a detriment to spiritual growth. And to joy.

Kodi perhaps knew this best. His eyes were open. And he tried his best to help the others see. He would step up and take Aron's place beside Nikal. Nikal could never despair, despite the two great losses in his life, as long as Kodi stood at his side. They truly, in every respect of the word, became brothers, privately sharing their thoughts and learning in the process. Tiliruf played a useful part with his own audacious brand of humor, and Curdoz the wise Sage and father-like figure, helped keep them all grounded.

When they arrived at Modela's pretty stone and timber cottage in its homestead, having followed a wide green trail through the island forest, it appeared to the crew and the friends that two hundred servants had arranged a grand affair like they might have done on the lawn at the imperial palace in Tirilorin. The sky overhead was growing slowly dark displaying stars increasing by thousands every minute. Torches, placed everywhere on carved wood columns, sprang to life.

Where the food for the banquet came from, and how Modela could brew such fabulous ales and craft such wines was a question that only had one answer. Magic. Upon a green lawn beside a crystal stream were cloth-draped tables piled high with every food that every man and woman and Etoppsis had ever delighted in or dreamed of. And barrels of ales and wines stood in a spring house where they were kept cool and marvelously palatable.

But before the revelry took place, the Bonding ceremony was witnessed by all. Though these did not travel with Idamé, a proper blue robe for Aron and a white one for Modela were 'discovered,' and these were placed upon the betrothed pair. A green mantle appeared upon Idamé, over which she wore her multi-colored shawl. Nikal stood tall and handsome at Aron's side, and Lyndz was given the honor of standing with Modela, whereas Ulna and Maru, with Curdoz' sagely permission, assisted Idamé in the place of absent Matrimonial Sisters. The Bonding party stood under an open canopy of white silk, and there were tropical white flowers in huge urns in strategic locations all around. The flowers glowed in the growing darkness though only a sliver of golden Orohmoon shown overhead. Solvermoon was new and absent. Yet overhead the celestial star bodies radiated not only white, but also reds and blues.

When Idamé pronounced the final blessing, the newly Bonded pair kissed passionately. Unexpectedly, white birds with long tail feathers streaked out of nowhere and flew in looping circles, and all the little crowd applauded. When above them soon afterward it grew fully dark, meteors by the hundreds streaked across from one end of the galaxy to the other. It was as though the heavens themselves celebrated the union and foretold of cosmic expectations. None among them would forget the Bonding of Aron of Nant and Vanayema of the Mold.

The grand festivity afterward could hardly be equaled, and though there were no servants, no one was bashful about filling his own mug or piling his own plate. Many simply stood at the banquet tables and stuffed their cheeks with scrumptious morsels. They had not eaten especially well on the ship, and yet few had ever eaten so well in any event. To Curdoz and Idamé the wine was as though it were made by the gods, and Kodi and Tiliruf praised the ales and drank their fill and more besides. Rainwing seemed always to drink ten times as much as any Human, and a clay mug of giant proportions appeared always to refill itself in her large hand.

Nikal determinedly cast aside all gloom, and he sat proudly at a table to Aron's right, whereas Modela was at the groom's left with Lyndz to her left. Modela made Lyndz feel as though they were best of friends, not unlike how Princess Isatura treated her at Carlomen's palace.

"Wherever did you acquire such a lovely emerald, my dear?" asked Vaneyema, looking intently for a moment at Lyndz' bosom.

"My father found it on the Tolosian Peninsula and had the jeweler craft the pendant for me!"

"Really?" she replied, with a gleam in her green eyes. "Well then I can assure you it is a treasure of treasures, my dear!"

All ate and drank and joked and laughed. It was as the revelry of the gods at the dawn of the world, the unfolding magic not allowing for any unhappiness. The night airs were warm, and after dinner many of the tipsy men jumped into the stream, fully clothed, splashing and whooping, with friends on the banks handing them more mugs. Lyndz jumped in holding hands with Kodi and Tiliruf, and then Ulna and Maru as well, setting off much laughter and glee. It was a memorable night, and all were enlivened not only by strong beverage, but also by the mystical enchantments of that island. Even Idamé could not find fault with the mirth-filled gaiety, her often raised eyebrow fully relaxed.

When four or five hours before dawn they all found beds of straw made up with bedclothes of linen and wool, they lay down and slept. And in the late morning sun, though Aron and Modela had long since disappeared, before them all were tables laden again with tropical fruits and fresh-baked loaves, goat cheeses and cool fruit-flavored waters in large clay pitchers. If any man awakened with the unpleasant aftereffects of too many pints, Ulna or Maru healed him instantly. The rest of the day was spent exploring the forested and watered land between Modela's farmstead and the beachhead.

By late afternoon all had gathered at the beach, where they found two extraordinary miracles had taken place: the sailor, whose crushed leg had to be removed by the Healers after the serpent attack, had been restored completely, the limb having astonishingly reappeared whole during a nap! The man was running and splashing ecstatically in the surf, and his friends were celebrating with him. Also on the beach were many crates packed with beautiful, imperishable fresh foods and full barrels of freshwater and even ales. The sailors had already rowed most of these to the ship where they found the virtually empty and stale barrels had disappeared by magic. When the ship had been fully loaded, the seven remaining friends, Nikal, Curdoz, Idamé, Lyndz, Kodi, Tiliruf and Rainwing, made their way back up the trail to Modela's cottage.

The two lovers met them on the lawn, both wearing clean, pale blue, linen garments. Their hair hung wet, and it appeared they had within the past few minutes emerged from a bath in the little stream beside the cottage. Modela had something very long, wrapped in cloths, in her hands. Aron stood with her, his shirt lazily open and untucked, and he was barefoot, and upon his face was a look that Tiliruf thought far too self-satisfied. He doubted even he himself ever looked that pleased after a particularly expressive night at his favorite North Bend brothel. He was just about to offer up a blithe comment about it when Modela spoke first.

The mood quickly changed to one of great somberness.

Indicating the object in her hands she said, "This Staff comes to you, Nikal, Prince of Nant and Sir Kodi of the House of Fothemy, yet with a price. Great treasures must be surrendered. The Prophecy of the Guardian must be fulfilled."

Nikal swallowed and nodded his head. Kodi followed suit, nodding as well.

"Do you know, Modela," asked Curdoz, "who the Alkhan and Alkhaness are? Where they came from? The origins of their dark magic?"

"I know much, more even than the Guardian, for the darkness in the Khestadone Realms blocks much of His sight. In His worlds He sees most clearly by way of the eyes of those who believe in Him and live by the Principles. Almost none in those places know of Meical the Guardian. Yet none of my children can hide from me. Though I am no fool and understand the dangers, within my heart there is not the capacity to assist you in war against any of my children, even when they have given over their own hearts to evil purpose. Vanayisu was the warrior. I am not. I am a mother, the mother of all. You must understand this. The ones whom you call the Alkhan and Alkhaness indeed have names, and they are my children as are you. You will learn nothing of them from me. This Staff I cannot claim because it was only entrusted to me for safe-keeping, otherwise I would be tempted to withhold it, for it is above all an implement of war. It is not I, therefore, who gives it to you, but Meical in his role of the Taxiarch. I have seen enough of war. I do not wish to watch again, even from afar."

"Will you at least tell us about the nature of the treasures we must give up?"

"Remember as does Kodi, the words of Vanaratu."

"*To lose is to gain,*" offered Kodi.

She nodded. "I can tell you very little more, and yet I think some of you already have an inkling. Am I right, Nikal?"

The prince did not mince words. "Do you not think some of us have suffered enough already?"

They then saw upon Modela's face a look of extreme compassion.

"Out of ignorance you misunderstand," she said softly. "I wish I could tell you more, but I cannot, or you will not grow as you must."

"So, you're saying we should buck up and keep hope?"

"Something very much like that, Kodi, Brother of Meical. Listen well then to your young friend, then, Nikal of Nant. Since it has already been understood I will confirm in part: that Nikal and Aron once they take their leave of one another today will have already made their sacrifices. Upon your return journey, along the way, the rest will then do so. Are you all committed, then? For once you do, there is no going back. At least not in the way you might think. From this point, you are required to go forward. You can never come back. You will either grow in your sacrifice, or you will descend into despair, and the world will grow dark, for the world depends on you. For some, the sacrifices will indeed be greater than others, yet perhaps the rewards therefore will be greater."

"*To lose is to gain,*" repeated Kodi.

"To lose is to gain," concluded Modela with a nod.

"Then I am committed."

"And you shall soon know why you are called Brother of Meical."

Kodi smiled and nodded.

"I commit. I must trust Meical. I do trust Him," said Lyndz, desiring to appear as ready as her twin.

"Then a recent foretelling for you will more likely come to pass."

Lyndz looked puzzled but said nothing.

"I commit, for I have already made the sacrifice," said Nikal looking at Aron. The two engaged in a long and meaningful soldier's grip and embraced.

Then Aron stood back and nodded. "I...I ah, alll...so commit. I give up a forrr...mer life. I commit my friend Nikal to Kodi and the others. I...I will miss yy...you, Yy...your Highness." Aron smiled and winked, but then the smile faltered, and suddenly big wet tears dropped unbidden from his eyes.

With this sadness displayed on the part of her new husband, Modela appeared much moved. She opened her mouth to say something but stopped herself. Finally, she offered one consolation. "The Guardian Himself is aware and honors you."

She then looked at Rainwing who spoke next.

"The war must be fought, or we lose. Meical wants Nikal and Kodi to have the Staff, therefore I commit," offered the Etoppsi female.

"For you then I can only say, Rainwing of Green Isle, to lose is to gain."

Tiliruf spoke next. "I don't know that I trust you, or Meical, or anyone, eh? Yet for the sake of friendship, I commit."

Modela quite shockingly replied, "I don't blame you for being untrusting, youngest child of Terianh the Great. For like you I too am aware that little is as it seems on the surface. Yet I will say that, 'for the sake of friendship,' I believe you have made a correct choice. You must not forget the reason, then, by which you are committed. For once you do, you will become the last of the great House of Terianh."

Tiliruf was torn between smiling cynically or swallowing apprehensively. Since the muscles in his face then refused to allow for the former, he swallowed.

Idamé breathed in deeply, and as she exhaled said, "I commit."

"And that is because despite your unease you have a heart that cares. Though all children are mine and you have never had a child of your own, you are more like me than anyone here. I honor you, Mother Idamé." She nodded respectfully to the Matrimonial.

"I committed to the trust and purposes of Meical long ago. I therefore commit again."

"Then I will say that Meical knew what He was doing when He changed your name...Wise One."

She then removed the bound cloths from the object in her hand. When she held it up, it shone with a light as white as Solvermoon. Made of holly wood, it appeared without a dent or scratch as though it were crafted of diamond-hard marble. The shaft was thick and straight, this without detail, yet ending at the head with a round ball which looked exactly like a perfectly cratered Solvermoon. Clutching this globe was a flawlessly carved, white eagle with wings lifted high. All looked at it with amazement.

"So, it *is* real!" said Tiliruf.

"You deny everything you do not see with your own eyes, much like your father Genehbro, at least until recently. It is your greatest fault, my son. Would that you had the faith instead of your great ancestor. Yet you do carry his blood in your veins. There is hope yet for you, Swordmaster."

Nikal placed his hand on Kodi's shoulder and the two of them stood forward.

Amazingly, tears dropped from Modela's eyes like they had from her husband a few minutes before. "Though I hate war, to see before me the confident pride of great warriors has always moved me. It is apparent why the Taxiarch has Called you, Nikal and Kodi. Like Vanayisu you appear, as he led the pride of the Three Peoples, his many sons, with the gods themselves against the Rebellious Ones. Reach out your hands then, and together take the Staff from me. I find I cannot let it go willingly."

And so Nikal and Kodi in tandem reached out and placed their four hands upon the Staff of Terianh and removed it from Modela's grasp.

Nothing more did she say, but rather she turned and looked at Aron. He took her hand.

Letti the grayhawk, who had been flying about freely since they arrived on the island suddenly landed on Aron's shoulder and appeared then to look intently at Nikal.

"She wants to stay with you," said the prince.

"No, that wouldn't be rr...right. Letti, go be with your master..."

"No. Let Letti be my last gift to you, my great friend. She will be happy here."

Aron acquiesced. The little raptor made a sharp squawk and flew off again in the direction of the mountain. The general nodded once more to the friends, and with his own met Nikal's eyes one last time. For a long moment the two looked at one another. Then Aron and Modela turned and walked away. All watched until the two disappeared into the cottage.

Idamé shed many tears.

Nikal and Kodi looked at what they held, and Tiliruf with immense curiosity came over also to examine it closer. For a long minute they all stared. Then Nikal took the Staff and handed it to Curdoz. "You must keep it, Lord Sage, until the time is right."

Curdoz nodded as he took it. He told Tiliruf to grab up the discarded cloths and string lying on the ground. "...but we will first allow the crewmen to see the Staff, as they have worked hard to help us procure it and sacrificed two of their own in order to do so. Then we shall put it away for the time being. The time and place to study or practice with it is surely not now or here."

"Then let us go," said the prince. "I don't know that I can stay in this place even another night."

Though its eternal beauty remained, the charms of that island had lifted for the seven. They all agreed with Nikal and made their way back to the beach and to the ship, upon which they soon set sail eastward.

As they looked back, in their eyes a red sun set, the night folded in, and Modela's island disappeared. Never would any of them see that land again.

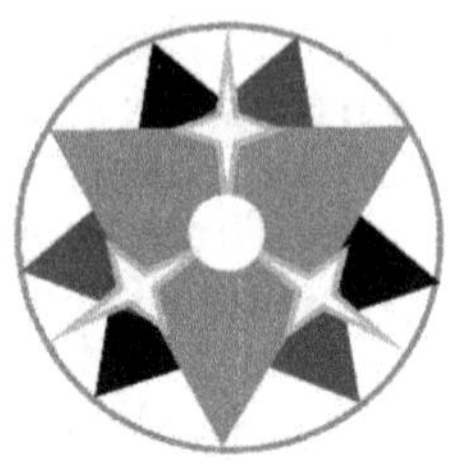

Chapter 22—Sacrifices

"Damn her!" yelled Tiliruf at the top of his lungs. "Damn her to the pits of that bloody volcano on that blasted island of hers! Malicious monster! I knew it! I knew it! Shaft her, vicious cur! Ram a dragon's spikeshaft up her rump!"

All came running to the men's cabin. It was the second morning after having left Modela's island. They had so far encountered no obstacles or storms, and under the guidance of Vanaratu, the Pearl Colossal was pulling the ship as it had before.

"SHAFT HER!"

"What is it!" exclaimed Kodi. "What's happened, Tiliruf?"

The other friends and Ulna and Maru were suddenly all there, along with several sailors who had heard Tiliruf's cursing. Not everybody could fit into the cabin, but those that could not were trying to peer through the door to try to determine what had caused the young man's outburst. No one had ever known him to be so infuriated. Any cursing was usually held in check by Nikal's disciplines.

The Tirilorine obviously didn't care at the moment.

"It's gone!" he yelled. "She took it! It's gone! Curse that WITCH!"

Strewn about the floor were the contents of his trunk, wrapped liquor bottles—one was broken—his hauberk and other gear, and Tiliruf was casting about his spare clothes furiously. The whole cabin which the prince insisted always stay in perfect order was instead a perfect mess. Nikal stepped past Kodi and grabbed the angry man and shook him. "What is it, Tiliruf! What did she take?"

"She took it! She took my sword!" He looked over at Kodi in pathetic desperation.

Kodi and all the rest took in their breath. "The Eagle Sword? Your sword is gone?"

The Eagle Sword of Terianh the Great, along with the beautiful new gold and silver scabbard that Genehbro and Jaden had had made for it was nowhere to be found.

"Oh, Tiliruf!" cried Idamé. She came over, but he shouldered her away.

It was when Kodi stepped in to try to help him that Tiliruf collapsed out of Nikal's firm grasp. Tears flowed from a reddened, pained face. "It had come to mean *everything* to me, Kodi! My father, my mother, Terianh! Everything!"

"I know it, Tiliruf. I know it did. It's awful. I'm sorry!"

Nikal ordered everyone but the seven to leave, and Curdoz shut the door.

Lyndz came over, and though Tiliruf was in such misery, he actually allowed her to hold him, and he let Kodi hold onto his shoulders. He cried like none of them had ever seen. If Tiliruf had ever cried, even Kodi didn't know. The young man nearly always portrayed a cocky, almost rebellious, self-confidence. He sobbed and sobbed until Lyndz' shirt was drenched. And then he apologized for having pushed away Idamé, and then she reached out and held him long as well.

Rainwing spoke. "I… I'm going to go for a fly. I'll see you all later." She then looked at Tiliruf. She opened her mouth again as if to say something to him, but then opened the cabin door, squeezed her huge frame through it, and disappeared.

They all gave Tiliruf as much time as he needed, and really none of them knew what they could possibly say to ease the pain. It was a terrible loss, a historical loss, even, for the world to forfeit such a legendary weapon. Finally, after a long time, he gathered himself together and sat up out of Idamé's arms.

"I just kind of felt it, eh?" he said quietly. "When we were walking back to the ship the other day, it came across my mind what it was she might take. I didn't say anything to anybody. I didn't want to believe it. Ever since the ceremony when Father gave it to me, I'd been latching onto Terianh's legend more than ever. I finally felt maybe I really was connected to it. Almost physically, you know? Not just my surname. It made me feel good, eh? Really, really good, and that, like the rest of you, I had a purpose in all this that's going on."

Nikal spoke with firm words of confidence. "Of course you have a purpose! You are a great Swordmaster, Tiliruf, perhaps the greatest in this world today. I know it, and Jaden knows it, and Aron believed so, too. And your father knows it. That sword had great symbolism, surely, and yet for you Tiliruf a'Terianh, to be great *you* need it not. Any sword in your hand, be it even a stick, will be a weapon no Khestadone knight in his right mind would ever want to go up against."

Kodi had been forming in his mind nearly identical words to say to his friend, and yet the fact that it was the stern and often critical prince who said them had greater value. They were a sharp contrast to his words back at the estate outside Tirilorin and had a positive effect on Tiliruf.

"Thank you, sir," he replied, nodding. He then wiped his face on his sleeve, and breathed in. "That's right good to know, eh?"

They all left him alone then with Kodi, who proceeded to help his friend drink himself into a silly sort of stupor. When later Tiliruf still couldn't fall asleep, Kodi stumbled out and begged Curdoz to come help. Though the drunken Tirilorine was resistant, Kodi held him down on Aron's mattress and the Sage used his magic to put him to sleep.

Kodi wasn't so drunk he couldn't answer the Sage's question.

"What do you think, Kodi?"

"I think he be a'right, Your Lordship, sir. Er, yeah, er, I mean Curdoz. Sorry 'bout tha'. Though he's gonna be really mad at that Modela wench for a long, long, long, long time. I mean a really long, long...long, long, long, long time. Know what I mean, Your Lordship? I, er, mean Curdoz, sir."

He put the mumbling Kodi to sleep, too, even though there were still several hours of daylight. It had been a distressing day, but the Sage couldn't help smiling at the two young men as they lay snoring. He suspected Kodi was right. Tiliruf, with regard to the sword, anyway, would hopefully be all right.

But what about the rest of us, he thought to himself. His smile faltered.

Rainwing had disappeared already that morning on another flight, an activity she had taken to regularly since Tiliruf's sword had gone missing two days ago.

The other females searched the cabin high and low.

"They're both gone," said Lyndz. "I'll have to face up to it."

When Idamé returned bringing with her the men, Lyndz told them. "My emerald pendant that Father had made for me is gone. It was in the box that Grandfather Yugan made for Grandmother. It's empty. And the gold buckle that the princess gave me."

"They're *both* gone?" asked Tiliruf.

She sat down with a despondent look. She cried a little when Kodi hugged her close.

No doubt both objects were treasured possessions, and Lyndz had lately taken to looking at them often. She had worn both to Aron's Bonding.

Nikal allowed Tiliruf a break from his work and his exercising, and he and Lyndz crawled about the ship for a couple of hours. Though Nikal would punish Tiliruf if he spoke uncouthly in the earshot of women by forcing him to apologize and do additional exercises, the prince held off today. In his odd way the Tirilorine was helping Lyndz deal with her loss, and it appeared to be working quite well, for she was kept in stitches by way of his forced hilarity. He taught her all sorts of colorful phrases as he expressed additional resentment toward Modela. Idamé, who could not bring herself to fault Tiliruf for his efforts with Lyndz, nevertheless had to keep her own ears plugged.

Eventually, the two sat on the aftcastle on a bench, the one Rainwing often sat upon. Either Tiliruf had run out of expletives, or he sensed Lyndz had grown thoughtful again. For a long time, they watched in silence as Rainwing soared among the clouds.

When the men awakened early on bathing day and it was discovered that the ambernut bow and the tooled quiver from the king were missing, though Kodi grieved in his heart at the loss, he could not pretend surprise.

He sat there as the three men watched him. They grieved for him, too. That bow in part defined him. He talked often of his grandfather, and they had all come to admire the bow as a unique and superior piece of art. Curdoz came and sat beside him on his bunk.

"I guess I knew it, too, like Tiliruf did," Kodi admitted. "Just kind of makes sense, doesn't it? I...I'm sorry if I've been so, I don't know how to put it. Cheerful? Enthusiastic? I keep trying to make people see a brighter side, but so many have given up so much. It's been awful, it has."

"But that's why you're important to us, mate," said Tiliruf benevolently. "When *you're* not cheerful, how are any of the rest of us supposed to be, eh?"

Kodi looked up. Nikal was smiling at him too. "Tiliruf states an important truth, Sir Kodi. Now listen. I have a fine bow in Sevarr in my rooms at the palace. Haven't used it in years. You are good with a sword, but the bow is your especial talent, and you mustn't be without one. It will come in handy, now. A good quiver I have as well. They will become yours."

"That's really good of you, sir." He then looked at Tiliruf. "Perhaps then you should have my sword, Ruffy. The sword of Bagarro. I can get another sometime."

"No, mate. You're getting better with it. You need it, eh? It was kind of a little miracle that it came to you, being your great-great-grandfather's and all. But thanks, mate. I really appreciate it."

"Hmm," intoned Nikal. He then went and pulled out the large drawer under Aron's old bed. "He left it! I thought so. He did not have it with him on the island. Seems like he's given up on the idea of fighting, anyway. Er, he's all about making love, now. Not all of us are so lucky on that point."

Nikal retrieved from the drawer a beautiful scabbard containing a blade, all attached to a belt. He handed it all to Tiliruf. "You must have this, Tiliruf. Aron would be pleased, he would. He believed, like I do, that your swordplay is inspired. He was a Swordmaster, too, as you know, though he learned under someone other than Jaden. He fought and killed one of the Alkhan's great bears with that. Made him famous."

"That's...that's splendid!" said the Tirilorine, gratefully accepting the scabbard and pulling out the high quality Nantian blade to examine it. "Ha!"

Curdoz couldn't help but to laugh too especially after all the generosity and kind words amongst the three men. He believed he was witnessing some of the best of human nature. "It *is* splendid, Tiliruf! It really is. May I apply a Blessing?"

"Eh? Absolutely, sir."

After bathing and breakfast, Nikal knew what Kodi needed. He ordered Tiliruf to spar and train with him for the rest of the morning. Physical exertion was what Kodi required to deal with his loss. Afterward, Rainwing took Kodi on an exhilarating excursion to the clouds and over the waves. And when it was time for sleep, Curdoz did not allow him even a moment to lie there and ponder, and with the green light penetrating his skull, put him straight to sleep.

Idamé owned five multicolored shawls. Each was a treasure to her. It was bad enough when she discovered they had vanished in the night. Yet none of them were prepared for Curdoz' declaration after he put the tearful woman to sleep again and emerged from the women's cabin.

"It wasn't just the shawls," he said sadly.

They all looked at him confused for a moment.

"No!" said Ulna, finally.

"You can't possibly mean it, Lord Curdoz!" said Maru, the realization having struck her at the same moment as her partner.

When he nodded, the Healers both had to manage tears and blow noses.

"Be plain, Lord Sage," said Nikal. "Tell the rest of us!"

"Her Gift has been taken from her."

They all expressed shock. Lyndz fought tears, too. "How can you tell, Curdoz? How would you know unless she never again was to see an Aura?"

"Our connection. The mind connection we often share. I can no longer reach her. It can only occur through mutual Gifted magic and only among some. Idamé and I were quite good with it. She can't achieve the Mode, either. But also, it could not be more plain what the shawls symbolize, and Modela knows it."

"She really is a witch. I keep telling all of you that, eh?"

"Listen to me, Tiliruf. No doubt Modela is a powerful magical creature. Yet you saw with your own eyes the tears she herself shed before we parted. I think she foresaw the pain we now experience, and it hurt her. She is nothing remotely like the Alkhaness, whom you might with complete truthfulness call a witch. And a witch wouldn't stock our ship with fresh water barrels and imperishable foods, not to mention giving Estader a new leg. Ask Estader if *he* thinks she's an evil witch. She essentially gave him his whole life back when he was, with good reason, perfectly convinced he would be an invalid the rest of his life. It is probably the greatest miracle any of us has ever witnessed. Modela has a mind so ancient and so powerful that we cannot know what her motivations are. Her methods are incongruent and troublesome to say the least, but I believe...I *have* to believe...she has a greater purpose. I think there is more to it than payment for the Staff."

"Allow me to test something, Kodi," said the Sage two days later.

Kodi did as he was told and lay back on his mattress in the alcove. He had taken over Aron's space at Nikal's insistence. However, when Curdoz placed his hands on his young friend's head no green Meicalian light came to his fingertips.

His stoles, like Idamé's shawls, had disappeared in the night.

"I am so sorry, sir," said the young man. "I never wanted any of this to happen when we left Solanto all that time ago. It wasn't what I envisioned at all! There was nothing in any of our Visions that showed us any of this, was there? Were we missing something?"

"No," said the Sage without emotion. Nikal and Tiliruf sat near. "Yet there was the Prophecy."

"Pecker-juiced Prophecy," spat Tiliruf, rolling his eyes. "Real bucking nut-kicker that was, eh?"

"And what about your communication with Vanaratu?" asked Nikal choosing to ignore Tiliruf's laced language. He himself felt exactly the same way about that Prophecy. "Does he still speak to you?"

"Yes. But that has nothing to do with my Gift, or lack thereof. He can communicate with whomever he wishes, or in his case, with whomever he is allowed. Indeed, he grieves for me and for all of us. He questions me constantly as to how everyone is coping. He is aware, and he is very sensitive. He has come to have great fondness for all of us, more than I would expect from a World God."

The Sage paced the cabin floor and continued. "It is the Gift that connected me, and Idamé, to Meical. Additional Visions for us appear unlikely. I'm not even certain we qualify anymore to be Members of the Orders. Perhaps Ralle can advise us. I should send a missive to the High Priest."

"Ralle has no more wisdom than you, Lord Sage!" said Nikal firmly. "It is your wisdom and your deep intuition and the symbolism you hold as a Servant of the Guardian that makes you who you are. Not even Modela can take that away!"

"To me you will always be the Sage of Solanto, and you will always be important, and not just to me, but to all of us," added Kodi. "There is no one, Mannago, Marco, Theneri, Danly, Xeno, anybody, not even King Carlomen, who would deny your authority in the Kingdom. And the common folk have you to thank for a better life. I don't know anything about your High Priest in the Valley, and we're a thousand miles away. He doesn't have anything to do with anything we're about, so I don't see any reason he has to even know about it."

Curdoz tried to smile.

"Eh, do you feel any less smarterly or less wiserly than you did yesterday?" quipped Tiliruf.

"No," he admitted. "I suppose I continue to have all my faculties."

"What I thought. And Mother Idamé still gives me that 'disapproving' look when I joke with Kodi and the sailors. I reckon the both of you are no different to me one whit. Who cares about stoles or shawls?"

Nikal looked at Tiliruf and glowered.

"Er, sorry. I mean, I'm not denying that you've given up a lot, Curdoz, really, sir, I'm not. I didn't mean to sound callous or anything, I swear. Don't tell Mother Idamé I said that about shawls, eh? She'll cry. Sorry. Er, maybe Lyndz can knit you a new stole, eh? I'll go ask her."

Curdoz could not help but to chuckle a little as Tiliruf stood up and walked out of the cabin.

Curdoz had lost his Gift, and so had Idamé. It was a horrible, almost inconceivable wrench to think that after forty years their mystical linking with the Guardian was severed. And yet the young men were correct. There was no change in their identity. There was no reason in the world to think Meical had abandoned either of them. He looked. The Staff still stood in its wrappings in the corner.

"Why is Rainwing gone on flights all the time?" Kodi asked of Lyndz the next day. They sat in the most private corner on deck they could find, away from the ears of the sailors.

"She won't say. She hardly talks at all, anymore. I'm really worried about her. I think she's very, very scared of what she might be required to give up."

"You don't think it might be something as simple as the ability to receive Prophecies or something..."

"Simple! Come on, Ko! It's a recent Gift she's proud of. It's made her feel all this time she's devoted to her study of Meical and Order history has had real meaning behind it all along! She feels connected because of it. Like Tiliruf with the Eagle Sword to Terianh's history and legend!"

"Sorry. You're absolutely right. I didn't really think of it like that. I only meant that she would still be who she is. Like Mother Idamé and Curdoz."

"I know. And it's not as though the same thoughts don't go through my head. Sometimes I have to stop myself thinking it might be as simple as me giving up...jewelry. I just don't know, though, what it could be. She is a very physical being. Her whole personality is wrapped up in her appearance, her physicality, her ability to be a fighter, her ability to do whatever she wants, quite frankly. And her fearlessness. Apparently, they're Etoppsi traits. She can't bear the thought of losing anything at all."

"You seem to know a lot, especially if you say she's being quiet about it."

"Just trying to suggest possibilities."

"No. I think you see things. I've told you it before. You're like Curdoz. You're like a Sage."

"I don't know. Did Rainwing say anything to you when she treated you with that flight the other day? When your bow and quiver disappeared?"

"No. She was quiet then, too. Although she would smile at me when I would look up in her face. Of course, she was trying to make me feel good after losing my bow. She knows how much I love to fly with her." He paused. "It's depressing. The pattern is obvious: every other day since Tiliruf lost the sword."

"I know. Tomorrow. It's unbearable." She looked at her brother. "Ko, you understand she brought absolutely nothing with her on this journey. No trinkets, no weapons, obviously no clothes, no books, no symbols of her Gift. Nothing. All she has is her person. I just don't know what Modela would take, if it's some possession Rainwing has back in Berug, and how we would even know about it. Maybe like you say it will be the Seer-like Gift, but I don't know."

Kodi swallowed. "Well. She has us. If you really think she's that afraid, then she's not going to sleep any tonight. We should stay up with her."

Lyndz considered a moment. "All right. I like that idea! We'll do that. I'll try to say something to her about it when she comes back."

Rainwing did come back eventually. It was nearing sunset. She tried to appear cheerful and ate her supper with several of them below deck where were located the huge crossbows and the weighted exercise equipment and where most of the sailors slept at night. But just as Lyndz turned to her to tell her that they all wanted to keep vigil with her, the Etoppsis spoke first.

"Lyndz, I want you to fly with me again tonight for a little. And Kodi, too. And Nikal. And anybody else who wants to, really. Tiliruf, you willing?"

The Tirilorine looked at her, appalled at first. He had always expressed to her his fear of flying. That she would ask again was annoying. And yet, suddenly, having become through his loss of the sword more sensitive to the others, he thought better of it, banished the consternation on his face, forced a smile and said, "Sure, Rainwing. Er, it'll be fun, eh? Er, can you carry a mate and me at the same time?"

She smiled and nodded. "Oh, yes. Easily."

"Then Kodi's up, eh? Er, but if you don't mind, take Nikal and some others up first. I think I want my supper to settle a bit."

In fact, Tiliruf put his fork down and didn't eat another bite.

As it turned out, after Kodi had made his suggestion, Lyndz had gone to all the friends plus Ulna and Maru, and they had all agreed to the idea of maintaining an all-night vigil with Rainwing. Nikal, who had grown to have quiet affection for Rainwing, was convinced the idea was excellent and said so. However, as they all sat about at supper, it appeared Rainwing had her own ideas, and they all were so attuned now that they were willing to follow along. Both the Healers and Curdoz agreed to fly with the Etoppsi female. Remarkably, even Idamé said she would try it if Rainwing promised not to go too far from the ship and return immediately if she suddenly felt too squeamish.

Rainwing was perfectly amenable to accommodating everyone's requirements, and every sailor whom the Etoppsis had pulled from the waters during and following the sea serpent battle were willing to fly with her. Plainly, everyone on board was attuned to what was going on. They all understood by now that the friends were each required to sacrifice something of great value in order for them to keep the Staff. The timing had been like clockwork: every two days, in the morning when they awakened, one of the friends had lost something precious to him or to her. If the magic of Modela held consistent, Rainwing stood to lose something of value...tomorrow morning. They had all grown fond of the exotic creature for her bravery and for her interesting personality. They might chuckle at her views about 'females,' and yet they never dared refute her on her position that Human females should be offered equal par with men. Most of them, being subject to Nikal and Aron, held women in high regard, for Nantians, anyway. Also, as commoners, most Nantian men thought their upper-class counterparts were unkind to their wives, and the sailors on Nikal's ship were no exception. Of course, Rainwing's suggestions went beyond what most of them thought was proper for the role of women, particularly the idea that some were strong enough to be sailors and courageous enough to be warriors. Even though they might agree with her at a sheer factual level, they still held chauvinistic views. But because they were forced to listen—it was impossible not to do so anyhow with her booming big voice—they listened. And though listening does not always lead to agreement, at the least it leads to mutual respect.

The sailors respected Rainwing. And they had good reason to, believing her a great hero. Because of their respect for her, they could tell she was...in need. If she wanted to take them on airborne excursions, thinking it might be a wonderful treat for them, they decided to banish their fears and participate.

The sun was dipping rapidly in a sky half filled with benign clouds, but it was like a grand party on deck. Nikal had the men lower the sails—it would not hurt anything for the Pearl Colossal to pull the ship without aid for an hour or two. Men were whooping and carrying on, drinking extra rounds of ale from Modela's barrels, encouraging their shipmates as the Etoppsi female launched herself, sometimes with one man, or woman, or two, depending. Most were awestruck by how powerful and gripping she was with those massive arms and hands, and they could not help but feel safe even if most of them were momentarily terrified when she would leap like a massive wildcat off the ship. After a minute or two of terror, even in Tiliruf's case crammed side by side with Kodi, they realized what sheer splendor it was to race through the winds, soaring high, dipping low just above the waters. She even accommodated the trick Kodi liked so well for a few—Nikal and Lyndz were two of these—splashing with powerful energy into the waters and back out again. Nobody cared how wet they got. Quite remarkably, Idamé found it exhilarating, returning to deck with a huge, Kodi-like grin on her face, declaring she liked flying far, far better than rolling up and down on a ship.

At midnight, as Rainwing sat in the men's larger cabin with the friends and the Healer pair, her grief poured forth. She could not cry, for Etoppsi did not have the ability to shed tears the way Humans did, and yet her body shook like one in deep sobs experiencing the death of someone she loved. They tried desperately to ease her pain with kind words. She refused to allow the Healers, who were just as capable of putting people to sleep as the Sage used to be, to do it.

She could speak no words or tell them precisely what she feared or suspected. They were determined, though, despite any awkwardness they might have felt, to share the pain. They were her friends. Unlike most Berugians, they were not prejudiced with regard to her odd life choices. She had come to love these Humans so well and had come to feel at home with them better than she did even in Berug with her own kind.

Along about sunrise the magic of Modela transpired. It was a sight none of them could ever have imagined, and every last one of Tiliruf's curses came into their minds and seemed perfectly appropriate.

As she sat on her hefty stool, her face heavy with pain, her magnificent silver wings suddenly vanished in a puff of air. The women screamed and Tiliruf cursed louder, far louder, than he did when his sword went missing, and poor Rainwing slumped over and fell with a screaming howl upon the floor.

None would ever forget the melancholy cry. It would linger in their minds and haunt their memories.

It was Nikal who helped Rainwing recover from the initial agony, though it took a long time. Those two, like Kodi with Tiliruf when the latter lost his sword, spent not one day, but two days and two nights together alone in the women's cabin. The other women were obliged to sleep with the men in Nikal's bigger space. Occasionally, the play of the winds would cause them to imagine echoes of howls issuing through the door of the women's cabin. In actuality, Rainwing was remarkably quiet after her first grief.

They all agreed that hers was, by far, the most devastating sacrifice of all, and even Curdoz was appalled by its seeming cruelty. It became obvious to them that Rainwing had predicted her specific loss, like Tiliruf had, and indeed had practically foreordained it long before, as Lyndz reminded them all. They were sitting in the men's cabin. Rainwing was still shut up with Nikal in the women's.

"Do you remember when she said, 'I'd give my wings for it,' back in Ralle's manor? For Nikal to gain the Staff, that is. I think *she* remembered she said it, and as things transpired the way they did on Modela's island, and especially when Tiliruf's sword disappeared, it came back to her."

They looked at her and nodded.

"It explains why she wanted to fly so much the last week," said Kodi.

"And why she wanted to share with everyone her gift the other night," added Curdoz. "She wanted all of us to at least try and understand the joy she experiences when she is aloft."

"It really was a magnificent gift, and I'll never forget it," agreed Idamé. "It was as though someone who feels death approaching crafts with her hands a beautiful shawl or a blanket for her beloved granddaughter, by which the granddaughter will always remember her. In fact, that was the case with one of my shawls—my first multi-colored one. My grandmother made it for me when I came home from my study in the Valley. She knew I would be advanced from a Sister to a Mother, someday."

The Matrimonial teared up, and when she reached automatically to dab her tears and realized her shawl wasn't there as usual to assist, she cried even more. Lyndz handed her a handkerchief.

"Well, if you haven't noticed, I'm making you a new shawl, dear," said Sister Ulna, showing them all the incomplete product in her lap as her hands worked feverishly upon the knitting needles. "Actually, Sister Maru and Lady Lyndz and I are working on it nonstop, taking turns. Lady Lyndz was inspired to have purchased all that yarn back in Sevarr before we left!"

"And we're planning a stole for Lord Curdoz when we're done with that," said her Healer partner. "It's unfortunate we only have the one pair of knitting needles!"

"I hope to have them done before we get to Sevarr. Or at least Tirilorin," assured Lyndz. "It was Tiliruf's idea, actually."

Idamé couldn't help but smile; she reached over and patted Tiliruf on his scruffy cheek. Though he didn't need it in the cabin, he had taken to draping the scarf the Matrimonial had knitted for him to wear in the winds on deck around his neck most of the time as an unspoken display of his affection for her.

"You know," said Kodi, "I can whittle you another couple pair of knitting needles. That's easy. I'll have them done for you by morning."

He got up to go find one of the sailors he knew who whittled regularly during his breaks to see if the man had some stock of wood to share.

"That's very kind of you," said the Sage. "All of you."

The next morning, the third from when her wings disappeared, Nikal emerged with Rainwing behind. She was gripping his shoulders to help her adjust to a new way of balancing on her feet without her wings.

Though the sailors had heard, they had not seen. Despite the initial shock of her missing wings and her much diminished appearance thereby, as they stood watching, one of the sailors who had been rescued by the Etoppsis during the serpent attack and had flown with her the other evening, started to clap his hands. And then two more began to clap until suddenly everyone on board was applauding and whistling. Some began to whoop and dance as though it were a party. Then they all crowded close, shouting jolly greetings, touching her and reaching up to slap her on the back—something they couldn't do before she lost her wings, and otherwise showing her how much they appreciated and cared for her. She would always be their 'female hero.'

"Rainwing Dragonfighter!" some shouted.

"Rainwing Serpentslayer!" others called. Expressive titles, perfectly Etoppsi, too.

Her anxious frown dissolved away.

THIS ENDS BOOK TWO

Continue with

Brothers of Myghal

Book Three of

Heirs to the Taxiarch

Enjoy a preview chapter of
Book 3

Brothers of Myghal

Brothers of Myghal

Chapter 1—The Kidnapping

Sunshine burst through swiftly dispersing rainclouds, and the escort of Solantine Kingsmen removed their cloaks, cheering the break in weather. Yet the sudden summer sun could not break through the clouds in the princess's mind. Traveling on the Northern Road not too far from Davvos, Isatura sat dry in her coach reflecting on the recent King's Council in Ferostro.

She had sat beside her father throughout, and despite her advice, and that of Grand Duke Mannago and Father Marco, his indecision upset her. Indeed, her father was growing old, she thought. Unlike the decades before when he deftly handled the barons during the Reforms, that former energy and once forceful personality had given way to a sweet old man who wanted nothing more than peace and contentment for all. The warning that Curdoz had brought to the king prior to leaving the country could not overcome Carlomen's desire to try to avoid conflict at all cost...even that of the honor of the kingdom, apparently.

Well, it wasn't quite that bad, she knew. At least not yet. Though that nasty Prince Filiddor threatened, the king had bought them all a little time by refusing a final decision for three months. Which left two more months remaining.

It was not what she would have done. Isatura would have made it plain that despite the old document the prince presented, centuries of history had intervened. Nor was anyone mollified by the fact that though the document also placed *Tulesk* under Hescian jurisdiction, the prince pretended he did not want it "out of regard for my brother, Duke Amerro." As if demanding the whole of the Tolosian Peninsula had not already been enough to infuriate the duke and turn him into his life-long enemy. They already hated each other, and so had their fathers before them.

If Duke Snoffit of Ascanti and some of his barons had not spoken in Filiddor's favor, the demand likely would have ended with a firm rejection the moment it was made. She was disgusted to think that at this moment she was on Ostin's turf as she traveled on the road towards Tulesk. The young baron was one of the more outspoken during the arguments. It angered her, for she knew that Ostin's father the former count had been one of the great supporters of the Reforms. The son's support for Filiddor was inconsistent with his family's former views. She suspected gold was involved. She would not seek lodgings at his estate and was glad Chernis was not on the main road. It would have looked bad if she had passed by without at least calling politely at his manor. She'd always had a good rapport with his wife.

Instead, she expected to make it to Thorune by nightfall. She trusted old Count Ilmore. It would be delightful to stay a night or two at the old castle; he and the countess converted it into a grand place after the last war, for with the acquisition of Stavenland from the Ice Tribes Thorune was no longer on the frontier. Ilmore had spoken in opposition to his own duke in the Council in favor of Amerro's position. Like the majority, he was opposed to Filiddor's demands and favored the status quo.

It was unfortunate that the minority was as vocal as it was, for that is what ultimately led to her father's indecision. Duke Snoffit's defense of Prince Filiddor's rights by way of the old Terianh document came as a surprise, and for whatever reason this made the king feel the need for a period of review and reflection on the issue.

The document itself absolutely came as a surprise. It was a great shock when it was presented and translated in Council. It was too bad Curdoz had not discovered it on his little spying expedition, for its existence, let alone its contents, muddied everything. And there was still the question of Ice Tribesmen. Mannago and Marco had told her everything. She knew it was sinister to begin with, but unfortunately her father did not. Carlomen had it settled in his mind that the presence of Tribesmen was nothing more than what that wily Filiddor had pretended it was: a trade delegation. The grand duke had called the prince out on it in the middle of the Council, and it came as a jolt to most, but her father was willing to give the prince the benefit of the doubt. She told her father it was wrong to take Filiddor's word over the warnings of Curdoz and the rest, but he dismissed her concerns.

It made her angry at the time, for she believed the king's position had been swayed by the arguments, yet she couldn't bring herself to fault openly her kind-hearted, peace-loving old father. Yet she herself was not deceived. She was absolutely on the side of Mannago and Marco: Filiddor was at the least attempting a diplomatic rapport with the dangerous northerners. She and the others worried there was more to it. Indeed, they were preparing for more.

She sympathized with Duke Amerro of Tulesk. She was on her way now to Felto in the guise of visiting the twins' mother, Elisa, to offer her friendship and cheer in the absence of her husband. Though it was only partly a guise, as Isatura was much intrigued by the whole Fothemry family now that she had met the twins and understood they were part of some great plan on the Guardian's part. She had a desire to know this family better. But she had arranged a secret meeting to take place with Duke Amerro while there. Felto was out of the way, and it would offer the privacy they all wanted to debate strategy.

She looked out the coach window. There was Matteo. The crinkle left her brow. A ray of sunlight shone into her mind.

Or more correctly, her heart. Mannago's eldest son was with her to represent his father at the upcoming meeting. She approved of her official 'escort,' Matteo and his younger brother Olaron who had come with him. She thought the brothers both handsome and dashing as they rode their steeds beside her coach, cloaks swung back in the sun, revealing them as the able young lords that they were. Matteo clearly enjoyed the company of his younger brother despite the two being several years apart; they spoke and laughed much together as they rode along.

Eyeing Matteo, a smile formed on her face. She was not unaware of Mannago's hopes on that front, he having insinuated much over the years, both to her father the king and to her directly. She so very much liked Matteo. Very much indeed. This journey had allowed them their first opportunity to spend useful time together, apart from all the eyes and ears of the court, though they had been dance and dinner partners at palace parties since they were quite young. They had come to enjoy one another's company on this trip, engaging in much conversation, both political and not. He was intelligent and engaging like his sociable father, with a hot energy and a warmly enveloping but non-domineering masculinity that drew her. Until recently, she had never allowed herself to feel this way about a man before. But lately when he would look at her—the confident smile he offered, the casual wink now and again, and his deep voice that she liked so well...there was a delightfully teasing ring to it when he would utter the words 'Your Highness'—she could no longer help the way her heart danced. She had had suitors over the years, including some promising young lords and princes from Eleni, but she had recently come to admit that Matteo was the best of the lot. When she became queen, he was just the sort of consort, and man, she wanted at her side.

Hmm, she thought. Did that mean she had made a decision? She turned from the window and began an analysis of her heart. She knew he was waiting for her to indicate something. He had, unlike most of the men in his father's clan, put off Bonding. Most of the grand duke's family and even their distant cousins Bonded quite young. As crown princess, of course, this was her call to make. He was much too gentlemanly to overstep his position with her and force the issue. Yet he had, she now concluded, waited long enough. He had retained his honor and held in reserve his passion. He was the subject of no little—or big—scandals, no liaisons or illegitimate progeny, according to the ears and eyes with which she communicated. It said something about him and his self-discipline. She knew he had done this...for her.

Yes, she said to herself in order to settle her mind. Looking out the coach window again, the sunlight seemed to grow even brighter. The time was right. She believed she was ready for such a commitment. Matteo understood what he was getting into; if he didn't, he would have aimed elsewhere years ago. He would be a powerful and influential consort considering his connections and personality, not to mention the father of a royal dynasty, though the way the kingdom's law worked the Grand Duchy of Escarant would instead pass from Mannago to Olaron in such an event. Matteo had surely weighed such pros and cons, had even insinuated that some things were more important to him than others. Again, he was referring to her.

Her father the king would be pleased she had finally made up her mind. Just maybe, she thought, a new sense of joy in their family after the loss of the queen so many years ago would give the king a new lease on life and snap him out of his near malaise, and even to face Filiddor's threats with more resolve. Bringing Matteo, and by extension Mannago, into the family orbit might solidify a union of minds in confronting Filiddor and the other dangers in the world.

Those threats appeared to diminish as she smiled to herself and allowed her thoughts to wander in bliss over the next few hours. She looked often out the window of her coach. At one point, Matteo happened to be looking at her from his position astride his horse, just as she was looking at him.

He winked.

Her heart leapt.

They came to Davvos, which she knew was the town where Lord Curdoz was from. Townsfolk came out, excited to see the princess's procession. She waved as they passed through. Before long they passed the more southerly of two side roads that led westward to Chernis, the seat of County Ostin. After a while an inviting green hill loomed out of the trees ahead on the east side of the road. Having basked in a hot sun since noon, she anticipated it would be dry enough. It was teatime. She called a halt.

"We shall picnic here," she said as she stepped from the coach. Matteo was suddenly there and held out his hand to her. She held to it a little tighter than she ever had before.

"Shall I escort you to the hilltop, *Your Highness?*" he asked. There was that playful ring again. "It should have an enjoyable view!"

"Surely!" she replied with a nod and a little wink of her own. "Indeed, my dear, there is something I wish to speak to you about!"

Some were surprised when she ordered that a little private affair be set up for herself and Matteo upon the hilltop, yet the servants did as they were told. Olaron considered the situation interesting, winked at his older brother and disappeared through the trees on his horse. Olaron loved to race off on his own and explore whenever he had a chance.

This country between Davvos and Thorune was lovely, with low green hills interspersed with stretches of forests. A little further north the Ascantian plains opened out again. At the tip top of the green hill upon which they had their picnic, the princess and Matteo could see far in the east the line demarcating the Escarpment. Despite that the unsavory Principality of Hesk was so near, the scene was beautiful with a dramatic sky. Birds flew overhead and cool breezes blew.

After the servants had set out everything and disappeared back down the hill to await by the road with the Kingsmen, Matteo himself poured Isatura's tea. They sat on a layer of blankets and engaged in small talk for a while, eating little sandwiches and treats out of a basket.

The small talk gave way to a bit of flirtation, and Isatura invited Mateo to sit a little closer. Shifting nearer, he seemed quite pleased by this.

"I have come to the conclusion, Matteo, dear," she began with a pretense at aloofness, "to honor your request."

His eyebrow shot up. Then he smiled quite knowingly. "Ah, *Your Highness,* but I have requested nothing of you, as you know quite well! I am but your devoted servant, of course."

"Perhaps then 'tis time for you to do so. Yet, I would prefer it should you address me in such settings as 'Isatura.' Do you not know?" She beamed and blushed, and then looked away for a moment. Then she looked back into his face with a sweet smile and waited. He had such a handsome look: black scruff on a face unshaved for a few days, on a chiseled, dark olive face. The Nantian descent demonstrated itself strongly in his family. He paused for a little. His eyes danced.

From his point of view, Matteo, though delighted at the portents of these last several minutes, was in a way taken aback. Protocol required a crown prince or crown princess to, as it were, 'do the asking.' And of course, he would never have presumed to press her. Did the princess harbor a little wish of the 'old fashioned' when it finally came down to the actual deed?

All hesitation melted as he realized she was offering him a little gift. He had daydreamed this moment for a long time, always playing in his mind phrases he considered both daringly rakish and chivalrously gallant. Tones and words he would never have really used in the actual presence of the woman who would one day be ruling Queen of Solanto, but rather for the woman of intelligence, of beauty, of charm, of...his many desires.

She apparently knew this and was allowing him an opportunity to...be himself. To be the daring and courageous man he hoped he was. And if that didn't, in a moment's time, double his devotion and love for her...

He stood. He breathed in a magnificent breath as he looked all around. Whether or not the servants and Kingsmen at the bottom of the hill were paying attention was irrelevant. The world around him had never seemed so extraordinary, and so exquisitely detailed, as it did at this moment. The sun seemed to light up a crystalline sky, the breezes were especially refreshing, the colors of the grass and trees bore shades of green he had not noticed before. He knelt before her and looked into her stunning green eyes. They were the verdant shade he knew best, for how often had he looked into them and noted their depth? He reached out and took her hand from her lap, in itself a daring move. The formality between them fell away.

"Darling Isatura! Oh, the subject of all my dreams. I love you with all that I have, and with all that I am. Would you, dear one, consent to Bond me? And, throughout our joint lives, face the joys and challenges of this world...together?"

There was nothing particularly rakish in that, yet it was from the heart. He then kissed her non-resistant hand and looked purposefully into her eyes.

"Yes, dear Matteo! I will!"

He could hardly believe his ears, nor could he contain his joy as they then kissed ardently on that sunlit hill. Perhaps he did employ a dash of the rake in that kiss.

Young Olaron was on his horse trotting through a stretch of forest. The road was off to his left, and, every once in a while, he could catch a glimpse of it if he strained his eyes in that direction. He always loved exploring the woods and countryside alone, enjoying being in harmony with his surroundings. He had a great love of nature.

Yet as he rode, something was odd. He couldn't put his finger on it. He pulled up and stopped, listening.

There were no birds singing nor any other sound. He also realized there had been no traffic on the road for some time. For whatever reason this did not please him. He decided teatime would soon be over anyway, and he had just turned his horse in the direction of the road in order to return quickly to his brother when he heard a voice. It was north and a bit east of his position.

In fact, there were several voices, all men.

Curiosity getting the better of him, he dismounted, tied the reins around a stump and made off in the direction of the voices. Before him was a low fold in the land. He descended, then climbed. The voices were just the other side of the hill. Not wanting to be seen, he lay flat at the top of the rise and looked down into a cleared hollow. Below were at least two hundred soldiers on horseback.

But they were not Kingsmen.

Suddenly, off to his right, a horsemen galloped over the rise and down to the others. Thankfully, Olaron was in such a position he was invisible to the rider.

When the rider reached the others, he began to talk animatedly and point, southward. Olaron could not hear what was said, but he knew this wasn't right. Not right at all. He crawled backward a little way, and in a few more minutes he was racing on his horse to the road and back to the others.

Kingsmen and palace servants were staring up the hill. Some were surprised and some were smiling. The maids were particularly pleased.

"Oh, I always hoped!" said one. "Lord Matteo is such a good one, too!"

"And so handsome!" said another.

Suddenly, Olaron galloped in, looking around. He quickly found the captain of the guard. "Hescian horsemen, Captain Cludder! At least two hundred of them!"

The captain was in shock for a moment, then suddenly began issuing orders, and everyone scrambled.

Olaron raced his horse straight up the hill.

"Olaron!" Matteo did not appreciate the interruption. "Whatever are you doing?"

Unfazed, Olaron leapt from his horse and bowed to the princess. "I...I am sorry! But there are Hescians ahead, Your Highness! Well-armed soldiers and knights on horseback!"

Matteo stood. "What! Where, Olaron? How many?"

"At least two hundred of them east of the road in the woods about three miles north!" Quickly he explained precisely what he saw, including the runner who had come up from the south.

"You mean they might be both south and north of us?"

Isatura spoke swiftly. "It is an ambush, Matteo! Don't you see? Consider the Council! Think what would happen if Filiddor had me as a hostage!"

Matteo's mind worked quickly. "Yet there are others traveling. It's a busy road! How could they get away with it?"

"But...but there is no one on the road!" offered Olaron. "I noticed it right before I discovered the Hesicans!"

"They've blocked the road?"

"That would be Count Ostin's doing," said Isatura. "You heard for yourself how he took Filiddor's part on that old boundary document!"

Matteo raised an eyebrow. "Of course! And between here and the Ramp are Nees and Mere. They are great supporters of Filiddor. But what a vicious turn of events for them to act in this way! It is treasonous, I tell you! We must get you out of here, Isatura!"

Leaving the tea things, they raced back down to the others. The captain had all the servants back in the coaches, and one of the maids had donned one of Isatura's cloaks and sat regally in the princess's coach.

A disguise was exactly what Matteo had in mind as well, and Isatura adopted a plain traveling cloak.

Then occurred the newly betrothed's first disagreement.

Matteo had mounted his horse and reached down for Isatura. His brother was ready to assist the princess. "Step up, dear! Quickly! We'll travel northwest and around! I must get you to Thorune. I know Captain Santher at the barracks, and you'll be safe in Ilmore's territory."

"No! I shall ride myself. Get me a horse, Captain Cludder!"

The captain went about choosing.

"But I can carry you more swiftly, my dear!" pleaded Matteo.

"Foolish. Of course, you cannot! But you shall defend me as we ride!"

Matteo nodded. This was not an argument he would win. Captain Cludder produced a swift gelding from among the Kingsmen's own.

She mounted. She was a good rider and had been since she was a little girl. "And hand me a longknife! The first Hescian that touches me I'll slash his throat!"

Matteo smiled. He appreciated her fierceness. He was then giving Olaron instruction to ride back to Davvos and see if he could get word south about what was happening.

"I will do no such thing! Send another! I am riding with you, Prince Consort!" Obviously, Olaron discerned quickly what had actually taken place on the hill while he was temporarily away and winked at his older brother. He mounted his own horse again and reached down to make sure his sword was in its place. "Oh. And congratulations, Brother!" And then he nodded to the princess. "And to you, Your Highness!"

It was determined that only a small number would accompany the princess, they to ride secretly through the woods and hills westward and northward with the hope of entirely skirting the Hescian force. It did seem better to try to get to Thorune which was much closer than any point south besides Davvos which was a part of County Ostin and could provide little protection. There was no stronghold or barracks there, whereas Thorune was a large town and offered several. The rest were to proceed on the road with the caravan as if everything were normal. Hopefully, should the Hescians surround the caravan, it would take them a little time before they realized the princess was gone.

Cludder dispatched four of his best to go with the Escarantine brothers and the princess. The seven set off immediately. It would, unfortunately, take them a little closer to Chernis and Count Ostin's seat, and there was the second Chernis road they would have to cross. Yet going east was surely even more dangerous considering that the Hescians apparently had that region under watch. They had definitely come from that direction; the Ramp lay that way.

They rode swiftly, though they tried to stay close together. Matteo was not pleased. "You are the only woman with us!" he called to her. "If they catch up with us, they will see through the disguise quickly. Would that it were night, and we could manage this more secretively."

"Would that I had time to dress up like a Kingsmen!" She pondered for a moment and spoke again. "I'm not happy about any of it, Matteo. Do you know what this means?"

"Yes. It means Filiddor is perfectly prepared for a war with the rest of the country if he doesn't get what he wants. Yet he can't, by himself. He must have help!"

Olaron put in. "You mean the Ice Tribes?"

Isatura nodded at the young man she hoped would someday be her brother-in-law. “Yes. Exactly that, Olaron. Your father suspected this.”

“Yet he expected no such aggressive move until long after the king made his decision about Tolos,” added Matteo. “None of us did.”

“Filiddor has become impatient,” said Isatura. In fact, she thought to herself, it was as if he were pressing the issue. “He actually wants to fight a war? But why? What if he could gain Tolos without a fight? Why does he not wait for my father to issue his decision on the matter?”

“Because Amerro would go to war against him in any regard. I don’t think we should pretend differently, Isatura. I know Amerro. He’s my cousin and a bit hot-headed. I like him, certainly, but as you and I have discussed before, it was an error for your father to grant him the Peninsula. At the least he should have given it to another. Despite Hess Fothemry’s exploration, Amerro doesn’t deserve Tolos anymore than does Filiddor. Your father should have granted it to Hess in the first place, if you ask me.”

“Kodi and I got to know each other well when he came through with his sister and the Lord Curdoz,” said Olaron as they rode. “He told me his father really didn’t want jurisdiction over such a large land. He was content with County Fothemry and the ambernut trade.”

“Yet men should respond to duty when called upon,” said Isatura. “He is clearly talented, and men follow him.”

“But that’s just it, begging your pardon, Your Highness,” said Olaron. “Kodi said his father would prefer to be his own man without always being subject to another, but he felt obligated to Amerro. He said that’s why he thinks Hess made Kodi stay at home so long, afraid that just like his father, he would subject himself and feel trapped into the bidding of others. Amerro especially. Of course, Kodi’s not like that. Kodi’s one to want to go out and conquer the world. In a good way, if you understand me.”

“Of course, I do, Olaron, dear,” said Isatura. “I discerned that in both the twins.”

“Sometimes I wish I could have gone off with him. He’s a cousin, too, you know. We kept calling each other ‘Cousin Ko’ and ‘Cousin O’ out of fun. We got to be good friends.”

Isatura smiled in his direction. He did have a certain amount of wisdom. Even so, Matteo was right. If her father had designated Tolos a new duchy and given it to Hess, or even to another if Hess refused it, then the current political situation might not be as volatile.

“If Filiddor has you as hostage, it would prevent your father from siding with Amerro. Surely that is what he is after,” said Matteo.

She considered as they rode through the woods. It was distressing to realize, but Matteo’s observations regarding Amerro and Filiddor were right. There would be war. It was mostly a matter of which of the two would begin it. Filiddor, it looked like, was desperate for an advantage. If he could in fact capture her, it would complicate her father's position and decision-making. She wished it would not. She didn't like thinking of herself as a pawn in a hostage negotiation.

She called a momentary halt, and the other six gathered in a circle about her. "Who's the fastest rider?" she asked, commandingly.

They all shifted. Most of them looked at Olaron—the youngest one there, though tough, muscly, and within a few months of traditional manhood. He grinned. "I am the best, Your Highness!"

The unabashed confidence of a fifteen-year-old boy, she thought, and yet presumed, particularly considering that Matteo did not argue, he was probably right. He did have a way with horses.

In fact, Matteo winked at his brother and admitted, "He wins all the races."

She issued Olaron a direct order. This time he didn't argue. He nodded his understanding, reached out and undertook the soldier's grip with his brother, and disappeared northwards through the woods.

Matteo looked at Isatura. "It is to be hoped still that we will outmaneuver the Hescians."

She nodded. "Yet if we do not, he will raise the alarm, and your friend Captain Santher may be our best hope. And if there is to be a fight, your young brother is out of the way."

"Thank you, Your Highness," he said. "It is a good thing you did not make that part plain, otherwise he would have resisted. But give him another year or two, and he will be a powerful knight-in-arms."

"Like you, my dear?"

He grinned boyishly.

"They will not harm me, you understand?" she added.

"What is your point, Your Highness?"

She trotted forward, and they continued on their way. She allowed Matteo to catch up. She spoke loudly enough that the other Kingsmen could also hear. "The point is that, if we are outnumbered, I want you to save yourselves, allow them to capture me, and then..." she paused and glared with a determined face when Matteo was about to protest, "I expect you to come after me. Whatever it takes, you will not allow Filiddor to keep me! He cannot be allowed to have his way. You must rescue me, Matteo, from that vile man!"

That last went without saying, yet what it did was give Matteo permission to ignore any orders to the contrary that might come from her father. "I am yours, Isatura."

"Yes, you are, Matteo," she said, with a bit of humorous condescension. She decided a moment of fun was called for, both to ease the tension, but also to make it clear to him exactly how she felt; their time on the hilltop was cut short. "You must preserve yourself, for the future of my House is in your hands, Matteo. Actually, it is in your trousers."

The Kingsmen guffawed. This was what she hoped. A joke of that sort would endear them to her and make her seem more human and not some distant, unseen royal in a palace. Matteo would need willing volunteers if events went badly.

Matteo grinned hugely. "I can happily manage that, Your Highness! Yet I suspect you will like what my hands do, as well!"

"I suspect I will!" she concluded with much additional laughter ensuing. "Now enough of this, and let us be a little quieter, shall we? We are attempting to elude capture, are we not?"

"You are the one creating a clamor, Your Highness!" said Matteo. "Houses and hands and...and trousers, my word!"

"You should not accuse a princess," she responded teasingly.

"Of course not, Your Highness! I am very glad to know your mind on..." he cleared his throat, "all these matters! It is quite arousing, I must admit."

She laughed. To have someone with which to drop her guard and play with in such a way was a new joy to her. She so hoped events would not turn out as grimly as they might. Then, for the first time she said the words, "I love you, Matteo."

He reached across for her hand and held it for a moment as they rode, "and I love you, Isatura."

Though they were ready to depart, Captain Cludder held the caravan in place for another quarter hour. Delay should aid the princess and the grand duke's sons. He could not send out any scouts, for if the Hescians knew he was scouting, they would realize he knew of their position and cause them to react too quickly. He only hoped they were not currently being watched, though he didn't think so based on Olaron's details. Smart boy, that one. Cludder was angry with himself for not having noticed that all traffic on the road had ceased. It should have been a quick clue that something wasn't right.

Eventually, he called the group to move. Additional delay would arouse too much suspicion. This was what Matteo and he had agreed upon beforehand. He had the caravan move at a snail's pace. There was no point in rushing this.

He looked around at his men. These were some of the best from King's Valley, he thought. He knew they would acquit themselves well if it came down to defending the princess's servants. Yet Isatura was convinced that this situation was all about her. She doubted the Hescians would fight except to get to her, and only if the Kingsmen insisted upon mounting a defense.

The question in his mind was whether they should initiate such a defense in order that it might gain the princess that much more time. Matteo had left that up to him to determine based on the situation as it presented itself. If the boy Olaron's information was correct, they were hopelessly outnumbered. He wished he had more men. There were only thirty of them. Twenty-six, now, he realized. He had sent off four with the princess. Thirty was thought to be plenty as an escort for a princess's caravan through a kingdom at peace.

This would change everything. There was nothing about this situation that remotely implied peace could prevail. War was coming, and that was assured whether the princess were taken or not. Obviously, Prince Filiddor was expecting it and even preparing for it. The princess as his hostage would give him leverage. To save the princess from Filiddor, the king would hesitate to side with Duke Amerro in the coming conflict.

Perhaps it was wrong of the princess to undertake this journey to Tulesk in the first place, considering recent events. However, it was the belief of the court that for the time being—at least until King Carlomen actually issued his decision on the Tolosian matter—all would continue as before.

Yet, with the exception of Thorune and County Ilmore, they were now in a part of Ascanti that was both geographically and historically tied closely to the Principality. And now there was a sizeable force of Hescians on horseback close by. Duke Snoffit was too easily bought, apparently, as were a number of his barons. He hoped Count Ilmore was still a friend. Matteo and the princess were insistent that he was. Santher, he thought, was the better hope. Cludder had known Santher for years and knew him to be an able officer. He had five hundred horsemen and two hundred foot soldiers and archers under his command in Thorune. Of course, many of the horsemen would be patrolling the roads and keeping the peace. In any event, if they could make it to the barracks in the middle of the town, the princess would be safe.

They had traveled only a half hour when suddenly before them was a contingent of perhaps twenty Hescian soldiers, most in the red and white colors of the Principality.

"Halt! Halt I say!" said the leader, a knight in chain mail.

The caravan halted and the captain rode forward. "Who are you to demand us halt on the king's roads? You are Hescians! What are you doing here in Ascanti? The roads are under the jurisdiction of the King of Solanto!"

"We will return them to your king," the man scoffed, "the moment you turn over to us Her Royal Highness, the Princess Isatura!"

"How dare you threaten the princess! She may travel wherever in her father's kingdom she pleases!" He drew his sword and the Kingsmen behind him immediately surrounded the coaches and took up a defensive posture. "I command you to turn about your mounts and return to the Principality!"

He spoke imperiously, pretending there were only the twenty Hescians before him.He didn't wonder but a moment where the rest were. Suddenly on all sides, coming out of hidden folds and forest growth and surrounding them in a thick ring, was the rest of the force. The boy was right. There were two hundred at least.

The Kingsmen all drew their swords and waited for a command. Despite the odds, they would willingly fight if the captain ordered it.

The Hescian knight in mail spoke again. "You are outnumbered, Captain. A fight between our forces is not required. Hand over the princess, and we will return to the Ramp forthwith. The rest of you may go free. His Highness Prince Filiddor promises to keep Her Highness Isatura safe from all harm."

"So, you intend to take her as a hostage?"

"Exactly that, Captain. I'm sure you are not stupid to the current political crisis."

The captain fumed. "I am not! And you must understand that it was not a crisis until you yourself appeared upon the road armed for war and with this outrageous demand! You are declaring open enmity with the king! Go back to Hesk, I tell you! Or better yet, turn yourselves over to me and I will guarantee your safety! Follow not a Prince of Hesk who dares to terrorize a royal lady on the roads!"

"That I cannot do, Captain. Now submit to my demand, or we shall be required to take her by force!"

There was little more Cludder could do at this point. He had tried to gain as much time as he could. Fighting was not a good choice; they would be overcome, and they would die without cause. If the princess were still with them, perhaps...yet there was still hope for her.

"Allow me to speak to Her Highness and see if she agrees to your demand."

"I am glad you finally see it my way, Captain."

He did not, of course, but he retained his silence on that subject as he trotted back to the princess's coach. He dismounted and stepped inside. After delaying several more minutes he stepped out of the coach and ordered his men to stand down. They all sheathed their swords and withdrew to the rear of the caravan.

The captain waited by the coach as the Hescian knight stepped forward.

"I would have your name, m'lord," said the captain.

"Tell His Majesty when you see him that it is Valgene, Son of Ultrech, Earl of Varn, who will escort his daughter in perfect safety to His Highness Filiddor." Then he turned to the coach and called out loudly. "Come out, Your Highness! I'm sure the good captain here has informed you what is afoot! Come out!"

With that, the chambermaid stepped out in Isatura's rich satin cloak. The man stared for a moment.

"You are not the princess!" Valgene was livid. He came forward and slapped the woman so hard she fell sprawling to the ground, blood dripping from her mouth. If he'd been wearing gauntlets, he'd have done much damage. As it was, he had removed them when Cludder ordered the stand down. He turned to the captain. "I have a mind to gut you!"

The captain ignored him and bent down to assist the poor maid. "Whatever did you do this for, brute? You are no lord and gentleman!"

"She is but a lowly servant and a woman; why do you care? Search the caravan!" he called to his men.

It took all of ten minutes, but finally the man named Valgene had to admit he had been duped.

"Where is she?" he yelled in the captain's face. "I've a mind to slaughter the lot of you!"

The captain laughed in his face. "You won't, though. Though war may come, I think you've been ordered not to begin the fighting. Suffice it to say Her Highness is not here. Now begone back to your Ramp! And once inside, I recommend you lock the gates, and should you ever come out of them again we'll see who guts who!"

Valgene ignored the provocation. The captain was right; he had been ordered at all costs not to fight unless necessary in order to take the princess into custody. He issued orders and within two minutes the Hescian force had disappeared.

It was over, yet the captain was unhappy. He said to the servants as they went about aiding the brave chambermaid and to the soldiers in earshot, "He realized the only place Her Highness would have gone is to Thorune. It's the only safe haven for her. He has sent them all in that direction. I'm afraid they will cut them off at the second Chernis road."

Olaron came abruptly upon the second Chernis road. There was no traffic here either. To his right he saw two horsemen, assuredly Hescians, in red and white. They were looking in the other direction, but the moment he began to cross they turned, yelled, and charged at him full gallop. Olaron urged his mount forward and plunged into the woods ahead. He had a good head start. *They'll never catch me,* he said to himself. In fact, they did not follow him far, and he was soon free of pursuit. It was to be hoped they would view him simply as a local boy on a horse. Nevertheless, he was much distressed. Their presence and their attempt to catch him meant the road to Chernis was being watched as well, though they expected it might be. He had no idea if his brother and the princess could cross it without being pursued and caught. They could not move as fast as he could by himself. He was tempted to go back and warn them to perhaps try a different route, but he knew it would likely lead the Hescians to follow.

He had to get to Santher in Thorune, yet he must return to the Northern Road at some point, or he'd never manage it in time for a warning to do any good. He didn't know this part of the country well enough to navigate without getting lost. Asking local folk and farmers to direct him on routes cross country would take too much time. In a few hours it would be dark. He wondered how far northwards the Hescians were monitoring the Northern Road. All he could do was guess, and after another half hour in the woods, he struck off in that direction.

Unlike Olaron, the princess's party approached the second Chernis road from a different angle and at a slightly more open location, therefore their approach was not as abrupt. They could see no one, and this cheered them. If they could cross without being seen, their chances of making it to Thorune safely were much improved. One of the Kingsmen, Kalob by name, was more familiar with this country and said there were many farms on the plains beyond the woods, and they could take refuge in a barn until nightfall. Once it was dark, they could navigate more secretively. Beyond the woods they would be in County Ilmore. It seemed their best hope, for they presumed Count Ostin and his folk in Chernis were now in the pay of the Hescians. They did not dare go that way.

The six crept to the roadside. From behind trees, Matteo dismounted and walked to the road. All was quiet as he looked this way and that. He returned to the princess and mounted again.

However, even as they began to ride across, they could hear suddenly eastward a troupe of horsemen galloping fast in their direction. They crossed quickly, but too late. A cry went up. They had been spotted.

Another cry came close from the west.

"Ride!" called Matteo.

They plowed through the trees, the Hescians pursuing. There were at least eight in red and white garb coming from the east and two from the west, angling towards them in the woods, and they were gaining.

"They're determined!" cried the princess. "They must realize who I am! Oh, Matteo!"

Her cry was desperate. She had not expressed real fear until now, and the panic on his betrothed's face set Matteo on fire.

"Halt!" he called. The four Kingsmen turned with him. Two had their bows quickly in hand and shot in the direction of the rapidly approaching Hesicans. One of the pursuers fell. He would prove the first casualty in this northern war. Then another.

Suddenly the rest were upon them, and the resulting swordfight was fierce. Two went after the princess—her cloak was a poor disguise. In the heat of the moment, the princess's courage returned. True to her word, when the first reached out to grab her, in a flash she whipped out the longknife she had been hiding under the cloak, and, swinging outward in a huge arc, slashed the rider's throat. Blood spurted everywhere and the man fell from his horse dead. There was a moment of shock for Isatura, and the other horseman was suddenly there and knocked the knife out of her hand.

Matteo plunged forward and unbalanced the man, stabbing him in the back as he fell. It was going well for the defenders, but suddenly there were more Hescian horsemen, at least thirty, bearing down on them.

They were quickly surrounded. At least twenty arrows were aimed at the men.

"Drop your arms!" called out a knight in mail.

"Do as he says!" screamed Isatura. "Remember what I told you, Matteo!"

Infuriated, Matteo tossed his sword to the ground, and the other Kingsmen followed suit. Remarkably, they were all uninjured. "Who by the Guardian are you? Why are Hescian cavalry pursuing us in the woods of Solanto!"

The knight smiled. "Matteo, is it? I've heard of you. You are the son of that interfering Mannago, are you not? Father said you both spoke hotly against him and His Highness at the Council!"

"You are Ultrech's son? I see the resemblance."

The knight nodded. "Very good. Valgene is my name! I have come, as you already realized, for the princess. Now back off! Or I'll slaughter the lot of you like pigs! You gave us the slip back there on the main road, but you won't do it again."

"You are starting a war, you realize, Valgene!" said the princess courageously. "My father will give in to no one's demands!"

Valgene looked at her scathingly. "What would you know! Keep silent, woman!"

He then pulled her forcefully from her horse onto his. It was all Matteo could do not to interfere.

Valgene sneered triumphantly at him. "Your captain already knows this, but you tell your old king that the princess will be kept safe. Her life is in no danger if you leave us alone. But tell him if he ever wants to see his daughter again, he had better make the right decision regarding His Highness Prince Filiddor's claim on the Tolosian Peninsula. There may be other demands, as well. We expect our messengers to be treated with respect and their safety assured, and His Highness promises likewise." Then to his followers present he said, "Retrieve their arms and those of the dead and gather up our own horses."

He had apparently said all he was going to say to the Solantines and turned to leave.

"Your days are numbered, Valgene!" exclaimed Matteo hotly.

"Really? That pathetic captain of the guard said much the same thing. This is what I say to that!" He came up to Matteo and backhanded him across the face. Matteo fell from his horse, face bloodied. However, he stood again. He looked first at the distraught princess to assure her he was alright, then he looked coldly at Valgene.

"You will regret that," he said, this time with deadly cold eyes.

"No. I don't think so," said Valgene unconcernedly. "Now ride for the Ramp, men! Let us leave this place!"

With that the Hescians took off eastwards.

They were without weapons, but at least Matteo and the four Kingsmen were sound and still had their horses. Valgene obviously didn't want even more riderless mounts to manage than those of the three dead Hescians, yet it was a wonder he didn't have the beasts shot. Maybe it was his contempt for Matteo, thinking he was no longer a threat. He probably thought a cowed Matteo would hustle back to the king in Ferostro with his message. Perhaps if he had known of the betrothal and Matteo's determination, he would have done otherwise.

Overlooked by Valgene's men, Matteo found the bloodied longknife used by Isatura. He looked at the man the princess had slain and felt an upwelling sense of pride in her willingness to fight. He presumed now since the Hescians had what they came for the entire force would vacate the area and head east towards the Ramp with all speed. Matteo hoped they themselves would not run into any of Ostin's people. He was in a murderous mood. He took a minute to drink from his water bottle, cleaned up his bloody face, and then the five men raced to find the Northern Road through the woods, even as Olaron had done an hour earlier. They eventually found it and before long had caught up with the caravan.

There was much disappointment when the servants and the Kingsmen realized Isatura had been abducted. Some of her maids wept.

"This isn't over," said Matteo grimly.

They knew the servants were in no more danger, and so the captain decided to leave only ten guards with the caravan. After discussing the situation with Matteo, it was determined that the procession should turn around and make their way back to Ferostro with all speed and spread the news as they went. The captain had already sent out two riders to Thorune earlier, as soon as he knew the Hescians had departed, but now he dispatched two more with the firm news that Isatura had indeed been taken by the Hescian force.

Matteo and the four with him were quickly armed again, and even as the sun began its descent in the west, the remainder of the Kingsmen, some sixteen, along with Captain Cludder and Matteo, rode cross country in pursuit of the Hescians. They did not plan to overtake them with so few to force a fight, yet they had high hopes that Olaron would get through to Santher, and if all went well, they would meet and engage the Hescian force before they reached the Ramp.

This course of action was their best hope in trying to retrieve the princess, for once behind the great gates at the bottom of the Ramp, it would be difficult to get her back other than through negotiations. Negotiations that would put King Carlomen and Solanto at a huge disadvantage. The old king would be heartsick. Despite Isatura's brave words to Valgene, Matteo foresaw the king giving in to any demand in order to get his daughter returned safely.

Even as they rode, Matteo kept plotting how he could keep his promise to Isatura. She had virtually ordered him to do whatever it took to rescue her. They did have some new spies in Aster, agents of his father Mannago. And he was privy to Lord Curdoz' little organization centering on that ancient librarian Theneri. He could try disguising himself. The problem with that was his obvious Escarantine looks. He was decidedly darker than most northerners; he might attract one too many second glances. A Monastic, maybe? There were Monastics and Healers in Aster that hailed from Escarant. Yes, that might work quite well. The biggest problem was how to get onto the Highland and into the Principality in the first place. After this kidnapping and the almost certain closure of the Ramp gates, what was he going to do? Climb the sheer Escarpment? And even if he could do that, how was he supposed to, if all went perfectly, get the princess out of Hesk? He could hardly drop her off the bluff. The only other good way in was the pass from Eleni on the other side of the Imperial Range, but it would take two or three months to get around to that point, and yet Filiddor would likely close that as well. It would be no easier than the Ramp.

Well, he thought, he'd figure that part out later. Maybe there were those in Ferostro who knew of some way north out of King's Valley over the hills and through the Durn marshlands. Yet even if there were such a path, it would be perilous to try to return with Isatura that way.

He hoped for a miracle. Maybe, if threatened with battle, Valgene would let the princess go. Apparently, he was under orders to avoid a fight if possible; Filiddor did not want a war to begin too soon.

In retrospect, it seemed hopeless. If Santher came and confronted the Hescians before the Ramp, what if Valgene threatened the princess's life in order to assure safe passage? The man was a brute. And as far as Matteo knew, there could be another force at the Ramp ready to assist Valgene. Not to mention Counts Nees and Mere.

"I'm stabbing that proud pecker Valgene," shouted Captain Cludder as they galloped along. It had been several hours, and it was dark now. However, the land though still hilly was more open here with fewer woods, and the moons and stars gave them light.

"Not before I take off his head," replied Matteo. His fury threatened to overcome him. He tried to settle it with a memory. But a few hours ago, he was newly betrothed to the woman he had carefully wooed for so long. It was a memorable moment frozen in time, and he would never forget how wonderful it was. He still felt their first kiss on his lips. How awfully it had ended when his brother raced up that hill with the news. If he went back there right now, he would find all the tea things and baskets still on blankets at the top. Some locals or travelers would find them. Would they even wonder what they represented: a moment when true love shown for a bright few minutes in the sunshine?

I will come after you, my love, he said both to himself and the mystical cosmos. *My princess.*

For him the sun would not shine again until he held her close once more.

Works by Terry Lee Martin

Fiction:

HEIRS TO THE TAXIARCH

Book 1: *Seeds of the Guardian* (2021 Silver Goblet Press)
Book 2: *Companions in Prophecy* (2021 Silver Goblet Press)
Book 3: *Brothers of Myghal* (Forthcoming in 2022)
Book 4: *Daughters of Vanayema* (Forthcoming in 2022)
Book 5: *Champions of Dumhoni* (Forthcoming in 2023)

Non-fiction:

"Love's Young Dream," The Letters of Dr. Edward Noel Franklin to Miss Nannie Hillman—1871 (2018 Silver Goblet Press)

About the author:

Terry Lee Martin is a graduate of the University of Tennessee at Martin with majors in history and psychology. With two more years of additional coursework at Tennessee Technological University, he received certification in secondary education. For many years, Martin taught high school social studies. He lives in Tennessee with his wife and sons. His first book, the non-fiction work, *"Love's Young Dream," The Letters of Dr. Edward Noel Franklin to Miss Nannie Hillman—1871*, explores two prominent Middle Tennessee families of the antebellum and postbellum South. The book received positive reviews by professors and historians. Martin has presented his research at various historical societies. Martin's venture into fiction began with his fantasy world-building in the early 2000s, coming to fruition in his *Heirs to the Taxiarch* book series. The first volume, *Seeds of the Guardian*, was published in 2021 by Silver Goblet Press. Contact Martin at the following email address: **tmartin@silvergobletpress.com**

Visit the *Silver Goblet Press* website to find Martin's blog, along with details and updates on his publications: *www.silvergobletpress.com*

www.ingramcontent.com/pod-product-compliance
Lightning Source LLC
Chambersburg PA
CBHW070542310726
48982CB00010B/1447/J

* 9 7 8 1 7 3 2 0 1 3 8 5 8 *